So Into Yo

"*So Into You* by Kathleen Fuller is an uplifting story about rising above your fears and letting go of your past. Secrets abound in this satisfying romance, and it's hard to look away when the house of cards comes crashing down. This satisfying tale will charm its way into your heart!"

—Denise Hunter, bestselling
author of *Before We Were Us*

Sold on Love

"The sweet third entry in Fuller's Maple Falls series (after *Much Ado About a Latte*) follows an unlikely romance between an ambitious realtor and an affable mechanic . . . their friends-to-lovers arc charms. Fans of wholesome romance will be eager to return to Maple Falls."

—*Publishers Weekly*

"Kathleen Fuller writes an 'opposites attract' romance that will leave you with a wonderful sigh and a silly smile. Harper Wilson overworks to cover up her insecurities, but when tenderhearted and gentle greasemonkey Rusty Jenkins enters her life to save her Mercedes, an unexpected friendship grows into something both of them need. Love-authentic and sweet, this small-town romance with wonderful heart and a delicious male makeover will have you cheering for two people whose lives look very different on the outside, but whose hearts are very much the same."

—Pepper Basham, author of
The Mistletoe Countess
and *Authentically, Izzy*

Much Ado About a Latte

"Fuller returns to small-town Maple Falls, Ark., (after *Hooked on You*) for a chaste but spirited romance between old friends with clashing entrepreneurial goals . . . the cozy atmosphere and spunky locals will leave readers eager to return to Maple Falls."

—*Publishers Weekly*

"You've heard of friends to lovers; now get ready for childhood friends, to coworkers, to fake-dating coworkers, to business rivals, to lovers. *Much Ado About a Latte* has it all—charming and sweet, with delectable dialogue and just enough biting tension to keep you on the edge of your seat. I fell in love with Anita's determined spirit, Tanner's kindness, and their slow-burning romance. A wide cast of side characters, including Anita's complicated but loving family, build the delightful feel of the town. Readers will love the beautiful setting of Maple Falls, the gratuitous food descriptions at Sunshine Diner, and Anita's adorable cat, Peanut."

—Carolyn Brown, *New York Times* Bestselling author

Hooked on You

"Sign me up for a one-way ticket to Maple Falls. If you love small towns, charming characters, and sweet, swoony romance, *Hooked on You* is your next favorite read. Kathleen Fuller has knit one wonderful story yet again."

—Jenny B. Jones, award-winning author of *A Katie Parker Production* and *The Holiday Husband*

"A charming story of new beginnings, family ties, love, friendship, laughter, and the beauty of small towns. Fuller invites you into Maple Falls and greets you with a cast of characters who will steal your heart, make you want to stay, and entice you to visit again."

—Katherine Reay, bestselling author
of *The Printed Letter Bookshop*
and *Of Literature and Lattes*

"A sweet, refreshing tale of idyllic small-town life, family, and unexpected romance, *Hooked on You* is the perfect read to cozy up with on a rainy day."

—Melissa Ferguson, multi-award-winning
author of *How to Plot a Payback*

"The quaint Arkansas town of Maple Falls could use a little sprucing up, and as it turns out, Riley and Hayden are the perfect pair for the job. What neither of them is counting on, of course, is that their hearts may receive some long overdue TLC in the process. Kathleen Fuller has knit together a lovable cast of characters and placed them in a setting so rich and dear you may find yourself hankering for a walk down Main Street on a warm summer's evening. I loved every minute of my time in Maple Falls, and I can't wait to return to visit the friends I made there."

—Bethany Turner, award-winning author
of *Brynn and Sebastian Hate Each Other*

So Into You

Other Contemporary Romance Novels by Kathleen Fuller

THE MAPLE FALLS ROMANCE NOVELS

Hooked on You

Much Ado About a Latte

Sold on Love

Two to Tango

So Into You

A Novel

Kathleen Fuller

THOMAS NELSON
Since 1798

So Into You

Copyright © 2024 Kathleen Fuller

Published in Nashville, Tennessee, by Thomas Nelson. Thomas Nelson is a registered trademark of HarperCollins Christian Publishing, Inc.

Thomas Nelson titles may be purchased in bulk for educational, business, fundraising, or sales promotional use. For information, please e-mail SpecialMarkets@ThomasNelson.com.

Publisher's Note: This novel is a work of fiction. Names, characters, places, and incidents are either products of the author's imagination or used fictitiously. All characters are fictional, and any similarity to people living or dead is purely coincidental.

Library of Congress Cataloging-in-Publication Data

Names: Fuller, Kathleen, author.
Title: So into you : a novel / Kathleen Fuller.
Description: Nashville, Tennessee : Thomas Nelson, 2024. | Summary: "Opposites attract when an introverted vlogger and a reformed party boy exchange lessons on art, confidence, and yacht rock"—Provided by publisher.
Identifiers: LCCN 2024018881 (print) | LCCN 2024018882 (ebook) | ISBN 9780840716125 (paperback) | ISBN 9780840716132 (epub) | ISBN 9780840716149
Subjects: LCGFT: Christian fiction. | Romance fiction. | Novels.
Classification: LCC PS3606.U553 S6 2024 (print) | LCC PS3606.U553 (ebook) | DDC 813/.6--dc23/eng/20240429
LC record available at https://lccn.loc.gov/2024018881
LC ebook record available at https://lccn.loc.gov/2024018882

Printed in the United States of America

24 25 26 27 28 LBC 5 4 3 2 1

To James. I love you.

Chapter 1

*L*ights? Check.
Sound? Check.
Script? Check.

Brittany Branch placed her hand on her fluttery stomach. Four hundred fifty-six videos, seven years on YouTube, almost five hundred thousand subscribers, comment sections filled with compliments and encouragement . . . and her nerves were still tap-dancing in her gut. She gave up hoping she wouldn't have stage fright or videophobia or whatever it was that made her anxiety reach unacceptable levels every time she filmed content for her channel. She was twenty-eight years old and an experienced vlogger. She shouldn't be fretting over her job.

She sighed and made the mistake she always made before filming her content—she glanced at her black computer screen and grimaced. No matter how she changed the lighting in her room, positioned her desk, or moved the monitor, she still caught her shadowed reflection. And even though her flaws weren't clearly visible, she knew they were there—the wiry curls she couldn't tame, one eyebrow that was clearly higher than the other, her elongated profile that had inspired her third-grade classmate Chase Anderson to call her "Horse Face," a nickname that stuck until eleventh grade when her fellow students finally decided to grow up a little. He'd even apologized—in a DM, of course, not in person—saying that she had never looked like a horse, and he'd been an idiot kid who liked to clown around in class.

She accepted his half attempt at an apology, but the damage was done. And it didn't matter how many commenters said she was "cute" and her hair was "beautiful" and claimed her squeaky voice was "adorable." She never forgot the sound of boys neighing behind her as she walked in the hallways.

Britt blinked, shoving the past aside. She took a deep breath, turned on her smile and her camera, and began filming.

"Hey, everyone! Britt here. If you're new to my channel, welcome. If you enjoy the content, hit Like and Subscribe!"

Today's video was a tutorial about perspective in anime art. Britt had recorded herself drawing a typical anime scene, so today she only had to be on camera for the intro and outro, and the rest was voice-over. Two hours later she finished and began the editing process, something that had initially been daunting when she'd started her channel, but she now did with ease.

She heard her mother's car door shut outside the window of her studio and glanced at the clock. Almost five? The video had taken longer than she thought. She would have to upload it tonight and then promote it on her social media channels, answer some comments, and take a stab at cleaning out her DMs and other private and public messages. Feeding the marketing beast was a never-ending job.

Britt went upstairs to start on supper as Mom walked through the door, her leather satchel slung over one shoulder and the other carrying her ever-present water bottle that said *Teachers Rock.* "Hey, hon," Mom said, setting the bag on the table and taking the water bottle to the sink. "How was your day?"

"Productive." Britt slipped the plastic spiral ponytail holder off her wrist and put up her out-of-control hair.

"That's nice. Did you go outside for a few minutes? The weather was gorgeous today."

"Um, no." She pulled out a skillet from the cabinet and set it on the stove. "I worked all day."

Mom stood beside her. "Now, Britt, we discussed how important vitamin D is, especially directly from the source. You need to sit on the patio for at least thirty minutes each morning."

"Sure." Britt walked to the fridge and took out the ground beef for Taco Tuesday.

"And wear sunscreen!" Mom grinned and went back to the sink. She washed out her bottle while Britt cooked, their typical post-work/post-school routine. As much as her mother's hovering and unwanted advice grated, Britt knew she was right. Staying cooped up in her studio wasn't healthy, as her pale skin made obvious. But she liked her studio. It was her space, and even though she was nervous before each video, that was the only negative feeling she had about her job. She loved drawing, loved coming up with content, and even enjoyed most of the marketing, except for the creepy DMs she occasionally received. A quick internet search had revealed that almost all content creators had to deal with problematic messages.

Mom made iced tea and they both sat down for supper. Britt shared her video topic of the day and Mom discussed the end-of-the-school-year scramble.

"My advanced calc class is almost all seniors except for two," she said, spooning salsa on top of her crunchy taco. "Things are crazy right now while we get them and all the other seniors ready for graduation, but next week I can take a breath."

Britt smiled. Mom might complain about some of the hassles that came with teaching, especially during stressful times of the year, like testing and dealing with senioritis. But she loved her job, even after twenty-five years.

She felt a tap on her wrist and glanced at her watch as a text popped up.

Phone call later?

She quickly gave the text a thumbs-up, then crunched into another taco. She could eat Mexican food every day of the week, but Burrito Monday and Quesadilla Friday didn't sound as clever as Taco Tuesday. Although she wouldn't mind if Sopapilla Saturday went viral.

"Who was that?" Mom asked, sprinkling a little queso fresco on top.

"A—" She was about to say friend, but she only had one real-life friend, Savannah, and if she told Mom it was her, a barrage of questions would follow. None of them too nosy, but usually conversations about Savannah led to the inevitable *"you should really get out and meet more people"* directive.

She couldn't tell her who was really texting, not unless she wanted to send her mother into orbit. "Just a spam call."

"Ew, I hate those."

They finished their tacos, with Mom still conversing about school and Britt interjecting a few things about her video channel. It had occurred to her more than once that both she and her mom were obsessed with their jobs. The only other activity they shared, other than watching movies together on Friday nights and going to church, was reading in their separate bedrooms.

"What are your plans for the evening?" Mom asked, getting up from the table.

Britt joined her as they collected the dishes. "The usual. Answering comments, organizing my email." After her phone call.

"You're being careful about who you talk to online, right?"

She fought the urge to roll her eyes. Her mother constantly asked her that question and had been asking since she first started her channel. The only thing that stopped Britt from making a snarky reply was . . . Mom was right. There were absolute creeps out there in the cyberworld, and she always kept in mind that whoever she was talking to, unless she knew them personally, couldn't be completely trusted. Since there were few people she knew on a personal level, she always had her guard up. "Yes, Mom. I'm being careful."

"Good." She opened the dishwasher, which was only partway full of dirty dishes. "I know you get tired of me nagging you about that—"

Truth.

"—but you wouldn't believe the things I hear from kids at school, their parents, even law enforcement, about what can happen online. Two weeks ago we had in-service about yet another way criminals are trying to steal personal information." She shook her head. "Technology is so helpful, but it has its downsides."

Britt rinsed the dishes and put them in the dishwasher, and a few minutes later the kitchen was clean. Between the two of them it didn't take long, and it had been the two of them for almost twenty years. They both liked things neat, and the house never got too out of control.

"I've got a stack of finals to grade." Mom yawned. "I'll be in the living room."

"Okay. After I'm done with a little work, I'm going to finish the novel I started last night."

"About dragons?"

She smiled. "Nope. Not this time."

"Anime?"

"That was last week. I decided to switch things up and read C. S. Lewis again."

"Ah, Narnia." Mom smiled. "Enjoy."

"I will."

They went their separate ways as they did every night. Britt entered her room and shut the door, then took her phone out of her pocket and found the number in her Contacts list. He answered on the first ring. "Hello?"

She lay down on her stomach on her twin bed. "Hey, Dad."

⌐

Buzz . . . buzz . . .

Amy Branch startled from a dead sleep. She sat up and looked at her cell phone on the side table, then at the crooked stack of papers on her lap. When had she fallen asleep? She took off her glasses and grabbed the phone without looking at the screen. "Hello?"

"Oh, hey. Did I wake you up?"

"No." She resisted the urge to yawn, settling back in her recliner to chat with her friend Laura. She was feeling every bit of her forty-seven years tonight. "You called at the perfect time."

"Fell asleep grading papers again?"

"Maybe."

Laura chuckled. "You know I'm an expert at snoozing over paperwork."

"Yeah, because legal paperwork is boring," she said, taking a dig at Laura's paralegal profession.

"That's where you're wrong, my friend. I would rather pore over pages and pages of writs than grade one single quadratic equation."

"These are calculus papers, not algebra."

"There's a difference?"

They both laughed as Amy glanced at the clock above the fireplace mantel. Ten thirty. She needed to get to bed before eleven or she would be groggy in the morning. "You're calling kind of late."

"I know and I'm sorry, but I had the best time tonight, and I have to tell you all about it."

Intrigued, Amy shifted in her recliner to get comfortable. "Do tell."

"I joined Single Mingles."

"What?" The papers on her lap almost fell on the floor with her jolt of surprise. "You didn't."

"I did. And guess what? It isn't as dopey as we thought. In fact, it was a blast, and you should join."

Amy rolled her eyes. "Not this conversation again."

"This is different. I'm not asking you to join another dating site," Laura said.

"Good, because that's not happening." Despite her warnings to Britt, and even though she knew the pitfalls of the internet, four years ago she'd agreed to sign up for a dating website and was promptly contacted by a slew of middle-aged guys who only wanted two things—sex and money. "I'm still getting over the trauma."

"These are real people. And they like having a good, clean time."

"That's nice. But no. I'm not interested."

"Amy, you can't live the rest of your life hiding from fun."

"I have fun. Brittany and I do lots of fun things." Well, not lots. But enough. Her daughter was twenty-eight and Amy didn't want to hover. Although she considered Britt closer than a best friend, they didn't have much in common, and never really had. Brittany had always been an introverted child, while Amy was more extroverted. Being around teenagers all day gave her plenty of interaction—in the case of the end-of-the-year scramble, *exhausting* interaction.

"Amy . . ."

She could feel her friend building up for another truth session, and she had to cut that off at the pass. "Laura, I'm really glad you had a great time with your singles and that you want to include me. But I have papers to finish grading and a bedtime to meet."

"But—"

"I'll call you tomorrow. At a decent hour." Amy smiled and hung up, knowing Laura wouldn't take it personally. That was one of many things she liked about her friend—she was levelheaded, intelligent, and logical. Above all, she was honest, and normally Amy appreciated that. But not tonight.

She finished the rest of the finals by eleven thirty and crawled into bed. As she turned off the light, their conversation came back to her mind. It had been seven years since Laura's husband's untimely death from a heart attack, and she had entered the dating market a year and a half ago. It was difficult to find romance in middle age, but she was persevering. *"I know my other Mr. Right is out there somewhere,"* she insisted.

Amy thought she'd had her Mr. Right, but he couldn't have been more wrong. The only good thing to come out of their relationship was Brittany. Daniel had killed her desire for a romantic relationship years ago. Twenty, to be exact.

She rolled over in bed. For years, she counted every day a blessing since she and Daniel divorced. He'd made her life a swamp of misery. To top it off, he abandoned Britt. Logically she knew all men weren't like him. She also knew people who had successful marriages. Her parents, for example. Lots of couples at church too. And Laura wasn't the only one wanting Amy to find a partner. It seemed everyone in her life, other than Britt, was eager for her to get married again.

She sighed. Although Britt didn't talk about it, Amy had to wonder if she was feeling pressure from anyone to start dating. While she wished Britt was more outgoing, she had to respect her nature, and she tried to gently encourage her to get out more. Her daughter didn't seem unhappy, or that her life was lacking anything. And her video channel was something to be proud of. She'd taken her degree in graphic design and turned it into a profitable and educational enterprise.

But will she live with me forever?

Amy had to admit, she wouldn't mind if she did. And Britt had never said anything about dating. In school she was more interested in art than boys, and Amy wasn't in any hurry for her to find a liar, cheat, and downright horrible man like her father.

Flopping over again, she closed her eyes and counted down from one hundred. If she continued to muse about Laura, Single Mingles, Britt, and—*shudder*—Daniel, she'd never get to sleep. Only two more weeks of school left, and she could relax . . .

⁓

"You still haven't told your mom that you're talking to your dad?"

Britt and Savannah were taking a walk around her neighborhood. It was a perfect day for a stroll. Savannah loved to walk, and every time she and Britt went on one, Britt promised herself that she would try to walk on a regular basis. But then she'd get caught up in her work or her art, and exercise fell to the wayside. She glanced at her friend. They had met at church youth group fifteen years ago, when they were both thirteen. She'd never had a friend like Savannah before, someone who understood and accepted Britt's quirks, particularly her annoying bouts of anxiety. Those had peaked during her school years, but she occasionally had issues when meeting new people and being around large groups in unfamiliar places. Social anxiety, her counselors had called it. She'd also read several blogs online to see if she was the only one who had that problem. Turned out she wasn't. It also turned out that most of the people online who admitted to having social anxiety had jobs where they didn't have to deal with people in person. Just like she did.

Savannah didn't have an anxiety problem, and she made friends easily. She was also beautiful. Her Hispanic, olive-toned skin took on a golden glow in the spring and summer months under the Texas sun, and she not only walked regularly, she also enjoyed going to the gym—something else Britt didn't want to do. But she appreciated her friend going at a slower pace so they could talk without Britt losing her breath.

"I haven't mentioned it yet," she said, finally answering Savannah's question.

"How long have you been in contact with him?"

"Three months."

Savannah shook her head. "That's a long time to keep such a big secret."

"It's not like I don't want to tell her. But you know how she would react if she knew." They turned right at the end of her street.

"She definitely won't be happy." Savannah tucked a lock of her long black hair behind her ear to reveal one of the gold hoops she always wore. Britt still couldn't get up the courage to get her ears pierced. "But maybe she wouldn't be quite as mad if she knew he was different now."

"I doubt she'd believe me." Britt was still coming to terms with reconnecting with her dad again. It was only last week that she stopped calling him Daniel and changed over to Dad.

"Aren't you worried she'll find out?"

Britt sidestepped a huge crack in the sidewalk. Her suburban neighborhood, while nice, wasn't without its problems, and aging roads and sidewalks was one of them. "Definitely. I'm being real careful. I still don't trust him completely. But so far, he's called me almost every night like he promised. We're still getting to know each other."

"I can't imagine talking to my dad every night."

"He's kind of busy being a veterinarian."

"Even if he weren't busy, I don't know what we'd say."

Britt sometimes had that problem with Daniel—Dad. Especially in the beginning, after he'd contacted her through her channel and asked if he could see her. It took a while for her to think it over, then she agreed and he'd stopped by the house during the day while Mom was at school.

She'd felt confused when she first saw him. In some ways he hadn't changed—he still had the same curly hair, although it was shorter than she remembered, and he was on the thin side. But he also seemed different. He looked healthy instead of gaunt, and there was a calm stillness about him, which was a huge contrast to his alcohol-induced volatility. He didn't ask her for anything, just told her he was sorry for the past and asked if it was all right if he could call her every once in a while. How could she tell her father no?

The sporadic phone calls became more frequent, and both of them became more relaxed. Now they never ran out of things to say.

She and Savannah changed the subject and chatted as they made the loop around her neighborhood. When they reached her house, her friend hadn't broken a sweat. Britt couldn't say the same. Wow, she was really out of shape. Being naturally thin, she didn't have the impetus to exercise to lose weight. But now that she was almost twenty-nine, she needed to do something. She couldn't rely on her genes forever.

They went into the kitchen and Britt filled glasses with ice water, and then they sat outside on the patio. Britt had just taken a gulp when Savannah spoke.

"Justin and I are engaged."

Water spewed out of her mouth. "What?" Britt wiped the back of her hand over her lips.

"I don't have a ring yet, but he proposed last night." Savannah beamed. "The ring is on layaway since we don't want to have any credit cards."

Engaged? Britt knew they had gotten serious pretty quickly—they'd only been dating for a few months.

Savannah's smile widened, showing perfectly straight white teeth. "We're planning to get married in August. I know it seems fast, but I've known all along that Justin and I would end up together. It was love at first sight for both of us."

Britt's head was spinning. "You never told me that."

She gave her a sympathetic look. "I didn't want you to . . . I don't know. Be jealous? And I definitely didn't want to be one of those friends who changes when they have a boyfriend."

She'd achieved that goal, because Britt was realizing she didn't know much about her best friend's relationship with her boyfriend. Scratch that—her fiancé.

Savannah turned in the lawn chair and faced her. "Will you be my maid of honor?"

Britt couldn't find the words to answer. More than anything she wanted to be there for Savannah's big day. But immediately, the obligation of the role plucked at her anxiety. She'd have to get a fancy dress and stand up in front of everyone. Then there were the bridal showers. And a bachelorette party. She'd have to coordinate things, talk to people, be around people . . . She rubbed her hand on the arm of the chair as she gripped the slippery glass in her hand. "Can . . . can I think about it?"

A flash of disappointment crossed Savannah's face. "Sure."

Suddenly a wave of regret washed over Britt. "I'm sorry. I . . . I want to say yes. I really do. But . . ."

Savannah reached for her hand. "I understand. And if you can't be in the bridal party, that's okay."

Britt squeezed her hand, fighting back the urge to flee. "I promise I'll let you know soon, okay?"

"Yeah. Sure." Savannah let go. "There's something else I have to tell you. Justin got a job in Missouri. It's with a prestigious architecture firm. He's getting a promotion, raise, the whole package. He starts work next week."

At first, Britt nodded, happy to hear that Justin had gotten a great job. Then the full meaning of Savannah's words sank in. "You're moving?"

Savannah nodded, her eyes sparkling with excitement. "That's part of the reason why we're in a hurry to get married." She glanced at her watch and stood. "Sorry, Britt, but I've gotta run. We have less than four months to plan the wedding and I've already got a list a mile long."

"Right." Britt stood and faced her best friend. Not only was Savannah tanned, gorgeous, and six inches taller than her, but she was also the sister Britt didn't have. Tears burned her eyes. "What am I going to do without you?"

Savannah's excitement dimmed for a moment as she seemed to register Britt's reaction. "We'll find time to hang out together before I move. I promise."

"That's not what I mean."

Savannah hugged her. "You'll be okay," she said, her voice thick. "You'll find your way."

Britt nodded, not wanting to let her go. But she had to. Soon Savannah would be embarking on a new chapter. *Without me.*

"Missouri isn't that far," she said, stepping away. "You can come visit. We'll be in Springfield, near the Ozark Mountains. Justin says it's really pretty there. Lots of trees and hills. And mountains, obviously." She smiled. "You'll always be my bestie, Britt. You know that."

Britt nodded and walked Savannah to her car, a used but still in good condition red convertible she'd gotten for high school graduation ten years ago. As her friend drove away, she swallowed the boulder in her throat.

Savannah's words were true—at least for now. But being an introverted wallflower had given Britt the opportunity to observe people, which was always easier than interacting with them. She'd seen her peers at church pair off, get married, have families, move away. They were living their lives, and she knew some of them didn't even talk to each other, despite being close while growing up. Missouri wasn't just around the corner, and even though Savannah had kept her relationship with Justin fairly private, Britt knew she wanted a family. She wouldn't marry him if he didn't want one too. She would move on from Allen, Texas, and create a new life in Springfield. That's how it always worked.

She stared at the convertible as it disappeared down the road. If she were Savannah's maid of honor, she would get to spend a lot of time with her before she left. Surely, she could get over her anxiety enough to be by her side. All she had to do was be . . . social.

Her stomach clenched at the thought. Now the nausea was coming in for a landing. Her palms grew slick, and spots danced before her eyes. It was all so ridiculous, but she couldn't help it.

If she couldn't overcome her social anxiety for Savannah, would she ever be able to? Or would she always be stuck in her small universe, engaging with the world from behind the safety of a computer screen or vicariously through adventure novels? *Will I ever grow up?*

Chapter 2

Hey! Watch where you're going with that forklift!"

Hunter Pickett blinked and quickly maneuvered the vehicle away from his coworker and roommate, Sawyer Campbell, barely missing him. He put the lift in Park and turned around. "Sorry!"

Sawyer shot him a hard look. "Did you fall asleep at the wheel or what?"

Hunter shook his head, but Sawyer was already back at work unpacking boxes of merchandise off the pile of pallets Hunter had just unloaded. He didn't blame him for being mad. He hadn't fallen asleep or even dozed off. But he was tired, and he'd been distracted—a common state of mind for him lately.

Sawyer was good-natured enough that he wouldn't hold the near miss against him. But Hunter expected some well-deserved ribbing was forthcoming.

He and Sawyer spent the rest of the afternoon unloading pallets at the warehouse where they worked, unironically called The Warehouse. They worked second shift, and as soon as ten o'clock rolled around, they met in the locker room, took off their safety vests, and clocked out.

"Wanna grab a bite on the way home?" Hunter asked as they walked outside and into the muggy Texas air. It was only May, but summer was already in full force.

"Rain check. You know Marissa?"

They reached Hunter's motorcycle. Sawyer's Subaru was parked next to him. "She works in the office, right?"

"I asked her out."

"Don't tell me she was dumb enough to say yes." Hunter lifted his helmet off the handlebars.

"Of course she did." Sawyer pushed his floppy bangs off his wide forehead, grinning as he got into the car. "Don't wait up, Dad."

Hunter shoved on his helmet as Sawyer sped away. Normally he laughed off his roommate's digs. But tonight it grated. He started his Yamaha, revved it up, and took off. He wasn't in the mood to go back to an empty apartment, so he headed for the local twenty-four-hour waffle house.

As soon as he entered, he was seated at a small booth near the window. He was the only patron in the restaurant. A waitress with short green and blue hair approached, carrying a pot of coffee and smacking her gum loudly enough to be heard in Dallas.

"Evening," she said. A white plastic badge with the name *Enid* handwritten on it was pinned to the lapel of her uniform. "Coffee?" *Snap.*

"Sure." He turned over the coffee cup in front of him and watched her fill it with the steaming brew. He hadn't slept well lately, and a little caffeine wasn't going to make a difference.

Snap. She gestured to the plastic-coated menu wedged between the window and the napkin dispenser. "I'll give you some time to decide on food." Giving him one last gum snap, she walked back to the counter.

Hunter glanced at the menu, even though he wasn't hungry. He took a sip of coffee, pulled out his phone, and scrolled through thirty-second videos on YouTube. There were the requisite silly dance videos, dumb viral challenges that would probably end up with someone getting hurt, and food. Lots and lots of food.

Snap. "Have you decided?"

He set down his phone and nodded. "A waffle and two strips of bacon." What else would he order in a waffle house?

"Crispy or regular?"

He frowned. "The waffle or the bacon?"

Enid gave him a patient half smile, revealing one incisor that was significantly smaller than the rest of her teeth. "The bacon."

"Crispy." The wrinkles at the corners of her lips and eyes made her look too old for multicolored hair, but who was he to judge.

Snap. Snap. She jotted a few scribbles on the pad. "Anything else, handsome?"

He flinched. "No."

"Coming right up." She flashed a more genuine grin at him before leaving again.

He let out a long breath. All he needed tonight was to get hit on by a waffle waitress who had a good ten, if not more, years on him. Again, not judging, but she wasn't his type.

Hunter slouched in the booth, pushing his coffee cup a few inches away with his index finger. The type of women he was interested in weren't eager to go out with a thirty-year-old entry-level warehouse worker with a GED.

Well, he *used* to be interested in those kinds of women. That was before his older brothers—top-notch attorney Payne and venture capitalist Kirk—had married two of them. His sisters-in-law were hot, with toned bodies, perfectly highlighted hair, unnaturally tanned skin, and pearly white even teeth.

They were also self-absorbed shopaholics who were bleeding his brothers dry.

He sat back up and ran his hand through his hair. He'd always been judgmental. About looks, about money, about everything. And now here he was, twelve years past high school, sitting alone at a waffle house on a Saturday night with few prospects—both personal and professional.

Whose fault is that?

He yanked out his phone again, desperate for a distraction. After scrolling through several kitten and puppy videos—they did warm his heart, he had to admit—a girl with a mass of curly, messy black hair popped up on his screen.

He paused. A week ago today she'd somehow appeared in his feed for the first time. *Britt Draws Everything.*

Out of boredom, he'd clicked on her video titled "Color Theory: Who Needs It?" and surprised himself by watching it all the way through, even though he couldn't draw a straight line. That sent him on a rabbit trail, and by the time he dozed off, he'd watched more than a dozen of her videos. Some were only a few minutes long, others were comprehensive art lessons. She was talented. She was also cute.

But not cute enough to keep his attention beyond wasting time on a dull Saturday night, and he'd avoided clicking on any of her other videos since then. But now here she was, smiling sweetly into the camera, her black squiggly curls framing a fair, thin face. He started to scroll past her, then went back up. His thumb hovered over the video for a few seconds before he tapped the Play button.

"I just had to try these." She held up a pack of fancy colored pencils, pushing them closer to the camera, influencer style. The case was crooked in the frame. "Oops." She quickly straightened it.

He smiled a little. Her high-pitched voice was soft, not grating, and she had a muted Southern drawl. Soothing too. He'd fallen asleep listening to her that first night.

She set the pencils down. "Want to see what I drew with them? Click here." She awkwardly pointed down, supposedly to the name of her channel or blog, but she missed it entirely.

"One waffle with crispy bacon." *Snap.* Enid set the plate down in front of him. "Anything else?"

"I'm good." As an afterthought he said, "Thanks."

"Sure thing, handsome." She winked at him as a group of customers entered the restaurant. She took off to tend to them.

His waffle and bacon forgotten for the moment, Hunter glanced at the video's view counter. Almost half a million views in less than a week. Wow. Unable to help himself, he clicked on the next one.

"Hi, I'm Britt." Her mouth turned up in a smile as her gaze moved downward. "Today I'm going to show you how to draw farm animals."

This wasn't the first animal lesson she had on her channel. When he watched the first one—"How to Create the Perfect Narwhal"—at first he thought he'd stumbled upon a kids' channel. Then he found out she was a graphic artist with a passion for animation. She was really good at it too. In this video, her hair was even mussier, as if she'd filmed it on a day with 150 percent humidity. Then she looked directly into the camera and smiled.

He paused the video and saw the reflection of the lights in her jade-green eyes. Her smile was endearingly awkward.

His thumb slipped and the video started again, the focus shifting from her to a sheet of white paper surrounded by cups of markers, pencils, and pens. He picked up his coffee and watched as she announced that today's animal was her favorite: a cow. Then she started to draw.

For the next twenty minutes, Hunter drank coffee, inhaled his waffle and bacon, and watched as Britt transformed a plain sheet of paper into an incredibly lifelike, detailed, and, oddly enough, colorful drawing of a cow's face. She worked fast and with skill, explaining everything as she went along. She did speed up the video in some places, but mostly it was all done in real time. Before he knew it, she was finished, and the focus was on her again.

"I hope y'all learned a few things today," she said, awkward smile back in place. "I'd love to hear about your favorite farm animal and the art projects you're working on. Until next time." She gave a little wave and turned off the camera.

He shut off the phone as Enid came over and handed him the check. He pulled out his wallet and gave her the cash. "Keep the change," he said, sliding out of the booth.

"Thanks." She looked him up and down. "Come back any time."

He gave her a quick, noncommittal nod, headed out the door, hopped on his bike, and sped off. When he reached his apartment building, he went upstairs and then inside. With nothing else to do, he headed to his bedroom, stripped down for bed, and turned off the light.

He lay on his back. Flipped onto his side. Tried lying on his stomach. Counted sheep. Counted sheep backward. Then gave up and grabbed his phone off the nightstand. Almost one in the morning.

After nearly running into Sawyer with the forklift, he couldn't afford another fidgety night. He started to put the phone back. Changed his mind. Turned it on and went straight to You-Tube . . . and *Britt Draws Everything.* He turned up the volume, hit Play, and set it back on the nightstand. Then he closed his eyes.

"Before I start with today's beachscape, I wanted to say a few words to those of you who are interested in drawing but haven't picked up your paintbrush or pen yet. It's okay to be afraid to try something new, or to come out of your comfort zone."

His eyes opened, then closed again. Her voice was so relaxing, he felt himself melt into his mattress.

"I've been thinking a lot about that myself. I've had a big change in my life recently, and I'm starting to rethink some things. Don't worry. I'm not giving up my channel. It's not going anywhere, and neither am I."

His breathing slowed.

"But have you ever come to a point in your life where you know you need to do something different or you need a change, and you're . . . scared?"

His eyes fluttered. She sounded different from her other videos. He wasn't sure why . . .

"Just know I understand. I also understand how hard it can be to make that change. It's easy to keep doing the same things, falling into the same patterns. It's safe. And we all like to play it safe, right?"

Safe. He rolled on his side, away from the phone.

"So maybe you can start with something small. Like drawing, and showing people your art. Or doing whatever it is you're interested in. Maybe it's a new job you're thinking about applying for, or possibly going out on your first date . . ."

Hunter half snored, half snorted.

"If you're thinking about doing something daring or new, don't overthink it. Just do it." She cleared her throat. "Now, on to today's lesson."

"Hunter!"

Pounding sounded in the distance. Hunter hugged his pillow. "Mmph." Then the door flew open. Light poured in as Sawyer burst through.

"Hey!" He shielded his eyes with his arm. "What the—"

"I've been banging on your door for five minutes." Sawyer flipped on the light switch, then walked to the bed and peered at him. "You okay?"

"I'm fine." He sat up, scrubbing a hand over his face.

"You sure?" Sawyer's gaze darted around the room.

"Yeah, I'm sure." He grabbed his phone. "What time is— Oh no." He scrambled out of bed, then noticed Sawyer was not-so-secretly opening the top drawer of his dresser. Hunter bumped him away with his shoulder. "You won't find anything there."

Sawyer stopped his snooping but didn't look convinced.

Hunter yanked a short-sleeved yellow uniform shirt out of his drawer. "I overslept." And had the best night's sleep he'd had in a long time. He didn't even remember drifting off. "That's all. I'll meet you at work."

"I can wait for you," Sawyer said.

He faced him. "Don't worry. I'm still clean."

"Just want to make sure."

"I appreciate it. If you insist on waiting, get out of here so I can get dressed."

Sawyer nodded. "Meet you outside."

Hunter headed to the bathroom for a quick shower, brushed his teeth, threw on his clothes and slicked back his damp, shaggy blond hair. He appreciated what Sawyer was doing. A year ago when they signed the lease together, he'd made a pact with Sawyer that he would stay clean and sober, and he'd kept it. That was in the past, and it was a road he never wanted to travel again.

He locked the apartment and went outside, and it hit him how long he'd slept. Now that he was fully awake, he felt better than he had in two weeks. He also remembered how he'd fallen asleep. *By listening to Britt.*

Jumping on his bike, he followed his friend to the warehouse. Some of the words she'd said flashed in his mind. Something about playing it safe. Up until recently, that had never been his MO.

But as he approached the warehouse, more of what she'd said came back to mind. *"But have you ever come to a point in your life where you know you need to do something different . . ."* That definitely applied to him. His life was at a standstill, and he didn't know how to change it.

He'd blown so many chances that he wasn't sure he could.

Chapter 3

Daniel Branch loosened the knot on his black tie and looked at Brittany, then took a drink of the half lemonade half tea she'd given him shortly after he walked inside the house. Not only was the drink delicious, it was also his favorite beverage, and he appreciated her thoughtfulness. Thoughtfulness he didn't deserve. But he was hoping to make up for the years he'd lost with her. And hopefully, someday, with Amy. *If she'll ever let me.*

"Thanks for agreeing to stay here today." Brittany tugged at the bottom of her white T-shirt. The graphic on the front was some kind of Japanese cartoon design he didn't recognize. Manga, he thought she called it. Whatever it was, he'd seen her draw similar-looking things on her channel that rivaled the commercially sold stuff. His girl had talent, and lots of it. "I didn't feel like going out today," she said.

"No problem." He shifted on one of two matching sage-green recliners.

Brittany was seated in the other one. He reminded himself that this was no longer his home and hadn't been for over twenty years. The walls were still the same shade of beige they'd been when he and Amy bought the three-bedroom home back in the nineties, soon after they were married. At that time, the city of Allen was starting to boom, and they'd gotten it for a deal. She was a first-year teacher and he'd just started his mechanic job at a garage around the corner that was no longer in business and was now a nail salon. They didn't have much money or experience. But they'd had a lot of love . . . and he'd squandered all of it.

"I'm sorry I haven't asked you this yet, but is it weird to be here after all these years?" Brittany put her palms on her knees.

"A little." More than that actually. There was nothing of him in this house anymore, other than her. He didn't recognize any of the furniture, pictures, or knickknacks. His ex-wife had even changed out the country blue carpeting for wood flooring. This house was all hers now, and she'd made it her home.

He glanced at Brittany. She was rubbing her palms over her knees, something she did when she was a little girl and was upset or anxious about something.

"Do you want to talk about it?"

Her head jerked up. "Talk about what?" She grabbed her glass and drained half of it in one gulp.

"Whatever's bothering you. Is that why you didn't want to go out and grab a bite to eat?"

"I didn't feel like being around . . ." She sighed and set the drink back on a coaster on top of a square glass-topped end table. "People."

"Ah." He settled back in the recliner. At least she was being honest. She might not have inherited her art talent from him, but she did have his introversion. Especially compared to Amy, who never met a stranger. "I get it."

"I don't." She stared at her lap, then gave the hem of her shirt one more tug. "Savannah's getting married."

Shortly after they started talking to each other a few months ago, Brittany had told him about her best friend. "That's good, isn't it?" he asked.

"Yeah . . . for her." She looked at him. "She wants me to be in the wedding."

"And you don't want to?"

"I do. But whenever I think about everything that goes with it, I get nervous. And then I feel guilty. The wedding isn't about me. It's about Savannah and Justin."

While he was glad she was sharing her troubles with him, he was already out of his depth. Their family had imploded when she was eight years old and Amy had filed for divorce. He hadn't exactly been present during the prior years either. He'd missed a lot of time and a lot of milestones. "What does your mom say?"

"I haven't told her." A thick lock of curly hair had escaped her ponytail, and she shoved it behind her ear. "I know what she'd tell me anyway."

"Do it?"

"Yeah."

"I agree with her." He shifted and faced her. "I know it will be hard for you, but Savannah is a good friend."

"She said it was okay if I didn't want to." She lifted her head and met his gaze. "I sound like a child, don't I?" Before he could answer, she said, "I'm going to do it."

He grinned. "That's the spirit!" At her eye roll he said, "Guess that didn't sound too hip."

For the first time since he arrived, she smiled. "You're forty-eight. You're not supposed to be hip." But she seemed more light-hearted as she took a sip of her lemonade tea. "Are you hungry? I made some tuna salad earlier today."

He hated tuna salad. But he would eat ten bowls of it if she wanted him to. "Sounds great."

They took their drinks into the kitchen, and he tried to keep his expression impassive. Just like the living room and foyer, every-thing was different except for the paint. He wasn't anything close to an interior designer, as his sparsely furnished, bare-walled, one-bedroom efficiency would attest, and he had no idea what Amy's style was, other than cozy. There was a serene, comfortable vibe throughout the space. They hadn't had much of that during their short marriage.

Brittany quickly made the sandwiches, adding a pickle spear on the side of each and a small serving of ridged potato chips. While he choked down the tuna, they talked about her channel, and a little more about the wedding.

"I'm proud of you, Brittany," he said.

"Thanks, Dad. But why don't you call me Britt like everyone else?"

"I don't know." He wiped his mouth with a paper napkin. "You've always been Brittany to me." He glanced at his watch. "Sorry, I've got to get back to work."

"Oh." Disappointment flashed in her eyes. "Well, I'm glad you could come over. Next time we'll definitely go out."

He was about to tell her that it was okay to stay here at the house, as long as Amy wasn't around. Not that he didn't want to see her. He was dying to. But she didn't even know he was back in town, and Brittany wasn't ready to tell her they were talking. He was allowing her to guide their relationship. She'd let him know when the time was right to reach out to Amy.

Then again, he didn't want to encourage her reluctance to leave the house. That was one thing he was concerned about—she had a fear of social situations. He wasn't a fan of them either, so there was a level of understanding there, along with more guilt. When Brittany revealed she'd been in counseling on and off for her anxiety, he knew he was partly to blame, even though she never said so. Considering how he'd abandoned her, he had to be.

"Right. We should go out," he said. "There's a new barbecue place in Plano I want to try." When she nodded, he was relieved. Maybe in the near future he would ask her about returning to counseling. Lord knows it did a lot for him. But not now. He didn't want to do anything to shake up their tenuous relationship.

He stood and took his dishes to the sink. After washing his hands, he tightened his tie. It was already approaching ninety degrees outside, and he'd left his jacket in the car. But he didn't want to forget about the tie. He had a strict uniform, and there was no deviating from it.

He turned to Brittany, who was wiping crumbs off the counter with a dish towel. "When are you telling Savannah?"

She paused, then folded the dish towel neatly into fourths. "Tonight," she said with a sharp nod. "I don't want to keep her waiting any longer."

"Good idea." He smiled, his heart full of pride and love for her. "By the way, you don't sound like a child. You're not acting like one either. When you do something that's hard on you to make someone else happy . . . that's maturity."

She tilted her head. "That's really wise. Thank you."

He wanted to pull her into his arms and tell her how much these moments meant to him. She was doing another hard thing by allowing him to prove she could trust him again. But he held back. They hadn't hugged yet, just shook hands the first time they met in person after he contacted her through direct message on her channel. There would be time for hugs. Right now, he would take anything he could get.

She walked him to the door and opened it. A barely year-old white Jaguar was parked in the driveway. "My dad, the chauffer."

He frowned a little. "Does that embarrass you?"

"Of course not. It's pretty cool. I don't know anyone else who drives a Jag."

"It is my boss's, remember." He wasn't going to mention that this was only one of his cars, and it was the cheapest and most common looking. He didn't dare drive the Bentley or the Bugatti by himself. He'd ridden in the Bugatti once, when his boss had driven it to the country club. Daniel had ended up parking it for him. Beautiful, amazing car. But driving the Jag was great too. "I better get back. He's got a meeting in two hours downtown."

"All right." She stood in the doorway as he went to the car. When he opened the door, she said, "Call me later."

He grinned. "Of course." He got inside and drove off, the rich interior cooling down quickly as he mulled over how good his life was now. A great job, fantastic boss, an apartment that suited him, and a relationship with Brittany. He would never have dreamed he'd be at this point in three short years. There was only one thing missing.

Amy.

All he could hope for where she was concerned was eventual civility. She had every right to be angry with him. Hate him, even.

But he wasn't the same man he'd been twenty years ago, or even three years ago. He'd changed for the better. He also had bridges to rebuild, and it was past time he did that.

～

"Oh, Britt, thank you! If I were there, I'd give you a big hug!"

Britt grinned as she FaceTimed Savannah, who was in Springfield with Justin looking at houses. Despite her anxiety over being maid of honor, it was worth it to make her best friend happy. She was glad she'd talked to her dad about it today. Confiding in him was a brand-new thing. As soon as he left, she decided to tell Savannah before she chickened out.

"I'll be home this weekend," Savannah said. "We can discuss all the details then. Oh, Justin says hi."

Justin's face appeared on the screen. "Hey, Britt. Thanks for making my girl's day." He grinned and disappeared from view.

"Isn't he the best?" Savannah put on her large-framed sunglasses. "We've got another appointment for a showing. This is the sixth—"

"Seventh," Justin corrected.

"Okay, seventh house we've looked at today. It's all running together."

"Any promising ones?"

"Not yet. But we'll find the perfect house, I'm sure. Thanks again, Britt. Talk to you soon!"

After Britt hung up, she went upstairs to her studio and looked at the large calendar on her wall. She had one more video to make this week, but she hadn't figured out the content yet. She was still fielding comments and messages about the last one she'd uploaded two weeks ago when she had admitted the need for a change.

She'd surprised herself by saying those words, and she had considered editing them out of the video. But she didn't, mostly to keep herself accountable. Now that they were out in the public domain, she needed to stand by them. Regardless of her father's excellent advice, she still might not have called Savannah and told her she would be her maid of honor if she hadn't been honest with her audience.

She sat down at her desk and started to doodle, something she did when she was looking for inspiration. But she wasn't thinking about videos. She was thinking about her father.

He always seemed uncomfortable when he walked into the house, no matter how much he tried to play it off. Although she was only eight when he left, she could remember the fights with Mom, the times he didn't show up to school or church events, the empty beer cans that littered the floor around his chair when he fell asleep drinking after work. There was one time when she got up before her mother, saw the cans, and picked them up so he wouldn't get into trouble. She was, what, five? Six?

Her heart pinched, and she stared at the doodle that wasn't a doodle at all. It was a pencil sketch of her father's eyes. Clear, bright, engaged. Like he was today. She hadn't expected him to figure out she was struggling with something. He'd told her he'd changed, and she could see it. But she also knew not to trust him—not yet. Even he'd said it would take time to build up their relationship. So far, it had been time well spent.

She did a quick fill-in of the rest of his features and set the drawing aside. She still didn't have a topic—she'd done many tutorials on faces and portraiture—but she didn't panic. There were endless ways to find inspiration. Eventually she would land on an idea, or several, she would want to explore.

Britt opened her laptop and went to her channel dashboard. One hundred new comments from yesterday, and twenty DMs, all from her "confession video" as she now referred to it. The unread DMs weren't all recent. Several of them arrived shortly after the video, and after the first three creeped her out, she'd avoided reading the rest. She was almost to the point where she wanted to turn off DMs. But not all of them were inappropriate or bad. There were good and kind people who complimented her art and gave her encouragement. It had also been the way her father had gotten back in contact with her.

Maybe some music would make the process of going through her messages less painful. She slipped in her earbuds, found one of her beloved yacht rock playlists, and jammed while she opened her inbox.

Hello dear. I like you videos and you are beiutyful. I am African prince with one billion dollers to give you . . .

Delete.

Dear Britt—while I do enjoy your videos, I wish you would do something about your hair and makeup. You would be so pretty if you would just add a little lipstick and mascara, and for the love of God buy a straightener—

Delete.

Wow look at u. So famous. Remember me? We went to elementary school togthr. U know, I have this business where I make 25k a day. U can too, just click here—

Delete.

"And I'm not famous," she muttered, even though she knew the message was a spambot. She didn't consider having a large audience being famous. She was just teaching what she knew, and she was glad other people were enjoying it.

The rest of the messages were similar, and she deleted all of them until she got to the last one.

Hi Britt. I hope this doesn't seem weird, but I wanted to let you know how much I appreciated your last video—the one where you talked about making a change. I can so relate. It's easy to stay stuck in a rut, even when it's uncomfortably comfortable. I've got some changes to make, but I'm not sure how to make them. I don't even know why I'm telling you this.

I just stumbled across your videos a little while ago. I'm not an artist. I can't even color in the lines.

Anyway, I'm rambling. Just wanted to say thanks and good luck with your art and the channel.

H.

P.S. That beachscape you drew was very cool. Made me want to go surfing.

Britt looked at the small circle to the left of the message. H's avatar was a digital drawing of a planet surrounded by purple, pink, and silver space dust on a black background. Then she read the message again. This wasn't the first time someone had written the words "I hope this isn't weird." It almost always was. And there were other people who messaged her and wondered why they were writing to her or confessing something. But there were two words in H's message that made her pay attention.

Uncomfortably comfortable.

That was her in a nutshell. She had nothing to complain about. She lived in a nice house, her mother treated her like an adult—most of the time—and she had a good job that was building a great nest egg. It helped that she didn't have too many expenses, although she did pay rent to her mother and footed her own bills for her phone, insurance, gas, etc. Not that she drove her secondhand car too often. Like everything else in life, driving gave her anxiety. She'd barely made it through the process of getting her license. She wouldn't have done it without Savannah's and her mother's encouragement.

Britt closed her laptop and went to the window. The bonus room she'd turned into an office six years ago faced the street and gave her an overview of the neighborhood. Beyond the house across from hers was a nice neighborhood park that had a pond complete with ducks, a walking trail, and a sand volley-ball court, along with the requisite playground equipment for kids. When was the last time she had gone to the park? Or gone swimming?

Her best friend was getting married, and Britt was . . . un-comfortably comfortable.

The playlist on her phone ended, and she started up another one. She'd never been into hip-hop, rap, or any pop music past 2000. Savannah always teased her about her "boomer music," but Britt didn't care. She smiled as a Seals & Crofts tune played in her ear while she opened her laptop again and reread H's message. She decided to respond.

Dear H,

She stopped, having no idea if H was female or male, and then realized it didn't make a difference.

Thanks for reaching out to me. I'm glad you liked the video—beachscapes are relaxing to draw, even though I've never been to an actual beach. One day I'd like to go, just to dip my toes in the ocean and collect seashells. I know that sounds boring compared to surfing.

I've discovered over the years that people who say they can't draw or paint or do any kind of art just haven't found what suits them. Coloring in the lines isn't easy, no matter what medium you use. I still miss the lines myself sometimes. And that's okay. You have to give yourself the freedom not to be perfect.

I hope you're able to figure out how to make your changes. I'm still working on mine.

Her fingers hovered over the keyboard. Now who was confessing things? She quickly signed off the message, and after a second's hesitation, hit Send. She'd probably never hear from H again. That happened too, where she liked a message enough to respond to it. Those were almost always requests for art help, and if she was able to offer advice, she gave it. It always surprised her how many people didn't bother to say "thanks" or "I got your message." She didn't want them kissing her feet, but a response in return would be nice.

She did some more doodling and internet searching, finally landing on an idea for her next video—a ten-minute art challenge. She'd done a thirty-minute one before and it was fun. She took out her planning notebook and decided on the subject—a seashell.

She made some production notes, a list of supplies, and a timeline, then practiced drawing a pale-pink scallop shell with pastels, all while timing herself. When she got down to ten minutes, she stopped, made a few notes about how she was able to accomplish the speed drawing, then began to shut down for the day and start on supper—a nice cobb salad with homemade dressing. On hot days like today, she and Mom preferred to eat light meals.

Just as she was logging off her channel, she saw a new message pop up. She paused, thinking it was probably another spam DM, then clicked on it.

Britt—I didn't really expect you to write back, so it was nice to get a response. I've got a few things to do before I head to work, but if you don't mind, I'd like to message you later. I've got some questions about art. Maybe you're right—I just haven't found the right thing yet.

She smiled and looked at the sign-off name. *Hunter.*

Chapter 4

Break time's over." Sawyer snatched Hunter's phone out of his hand.

Hunter shot up from the chair at one of the wobbly tables in the warehouse break room and grabbed for his phone. "I've got three minutes left. Who put you in charge of the clock?"

"Me, myself, and I." Sawyer, who was at least four inches shorter than Hunter but twice as fast, ducked under his arm and dashed to the other side of the empty room. "What do we have here?" he said, looking at the screen.

"Give it back, Campbell," he warned.

"In a second. I want to see what—or *who*—has been consuming your life for the past week." He frowned as he brushed the screen with his finger. Then he looked up. "Art videos?"

Hunter jerked the phone out of his hands. "Yeah. What did you think it was?"

"Nothing that innocent." Sawyer shoved a nearby chair under a table with his hip. "Since when have you been interested in art?"

"That's none of your business." He put his phone in his pocket and clocked back in to work. "Next time you pull a stunt like that, you'll regret it."

Sawyer held up his hands, palms out. "Okay, okay. It was just a joke. Don't get so touchy."

They walked out of the break room. Hunter didn't think he was being touchy at all for getting annoyed about Sawyer looking at his phone, even as a joke. Before he was so unceremoniously interrupted, he'd watched Britt for over five minutes as she departed from her usual drawing and painting and sculpted a clay figurine.

"It helps to visualize the object in three dimensions, adding more realism to the project. If realism is your goal." She shrugged, giving the camera a shy smile. *"For you impressionists out there, just have fun with the clay."*

Until he'd started watching her channel, he hadn't given any thought to all the ways there were to create art.

"Later, man," Sawyer said, clapping him on the back. "And hey, sorry about the phone. I'll keep your art obsession between you and me."

"It's not an obsession," he said, but Sawyer was already heading for the back of the warehouse.

Hunter shook his head and walked over to the forklift. While he'd spent a lot of time over the past two weeks watching Britt's channel, he wouldn't call himself obsessed. She had hundreds of videos and tons of content. He was learning a lot too. Besides, it was a much better way to pass the time than scrolling through thirty-second videos of birds dancing and people doing stupid stuff.

Slipping on his earphones, he cranked up the latest top twenty hip-hop list and focused on his job. Four hours until quitting time. Over the past two weeks he hadn't bothered asking Sawyer if he wanted to get something to eat or to play a video game after work. Sawyer's date with Marissa had been a bust, and now he was seeing a new girl he'd met in the chip and dip aisle at the corner convenience mart.

Without his roommate as a distraction, he could concentrate on Britt's videos.

After Hunter clocked out, he jumped on his bike, headed back to the apartment, and fixed two grilled cheese sandwiches—extra cheesy. Popping the top on a can of Coke, he sat at the small table in the kitchen and opened his laptop. He wasn't satisfied only watching her videos on his phone anymore.

Thirty minutes later he'd polished off his dinner, drained the Coke, and finished the sculpting video. He was about to click on another one, but stopped when he saw a new notification. He grinned and immediately clicked on it.

Hi Hunter,
Are you sure you want me to tell you all about anime and manga? I could write a book!

He settled in and read Britt's detailed explanation about the popular Japanese art and literature form. Since he'd first given into his impulse and dashed off a message to her a little more than a week ago, they had "talked" every day, mostly about art, of course. He was full of questions, especially after she'd told him he just needed to find the right thing, whatever that was. Not that he imagined art would be his thing, or even a hobby. But he did enjoy her videos . . . and he was starting to enjoy her. She wrote like she talked in her videos—concise, down to earth, easy to understand. Even reading her essay on anime and manga was interesting.

I hope I didn't give you too much information. I tend to go a little overboard when I'm passionate about something.

Hunter blinked, then smiled. *What else is she passionate about?* He shook his head, stunned at the thought, reminding himself that he was only interested in her content, not her—even though she was cute, smart, and extremely talented.

I just uploaded my ten-minute art challenge. Why don't you give it a try? You can send it to me when you're finished. If you want, that is. You don't have to. B.

His phone buzzed and he tilted it up to look at the screen. Why was Payne calling him at 11:45 on a Thursday night? "Hey," he answered. "Everything okay?"

"Yes. I'm working late at the office and time got away from me. I meant to call you earlier today."

Hunter put the phone on speaker, then stood and went to get another Coke out of the fridge, only to change his mind and grab a clean glass out of the dishwasher. "What's the special occasion?"

"Father's sixtieth birthday," Payne said in his usual matter-of-fact tone. Either his brother didn't get Hunter's sarcasm, or he was letting it pass without comment.

Hunter turned on the tap. "That's next month, right?"

"Yes. The family is throwing him a party."

Uh-oh. He filled the glass with water and sat back down. When the Pickett family threw a party, they threw a *party*. The kind that ended up in the society section of the *Dallas Morning News*—if they even had a society section anymore. He hadn't read a newspaper in ages.

"You're invited," Payne said.

"How kind of you to allow me to come to my father's own party." He couldn't hold back his snide tone.

"You're reaping what you sowed, Hunter."

He was painfully aware of that. After his last run-in with the law, his parents had cut off all contact, and he didn't blame them for doing so. "Let me guess, you drew the short straw and were tasked with not only inviting me, but telling me to be on my best behavior."

"And to warn you if you do anything to upset Mother, embarrass Father, or ruin this party, Kirk and I will never *allow* you to attend another family event. We're only allowing it this time because Mother insisted Father would want you there."

That was a surprise, considering their current no-contact status with him. Well, at least one of his family members still cared. Or they were all trying to keep up appearances. Each time he'd crashed and burned, his parents were there to clean up his mess and keep it out of the papers and away from all media. Not for his sake, but their own. *Until that last time . . .* "When is it?"

"June thirtieth."

"Well, look at that, I happen to be free." He was always free.

"I'll text you the details when they become available," Payne said. "Do you have a tuxedo?"

"No. The Warehouse frowns upon them."

"Huh?"

Hunter grinned a little. "I'll rent one."

"Make sure you do. We all want this party to be perfect."

Like Payne was. And Kirk. And his parents. *But not me.* "Don't worry. I won't mess this up for Father."

"Make sure you don't."

And then there was silence. He stared at the blank screen and leaned back in his chair. *One big happy family.* They *had* been, at one time. Before he was a teenager and had gone off the rails. But even when he was a kid, he knew he didn't measure up to his older brothers and his parents' expectations of him. And maybe it was a self-fulfilling prophecy, or rebellion, or just his nature at the time, but between the ages of thirteen and twenty-eight, he'd reinforced every single doubt they had about him.

A chime rang from his computer. He glanced at it and saw there was another message notification from Britt. He clicked on it.

I don't want to pressure you about the challenge. I probably shouldn't have said anything about it. Don't feel like you have to do it if you don't want to. B.

Quickly, he tapped out his response.

No pressure at all. In fact, I think

He paused, mulling over his decision.

it's a great idea. I'll send it to you when I'm done. H.

He hit Send. Now he was committed. And maybe this was what he needed to try his hand at something new—a challenge. He clicked on the video and made a mental note of the supplies he would need to pick up tomorrow before work: paper and some crayon-looking things called pastels. There was an art store in Plano—K&B Art Supplies—where he could stop by and get what he needed. They had sponsored a few of her videos.

At the end of the video, she was on camera again. "If you're a beginner artist, this is the perfect project to practice your skills. And you don't have to use pastels. You can use colored pencils, charcoal, even markers if you want to. The point is to challenge yourself. I sure did with this seashell."

Her seashell was perfect, and as familiar as he was with her artistic talent, he knew she was being humble. Another point in her favor.

She signed off with her usual shy little wave. And as usual, he smiled back. He couldn't help it—she was too cute when she did that. He was about to shut down the laptop, then froze. K&B Art Supplies. In *Plano.*

Did she live in the Dallas area? Why else would a Plano art shop sponsor her videos? Then again, any art store in the country would, particularly the ones who had online shopping and shipped their supplies. He worked in a shipping company warehouse, but he rarely paid attention to the boxes he moved around and organized, other than their shapes and quantities, so he couldn't say if he saw K&B Art Supplies' name on any of the packages.

Hunter closed the laptop and headed for the shower. There were over six million people living in the Dallas-Fort Worth area. Even if she did live here, the chances of running into her were almost none, other than hanging out at K&Bs to see if she showed up. She might not even buy anything from there, although she did use and recommend supplies from her sponsors. K&B was only one of them.

Shaking his head, he turned on the water and stood under the spray. It didn't matter if she lived close by. He never intended to try to meet her. He was just killing time, watching videos.

Then again, he never intended to contact her either. *But I did.*

He finished his shower and slipped on a T-shirt and boxers, then played a few video games on the TV in the living room. But his curiosity about where Britt lived was piqued. There was a simple way to find out. *I could just ask her.*

"No." He switched to another mind-numbing game. From his very first message, he took great pains not to come across as weird, creepy, or stalkerish. And now that he'd made the decision to do the ten-minute challenge, he didn't want to do anything to give her cause to shut him out. All the hours spent learning from her would go down the tubes.

Funny how up until now, he'd only considered watching her channel as a time waster. For sure he was no artist, but he could have some fun and do something more productive than play video games.

His leg jounced as he engrossed himself in the game. But no matter how much he tried to get into it, he couldn't stop looking at his closed laptop.

~

Britt shut off her computer and went downstairs. She'd spent more time working tonight than she'd intended to, but she was eager to upload her ten-minute challenge video. She thought it was one of her best ones, and she planned to do at least one challenge every three months, if not more often. Even if she didn't get an enthusiastic response from her viewers, she had enjoyed the project.

She went downstairs to fix a snack of celery and carrot sticks with hummus and headed for her bedroom. When she passed the living room, she saw her mother conked out in the recliner again. School ended last week but there was still one more day of meetings and professional development before she wrapped up the year.

Britt paused, wondering if she should wake her, then decided not to. Anytime Mom fell asleep in the chair, she always got up and went to bed soon after. There was no reason to disturb her.

Once Britt was in her room, she settled into a vintage chair from the seventies, complete with brown and yellow plaid upholstery. She'd fallen in love with it years ago when she and Savannah had gone to a thrift store looking for an old dress for a costume party Savannah was attending. It took some elbow grease to clean it up, including shampooing the fabric and polishing the wooden arms. When she finished, it looked like an odd mix of dated and brand new. It was comfy, it was hers, and she loved it.

She set her food and a glass of water on the upside-down apple crate she used as an end table and picked up her well-loved copy of *Prince Caspian*. A few pages in, the celery and almost all of the carrots and hummus were gone, but she couldn't focus. Her mind wasn't on her favorite book in the Narnia series. It was on Hunter.

Right after she'd sent her looooong message about anime and manga, she cringed. Surely he hadn't expected her almost textbook explanation. Then she'd gone and invited him to do the challenge and, immediately, doubts set in. She didn't want him to feel obligated. But then he responded so quickly, saying that it was not only totally fine, but he was going to do the challenge.

A tiny thrill went through her when she read that.

There was no use trying to read when she was so distracted. She shut the book and munched on a carrot as she used her phone to check on her channel. She could barely admit to herself that she was hoping for another message from Hunter tonight. Why, she didn't know, only that she liked talking to him about art. From his questions, she guessed he was a beginner and possibly a complete novice. He also passed her personal private message test—he was courteous, stayed on topic, and kept all communication appropriate.

For some reason, she found herself wishing she knew a little more about him. Like what state or country he was from. What he did for a living. His age even. Not that age mattered during professional correspondence.

But she couldn't help but want their correspondence to be a little more personal.

Mom poked her head inside the doorway. "Still up?"

Nodding, Britt set her phone in her lap. "I worked late tonight, so I'm not quite ready for sleep yet."

"That's definitely not my problem." She yawned. "Everything going okay? I feel like we haven't talked much lately."

That was true, and right now Britt was fine with that. A part of her felt extremely guilty for seeing her dad on the sly. But now wasn't the time to bring him up to Mom. She was in the middle of ending another school year, and her focus should be on that. There would be time in the future to tell her about him. "Everything's fine. Good actually. I told Savannah I'd be her maid of honor."

Mom's eyes grew wide. "Really? Britt, that's wonderful! I'm sure she's happy about that."

"She is." Britt smiled.

"You're doing the right thing, honey. I'm proud of you."

"Thanks." But her smile dimmed a little. First Dad, and now Mom, expressed their pride in her. And she'd be happy about that if she were actually doing something impressive instead of what any normal best friend would do for the bride-to-be.

"Why don't we do something fun this weekend? We could go to Grimaldi's, maybe do a little shopping after?"

"Sure."

Mom yawned. "All right. One more day. I can do this." She gave Britt two thumbs up. "Good night. See you tomorrow."

"Night, Mom. Love you."

"Love you too."

Britt yawned, surprising herself. Guess she was tired after all. One more check of her channel and she'd call it a night. She picked up her phone, went back to YouTube . . . and saw three new notifications. Quickly she looked through the first two that alerted her to new comments on several of her videos. Then she clicked on the third one.

> Hi Britt. One more thing, and I hope I'm not bugging or bothering you. I noticed one of your sponsors is K&B Art Supplies. I was thinking about buying my supplies from there. Do you have any recommendations?

While it was great he wanted to patronize a sponsor, she wondered why he chose them. She had several art companies sponsoring her videos, and she appreciated every one of them. But K&B was special. It was where Mom had bought Britt's first paint for her set when she was a child, and she was good friends with Maude and Xavier—X, as he preferred to be called—the eccentric, long-term owners of the store. She shopped there at least once a week, often more. It was one of the few places where she didn't feel anxious.

Did he live in Plano? No, that would be too much of a coincidence. Maude and X had a thriving online business. That made them a perfect place for him to order his supplies.

She messaged him back with a list and their website.

> Thanks for purchasing from them. I've been going there for a long time. They're my favorite art store. B.

Nibbling on the last carrot, she waited to see if he would reply right away. Ten minutes later, he hadn't, and she started to log off—

Thanks, Britt. Have a good night.

You too, Hunter.

She smiled and turned off her phone.

Chapter 5

Y ou didn't have to take me to lunch today, Mr. Pickett." Daniel opened the Grimaldi's menu as the tangy scents of tomato sauce, oregano, and pizza dough surrounded them.

"It's my pleasure." He rolled up the sleeves of his white shirt, one that probably cost as much as Daniel's biweekly paycheck. "Lila won't allow a sliver of pizza past her lips, so any time I get a chance to eat a good pie, I'm going to take it."

Daniel smiled and perused the menu. When his boss had suggested they go to lunch after his quarterly Saturday morning investor meeting, he was surprised. After being in Arthur Pickett's employ for almost nine months now, he was coming to expect the man to throw him a few curve balls occasionally. Unlike his wife, Mr. Pickett didn't mind the occasional change in schedule.

"Have you been here before?" his boss asked.

"More than I can count. The food is excellent."

"Any recommendations?"

"Do you like pineapple on your pizza?"

Mr. Pickett gave him a pinched look. "That's unnatural, Daniel."

Daniel chuckled. "It's definitely controversial. I suggest getting the make-your-own. You can pick your crust, sauce, and toppings."

"Done."

The waitress came over and placed glasses of water in front of them, the diamond stud in her nose twinkling. "Can I take your order?"

Letting his boss go first, Daniel looked around the crowded restaurant. Grimaldi's was always packed on a Saturday, and today was no different. Although their main attraction was pizza, the restaurant also served several authentic Italian dishes and desserts. Grimaldi's wasn't fancy, but it wasn't a hole-in-the-wall pizza parlor either.

"And you, sir?"

"A personal pan Hawaiian and sweet iced tea."

She jotted it down, picked up their menus, and left to put in their orders.

Daniel took a drink of water. This was the first time he and Mr. Pickett had shared a meal together, and he didn't know what to talk about. Other than being his chauffeur, their worlds didn't intersect. Well, that wasn't exactly true. When Daniel had been in legal trouble seven years ago, Mr. Pickett took him on as part of his ongoing commitment to have a percentage of his case load be pro bono, and he managed to get Daniel a reduced sentence and parole.

That was Daniel's wake-up call, and he'd been on a clean and sober journey ever since. No one was more surprised than he when Mr. Pickett reached out and asked him if he wanted a job. When he was hired, he didn't dare ask why.

Mr. Pickett glanced around the restaurant. "I like it here. Nice décor, not too swanky, reasonable prices. No Perrier, though. Club soda will have to do." He folded his hands on the table. "You're probably wondering why I suggested lunch today."

Although it seemed far-fetched that Mr. Pickett would fire him over pizza and breadsticks, Daniel couldn't stop the dread from surfacing. He mentally searched for what he could have done wrong. He was never late, always kept the cars washed and detailed, the engines running at top capacity, and had even worked late several times, almost always at Lila's insistence. "It had crossed my mind, Mr. Pickett."

"Please. Call me Arthur."

Daniel rubbed his hands over his legs underneath the table. "Sure. Arthur."

His boss sat back, his gaze serious. "How are you liking your job?"

"I really enjoy it," he said, telling the truth. "I've always liked driving and working on cars. I see this as the best of both worlds."

"Glad to hear it. You're the best chauffeur I've ever had. I want to make sure you're happy. Consider today a celebration."

"For what?"

"Your 30 percent raise." Arthur grinned.

Daniel's jaw dropped. "Seriously?"

"I'm always serious about money. You'll also be getting paid vacation time."

He fell back in his chair. This was more than he'd ever hoped for. With his record, job opportunities were limited. Not only did Mr. Pickett—Arthur—pay well, he also provided health insurance coverage. That had been enough. Now he was offering a raise and paid vacations too? Daniel's hand shot out. "Thank you, Arthur. Thank you so much."

Arthur shook it as the waitress brought their drinks. "Your pizzas will be right up," she said, giving them a smile.

Arthur took a sip of the club soda. "Excellent"—he peered at her name tag—"Stormi. Excellent club soda."

She beamed. "We aim to please."

As Arthur continued to butter up the waitress, Daniel was still processing. He'd only done what was expected of him, with a little extra due to Lila Pickett being quite demanding when it came to punctuality, scheduling, and keeping the cars in spotless, pristine condition. But even during those times, she was fine to deal with and always pleasant to him. Just as he didn't understand why Arthur had hired him, he was clueless why he was getting such a hike in pay.

The waitress left, and Arthur turned to him. "You look puzzled, Daniel."

"I am." He hesitated, not wanting to ruin a good thing if his next question upset Arthur. But he had to know the answer. "Why did you take a chance on me?"

Arthur stared at the bubbles in his glass for a moment. "After more than thirty years of practicing criminal law, I've developed a level of discernment. Some of my clients are not only true criminals, they also relish their criminality. Others are sorry for what they've done but refuse to change their ways. Then I get a few, like you, who learn their lesson and transform their lives for the better." He shrugged and looked at Daniel. "You can call it a gut feeling too. After I fired my last driver, you came to mind. To be honest, I was sure you weren't going to take the position."

"Why?"

"It's not exactly a glamorous job. And I know Lila can be a bit much sometimes. But I'm impressed with how you handle the position, and my wife. I believe good work should be rewarded."

Daniel grinned. "Thank you, Arthur. That means a lot. I'll stay on as long as you want me to."

"That's good to hear." He grew serious again. "I wish more people would make the effort to turn things around."

He said the last sentence in a voice so low Daniel could barely hear him.

The waitress showed up with their pizzas and they dug in. From Arthur's muffled sounds of approval as they ate, Daniel could tell he'd made the right recommendation. They chatted during the meal, mostly about the investor meeting, with Daniel saying few words and nodding at appropriate times. He'd learned a while ago that sometimes all Arthur wanted was a sounding board.

As he was about to finish off the last bite of pineapple-laden pizza, he looked up at the entrance. He froze at what he saw— Brittany and Amy walking into the dining area.

Arthur turned around to see what he was looking at. "Friends of yours?"

He was tempted to drop his pizza and run over to them. But he held back, and fortunately neither of them spotted him as they were seated at a table on the other side of the restaurant. He exhaled. If Brittany had been alone, he wouldn't have hesitated to go to her. But he couldn't, not with Amy there. It wasn't time, not yet. *Hopefully soon . . .*

"Everything all right?" Arthur asked.

Collecting himself, Daniel said, "Yes." His boss didn't know anything about his family life. At the time of his conviction, he wanted to leave Brittany and Amy out of it. He hadn't even told Brittany his boss's name. "I just thought I saw someone I know." Disappointment filled him. "My mistake."

Britt gripped the edge of the red-and-white checkered tablecloth as her mother perused the menu. The trunk of Mom's car was half-full of packages from their morning shopping spree. The stores hadn't been too crowded for the first two hours, and she was able to relax a little. But after more shoppers appeared, she started getting anxious, and then she got annoyed with herself because she was anxious.

Her nerves were heightened even now, since Grimaldi's was jam-packed with people. They were lucky they'd gotten a table. At this point Britt would have been happy to go home and have a PB&J, but she couldn't keep running away and avoiding everything that made her uncomfortable. This was good practice for Savannah's wedding.

"Everything always looks so delicious." Mom smiled and kept reading. "I always have a hard time choosing what to get."

Britt didn't. She always got the same thing.

"Okay," she finally announced, "I'm getting the fried tortellini with clam sauce." She shut the menu. "YOLO. Isn't that what all you cool kids say?"

"Yeah," Britt said, laughing. "Ten years ago." But her mother's attempt at being cool made her smile. Both her parents could be such dorks sometimes. It was cute.

A waiter came over, his face flushed, glasses of water balancing in his hands. "Sorry for the wait," he said, giving them the drinks. "Today has been crazy." He shoved back his blond bangs and pulled out a pad from the black apron around his waist. "Have you decided?"

Mom gave her order, along with a Diet Coke with lemon to drink. "Clearly I'm counting calories," she said with a grin.

The waiter smiled and turned to Britt.

"Hawaiian," she said.

He leaned forward. "Sorry, I didn't hear you."

She gulped and spoke louder. "Hawaiian. Personal pan."

"Ah, got it. Anything to drink?"

Britt shook her head. Water was fine. As he walked away, she looked at her mother, noticing she wasn't smiling as much. "Is something wrong?"

"No." She quickly arranged her silverware, not looking up. "I've never understood why you and your . . . why you like pine-apple on pizza."

"I don't know. I've just always liked it."

Mom went to pick up her cloth napkin and it slipped through her fingers and dropped on the floor. She reached down to get it at the same time a man passed by, bumping into her.

"Oh," he said, stopping as she sat up. "I'm sorry." Then he paused. "Mrs. Branch?"

Her brow furrowed slightly.

"Arthur Pickett." He held out his hand. "You had my youngest son in algebra class."

"Ah, right." Mom shook it and smiled. "I remember now. That's been, what, fifteen years ago?"

"Fourteen."

Britt watched the exchange. He was handsome for an old man, with almost totally gray hair and deep wrinkles at the corners of his blue eyes as he smiled. His white dress shirt was rolled up at the sleeves, and she liked the casual look.

"I can't believe you remembered me," Mom said. "That was so long ago."

Arthur tapped his temple with his finger. "I've been blessed with a steel trap." He turned to Britt. "Hello."

"This is my daughter, Brittany." Mom gestured to her. "We're just out shopping and decided to break for lunch."

"It's a great day for it," he said. "But just wait, the real heat is coming." He grinned, giving Britt the impression that he knew exactly how to work a room. "Lovely to meet you, Brittany. And good to see you again, Mrs. Branch. If you'll excuse me."

After he was gone, Mom looked at Britt. "That was a surprise," she said, leaning forward. "Don't tell anyone, but I can't remember his son's first name."

"You've had a lot of students over the years."

"The names run together, that's for sure. But I do remember him." She frowned. "Handsome kid, popular with the girls. Liked sports but rarely paid attention in class. He was suspended for smoking pot in the boy's bathroom right before Christmas and didn't return. Later I found out he transferred to another school." Her frown deepened. "Oh, this is bugging me. I hate when I can't remember a student's name. Hudson? Hayden? It will come to me later."

Britt relaxed her grip on the tablecloth. It didn't matter if she remembered or not since they wouldn't run into Mr. Pickett in the future. Considering how many people lived in the Dallas metro area, it was a miracle they had today.

"Is there anywhere else you want to go?" Mom asked.

"I might stop by K&Bs later," she said. After Hunter had mentioned it, she realized she hadn't been there in a couple of weeks. She was overdue for a visit.

"We can go together."

"That's okay." Britt laid her napkin neatly on her lap. "You know I like to browse around. I don't want you to get bored."

Mom nodded. "I wish I could get as enthusiastic about colored pencils as you do, but alas, I can't. Just like I can't get you to understand the bliss of a perfect equation."

Britt chuckled, relaxing a little more. Being with Mom always made things easier. Over the years her mother had been willing to do whatever was necessary to help Britt's anxiety. She always had her back.

Soon their drinks and food arrived, and they dove in. There

were so many people going back and forth from the restroom that neither of them saw Mr. Pickett return, and when they finished and paid for their meal, he was nowhere to be seen.

"Do you mind if we stop at that new shoe store at Willow Bend?" Mom asked as they headed to the car. "I can't remember the name of that either." She frowned and unlocked the door. "Guess I still have school-year brain drain."

Britt got in the car and pulled out her phone while her mom cranked up the AC. A few swipes and she found the shop. "Barker's Shoes," she said, clicking on the address.

"Wonder if that's a pun?" Mom put the car in drive. "You know. When your feet hurt, they bark?"

Britt blinked at her.

"Never mind." Mom chuckled and they drove off. "After we finish there, we'll go home. Just let me know when you leave for K&Bs, okay? And since I'm forgetting everything today, make sure to tell Maude and X I said hi."

"I will." Britt settled in the seat. After a fairly stressful but ultimately enjoyable day, she was looking forward to spending some time at K&Bs. Nothing unexpected ever happened there.

～

Hunter pulled his motorcycle into one of the spaces in front of a short strip mall in Plano, then removed his helmet and stuck it in the saddlebag, locked it, and looked at his watch. He had a few hours before he had to be at work. He shielded his eyes from the setting sun behind the storefronts.

Normally he would still be asleep, but ever since he'd been playing Britt's videos at night, he slept better than he had in months. Her voice soothed him for some reason. Or maybe he was overtired from his long spell of insomnia. Didn't matter. He felt better, and that's what counted. He looked straight ahead at the K&B store in front of him.

Armed with Britt's list, he walked inside and was immediately hit with a riot of color. Different types of art covered the wood-slatted walls—modern, classical, mixed media, and stuff he didn't recognize. There were shelves, bins, baskets, and other containers filled with different art supplies. He scratched his head. He had no idea where to begin.

"You look lost."

He turned to see a woman about his parents' age, dressed straight out of Woodstock. Her long, gray hair was pulled into a ponytail, and she wore a crazy-colored, long, flowy dress over her plump figure. Red square glasses covered in rhinestones perched on her nose, a beaded chain dangling from either side of the lenses. She took off the spectacles—yes, they were a spectacle—and smiled. "That's what most people look like the first time they visit us. I'm Maude. Can I help you find anything?"

"Uh, yes." He pulled out his phone and showed her the list. "A . . . friend of mine recommended I get my supplies here."

"Wonderful. Word of mouth is the best publicity." She put her glasses back on and peered at the list. "This is fairly simple. The paper's over there," she said, pointing to the back of the store. "The pastels are here behind me, and you'll find charcoal pencils and erasers on the other side. If you need help finding anything, just give me or my husband a holler. He's in the back. Just call out for X."

Hunter nodded, at a loss for words. He was still trying to comprehend her outfit, never mind her chaotic store. "Thanks," he finally said, then went on his quest to find the supplies.

As he made his way through the store, he started to see

some rhyme and reason to the layout. He was impressed with all the different offerings. The paper section was almost overwhelming, and he was glad Britt had been specific about what he should purchase. When he found the right type of paper, he hunted down the rest of the supplies. He even grabbed one of the canvas reusable shopping bags with the K&B logo on the front. Surprisingly, it was in black on wheat-colored canvas. Staid, compared to the rest of the store.

When Hunter reached the checkout, Maude was nowhere in sight. Instead, an extremely tall, extremely thin man with a bald pate and a ring of longish gray hair around the nape stood behind a register. "Find everything?" he asked as Hunter placed his items on the counter.

"I did." He glanced around. "This sure is an interesting place."

"Thank you. It's a labor of love." He tapped on the number keys. "Did you have a chance to look at the art? We like to support local artists. Every piece on the walls is for sale."

"I didn't, but I'll take a look." He had some extra time before he had to leave. "I take it you're X."

He grinned. "You've met my wife then. Xavier Cornelius Von Poffenberger, at your service."

Hunter gave him a slow nod. No wonder the man went by X. "Ah, yes. She was very helpful."

"That's my job," Maude said, coming up behind Hunter. Her glasses were hanging around her neck again. "I meant to ask you—who can we thank for recommending us?"

He opened his mouth to speak as the bell above the store rang and a woman walked through the door.

"Oh my goodness!" Maude rushed over to her and pulled her into a huge bear hug. "X, looks who's here!"

Hunter's jaw dropped. *Britt.*

Chapter 6

Britt allowed herself to be swallowed up by Maude's engulfing hug. She smiled, hugging her back. The second she walked into the store and inhaled the familiar scents of art supplies and a mysterious combination of essential oils that X insisted on diffusing near the front door, she felt at home. With Maude's patchouli perfume filling her nose, every muscle in Britt's body relaxed. Other than her house, this was her safe space.

"Good to see you too," she said, moving a little out of Maude's embrace but still keeping her arms around her.

"So, tell us what you've been doing that's kept you away from us for so long." Maude beamed. "Of course, since we always watch all of your videos, we know you've been busy with your channel."

"Loved the ten-minute challenge," X said from behind the register. He was putting art supplies in a bag for a customer . . .

Britt stilled. *Thump. Thump.* Standing at the counter was the most perfect-looking guy she'd ever seen. Thick, shaggy blond hair with sun-kissed highlights, a white T-shirt that fit tight in all the perfect places, jeans that weren't too baggy or too slim, and black leather boots. *Thumpity thump.*

X handed him his bag and the guy promptly dropped it on the floor.

"I'll help you with that," Maude said, floating over to him.

"I got it." He swooped it up. "Thanks, though."

Wow, even his voice was perfect. Deeper than she'd expected, and that wasn't a bad thing. Her pulse thumped again. She'd seen handsome men before, but she'd never had this reaction—at least not since she was a teenager. To be fair, most of her adulthood was spent inside away from crowds, so she hadn't seen that many men in real life, period. But this one . . . *Oh my—*

"You're looking at a genuine celebrity here." Maude fluttered back to Britt and took her by the hand, parking her in front of the man. "Brittany Branch," she gushed. "The greater Plano area's premiere artist."

Not only did Britt's face heat up like a pizza oven, but her palms grew damp, her mouth turned dry, and her stomach twisted, all at the same time. Her upper lip was also perspiring, and not a delicate, feminine glow, but an outright ugly sweat. Talk about embarrassing. She wiped her mouth and stared at her feet, unable to look at him.

"Maude, you know Britt doesn't like us making a fuss over her." X moved from behind the counter and put his arm around her. "We're just excited to see you, sweetie."

She gulped, still staring down, her palms so slick she wanted to wipe them off on her shorts, but didn't dare.

"And we do love to brag about you." Maude flanked her on the other side. "We're so proud of our Britt. From the moment she started taking art lessons from us ten—"

"Eleven," Britt mumbled, unable to stop herself. She managed to slightly glance up.

"—years ago, we knew she was gifted. We even have our own Britt wall of fame." She gestured to the wall behind the counter, covered in art projects Britt had made over the years. K&B's equivalent of a proud parent's refrigerator.

She was dying inside. Normally Maude didn't go overboard

like she was doing now. She would sometimes mention Britt's channel to a customer or point out her favorite work on the wall of fame—a mixed media, Picasso-inspired modern portrait of her and X's wedding day at his parents' bowling alley in Middlebury, Vermont. Maude bowled a perfect game at the reception. When Britt first saw the photo of her in a wedding dress, him in a tux, and the six attendants all holding colorful bowling balls, she had to create her own interpretation.

"That's . . . great," the man said.

That voice. So smooth, like honey over glass. She was terrified to look directly at him, knowing he was probably more than ready to get out of the store but now had to act interested to humor Maude. She desperately needed an escape. "I, uh . . . gotta go to the bathroom."

She dashed off to the back of the store, alternately wincing and cringing the whole way. She could have said she needed new brushes or wanted to look at watercolor options for an upcoming video, or she could have pretended her phone buzzed in her pocket and she had to take the call.

But no. She chose to run to the bathroom.

Britt entered the one-person restroom and nearly slammed the door. She leaned against it, squeezing her eyes shut and willing her pulse to slow. Then she pressed the heel of her damp hand against her equally perspiring forehead and cringed. Her whole face felt *moist*. How pathetic.

She couldn't even look at a handsome guy without turning into a boiling cauldron of nerves. How was she going to handle being in Savannah's wedding? Surely there would be some handsome men there, although probably not any as gorgeous as that guy.

She went to the sink, grabbed a length of the brown paper

towel from the dispenser, and ran cold water over it. Dabbing it over her forehead, she looked into the mirror and grimaced. To top it off, her hair was a mess. She'd put it in a loose bun earlier in the day and hadn't thought to check to see if it needed attention. Twirls of curls were falling out of the scrunchy, making her look like she'd just rolled out of bed and out the door.

Britt threw the towel away and leaned against the sink. Finally, she was cooling off, her heartbeat steadier. She didn't feel like throwing up anymore either.

"It doesn't matter," she whispered, looking in the mirror again. Odds were next to zero she'd ever see that guy again, and X and Maude knew about her problems with anxiety. Maude was probably in the break room now, fixing Britt one of her calming tea blends. Although they were nice to drink, they rarely made a dent when she was really agitated.

After deciding she might as well make use of the facilities, she finished up by washing her hands, in control of her emotions again. She really didn't want to waste time in the bathroom when she could be visiting with X and Maude. Now that she was able to think clearly, she wasn't even sure why she'd had such an extreme reaction to him.

"So what if he's handsome?" she said aloud, her voice echoing off the subway-tiled walls. "For all you know, he could be an axe murderer." Managing a small smile at her lame comment, she straightened, threw her shoulders back, and blew out a breath. Crisis over.

Ready to visit with her friends and apologize for being the weirdo she was, she threw open the door . . . and saw the handsome stranger standing right in front of her.

Those eyes . . .

Hunter had known from Britt's videos that she had pretty eyes. But their beauty in real life was on a whole other level. Variegated shades of jade green, with thick black lashes lining them. He couldn't take his own unremarkable eyes off her. She was cute on screen but downright adorable in person. Even the way she kept looking down while Maude was singing her praises appealed to him. She really was as humble as she seemed to be in her videos.

But right now, her stunning eyes were wide and filled with shock. He suddenly hoped she didn't think he was following her, even though he totally was. Then her gaze darted down again.

He knew from her videos that she was somewhat shy, but the sides of her neck were dark red, bordering on purple. Her visual focus was still downcast, as if she didn't want to look at him. Now he was second-guessing his impulsive decision to wait for her to come out of the bathroom and tell her who he was. She seemed extremely uncomfortable around him.

"I, uh . . ." he stammered, shoving his hand through his hair. Then he saw the commode behind her. "Gotta go."

Her gaze whipped up. A wayward curl fell out of her casual bun and joined several others that were loose around her face and neck. She took a step to the side but remained in the doorway.

He almost smiled but kept it to himself. He wondered if she knew she was staring straight at him. Then he realized she was looking almost through him, which made his internal grin disappear. Better to just end this now. He moved to squeeze past her, but she stayed in place. He caught the scent of fresh soap and . . . oregano?

When his body brushed against hers, a pleasant, intense shock went through him. He froze. *Whoa.* Her rosy cheeks, thick eyebrows, and pale skin were a dynamite contrast to her wild black curls. But that wasn't what hit him. It was the fervent way she was looking at him when their eyes met. She wasn't seeing through him now.

Then her brows shot up. "Oh! Sorry!" She flew out of the doorway and scurried off, much like she had minutes before, and disappeared into the woodworking and leather tools aisle.

Hunter turned and stared at the empty bathroom. He didn't have to go, but he couldn't just walk back up front without waiting a few minutes, or she would for sure think he was following her.

He closed the door and shook his head. Despite discovering how pretty she was in person, never mind whatever that electric jolt was that hit him when they touched, it was probably best that she didn't know who he was. She was a successful artist who had her act together, and he was a warehouse worker. Not that working in a warehouse was bad or anything to be ashamed of. It was his chronic lack of direction he didn't want her to know about. Better to just keep their correspondence online with quick, surface messages.

When enough time passed, he exited the bathroom and went to the front of the store, expecting to see her with X and Maude. He intended to just nod goodbye to her and move on. Maybe he wouldn't bother with the ten-minute challenge either. There wasn't any reason to get involved any deeper with her than he already had.

But when he reached the front, a troubled-looking Maude and X were there, but no Britt. "Everything okay?" he asked.

"Oh, sure." Maude's smile didn't reach her eyes, and she glanced at the front door.

"I said you were over the top," X muttered, frowning. "You know she isn't comfortable with attention."

"I just . . ." Maude looked directly at Hunter, then shook her head. "You're right."

Hunter paused, wondering why the woman was giving him a

strange look. Not that it mattered—he didn't plan on returning to the store anyway, although Maude and X seemed like good, enthusiastic people. But because he couldn't leave well enough alone, he asked another question. "Did Britt leave?"

"Yes." X pointed his thumb unnecessarily at the front door.

"She hustled out of here like her pants were on fire," Maude said, now sounding distraught. She put her hand on X's arm. "I'll go check on her—"

"No." He took her hand. "She'll be fine. You didn't chase her off for good."

"I hope not."

"She obviously needs some space."

Now Hunter felt like he was intruding. "Thanks again," he said, lifting up his bag.

"Oh! Thank you." Maude smiled, and this time it was more genuine. "Please stop by again."

He gave her a tepid wave and left the store. As he headed for his bike, he passed a light-blue compact car parked three spaces over and glanced at it, stopping when he saw Britt in the driver's seat. She was staring straight ahead, and she hadn't even started the car. Maybe there was something really wrong with her. He hesitated, then tapped on her window.

Chapter 7

Britt startled when she heard the tap on her window, then slid in her seat when she saw the man from K&Bs peering at her. *Oh boy*. She hadn't made enough of a fool of herself by running to the bathroom and standing in his way when he needed to go. She'd been so out of sorts, she only waved goodbye to X and Maude and dashed out of the store and jumped in her car. She was planning to go home and melt into a puddle of humiliation.

But she couldn't just leave Maude and X hanging without saying a proper goodbye. She was just about to go back inside, deciding that if she did see him, she would pretend she hadn't inadvertently blocked him from using the restroom, and they hadn't just had their bodies pressed against each other.

Now he was here, with only her car door separating them. All she could think about was how he felt, how he smelled—completely yummy—and how he had to think she was the weirdest person on the planet. Probably the entire universe.

He tapped again, and she pushed the button to roll down the window, only to fail since the engine wasn't on. She started the car and tried to roll down the window again. Instead her back windows went down. Good grief. She quickly rolled them up. Forget the windows, she'd just open the door—

"Oof!" He took a step back.

"Sorry!" This was going from bad to worse. She got out of the car and shut the door. "Are you okay?"

He rubbed the center of his chest. "It's gonna take more than a car door to put a dent in me." He smiled.

And her knees swayed. Literally, she had to grab the hood of her car for balance. Hopefully he didn't notice.

He took a step forward, his smile shifting to a concerned look. "Are you all right?"

Too late. "Me? Oh yeah. I'm fine. Perfectly fine." She tried to play it off by putting her hand on her hip and draping her other arm over the top of her car, hoping the position didn't look as awkward as it felt. From his frown, she could see it did. She straightened, her hands drifting to her sides.

"Glad you're okay," he said, but he looked unconvinced.

Uh-oh. Sweaty palms, galloping heartbeat, sour stomach . . . It was coming back with a vengeance. Again, she needed to escape. "I better get back inside. I was just checking on something in the car." Not exactly the truth, but it would work.

He nodded. "Maude and X looked a little worried about you."

Her friends' concern cut through her nerves enough to make her smile a little. "They're really sweet people. Eccentric, but sweet."

"I could tell." He glanced at the Yamaha motorcycle behind him. "Guess I'll get going," he said, moving away from her.

She made her own move to walk away, only to pause. "Thanks for checking on me," she said, and she meant it. "You didn't have to do that."

He stopped. Nodded. "No problem."

Now that they were talking and she was acting somewhat normal, she could see his features in the fading light of dusk and took a more detailed inventory. Straight eyebrows hovering over hooded eyes. Light hazel irises ringed with brown. A sloped, even nose. Full lips, with the top one a little larger than the bottom, but not enough to distract. At least a two-day five o'clock shadow covered a square, proportional jaw. This man was not only incredibly good-looking, but he'd been blessed with almost flawless features. In her mind she imagined how she would draw him—

She blinked. Twice. Then realized he had tilted his head and was staring at her.

"I . . ." *Brother.* How was she going to explain that she was fantasizing about drawing him? She asked the first question that came to mind. "Are you a model?"

He broke out in a laugh. "No. Not even close."

"You could be," she blurted, then resisted the urge to face-palm herself. "I mean, I draw portraits sometimes—"

"I know."

"How . . . Oh yeah. The Wall of Britt." She leaned against the car. "Maude and X are good teachers. I'm not the only one whose artwork they display."

He hooked his thumb into his beltloop, letting his bag of art supplies dangle by his leg. "Do they have their own walls?"

"Um, no." She scratched the back of her neck. "I'd be happy to share, though."

He didn't say anything else. Traffic hummed from the street by the lot. A horn honked in the distance.

And here comes the awkward silence. "Uh, have a good evening. Night, I mean." What time was it even? She reluctantly pulled her gaze from him and started for the store, committing every detail of his face to memory the best she could. She definitely wanted to draw him. Was that creepy? She wasn't sure.

"Britt."

She halted, stunned he'd called her name. Then she tried to

turn on her heel, only to stumble on a piece of broken blacktop. Regaining her balance, she yanked at the hem of her multicolored flower power T-shirt. "Yes?"

He walked toward her, and for the first time since she'd met him, an uncertain expression crossed his face. He stopped a few feet away. Shifted his bag to his other hand. Looked away for a moment before he extended his hand to her. "I'm . . . Hunter."

$$\smile$$

When Britt's jaw literally dropped and stayed open for a few seconds, Hunter wanted to touch her chin with one finger and push it closed. He could almost smile at her shocked expression if he wasn't so concerned he was making a terrible mistake. He didn't know why he'd told her who he was when he'd been so sure he shouldn't. But as she walked away from him, he couldn't just let her go. Even if they never spoke or wrote to each other again, at least he'd had these few minutes with her. Still, he hoped this wasn't the end.

She finally closed her mouth. "Hunter. From—"

"Your channel." He lifted his bag and half smiled. "Just bought my supplies for the ten-minute challenge."

The parking lot streetlamps turned on as her eyes widened. "You live here?"

"Yep. About fifteen minutes west."

Now she was blinking, as if she were trying to comprehend what he was saying.

"Me showing up here tonight was just a coincidence, I promise. I don't want you to think I'm stalking you. Or that I'm an axe murderer." He tried to smile, letting her know he'd heard what she said when she was in the bathroom.

Britt took a step back, her expression now guarded. "How do I know you're telling the truth?"

She had him there. His smile disappeared.

"I guess you don't." He backed away. "Don't worry. I don't know where you live, and I'm not going to try to find out. Like I said in my messages, I came across your channel, started to watch the videos, and liked them." He left out the part where he listened to her as he fell asleep. She would really be freaked out about that.

She took another step away from him.

"Yeah . . . this was a horrible idea," he muttered. "I shouldn't have told you."

"I don't know," she finally said in a timid voice. "It might have been weirder if you hadn't." She wrung her hands together. "I get a lot of creeps who message me."

"I'm not surprised."

She lifted an indignant brow. "What's that supposed to mean?"

He held up his hands, palms out. "Just that you're—" He almost said cute, and if he had he was pretty sure she'd be dialing 911 right now. "Talented. You have a lot of subscribers and tons of comments. Considering the law of averages, you're bound to have some oddballs reaching out to you."

She crossed her arms. "What would the law of averages say the chances are that we just happened to be here at the same time?"

"I don't know." He dropped his hands. "Never made it past pre-algebra in school. But I'm serious when I say it's complete chance that we both decided to go to K&Bs today. And I did tell you I wanted to patronize one of your sponsors. I picked this store because it's local to me."

"I suppose that could be true."

This would be an ideal moment for him to hop on his bike, drive away, and forget all about Britt Branch so she could forget all about him. But as he'd done when making all his decisions since she'd walked into K&Bs, he continued to ignore common sense.

"I can prove it to you. Why don't we meet back here, let's say Monday afternoon around two or so. I'll work on my ten-minute challenge, and I can show you my work in front of X and Maude, so we'll have witnesses. Until then, I won't message you online. How does that sound?"

She rocked back and forth on her heels, her gaze remaining on him. Finally, she nodded. "Okay. Two o'clock. Monday, in front of my friends."

His shoulders relaxed. "Sounds good." Then he added, "Thanks for giving me a chance."

Her expression still shuttered, she nodded, then turned and hurried to the store.

He didn't blame her for running off. He also couldn't help but smile. He would prove to her he was genuine about learning from her. More importantly, she would see he wasn't a stalker or a creep.

Then his smile faded when he realized he'd truly committed himself to drawing a seashell in ten minutes. Oh boy. He hopped on his bike and headed back home. He had a lot of practicing to do.

Chapter 8

What am I doing?

Amy sat in her car and stared at the building in front of her. Ike's Hometown Tavern. She shouldn't be here. Not only was she absolutely not a tavern type of woman, she also had better things to do on a Saturday night than attend—shudder—a Single Mingles get-together.

The blindingly bright sign to the right of the tavern advertised karaoke Saturdays. She hated karaoke. But she didn't used to. Daniel had killed that for her too.

Her hands were still on the steering wheel, the engine running. She should just go back home. Britt might have returned from her trip to K&Bs by now, and maybe they could settle in with a movie and some homemade popcorn. Lightly salted, no butter. The way they both liked it.

It had been great to spend time with her today. During the school year, most of Amy's weekends were spent recovering from the week and doing the never-ending chores around the house. Britt was always a big help with cleaning and yard work. But Amy wasn't a spring chicken anymore, and she couldn't afford to hire a lawn service. By Sunday afternoons after church, she was mentally preparing herself for the next school week. Spending a Saturday doing something fun and carefree was a treat, even if she did spend a little more money than she should have.

Listening to karaoke at a tavern did not sound fun. Not even close.

Her phone buzzed and she released her death grip on the steering wheel to look at the text that popped up.

Running late. There's a table for eight already reserved at the left of the stage so go on in. See you in a bit. Thx.

Amy tossed her phone in her purse and reluctantly shut off the car. Laura was supposed to meet her here, and now she would have to face the singles on her own until her friend showed up. This was the one and only time she was going to do this, and the sole reason was because Laura had been relentless ever since she'd taken over the group. Even though she'd just joined a couple of weeks ago, the former leader had since gotten engaged. Laura was a good choice because she was highly organized. She was also the only one who volunteered.

Amy sighed. Better to get the impending disaster over with than have Laura spoil her summer by constantly insisting that Amy needed to attend their events and have some fun.

"Not going to happen," she muttered, grabbing her purse and exiting the car. The lot was full, the scent of greasy fried food hung in the air, and she could already hear muffled music coming from the building. A knot formed in her stomach. Unlike Britt— bless her daughter's heart—Amy had never had a problem with social situations. She loved eating lunch in the faculty lounge, although at times the gossip could get a bit much and that's when she excused herself, pronto. She enjoyed open house, going to ball games and supporting her students, and she hadn't missed chaperoning a dance in more than six years. There was even a tradition at prom where everyone did the Ms. Branch Boogie at the end of the night, with her leading the dance. But meeting single people whose main interest was finding love again? The whole idea made her unfathomably uncomfortable.

Now that she was committed, there was nothing left to do but get it over with. She walked inside and was a little surprised at what she saw. Instead of the darkly lit, alcohol-soaked bar she'd imagined, she could plainly see the tables and chairs that were filled with people talking and laughing. Waitresses and servers wearing red short-sleeved shirts and khaki shorts circulated around the place, which she could see was more restaurant and less nightclub. A pale wood-planked dance floor was in the middle, and an empty stage was up front with a string of colored lights draped over a white curtained background.

She looked around for the table Laura was talking about, then located it. She scooted by several tables and sat down, frowning a little as she glanced at her watch. She was on time, so where was everyone else? Menus and silverware were in front of each empty chair.

A waitress appeared and placed a cardboard coaster in front of her. "Can I get you something to drink?"

"Water, please."

She nodded and walked away, while Amy tried to relax a little. At least the music wasn't too loud, and the karaoke thankfully hadn't started yet. She felt like a little old lady shaking her cane at kids running across her lawn, but she couldn't help it. Even now she was trying not to wonder if Daniel had frequented this place during their marriage. She knew he'd hit numerous bars over the years they were married, usually after they had a fight about his drinking.

She shoved her ex out of her mind. Even though she didn't want to be here, she would make the best of it. She just hoped Laura would arrive soon.

"Is this seat taken?"

Amy looked up to see a clean-cut man with black thick-framed glasses standing across from her. "Uh, kind of?"

"Are you with Single Mingles by any chance?"

"Ah . . . yes." She so badly wanted to say no, but obviously he was here for the group.

"Good, I'm at the right place." He paused, half smiling. "At least I think it's good. Mind if I sit down?"

She shook her head and he lowered himself into the chair. "Max Monroe," he said, holding out his hand. "I'm brand new to the group, so I'm not sure what I'm doing."

"Amy Branch. And ditto."

The waitress brought out her water, and Max told her he'd have a Coke. As he ordered, Amy got a better look at him. The frames were trendy, not nerdy, and he wore a crisp white shirt, sans tie, with a nice gray jacket and navy blue pants. His short brown hair had gray threaded through the top but was completely white on the sides. She had to admit he was a good-looking man.

The waitress went to get Max's drink, and he glanced around the tavern. "I've never been here before either. Seems like a nice place."

"This is my first time too." She pulled her phone out of her purse to check her messages. Nothing so far. "My friend Laura should be here any minute. She's running late."

"I figured I'd be the tardy one." He scooted his chair a little closer to the table and leaned forward.

"How did you find the group?" she asked.

"Online, I'm embarrassed to say." He ran his thumb across the edge of the table. "My wife died five years ago. I figured it was time to join the world again. Socially, I mean."

"I'm sorry for your loss."

"Thanks. Crystal would have wanted me to move on . . ." He looked up. "I'm doing exactly what I told myself I wouldn't do— jump in with my sob story."

"It's okay." She smiled. "How long were you married?"

"Thirty years. She died of breast cancer." He cleared his throat. "Anyway, tell me a little about yourself."

"I'm divorced and I'm here against my will." At his wide-eyed expression, she laughed. "I've been happily divorced for a little over twenty years. My friend Laura seems to think it's past time for me to mix and mingle, and I'm here so she'll shut up about it."

"I see . . . I think."

Her smiled faded. Maybe she shouldn't have been so honest. "Don't get me wrong. I love being around people. I'm just not interested in romance."

His shoulders relaxed and the waitress returned with his drink. "Thanks," he said to her, then looked at Amy again. "I'm so glad you said that. I'm not looking to date either. But I've got all these well-meaning people in my life who are so pushy. Including my former mother-in-law, if you can believe that."

"Oh, I believe it. It's like no one's allowed to be single and happy."

"Exactly." He grinned and lifted his drink. "To being single."

"Here, here." She tapped her glass to his just as her phone screen lit up and Laura's text appeared.

Still running late. Tell everyone to order without me.

"Hang on a minute," she said to Max, picking up her phone. "Laura sent me a message."

Amy: There's only me and one other guy here. His name is Max and he's new. Where is everyone else?

> Laura: I'll check the online group.

"I asked her for an attendance update," Amy explained.

He nodded and picked up the menu. She followed suit and had decided on a cheeseburger with blue cheese and bacon when her screen lit up again.

> Laura: They all cancelled. Every one of them.

> Amy: Really? Has that ever happened before?

> Laura: No. Usually at least two or three show up. Most of the time it can be up to twenty. I just reserved for eight because that's how many said they were coming. I don't know when I'll be there either. Farah's softball game is in extra innings, and then I have to drop her off at home. I don't want you to have to wait so go ahead and leave. We'll do this another time. Sorry!

Amy glanced at Max, who was still perusing the menu. She'd only ordered water and she could still leave without putting the waitress out too much.

> Amy: Don't worry about it. I hope Farah wins!

> Laura: Me too! It's an exciting game!

She slipped her phone back into her purse. "Bad news. No one else is coming."

"Really?"

"Yeah. I'd understand if you want to leave."

He closed the menu. "If you're staying, I will too."

She smiled. "Then it's a nondate."

"Those are the best kind."

For the next hour, she and Max ate—he had a cobb salad—and talked about their lives, which couldn't be more different. "I'm a corporate attorney," he said, spearing a bit of avocado. "Have you ever heard of Pickett & Jones law firm?"

She shook her head. "Nope. Haven't had to deal with a lawyer since my divorce."

"I joined the firm last year. They primarily do criminal law but now they're branching out into different sectors. I work in the McKinney office. I don't see Mr. Pickett or Mr. Jones that often, but they occasionally stop by the office and shake hands. They're decent people." He gave her a sheepish grin. "I get a little defensive about my profession sometimes."

"I understand. I don't watch much TV, but when I do, I'm inundated with ambulance-chasing ads."

"Yeah, those are the worst. But we aren't all like that."

Amy nodded, selecting a thick french fry from her plate. "Sometimes I feel a little protective of my profession too. Teachers get a bad rap, and some of them deserve it. But most of us love what we do and want our students to succeed. I can't imagine doing anything else."

"I had some excellent teachers throughout my school years." Max sipped his second Coke. "I often thought about teaching law after I retire."

"When will that be?"

"I'm fifty-seven, so I've got several working years left. Crystal and I had planned to tour the world after we both retired. She was a nurse and worked for almost two decades at Children's Medical Center before she moved to work in a private practice." He pressed his lips together. "Plans have changed, obviously."

Amy's heart went out to him. She'd had plans with Daniel too. Lots of them. Other than buying the house in Allen and having Britt, none of them had come to fruition. But she'd had lots of time to mourn those losses.

"There I go again." He shook his head. "Turning a perfectly fine conversation maudlin."

"Thirty years and a tragic death are hard to get over," she said gently. "It's understandable."

"Thank you." He smiled. "I have to admit, tonight's turning out much better than I thought it would."

Amy smiled. Agreed.

As they finished their meals, Amy told him about Britt and her channel, and he said he would check it out. He didn't have any kids, but he had lots of nieces, nephews, and now a grandnephew to spoil. They learned they both went to different churches on the opposite sides of the metro area, and they had landed on the topic of hobbies when the karaoke cranked up.

Amy couldn't hide her grimace or her snarky comment. "And here the evening was going so well."

Max raised an eyebrow. "You don't like karaoke?"

She'd been honest with him all night—no need to sugarcoat it now. "I detest it. With a passion."

"I don't mind it. But it's not conducive to conversation." He eyed their empty plates. "Want to go somewhere a little less—"

"Annoying?" She covered her mouth with her fingers. "Sorry. Slipped out."

He motioned for the waitress to bring their checks.

Her stomach knotted up again. So far, she was having a great time. From all accounts, Max seemed to be a nice guy, and she was enjoying their conversation. She wouldn't mind continuing it, but where did he want to go? Again, honesty was the best policy. "If you want to go to a bar, I'll have to decline. I don't drink."

"Me either," he said without hesitation. "I was thinking about Madeline's Coffee House. Are you familiar with it?"

"Overly." Her smile returned. "Unfortunately, it's on my way to work, and I've spent more than my fair share in their drive-through on bleary-eyed mornings."

"I think they're open until eight. I'm partial to their cortados. Just espresso and milk. Simple and satisfying." He looked at her for a moment. "Let me guess. You're an iced-coffee kind of girl."

She almost laughed at him calling her a girl. He wasn't that much older than her. But it was nice to hear. "Wrong. Red eyes for me."

"Coffee and espresso? Bold choice."

"I teach high school kids—I need the fortification. But tonight, I'll take it easy and have a chai latte."

The waitress returned with two checks. Max reached for them but Amy intercepted.

"This is a nondate, remember?" She looked at both checks and handed him his. "Nondates always go dutch."

"As a man, that goes against my grain," he said, grinning a little. "But I'll acquiesce."

They paid their bills and headed for the door just as the cater-wauling began. Amy mentally chastised herself. She wasn't being fair. There were plenty of fine karaoke singers, and even those who weren't talented were having fun. Just because Daniel had ruined the experience for her didn't mean she had to be a jerk about it, even in her own mind.

"I'm parked here," she said as they left the tavern, gesturing to her silver sedan parked two rows back.

"I'm right behind you then."

Her eyes widened when she saw his sleek black Mercedes gleaming under the parking lot lights. "Nice," she said.

"It'll do. See you in a few minutes?"

"I'll be there."

Amy got into her car and paused, once again asking herself what she was doing. There hadn't been a single second tonight when she'd felt an attraction for Max. He was handsome, smart, and gentlemanly. But although there wasn't a spark—thankfully, because she seriously wasn't interested—he was nice to talk to. It had been so long since she'd had a male perspective on anything. Most of the teachers at the high school were women, and the men who did teach were mostly coaches, mostly married, and understandably hung out with each other. Her church friends were all women too.

She shrugged. There was a good chance Max wouldn't show up anyway. They both had twenty minutes to change their minds and forget about the coffeehouse. Surprisingly, she felt disappointed at the thought. And she definitely wasn't going to back out of her commitment. Once she gave her word, she meant it. Unlike Daniel.

Frowning, she started her car and headed to Madeline's. She wished she could say there was a day that went by that she didn't think about him, but she couldn't. Britt looked so much like him it was jarring sometimes, but she never blamed her daughter for something she couldn't help. And there was always something that came up that reminded her of him. Like karaoke tonight, or just thinking about how Daniel never kept his promises.

Even now as she went to hopefully meet Max, she was a little envious of his marriage. She wasn't naïve enough to think his relationship with Crystal hadn't had its rough spots. But hers had been awful almost from the start.

Amy turned on the radio to escape her thoughts. When she pulled into Madeline's parking lot, she didn't see Max's Mercedes. Her spirits sank and she tried to be practical. Maybe he'd realized on the way here that supper had been enough. Or maybe he'd gotten an emergency call from a client, if that was a thing. She'd prefer anything but that he'd changed his mind because she said or did something wrong. She hated second-guessing herself.

Headlights appeared behind her car, then turned off. The Mercedes emblem shone in her rearview mirror, and she saw Max get out of his car. Yes! Then she settled down. It's a nondate, remember? No sparks, remember?

But when she got out of the car and saw him standing there with a grin on his face, she couldn't deny the fluttery sensation she felt inside. She was never going to doubt Laura again.

Chapter 9

H e's quite the dish, isn't he?"

Britt shifted on the mustard-yellow plastic shell chair in the back room of K&Bs, struggling to act nonchalant and unaffected by Maude's assessment of Hunter. She gulped down the rest of her third bottle of water. She had to stop drinking or she would be running back and forth to the bathroom for the next two hours. Managing a shrug, she said, "If you say so."

Maude grinned and sipped a cup of tea. Today's flavor: Japanese orchid sencha. "I'm sure I'm not the only one who says so."

She fidgeted in her seat again. This style of chair was ubiquitous in the sixties and seventies, and they weren't comfortable at all. At least in the teaching area, Maude and X had regular folding chairs, complete with padded seats. Why they insisted on still using these things was a mystery.

When Britt had gone back into the store on Saturday, she reassured Maude and X that she was okay and explained about Hunter. They'd both been relieved, and Maude had seemed quite excited that he was returning to the store to see Britt.

When she arrived today, the two of them headed to the back room that doubled as a break room and an office. Britt had been a bundle of nerves all day, although she managed to hide her state from Mom, who spent the morning weeding around the back patio. Finally, she couldn't take it anymore and went to K&Bs

more than an hour early. Although that gave her some time to visit with Maude, she still couldn't relax.

For the fifth time since she arrived, she glanced at her watch. Ten minutes to two.

"Worried he won't show up?" Maude asked.

"I'm not sure I want him to." There. She said the one thing that had been bothering her since Hunter had introduced himself.

Maude took another sip and set the teacup down on a matching saucer on the coffee table in front of her. "That's understandable. You can never be too careful nowadays. But my gut says you don't have anything to worry about." She patted her rounded stomach that was covered with a turquoise, white, and red paisley caftan. Maude rarely wore pants, and when she did, they were bell bottoms. Britt loved her style.

But she wasn't sure she could even trust Maude's sixth sense. After Hunter had told her who he was and said he wanted to convince her that he wasn't a creep, she still couldn't believe that a) he lived in her vicinity, b) he was so ridiculously good-looking, and c) he seemed nice. Really nice.

Ugh, her mouth was parched and when she looked at her hands, she realized she was tugging at her shirt hem again. She'd made three different outfit changes before deciding to choose comfort over fashion and selected a loose-fitting navy blue T-shirt, her favorite pair of high-rise jeans, and white tennis shoes.

When Britt glanced at her watch again, Maude stood. "I can feel the nervous energy coming off you." She gestured for her to stand up.

"I'm sorry." She rose, feeling guilty that she was making her friend uncomfortable. "I can't help it."

"Oh, sweetie." Maude put her arm around her shoulders. "I

know it's a struggle for you. In this case, you have a good reason to be nervous. I'd be on pins and needles too if I were waiting for Mr. Dreamy to walk through the door and wow me with his seashell."

Britt laughed, releasing some of her tension. "What would X say?"

"Oh, I'm sure he wouldn't mind. Not too much anyway. Have you been doing those deep-breathing exercises you learned in therapy?"

"No," she admitted. "I've been too anxious." Which sounded dumb now that she said it out loud. The diaphragmatic breathing did calm her. So why wasn't she doing something that worked?

"Let's practice." Maude lifted her ample chest, closed her eyes, and took a huge breath through her nose. Then she exhaled. "Breathe in . . . breathe out . . ."

Britt followed suit. *Breathe in . . . breathe out . . . breathe in . . . breathe out . . .*

After they did that for ten more breaths, Britt opened her eyes. That was better. But she couldn't exactly do that in front of Hunter, not without him thinking she'd lost her marbles. Then again, she still wondered if he was the weird one. "Thanks, Maude."

"It's two o'clock." She spun Britt around and gave her a gentle nudge toward the door. "Your budding artist awaits. Oh, I asked X to put some lavender in the diffuser. It's such a soothing scent."

Britt nodded and entered the showroom floor. Mondays were usually slow, and today was no exception. Carrie, their part-time employee, only worked on Tuesday, Thursday, Friday, and every other Saturday. The shop was closed on Sunday. Right now, the store was empty—the way it had been on Saturday afternoon.

Breathe in . . . breathe out . . . breathe in . . . She started to yank on her shirt again, then realized what she was doing and put her hands in her pockets. *Breathe out . . .*

When she reached the front of the store, she stopped breathing altogether. True to his word, Hunter was there, standing at the counter and talking to X, who then noticed Britt. He nodded to Hunter, who turned around . . . and smiled.

The thumping started again, and now she was seeing spots before her eyes. Oh, right. *Breathe!* A huge amount of air whooshed from her lungs and out of her mouth.

He tilted his head, a small frown tugging on his lips. "Uh, hey."

"You're here," she blurted.

His smile returned. "So are you. Thanks."

"For what?"

"Showing up."

"Helloo, Hunter!" Maude appeared, her caftan flowing behind her as she hugged his waist like they'd known each other forever. "Britt told us you did the ten-minute challenge."

"I tried." He turned and grabbed a manila file folder off the counter. But when he started to open it, she pinched it shut.

"Britt should be the first one to see your masterpiece." Maude beamed, then glanced at X. "Right, dear?"

X rolled his eyes, then smiled at Britt. "Whatever you say, my love."

"Why don't you show him our education room, Britt," Maude said, prodding Hunter toward her. "You two can talk about his drawing alone—I mean, without distractions."

There weren't any distractions in the empty store. And Britt didn't think she was ready to be alone with him. Maude and X were supposed to be witnesses after all.

"I can show her here." Hunter looked at Britt. "There's not

much to talk about anyway." He shoved his bangs off his forehead, appearing uncertain again. "It doesn't resemble a seashell at all."

"I'm sure it's better than you think." Britt took a step toward him, not wanting him to disparage his work and get discouraged.

"Britt can give you some extra tips." Maude put her arm around them both, and they all moved in tandem toward the education room. "I've been trying for years to convince her to teach classes here," she said as they squeezed down the scrapbook and photo storage aisle.

"I prefer being online," she mumbled. If she'd known Maude was going to be so pushy, she wouldn't have agreed to meet Hunter here.

Maude finally dropped her arms and walked into the room. Britt and Hunter had no choice but to follow. Britt did like this room, and it was ideal for teaching all kinds of classes. Maude and X taught their fair share of them. X was an expert on sculpture, pottery, and kids' crafts, while Maude was skilled in all paint mediums, jewelry, and yarn crafts.

"Make yourselves at home." Maude grinned, then disappeared.

Breathe in . . . breathe out . . .

"This is a cool room." Hunter glanced around at the art displayed on the walls, shelves, and small display cases. "Any of your pieces in here?"

She faced him, taking in his gray V-necked T-shirt, jeans with small holes in the knees, and the same boots he'd had on the other day. Again, they were all a perfect fit. "Uh . . ." Oh no. What had he asked her?

Hunter moved to stand in front of her, his expression serious. "We don't have to do this," he said. "I don't want you to be uncomfortable."

He seemed sincere, and his kindness helped her find her

words. "I'm always uncomfortable in new situations," she admitted. Then she stilled. She'd never confessed how she felt to a stranger before. And that's what they were, even though they'd exchanged messages. She didn't know anything about him outside his questions about art and the magic words he'd written in his first message—*uncomfortably comfortable.*

"Been there myself," he said. "More than once. Like now, showing a famous artist my ten-minute attempt at a scallop."

"I'm not famous."

"Famous enough." He blew out a breath and presented her with the folder.

~⁀◡

Hunter was surprised at how tense he was as he handed her his artwork. Tense and a little embarrassed. He'd practiced all Saturday night and also when he got off work on Sunday, rewatching her ten-minute challenge video so many times he'd lost count. With each viewing, he learned something new, and finally, three hours ago, after filling a trash bin with failed attempts, he came up with something that looked like it might live in the sea— emphasis on *might.*

But this wasn't the only time he'd been nervous since meeting her on Saturday. His anxiety had heightened throughout the weekend, and he'd had to double focus at work on Sunday so he didn't make a mistake. What if she didn't show up? What if she laughed at his shell? What if she showed up, didn't laugh at his shell, but still thought he was a creep?

All that had been simmering inside him when he drove into K&Bs parking lot. When he saw her car, he was relieved, but still nervous. He was ten minutes early and glad that X had engaged him in small talk right away. That helped calm him a little, along with whatever smell was in the air the second he walked into the store.

Then Britt appeared. Her hair was in a fluffy ponytail, and she looked comfy in her casual T-shirt and jeans. But her expression was what had him back on edge. She was tense—extremely so—and her wide-eyed stare had unnerved him a little. When Maude suggested they go to the education room, she looked like a deer standing in front of headlights.

She might have shown up, but he was sure she didn't want to be here.

Even now as she looked up at him, then back at the folder, she seemed at a loss. He'd tried to set her at ease by sympathizing with her. He really did understand. Since he was a kid, he'd learned how to hide his insecurity with a veneer of bravado.

Finally, she took the folder and opened it. He held his breath as she studied his drawing, her expression blank. In fact, she studied it so long he started shifting on his feet. "That bad, huh?"

She lifted her head, her gaze connecting with his. Then she smiled. "No . . . it's good. Really good." She motioned for him to sit with her at one of the tables. When they were seated, she laid the drawing on top of the folder. "This only took you ten minutes?"

"More like ten hours."

Britt smirked. "It was supposed to be ten minutes."

Hunter lifted his hands. "I'm new to this. I wanted it to be . . . presentable. Trust me, none of them were except this one."

"The shell is a little wonky." She pointed to the imbalance between the two sides, something he hoped she wouldn't notice.

"Yeah. I could never get them to look the same."

"Well, they don't have to. Nothing in nature is absolutely perfect. But I can give you some pointers." She got up from the chair, went to a closet, and walked inside. When she came back out, she had a short stack of paper and some colored pencils. She sat back down and handed him a few sheets of paper. "I didn't put this in the video, but when I was learning how to make things look even, I used to fold my paper in quadrants."

He watched as she creased the paper into four sections, then picked up a black pencil and started sketching. "This helps to center the drawing, and then you can see how each side fits in the different areas."

"Is that something you learned in art school?"

She shook her head, still focused on drawing. "No. It's just something I tried out that helps me." She picked up a dark-blue pencil and handed it to him. "It might not work for you, but you can try it if you want."

Hunter took the pencil from her and picked up a clean piece of paper. It didn't escape his notice that her discomfort seemed to vanish as she was talking about art. He folded the paper and started outlining the shell. He didn't need a visual aid anymore. The shape was cemented in his brain.

They were both quiet while they worked, and he forgot about his own nerves as he delved into the task. He switched out the dark blue for a light blue and started shading the ridges the way she'd demonstrated in her video. When he finished, he looked up, wondering if she was done with the black. But she wasn't drawing. She was watching him. Or rather, she was looking at his picture.

"Now they're more even." Britt smiled. "You catch on fast."

"I've got a good teacher." He turned his body a little so he could face her. "I can see why Maude wants you to teach classes."

Her gaze moved to her own picture, a much fancier shell surrounded by a sketched-in beachscape. "I couldn't do that. I'd be too nervous."

"You're not nervous with me."

Britt paused, giving him a small nod.

He leaned back in the chair, hoping he'd redeemed himself and she no longer thought he had ill intentions toward her. "This is fun after you get the hang of it."

"Satisfying too." She took an aquamarine pencil and started coloring the sea behind the scallop.

When he reached over and picked up the black pencil, he accidentally brushed against her. "Sorry," he said, pulling back a little.

"It's okay." She handed him the pencil, then went back to drawing.

By the time he finished his scallop, an hour had passed, and he had something that looked much better than what he'd done before. She'd given him a few more tips on shading and colors, and he had to admit he had done a decent job. He held up the picture at eye level and examined it. "Not too bad."

"Make sure you sign it."

"It's not that good. I'll probably just toss it in the bin." He started to ball it up when she laid her hand on top of his.

"You shouldn't do that." She took the crinkled paper and smoothed it out. "This is your first piece. It's special."

"Technically it's my second."

Her cheeks turned pink. "That's right. Well, they're both special. You should keep them in a file. As you improve your skills, go back and draw a new shell. That's a great way to see your progress."

He never would have considered saving any of his pictures. He glanced at her. She was assuming he would continue to draw. Of course she would think that. That was the reason he was here, right? To get her opinion and improve?

Yes. He really enjoyed the project, including all the mistakes he'd made. He was honest with her about finding it relaxing. And now that she was in her element, she was great to be around. Just sitting next to her as they both drew and colored their seashells was nice. Even better—she was turning out to be exactly what she was on camera. Shy, humble, talented . . . and fascinating.

She started gathering up the pencils and put them back in the box, a cue that they were finished. Disappointed, he straightened the sheaf of extra paper and handed it to her. "Thanks for the lesson," he said.

Turning to face him, she smiled. "You're welcome."

He wasn't ready for their time together to end, but she seemed to be. He couldn't leave without being sure of one thing, though. "Do you still think I'm an axe murderer?"

"You heard me say that in the bathroom, didn't you?" She stood and picked up the box.

"Yep." He scooped up the paper. "Although I have no idea why you'd think that. We hadn't even officially met yet."

"That's so embarrassing." She tucked her chin against her chest and looked down. "I was just trying to . . ."

He got out of his seat. "Trying to what?"

"Calm myself down." She lifted her gaze.

"Did I say something to upset you?" He couldn't remember, she'd left so quickly after Maude had mentioned Britt's Wall of Art. "If I did, I'm sorry."

"No, you were fine." She took a deep breath. "It's not your fault you're so good-looking." She scurried past him and rushed to the art closet.

He stilled. Well, he hadn't expected her to say *that*. He smiled and grabbed the paper off the table. When he poked his head into the closet, she was straightening up an already neat shelf of boxes of colored pencils. "Thanks for the compliment."

Britt looked over her shoulder, a little smirk on her cute face. "Don't act like no one's ever said that to you before."

They had, all his life. And he'd skated on those looks too. Coupled with a charming smile, he was able to manipulate situations and people to his advantage.

And where did that get him in the long run? A criminal record, a less-than-stellar education, and zero idea what he wanted to do with his life.

She faced him, her smirk replaced with concern.

Only then did he realize he was frowning. He shrugged it off. "That's me. Mr. Hot Stuff." He turned on a grin that made girls, and more than a few teachers, swoon.

But she wasn't swooning. Far from it.

~

Britt didn't say a word as she saw Hunter's smile slip from his face. When he first flashed that Hollywood-worthy grin, her stomach did a backflip. But she instantly noticed it wasn't real. He didn't believe he was hot stuff. Not for a minute. She'd spent a lot of her life avoiding looking people in the eye until she was comfortable with them, and she was no expert on reading facial expressions or emotions. But the self-doubt she saw in Hunter's eyes as he tried to play off her impulsive comment about his looks was easy to see. It was only there for a second, but it was real.

And it confused her.

His grin reappeared, less bright this time. "Since we're done with our lesson, you want to go grab some coffee? A bite to eat?"

She grabbed her shirt hem again, but at least she wasn't compelled to stare at her sneakers. "I . . . I don't think that's a good idea."

"Oh." Disappointment crossed his features. "I guess I thought I'd convinced you I was harmless."

He had. Once she forgot her anxiety, their impromptu lesson had been fun. And she'd been truthful about his picture being good. His color choice, symmetry, and shading showed sparks of innate talent. But drawing and coloring seashells was way different from sitting in a restaurant over a meal.

"Sorry." He continued, stepping back and shoving his hands in his pockets. "I don't mean to be pushy."

She pressed her lips together. "You're not pushy. You're really . . . nice."

A glimmer of hope lit up his eyes, only to fade. "Just not nice enough to go out with."

Did he mean a date? Her stomach fluttered, only to calm when she reminded herself that a meal didn't equal a date. It was ridiculous for her to even think a guy as handsome and nice as Hunter would ever think of her in romantic terms. "It's not you, it's—"

"Me. Got it." His expression shuttered. "Thanks for your time. Don't worry. I won't bother you again." He turned to leave.

Although she was sure his ego was bruised—he'd probably never been turned down before—she couldn't let him leave thinking he was the reason she said no. She went to him and touched his arm. More accurately, his bicep. And what a bicep it was.

"Hunter . . ." Oh no. Her mouth was drying up again, her words evaporating. Worse, she was still touching him. She should stop, but she couldn't make her hand obey.

He turned, forcing her hand to shift off his arm, his face still unreadable.

"I . . . I'm sorry." From his frown she could tell that wasn't the right thing to say. "I . . ." Her gaze landed on their shoes, her white sneakers almost toe to toe with his leather boots.

"Britt."

She looked up at him, her gaze locking with those incredible eyes that she still longed to draw.

"It's okay, really." His expression softened a little, and a small, genuine smile appeared.

She shook her head so hard her ponytail slapped her ears. "No, it isn't." A lump formed in her throat, and she couldn't stop herself from admitting the truth. "I'm a mess, Hunter. A huge mess."

Chapter 10

Hunter fought the urge to reach out and put his finger on Britt's lower lip to stop it from trembling. The movement was slight, but noticeable. She was staring at her feet again, and even though he couldn't see her entire face, the back of her neck was scarlet. He pulled his hands out of his pockets and ducked his head so he could look at her. "Hey," he said, gentling his voice. "You don't have to say that to make me feel better."

"I'm not." She moved away, then turned her back on him. "I'm telling you the truth."

"Who isn't a mess, though?" He circled around to face her again. "I sure am."

Britt lifted her head slightly. "Are you a constant ball of anxiety that avoids people and social situations at all costs?"

She had him there. "No. But I've had my fair share of problems." Ones he wouldn't admit out loud. Even his roommate had no idea how much trouble he'd been in, only that he was a recovering alcoholic. "I've been nervous before. Plenty of times."

"This is different." She was looking at him again. "I don't just get nervous. I break out in a sweat, my palms get slick, my stomach turns sour, I forget my words, and sometimes I almost pass out. And that's on a good day."

He noticed her fingers were shaking as she yanked on the bottom of her shirt so hard the material was stretching, making him want to take her hands in his and soothe her. But he couldn't. She was like a frightened little bunny right now, and he didn't want to do anything to make her scamper off.

"The only times I feel calm are when I'm creating something or hanging out with my mom or my friend Savannah," she continued. "Otherwise, I'm a jumbled wreck and no fun to be around."

"Then we don't get coffee. We stay here and order something in."

She shook her head. "You don't understand. It's not just crowds. Sometimes it's just one person."

"I make you nervous."

"Yes," she said in a small voice.

"You weren't nervous when we were working on our drawings."

"No. But that was different."

He spotted a stool in the corner of the supply room. Quickly he picked it up and put it in front of her, then sat down so they were face-to-face. "Remember that video you made, where you talked about taking chances?"

"Yeah." She rocked back and forth on her heels. "I know. I'm a hypocrite."

"No, you're a normal human."

Irritation flashed in her eyes. "Being anxious all the time isn't normal, Hunter."

"True. But being afraid to take a chance or a risk is something everyone struggles with. Including me."

"But you're so confident."

He almost laughed at that. She had no idea about his internal struggles, and he wasn't going to dump them at her feet. This conversation was about her. "I play a good game," was all he'd admit. "I think this might be an opportunity to help each other, though."

"What do you mean?"

"I'm pretty sure I've got the art bug." Which was true. After today he was ready to learn as much as he could about drawing. He chuckled.

"Why is that funny?"

Hunter pointed to himself. "Me, an artist. I never could draw a straight line." He also hadn't had the patience to really try, up until now.

"You didn't take art in school?"

"Only in elementary and middle school. After that I always thought art was for weirdos and hippies."

"Yoo-hoo!" Maude's voice came from the other room. "You two okay in there?"

Hunter's brow shot up and Britt covered her mouth with her hands, letting out an adorable giggle. "We're fine," she called out. "Just putting up our supplies."

"Oh, I *see*. Well, I'll leave you to it."

A few seconds later, Britt peeked out of the closet and into the art room. "She's gone," she said, looking at him again. The lines of tension around her mouth and eyes had disappeared too.

"You don't think she heard me, do you?" he asked, a little concerned. "I was just making a joke."

"Even if she did, she wouldn't care. She and X are still living in the seventies and loving every minute of it." She tucked a loose curl behind her ear. "It must be nice to be so confident in your own skin."

I wouldn't know. "Back to my art bug."

Britt smiled.

Which made him smile back. *So pretty.* He shoved his focus back on the topic. "You mentioned that you're comfortable with your mom and Savannah."

"Maude and X too. And . . ." She cleared her throat. "That's it."

"You're not nervous around me when we're working on art."

He didn't bother to point out that she didn't seem anxious now either. That would work in his favor. "I propose this—in exchange for art lessons, I'll help you with your social anxiety."

"How?"

"When you're ready, we'll go out for coffee. Then we'll move on to a meal, and after that maybe a museum or shopping." The more he talked about this, the more he liked it. If she agreed, they'd be spending a lot of time together, something he didn't mind one bit.

"Why would you do that for me?" She frowned, the tension returning.

"I'm not being completely altruistic," he pointed out. "I'm getting art lessons from one of the best artists in return."

Britt glanced away.

"You don't have to decide now." He got up and went to put the stool back in its original spot. "There's no rush—"

"Yes."

He turned around. That was quick. Then he saw the uncertainty in her eyes, and he walked over to her. "I'm serious. Take some time to think about it."

"I don't need to. I'm tired of being like this. I've had counseling, taken medications, tried different therapies. They all work for a little bit, and then I go back to being . . . me. But no one's offered to help me like this. I'd be stupid to turn it down." Her hands moved to her shirt again.

He intercepted them, then gently moved them to her sides. "And it's not every day that a schmuck like me gets premium art lessons. It's a win for both of us."

"You're not a schmuck."

"About three hours ago you thought differently."

"No," she said, tilting her head and smiling a bit. "I thought you *might* be a creep. That's different."

He laughed. "I stand corrected. All right, it's a deal then."

Britt nodded. "As long as you don't mind hanging out with a nervous ball of anxiety with a perspiration problem when under stress."

"I can handle it. But are you sure you want to spend time with a thirty-year-old warehouse worker who only has a GED and lives with another guy who is barely out of high school?"

"What's wrong with a GED?" she asked without hesitation. "And warehouse workers are crucial members of the workforce. Without y'all, commerce would grind to a halt. Your living situation sounds practical too."

He truly hadn't looked at it that way. "Thanks, Britt. I appreciate that."

"At least you don't live with your mother." She headed out the door.

"Do you two get along?" he said, following her.

She nodded and pushed the chairs they'd used under the table.

"Do you like living with her?"

Britt turned around. "I do. I pay my fair share too. But I'm twenty-eight years old. I should be out on my own."

"Who says?"

"I do." She waved her hand. "When do you want to meet again?"

They set up a time for the following Monday—his next day off. "Okay, you come up with an art assignment, and I'll figure out some things for us to do—when you're ready," he emphasized.

Nodding, she said, "That sounds like a plan."

After collecting their drawings, they headed to the front of the store. X was straightening an endcap filled with mini canvases while Maude stood behind the counter scrolling on her phone. "Mondays," she sighed. "They're so slow, it's almost not worth being open." Then she looked up, her eyes brightening. "All the *supplies* in order?" She gave them a cheeky grin.

"Maude," X said, his tone holding a slight warning edge.

"I'm just teasing them." She came around the counter. "Let's see the masterpieces."

Britt easily showed them hers, and Maude made the appropriate awe-filled comments without going overboard.

Hunter held back, folding his into quarters on the creased lines. "Mine needs more work."

"Oh, I'm sure it's wonderful." Maude stepped beside him. "I'd really like to see it."

He looked at Britt, who nodded and smiled.

Reluctantly he unfolded it, and Maude took it from him. She studied it for a second, and he regretted giving in.

Then she grinned. "Marvelous. This is really impressive."

He glanced at her, wondering if she was buttering his biscuit a little too much. But she seemed genuine. "Thanks," he said, unable to hide his grin. It had been a long time since someone had showed so much appreciation for something he'd done. A very long time, and he soaked it in.

Britt's phone buzzed and she pulled it out of her pocket and looked at the screen. "It's Savannah," she said. "I've got to take this." She walked away and answered the phone.

"I offer a beginner drawing class on Saturday mornings, if you're interested." Maude handed him back the seashell drawing.

"Thanks, but I can't. I work on Saturdays. Second shift." He was about to tell her that Britt had agreed to give him lessons but decided not to. Britt could give them the news if she wanted to. They'd find out anyway when he showed up next Monday.

Britt returned. "I've got to go," she said, her nervous expression back in place. "Savannah wants to look at dresses this afternoon before the shops close."

"Ah, a summer wedding." Maude clasped her hands together. "I do love those."

"Not me," X said. "I never understood why any sane person would get married during the boiling Texas summer."

"True love doesn't care about temperature," Maude said.

X frowned. "That doesn't make sense."

"It does to me. Besides, that's why we have air conditioning." She gave Britt a quick hug. "Have fun. I hope you find something beautiful to wear."

It didn't take a genius to deduce that Savannah was a bride-to-be, and Britt was involved in the wedding in some way. That explained her anxious expression, and why she was fidgeting with her shirt hem again.

She looked at Hunter. "I'll see you later," she said.

"Hold up, I'll walk out with you." He said goodbye to X and Maude, ignoring Maude's giddy expression. She wasn't exactly being subtle.

Fortunately, it wasn't boiling hot outside as he and Britt left K&Bs and walked to their vehicles, but it was still May and soon the heat would crank up. He was parked a few spaces away from her compact car, and he walked to it with her. "You gonna be okay?"

She turned and nodded. "I've never shopped for a fancy dress before. I'm Savannah's maid of honor."

"I too have never shopped for a fancy dress." He grinned and she smiled. "But I have worn a tux before."

"Really? When?"

He stilled, wondering if he should tell her about his family.

No, not at this juncture. If she found out his father was crazy rich, she'd wonder why he wasn't working for him and why he was living with a roommate. Too much info too soon. "Prom," he lied. He'd never been, although he'd had dates for every regular dance at every school he'd attended. Usually by prom time, though, he was either suspended or had been transferred to yet another school. By the start of his senior year, he gave up and got his GED.

"Oh, right," she said. "I never went to prom."

"You didn't want to go?"

"No one asked me." She quickly opened the door. "See you Monday," she said, jumping inside.

Hunter waved as she sped off. He went to his bike, took the helmet out of the saddlebag, and put it on. If she would have told him even an hour ago that no one asked her to prom, he wouldn't have believed her. But knowing she had crippling anxiety, it made sense. Even if she'd been asked, she probably would have said no. But to not even have had the chance . . .

He got on his bike and made himself a promise. Whatever he had to do to help her, he would—whether she gave him art lessons or not.

Chapter 11

"Okay, girl. I want details. Every single one."

Amy raised an eyebrow and sipped her homemade virgin piña colada as she and Laura sat on her freshly weeded back patio. It had taken most of the day to conquer every single intruder. Britt would do a little weeding here and there, but once Amy attacked the job, she was determined to yank out every one of those suckers. "I have no idea what you're talking about."

Laura set down her drink on the round patio table and twisted her body until she faced her. Her curly auburn hair was pushed off her forehead with a tortoiseshell headband, and she narrowed her blue eyes. "Supper Saturday night? With Max, the hottie?"

"How did you know he was hot?"

"Is he?"

"Yes . . . hold on a minute." She scowled at Laura. "That was a trick."

"Of course it was." Laura gave her a triumphant grin. "But I knew he was good-looking. One of the perks of overseeing the Mingles is that I see all the signups. I also do a quick internet search to find out a little about them."

"Isn't that spying?"

"No. It's gathering intel. And I don't go deep. I check if they have a Facebook profile, then hop on LinkedIn to see if they have a presence there. If there are red flags, I might do an actual search. You can never be too careful these days."

"True." Hadn't she warned Britt enough times about the dangers of interacting with strangers on the internet? "Any red flags with Max?"

"Nary a one."

That was a relief. They'd closed down the coffee shop on Saturday night, and surprisingly, she'd been reluctant to leave. As soon as she walked through her door, she got a text from him.

I had a great time tonight. Maybe we can do it again.

She'd paused before answering. One evening with him hadn't changed her mind about steering clear of romance. But there was nothing wrong with male companionship, was there?

Sure. Hit me up sometime.

"You're smiling again."

She blinked, Laura's words bringing her back to the present. She tried to cover. "It's a lovely evening, my patio is weed free, and these piña coladas are delicious. Why wouldn't I be smiling?"

"Indeed." Laura grabbed her drink and took a sip. "I'm still waiting, by the way."

"For what?"

"Details!" She rolled her eyes. "It's like yanking out a molar getting info from you."

While keeping her friend hanging had its fun side, she didn't want to irritate Laura too much. "I will, after you answer one question."

"Go."

"Did you set us up?"

Laura looked genuinely surprised. "No. Promise. I can show the messages on the group where everyone cancelled. And I couldn't have made Farah's game go into extra innings."

"I'm glad she won." Amy twirled the little pink umbrella in her drink. She'd been surprised to find them in her junk drawer. They were left over from two years ago when she decorated her classroom in a Hawaiian theme for the last week of school. "It's just hard to believe it was a coincidence."

"Because he's perfect?"

Now it was her turn to roll her eyes. "No." Although he seemed pretty close to perfection. She hadn't noticed in the tavern, but when they were in the coffee shop and sitting at a smaller table, she could smell the woodsy scent of his cologne and see the smoky gray of his eyes. If he was this good-looking at fifty-seven, she could only imagine how handsome he'd been in his younger years.

"It's okay, Amy. You can admit I was right about Single Mingles." Laura took a slurp.

"You were sort of right." She turned serious. "I did have a good time with him. He's easy to talk to."

"And easy on the eyes. You should see his LinkedIn profile picture."

"Looks aren't everything." Daniel had been stunning in his twenties. Black curls he'd kept longer than his chin, pale-green eyes that sparkled when he laughed, and a lean physique that had made her sixteen-year-old knees turn to goo the first time they met. No, looks meant nothing when the person who had them was a raging alcoholic, a selfish husband, and a deadbeat dad.

"When are you seeing him again?"

"Max?" She shrugged. "I don't know."

"Did he text you?" she asked.

Amy nodded. "Three times." The other two had been to wish her a good day. So far, no mention of a second date—er, meeting.

Laura took her white umbrella out of her drink and waved it. "I surrender. You're obviously not going to tell me what happened." She pouted. "Even though I'm the one who made it happen."

"I'm sorry. I was just yanking your chain a little."

"I know, but this is serious. You haven't been on a date—"

"—it wasn't a date—"

"—since your divorce. As your best friend, of course I'm interested."

"It wasn't a date," Amy said again, more firmly this time. "And nothing happened. We went to Madeline's for coffee after karaoke started."

"You've got to be the only person I know who doesn't like karaoke."

If Laura had experienced a drunk Daniel making a fool of himself on karaoke night—not once, but four times—she'd understand. Amy had to take some responsibility for believing him when he said he wouldn't drink or misbehave again. But his words were hollow. First there would be only one or two drinks. That turned into several, and by the time he got on stage—after Amy begged him not to—he could barely say a coherent word, much less sing a song.

They'd even gone to other karaoke nights at different bars, and he'd embarrassed her and himself at each one. The last straw had been the final night, five years into their marriage and after two years of supposed sobriety. He'd been so drunk he started cursing at everyone, including her. She'd left him there that night and found out later the owner had to call a cab to take him home. There was some guilt over that, but not much.

She clenched her drink. She hadn't been to a karaoke night since.

"So you just talked?" Laura asked. "Nothing else?"

"Yes, that's all we did. You know I'm not that kind of girl. You're not that kind of girl either."

"I didn't mean you slept with him." Laura plopped her umbrella back in her drink. "If you had, you would have gotten a huge lecture from me. But there's nothing wrong with a little kiss or two."

Amy held up her hand. "No kisses. Or hugs. We shook hands, though."

"How scintillating."

Amy chuckled. "That's about as scintillating as I get. I did have a great time with Max. I wouldn't mind seeing him again." She held up her hand as Laura started to speak. "As friends. That's all I'm interested in." *And ready for.*

Laura grinned. "That's progress." She paused. "I do envy you. I wish . . ."

"What?" She leaned closer to her friend.

"That I wasn't so lonely." She sighed. "I miss being married. I miss having a man in my life to share the burden. Farah's a huge help, but she's so young and still getting over her grief. She misses Gary so much. We both do."

Amy took Laura's hand. Farah was only sixteen and had taken her father's death extremely hard. Britt was eight when Amy and Daniel had divorced. It was hard on her. *And on me too.* But they made it through together. Her daughter had been her constant companion. Maybe that was the reason Amy wasn't looking for anyone else. She wasn't lonely . . . at least not too much.

Laura squeezed her fingers and let go. "I'm not happy being single. I want to fall in love and get married again. I'm too young to live the rest of my life alone."

Her words hit Amy square in the chest. She hadn't realized her friend was suffering so much. "I'm sure God has the right man in mind for you."

"Then I wish he would hurry up." Laura leaned back in her chair. "Or maybe he's trying to teach me patience."

"Is there anyone in the group you've hit it off with?"

"Not romantically. They're all nice, but there's no spark."

"If Max were interested in dating, I'd set you two up," Amy said.

She smiled. "Now that's a true friend. Just give me advanced notice. I need to lose twenty pounds first."

"Hardly." Amy wagged her finger at her. "Besides, Max doesn't seem to be a shallow guy."

"How would you know? You look the same as you did in high school."

"Another lie." But Amy was lucky she'd kept her figure somewhat trim over the years. She chalked it up to hustling after high schoolers for decades. But gray hairs were coming in fast, there was more sag in her upper arms than she liked, and her crow's feet were spreading. *Welcome to middle age.*

For the rest of the evening, she and Laura abandoned relationship talk, and over a fresh, crisp salad and garlic bread, they played cards outside until the string of soft white lights draped across the patio eave came to life.

Around seven, Laura's Taylor Swift ringtone sang from her phone. She picked it up. "All done? Good. I'll be there in twenty. Love you too." She ended the call and stood. "Pool party's over. I've got to pick Farah up in McKinney."

McKinney. Where Max worked. He lived in Fairview, though. A very expensive town that wasn't far from Allen. Although, with Dallas metro traffic, it seemed a long way. Wait. It didn't matter where he lived, or how far away he was. She wasn't going to obsess over whether she saw Max again.

When Laura started to gather up the dishes, Amy stopped her. "I've got it. You go get Farah."

"You sure?"

"Of course. It's not much."

Laura gave her a hug. "Thanks for a great night." As she walked away, she added, "I'll let you know when we have another Mingles activity."

"I said I was one and done—"

"Ta-ta!" She opened the privacy fence gate and left before Amy could lodge another protest.

Once Amy finished the dishes and tidied the kitchen, she glanced at the time on the stove: 8:13 p.m. Britt had texted her earlier, telling her she was going shopping for wedding dresses with Savannah, so Amy wasn't too worried. In fact, she was glad her daughter had agreed to be her friend's maid of honor.

But as she walked to the living room and sat in the recliner, she wondered if she should text her. Were specialty dress shops open this late? Maybe they had gotten a bite to eat, although she wasn't sure if Britt would agree to that.

Amy had been so focused on school this year that it had escaped her notice that Britt was spending more and more time at home than she had in the past—and that wasn't counting the hours she spent on her online job. Now that Amy was off work and had more time to think back, and to pay attention to the present, she could see Britt was really struggling with her anxiety again. Their Saturday shopping spree had been fun, but Britt was tense the entire time, even though she valiantly tried not to show it. She'd hesitated going into Grimaldi's too, but gave in.

Amy's heart ached. Over the years, Britt had been in and out of therapy and had taken and abandoned several prescriptions. She didn't blame her daughter for not taking them. If they weren't working, she shouldn't. Her teen years were the worst, but as an adult she still wrestled with anxiety disorder. However, Amy had thought this last counselor had been tremendously helpful, and when Britt stopped seeing him two years ago, she seemed less nervous and more willing to be in social situations.

Amy was proud of how her daughter built up her business to be such a success, but at what cost? The counselor had pointed out that Britt's occupation choice could impede her growth. *"The best thing for social anxiety is to be social,"* he'd said. And she was—a little bit. Amy frowned. Or maybe she'd thought Britt was more social because she did a few volunteer activities at church. *Actually, just one.*

Picking up her phone again, she glanced at the time. Eight thirty. She frowned. She was being ridiculous. Britt was close to thirty years old. *But I'll always be her mother.* Some days she longed for the time when her biggest concern about her daughter was whether she wanted apple or orange juice, and how to keep her curly hair tamed for her yearly school picture. No one warned her that the problems and worries got bigger as children got older.

She started to set the phone down when a notification popped up. *Britt?*

But it was a message from Max.

Stemming her disappointment, she clicked on it.

Max: Hi.

                                          Amy: Hi.

She waited for him to respond. And waited . . . and waited. Well, this was weird. Had he accidentally texted her? After another five minutes:

Max: Sorry. Had to take a call.

Amy: A lawyer's work is never done.

Max: True. But this time it was the pizza delivery guy. He's lost.

Amy: Hopefully it won't be too cold by the time it gets there.

Max: If it is, I'll just warm it up. Anyway, I'm not sure how this nondating thing works, but I've got two tickets to a movie at the Mango Movieplex. My admin couldn't use them, so she passed them on to me.

Amy: What's playing?

Max: New movies I've never heard of. One Alfred Hitchcock: Vertigo

She paused. She liked old suspense movies, and she hadn't seen that one.

Max: Want to go Monday night? That's the only night Vertigo is playing.

Another hesitation. This was getting close to dating territory. Or not. Friends went to movies too.

Amy: Sure. As long as I pay for my ticket.

Max: No can do, they're free.

Amy: Then I buy the popcorn.

Max: And I'll get the Milk Duds.

Amy: Junior Mints for me.

Max: Great. I can pick you up beforehand.

Amy: I'll just meet you there.

Max: . . .

Uh-oh. Hopefully she hadn't insulted him. She waited as the dots disappeared, reappeared, and then went away for a few minutes altogether. Nuts. She should have just told him to pick her up. Friends picked up friends too. She shouldn't be overthinking it—

Max: Sorry again. Pizza's here. Sure, we can meet there. Movie starts at 7. I'll be outside waiting.

Amy smiled.

Amy: Thanks. See you then.

She set her phone down, continuing to grin. Then she felt a little guilty. Laura had just admitted to feeling lonely, and here Amy was going out with a man when she could take him or leave him. A friendly outing, but still. She really wished she could fix Laura up with him, but that wouldn't be fair to her since she wanted romance and he didn't. Maybe next time he suggested going somewhere she could ask Laura to join them.

Another idea occurred to her. She could ask Britt to go with them. That would get her out again, and she could probably get another ticket. Then she discarded the thought. Britt didn't like going to movies. They'd always watched them here at home.

Amy rose from the chair, taking her phone with her. She needed to stop worrying and let Britt find her way. *Easier said than done.* She entered her bedroom and decided to take a hot bath. Her muscles were starting to ache from her war on weeds. And she'd leave her phone on her nightstand, so she wasn't checking it every five—make that two—minutes.

Britt was fine. She was with Savannah, and Amy was sure they were both having fun.

"Wasn't that so much fun?"

Britt glanced at Savannah, who was driving her back to the first dress shop they'd visited more than four hours ago. Britt had left her car there and they went to three other bridal shops, stopping for a bite to eat in between the last two. It turned out Savannah's favorite dress was at the first shop, and she intended to go back in the morning and put down a deposit. They didn't even talk about Britt's or the bridesmaids' dresses. Today was all about Savannah.

"It was . . ." Britt wanted to say okay, which was the truth. Instead, she perked up her tone. "Great. Really great. I'm glad you found your dress."

"Me too. Thanks for your input, Britt. I wouldn't have been able to decide without it."

That made the whole ordeal worth it. While going to bridal shops hadn't been socially stressful since there weren't very many people in the stores, she hadn't realized until now how picky Savannah was. True, it was her wedding and she wanted it to be perfect, but she rejected dresses for the most insignificant reasons—the hem was a quarter inch too short, or the lace pattern was too lacy, or the color wasn't pure white. Britt's life revolved around color and even she couldn't tell the difference between the shades of the dresses. But Savannah could. Britt wondered if part of the "fun" of shopping for her friend was to keep the sales ladies hopping.

The only saving grace was that Savannah had been so singularly focused, she hadn't noticed that by the time they got to the second store, Britt was only half paying attention. She'd tried to be involved, but Hunter kept popping up in her mind. She still couldn't believe she'd agreed to give him art lessons. But the bigger shock was that he wanted to help her with her anxiety. She was still kicking herself for telling him about that, but not too hard. What if he really could help her?

And she had to be honest—she wanted to spend time with him. That had to be the biggest shock of all. His gorgeous looks aside, he was nice. At least he seemed to be. She was still going to keep her guard up, and if he made one wrong move, she was cutting bait. But she sensed he was trustworthy. He must really be serious about learning how to draw if he was willing to help her with her problem. It seemed like an unbalanced deal in her favor.

"There you go again." Savannah turned into the store's parking lot and put her convertible in park. "You've had something on your mind all day."

Oops. She considered denying it, but Savannah wouldn't believe her. "I'm sorry. I should have been completely focused on you."

"I had plenty of attention." Savannah whipped her hair in an exaggerated motion. "I just hope you weren't too bored."

"No. I'm just . . ." Should she tell her about Hunter? Her gut said no. There would be too many questions and she wouldn't have all the answers. So she told her another truth. "I'm worried about disappointing you."

"Britt." She took her hand. "I know I had high expectations for the dress. And the cake and the flowers . . . Well, the whole thing now that I think about it."

"You'll need to keep them low when it comes to me." Britt's stomach twisted.

"No, I don't." She squeezed her fingers. "You don't have to worry about disappointing me. I know this is difficult for you and I'm so grateful you'll be by my side. No matter what happens, I'm going to be happy."

"Even if the flowers start wilting?"

"Well, that might send me over the edge." Savannah grinned and let go of her hand. "Thanks again for coming with me."

"Thanks for asking me. And for being the best friend in the world." She relaxed some. "Can you send me the list of your bridesmaids? We need to start planning your shower."

"Yes, I can't believe I've forgotten to do that." She pulled out her phone. "I've got the list here. Texting it to you now before it escapes me again." When she finished, she said, "Do you need any help?"

"Yes, but not from you." She smiled and heard her phone in her purse buzz with the notification. "I might ask Mom for a little assistance, though."

"That would be great." She hugged Britt's shoulders. "Next challenge: bridesmaids' dresses! Are you free next Saturday?"

She was always free. "What time do you need me?"

"I'll text you." Her phone rang. "It's Justin."

"Say no more." She opened the car door as Savannah waved goodbye and put her phone to her ear. "Hey, babe. You won't believe the dress I'm getting—"

Britt shut the door and went to her car. She set her purse on the empty seat and started the engine, glancing at the clock on the dash. Almost ten o'clock. She hadn't expected to be gone that long, and she should have let Mom know she was running late. Then again, she was an adult. She didn't need to check in with her mother all the time.

As she drove home, she thought about Hunter again. No doubt he had tons of girls interested in him. He seemed so sure of himself, she had to assume his social calendar was full. And yet he was willing to spend a lot of time with her.

Does he like me?

She slammed on her brakes, almost running a stop sign. She blew out a breath and gathered her senses, forcing herself to pay attention to driving until she arrived home. When she turned off her car, she sat for a minute. Hunter liking her? Impossible. Men like him didn't give women like her a second look. Crazy-haired, pale-skinned, anxiety-ridden women. *Don't forget horse-faced.* Ugh.

No, he was just a nice guy interested in art. That was all there was to it. And she needed to get her attraction to him under control. Just because he was gorgeous and kind didn't mean she *had* to like him. She *shouldn't* like him. It would be a monumental waste of time, and she had other things to focus on. Her channel, her maid of honor responsibilities, and . . . and . . .

Well, those two. But they were enough.

Only the living room light was on when she walked inside. She turned it off and headed for her room. Her mother's room was down the hall, and she didn't see light coming from underneath the door, so she assumed Mom was asleep. After she changed out of her shirt and pants and put on a pink Manga T-shirt and candy-striped cotton shorts, she pulled back the covers on her bed and snuggled underneath them. One last look at her channel and she'd go to sleep.

She had seven DMs. One of them was from Hunter.

I forgot one thing, and I hope it's okay to ask this. Can I get your number? H.

Her stomach turned into a butterfly garden. *He wants my number!* Then she shook her head. Art lessons, remember? She tapped her number into the message.

A minute later she got a text.

Thanks. See you next Monday.

She couldn't help but smile as she quickly deleted the DM with her number in case she got hacked.

See you then.

Chapter 12

Daniel's jaw almost hit the floor when he read the price tag hanging from a navy blue wool suit. Almost one thousand dollars. Unbelievable. And that was less than the last suit he'd looked at. *I should have just stayed in the car.*

He tugged on his plain black tie—a splurge at thirty dollars from a chain department store—as Arthur strolled through the store, an attentive employee at his heels. His boss's schedule was usually light on Fridays, and Daniel always prepared himself for Arthur's call requesting he pick him up at work early. Today when he'd left the Picketts' house in University Park it was a little past eleven thirty. He was promptly instructed by Arthur to bring him to Dan Hutton's, a high-end haberdashery in downtown Dallas. Until now, he'd had no idea how high end it was.

"We have some recent Jack Victor arrivals, sir." The haberdasher, a sixty-ish, impeccably dressed gentleman without a hair out of place and a mustache to rival Burt Reynolds, gestured to another suit display.

Arthur slowly looked them over, then selected a camel-colored one.

"Excellent choice." The man smiled and took the jacket off the hanger. "Cashmere is always in style."

In his several months of employ, Daniel had yet to see Arthur wear the same ensemble twice. He couldn't imagine the money his boss had spent on his wardrobe, especially if he frequently shopped here.

While Arthur continued his extravagant retail therapy, Daniel wandered through the store. He couldn't even afford a pair of socks from here. Which was fine. He'd never been a fancy guy, and while he didn't mind wearing a suit for his job, he did find it stifling at times. He stopped in front of an impressively displayed circle of ties fanned out on a table, a male torso stand in the middle wearing a neutral-colored shirt. He didn't even bother looking at the prices.

Arthur appeared to be settling in, so Daniel parked himself in a leather chair near the door and pulled out his phone. He set the speaker to mute and went to YouTube. Britt hadn't posted anything new so far this week. She'd told him that she didn't really have a set filming or uploading schedule, just that she had to post content fairly regularly.

He clicked one of her older videos he hadn't seen before and started to watch, immediately smiling when she showed up on screen. He turned down the volume so low it was nearly inaudible as he watched her demonstrate how to make a basket using pine needles. She filmed herself weaving it and had sped up the footage, which made it even more impressive. It amazed him how she could master any creative medium.

He was about to click on another video when a young man entered the store. He stopped a few feet from the entrance and glanced around with a wary look, as if he'd just walked into a strange new world. Daniel sure could relate.

The guy was tall with shaggy blond hair and was wearing a form-fitting white T-shirt and shorts. He was extremely fit. Daniel inwardly sighed. Once upon a time he'd been in that kind of shape.

But he'd abused his body with alcohol, bad nutrition, and other horrendous personal choices. Now he was forty-eight, and middle age was having its way. He wasn't decrepit, but he sure did feel old.

He clicked on another one of Britt's videos while the guy walked over to the tux section of the store. A minute into Britt's introduction, he received a text.

Arthur: I need a third opinion.

Daniel: Right away.

He stood and pocketed his phone, then went to the back of the store, passing the young man who was now rubbing the back of his neck as he stared helplessly at the tuxedos in front of him.

Daniel arrived to see Arthur preening in front of a three-way mirror, the haberdasher standing to the side and nodding his approval. The suit wasn't a tailored fit, but it looked good, and the shirt and tie underneath were a flawless choice.

"What do you think?" Arthur pressed his palm against his midriff, over the two fastened buttons.

Daniel didn't respond right away, even though he was planning to say the first thing that came to mind—that it was a nice suit that he wore well. He'd learned Arthur liked more measured responses, and Daniel understood that. When he first started working for him, he thought the man was a little full of himself. He quickly realized that Arthur was plainspoken and straight to the point. Arthur Pickett knew he looked good. There was no reason to deny it.

After pausing the appropriate amount of time and giving him a visual once-over, Daniel said, "Nice suit. You wear it well." He held back a chuckle, keeping a straight face while his boss conferred with the haberdasher and scheduled a fitting.

"Excuse me."

Daniel turned to see the young man holding up a tux jacket as he walked toward them. "Can you help me with—" His face turned chalk white.

"I'll be right with you," the haberdasher said. "I apologize, we're short staffed today."

But the kid didn't respond. He clutched the jacket and stared . . . at Arthur.

Arthur's expression was unreadable, but his hand started to tremble as he touched the knot of his tie. He blinked, then shoved his hand into the jacket pocket and moved toward the young man, stopping a few inches from him. Clearing his throat, he said, "Hello . . . son."

~

Hunter's knee bobbed up and down as he sat in the back seat of his father's twelve-year-old Bentley while the driver whizzed through downtown with some serious skill. This was a mistake. A massive one. This morning he planned to rent a tux for his father's upcoming birthday party before he headed for work. Although it was still a little over a month away, he wanted to make sure he reserved it. He knew he couldn't go to just any man's store. He had to go to Hutton's, a place he hadn't stepped foot inside since his brother Payne's wedding six years ago. He'd gotten drunk and made a complete idiot of himself at the reception. That was the last time he'd been invited to a family event, until now.

As soon as he walked inside the boutique, he regretted it. He wanted to go to Dad's party, and he wanted to dress as he was expected to. But inhaling the mix of leather, luxury fabrics, and several kinds of expensive cologne reminded him that he was no longer a part of the elite society that could afford to shop here. He almost walked out, and he'd caught the guy in the chair staring at him before he pulled up his big boy pants and went to the tuxedo section.

Turns out that guy was Dad's driver, and as soon as his father had settled with the haberdasher, he asked Hunter why he was there. Lying had been second nature for most of his life, so he said he was on an errand for a friend, but they didn't have his size. The party was a surprise, and he didn't want to blow it. Hunter thought that was all he had to say, that he and Dad would part ways like they had two years ago—the last time they'd been in the same room together and his parents had cut all ties with him. That parting had been a lot more acrimonious.

Instead, Dad said, "Let's go for a ride."

Those words never boded well for knuckleheads in gangster movies, although Hunter didn't think his father had ill intentions. But his expression and tone didn't give him a choice, and he followed Dad and his driver to the car. On Dad's signal, the driver opened the back door, and Hunter climbed inside, followed by his father.

"How long has it been, Hunter?" Dad asked.

He shrugged and stared out the window. *Two years, five months, ten days. But who's counting?*

"It's—" Dad cleared his throat. "Good to see you."

A little ice melted around Hunter's heart. He looked at him. "Good to see you, Father."

Dad scoffed. "You and your brothers. Always so formal with me. Well, that's your mother's doing."

"How is she?" Hunter couldn't stop himself from asking.

"She's fine. Had a knee replacement last year. Also a little nip and tuck around her neck, if you know what I mean." His eyes softened. "She didn't need it. Wrinkles and all, she's beautiful to me."

He smiled a little. He loved his parents, despite the horrible way he'd shown it. They finally put a boundary up, and it worked. But that didn't mean he'd ever be permanently welcomed back into the fold.

"Still seeing your parole officer?"

Hunter cringed and glanced at the driver, who was staring straight ahead, sunglasses covering his eyes and the rest of his face unreadable.

"Don't mind Daniel," Dad said. "He's completely trustworthy."

Sinking against the supple leather seat—he had always loved this car—he nodded. "Haven't missed a check-in."

"Good. Still sober?"

"Yes."

Dad paused for a moment. "Are you telling me the truth?"

Hunter ground his back teeth to keep from snapping back at him. He was the one with the problem, not his father. "Yes. I am."

After his dad eyed him for a minute, he said. "I believe you."

Hunter blew out a breath he didn't know he was holding.

They didn't say anything for a long moment. The silence was stifling, the smooth purr of the engine the only sound in the car.

"Maybe . . ." Dad glanced away and stared out the window for a second before turning to him again. "Maybe we could—"

His phone rang, and he reached into his suit jacket pocket. "Hello. Now? Can't it wait until tomorrow? I'll be in at eight in the morn— Okay. I'll head on over there now." He hung up and put the phone away. "I've got to return to the office. A crisis of some sort. Where can I drop you?"

Hunter told him where his motorcycle was parked, a block away from Hutton's. When they reached the destination, Daniel maneuvered the car close to the bike.

"You still don't have a car?" Dad looked shocked.

"I like the Yamaha." He opened the door and started to get out, then turned to him. "Glad to see you again . . . Dad."

"If you need anything . . ." He shook his head and faced the front.

Hunter waited to see if he would say anything else. When he didn't, he got out of the car and shut the door. The Bentley sped off.

He stood by his bike, still trying to process what had happened. For the first time in years, he'd had a conversation with his father that hadn't turned into a fight. Granted, it was only for five minutes, but that was a start. And he realized something else—he truly missed him. And his mother. Payne and Kirk, too, although not nearly as much.

He walked back to Hutton's, having avoided his father asking more questions about his "friend's" interest in a tuxedo. And avoiding more lies. He'd made a vow to stop lying shortly after he was jailed, but this was an exception. After the party, he was never going to lie to his family, or anyone else, again.

～つ

"We'll be at your office in fifteen minutes," Daniel told Arthur as he merged onto the freeway. He glanced at his boss in the rear-view mirror.

"Just take me home."

Daniel frowned. "But what about the crisis?"

"There isn't any." His boss sounded defeated, something Daniel had never heard from him before. "It was a spam call. Lila and I have put up strict boundaries where Hunter is concerned. If she found out I'd even talked to him, much less invited him into my car . . . I saw the opportunity to cut off engagement, and I took it."

Daniel got off the freeway and turned in the opposite direction.

The tension in the car had eased the moment Hunter left, but Daniel was still reeling from the news that Arthur had another son. He thought there were only two—Payne and Kirk. Even in the main house there weren't any pictures of Hunter, and no one had ever mentioned him. Then again, he realized that the only pictures he did see of the family were recent ones. No baby or school pictures of the kids. Just wedding photos from Payne's and Kirk's nuptials, along with a large oil painting of Arthur and Lila on the wall in the formal living room.

"I guess you're wondering what all that was about," Arthur said, sounding slightly more collected.

"No, sir." He inwardly cringed at the fib.

"I'm wondering about it myself." He sighed, and Daniel heard him shift in the seat. "Hunter's my youngest son. I think he was about eleven, maybe twelve, when he started rebelling. I'm still not sure why. His personality was always so different from Kirk's and Payne's. More free-spirited, but still intelligent. He just refused to apply himself unless sports or girls were involved."

Daniel turned on his blinker.

"We tried everything to get him to take his studies and life seriously, but he defied us at every turn. Getting kicked out of schools. Drinking all the time. Drugs too, although he never did those on a regular basis, thank God. He even stole from one of his teachers—a spiral notebook, of all things." Another sigh. "Sorry. I don't know why I'm telling you this."

"Maybe because I understand. My past certainly isn't lily white."

"What caused you to drink so much— I'm sorry, don't answer that question. That's none of my business."

Hearing the pain in Arthur's voice, along with the desire to possibly understand what happened to his son, was surreal. It also tugged at Daniel's heart. "I don't mind telling you," he said. "The answer isn't a good one, though."

"What do you mean?"

"I don't know why I became an alcoholic. Or why I kept messing up my life over and over. I guess there was something inside me that was deeply unhappy, and I was looking to numb the pain." He gripped the steering wheel. "At first you don't expect to fall into the abyss. A few drinks and you feel better. But soon that turns into more, and then before you realize it, you're out of control. Then the only thing that can block out the shame of continually screwing up your life is more of the same. It's a cycle. And it's unbelievably difficult to break."

Arthur didn't say anything.

When they reached his house, Daniel wondered if he'd revealed too much. Dread seized him again. Now that Arthur knew how weak he was, he might not want him as a chauffeur anymore. He pulled into the circular drive and in front of their grand house that he wouldn't be able to afford in twenty lifetimes. He put the car in park and got out, attempting to settle his nerves. *I should have kept my mouth shut.*

He opened the door and Arthur stepped out, looking as composed as he'd been in Dan Hutton's. "My family can't find out that I talked to Hunter today. Understand?"

He nodded. The promise would be easy to keep. Payne and Kirk acted like Daniel didn't exist, and their wives were worse. Payne's wife, Everly, once had Daniel take her to Starbucks five minutes away—after she'd driven to the Picketts' in her BMW. When they got to the coffee shop, she changed her mind and ordered him to drive her back to the Picketts'. But Daniel never complained. Dealing with mercurial family members was part of the job.

He shut the door and headed for the Bentley's driver side.

"You were wrong, Daniel," Arthur said.

Wincing, he gulped and turned around.

Arthur's eyes were filled with pain. "Your answer. It was a good one." He turned on his heel and headed for the house.

Daniel exhaled, then hopped into the Bentley and drove it into the multibay garage. When he parked the vehicle in its spot and shut off the engine, he bowed his head with relief.

Then compassion filled him. He couldn't imagine watching a child suffer with addiction. Seeing Britt's struggles with anxiety broke his heart, but she was coping. And from what he could tell about Hunter, he was doing okay. He looked healthy, which was a good sign. And although Daniel tried not to listen to their conversation, he was glad to hear he was sober and keeping up with his parole officer. But it wouldn't take much to topple off that wagon and plunge right back into the nightmare.

Daniel knew that better than anyone.

On Monday, Britt placed a bowl of fuji apples on the table in the K&Bs education room. She took a step back, scrutinized it, and moved one of the apples over half an inch. There. A perfect still-life subject. A sheaf of drawing paper and two packs of colored pencils lay near the bowl.

"That's going to be a challenge for him, don't you think?" Maude set out a Bundt cake next to the tea set in the corner of the room.

She turned and looked at Maude. "Bundt cake?" Britt raised a brow. "We're having an art lesson, not a coffee klatch."

"Where did you hear an old-fashioned word like that?"

"Books, Maude. I read lots of books."

"Oh, that's right." She lifted the lid off the pot and sniffed. "Ah. Good old Earl Grey. It will go nicely with the orange dream cake."

Britt started to protest, then just smiled. When she'd told Maude and X that she would be giving Hunter a few art lessons, their reaction was typical—Maude shrieked, and X calmly nodded. Maude had wanted to do a whole tea service, complete with dainty sandwiches and scones. "I'm sure Hunter isn't a dainty sandwich kind of guy," Britt pointed out.

"Oh." Maude got a dreamy look in her eyes. "Probably not. His hands looked quite big—"

"Will you leave the kids alone?" X shook his head, but he was chuckling.

They had compromised with Earl Grey and Chips Ahoy! cookies, but Maude pulled a fast one and brought the Bundt cake. Oh well, she was an excellent baker. The snack would be good.

"He should be here any minute," Maude said. "I'll give him a proper greeting and send him your way." She peered at Britt. "How are you doing?"

"Okay." Surprisingly she wasn't as nervous as she thought she'd be, probably because she was in her element and knew exactly what she was going to teach Hunter. Her friend was right—it was a challenge. But from what he showed when he drew that second seashell, she didn't think it would be that hard. If it was, they'd just work on one apple. No rush.

Once Maude left, Britt glanced at the clock. Almost two. She hurried to the bathroom to check her hair. She'd swept it up in a bun and wrapped a neon-yellow-and-pink scarf around it. It was hot today, so she wore white and gray gingham shorts, a white T-shirt, and tan sandals. Several curls had slipped out of the bun, and she tucked them back in. She stared at her reflection. Yep. Her face was still long and her skin still pale. However, she could do something about that last flaw.

Not wanting to waste time staring at herself, she left the bathroom and went back to the education room. Hunter was already there, sitting in the chair and staring at the apples, looking pensive. *Uh-oh.* Maybe Maude was right, and she was too ambitious in her still-life choice. "Hi," she said, walking toward him.

He turned to her and smiled, but it didn't completely reach his eyes. "Hey." He looked at the fruit again. "Is that today's lesson?"

"It doesn't have to be." She tugged at her hem, then put her hands behind her back. "We can draw something else."

"No, it's fine." He stared at the bowl again.

Something was wrong, and that started up her anxiety. She sat down next to him and tugged on her fingers. "W-we really can do something else."

He turned to her. Glanced at her hands, and then covered them with one of his own. "I want to draw the apples."

Britt glanced down at his large hand covering both of hers. *Maude was right.*

Hunter removed it and sat back in the chair. "Can I ask you something?"

"Sure." She tucked her hands underneath her thighs. Problem solved.

He rubbed the back of his neck, then stopped, as if he realized he was performing his own nervous gesture. "How do you handle stress?"

"Not well, obviously."

He jumped up from the chair and walked a few paces. "I'm not just talking about anxiety or nervousness. What do you do when you get upset?"

She tilted her head and looked at him. "We're starting with *my* lesson?"

He froze, his eyes widening. "Uh, no." He sat back down. "This is actually about me." Then he quickly grabbed a box of pencils. "Never mind," he mumbled, opening the box. "We use red first, right?"

Britt watched him fumble with the tab. She scooted closer to him, took the box from his hand, and set it back on the table. "My therapists always recommended exercise." She gestured to her less than sculpted body. "But as you can see, I'm not a fan of that."

His gaze flitted over her. He grinned, and it looked genuine. "You look fine to me."

Warmth washed over her, but she set it aside, her cheeks flaming. He was nice—of course he'd tell her a white lie. She'd practically asked for a compliment anyway. She averted her gaze and put her hands under her thighs again. "Maude is a big proponent of calming teas. Chamomile, kava, things like that. X likes his essential oils, as you can tell."

"Is that what I smell when I walk in the door?"

"Yep. He says it 'enhances the customer experience.'"

Hunter chuckled. "I don't know about that but whatever he's spraying, it smells good."

"Diffusing," she corrected, her neck muscles relaxing. "My mom starts cleaning house when she's upset. Or 'dysregulated,' as my therapists called it."

He nodded, his good humor evaporating. "I run three or four times a week. I've got a physical job too. So exercise isn't a problem."

That explained his phenomenal physique.

"I don't like tea," he continued, "although I'm not opposed to trying it again. My roommate would ridicule me without mercy if I started spraying—excuse me, *diffusing*—essential oils in our apartment."

She tried to think of something else. "Distraction can work." Lord knows she used that enough, especially with her art.

"I've done plenty of that," he mumbled.

"Well, there's always talking about it too." Britt moved her hands and set them on her lap.

Hunter scoffed. "That wasn't done in my family. If you weren't a certain way, you—" He pressed his lips together. "I'm sorry. I'm hijacking the lesson. And I'm supposed to be helping you feel better."

"You are." She held up her hands. They weren't trembling, and she wasn't tugging or pulling or sitting on them. "See?"

"Yeah," he said softly. "I'm not sure how that happened."

She had a sudden epiphany, but it wasn't going to paint her in a good light. "I think one of the reasons talking to someone else helps is because it takes the focus off ourselves and our own problems. It's a form of distraction too. While I'm focused on you, I'm not so focused on me."

"Did you learn that in therapy?"

"Kind of. My counselors wanted me to get out and do stuff. Help other people. Which I want to do, but that means I'd have to be around . . . people."

He smiled, another sincere one. "You've helped me. I feel better than I did when I walked in here. And now I have a list of things I can do when I'm feeling on edge. Except the oils. Ain't gonna happen."

She laughed. "I don't blame you there."

"Thanks," he said. "Really." He picked up the box again, more calmly this time. "Now, how about we draw some apples?"

Chapter 13

Hunter continued shading the bottom of the blue-and-white ceramic bowl. He thought they would be drawing the apples today, but Britt focused on the bowl first. He'd had no idea how colors could be used for different effects, and most of them had to do with light or the absence of it. Ninety minutes had gone by, and he was still working on the bottom of the bowl.

Britt leaned over and inspected his progress. "That looks good."

He couldn't help but breathe in her scent—clean, a little flowery, but nothing overwhelming. Definitely alluring. He cast a side glance at her as she continued to evaluate his drawing, which wasn't much of anything. As far as he could tell, she didn't wear any makeup. And when she'd made a comment about not liking exercise, he noticed her insecurity about her figure. He thought her body was just right.

"We can stop now and finish up the bowl next week." Her gaze moved up to his face.

He marveled at how different she looked when she was completely relaxed, like she was now. Even on her channel she didn't have the same gleam in her eyes or the easy smile he was seeing in front of him. She seemed completely . . . *comfortable.*

"It's up to you." He wasn't in any hurry to leave.

She paused and looked at her watch, then at the apples. "We should stop."

"Okay." He tried to hide his disappointment by poking the pencils back into the box. It wasn't just that he didn't want to leave her, but he really was enjoying the lesson.

"You can take those with you if you want," she said. "And you should snap a picture of the still life. You can practice during the week."

"Yes, Ms. Branch." He gave her a salute, and grinned when she smiled.

As he took the picture, she started neatly putting her pencils away. "Funny, I never thought anyone would ever call me Ms. Branch. That's my mom. She's a teacher."

He stilled, his phone facing the apples. Ms. Branch? Didn't he have a teacher named— Oh, wow. Ninth grade, remedial math. He'd only had her for a semester before he was suspended and sent off to another school. He didn't even remember what he'd done to get into trouble. Had he been drunk? High? Probably both.

Familiar shame filled him as he looked at Britt, the urge to dull his feelings almost overwhelming. He hadn't experienced that temptation for almost two years. Now he'd felt it twice in several days, the first being after he'd talked to his father. He'd reserved the tux and gone to work, but he couldn't stop thinking about how he was separated from his family, and it was his own fault.

He'd been on edge ever since, enough that his coworkers and roommate noticed it. Sawyer had asked if he'd been drinking again, and Hunter truthfully denied it. But he had to admit to himself he'd been thinking about it. A lot.

He glanced at Britt, who was still focused on carefully sliding the pencils inside the box. Just being around her made him feel better. But the fact that he knew her mother was one of his teachers, and an eyewitness to the grand beginnings of his immature, self-destructive behavior, rattled his nerves. If Britt learned about that or anything else regarding his past, she wouldn't just think he was a creep but a complete reprobate.

At one time, he was.

Britt closed the lid on the slim box and picked up the rest of the materials, including his drawing. "We'll keep these here," she said, adding her beautifully finished rendering of the apple bowl on top of the pile.

"Sure." He watched her walk to the storage room, and when she went inside, his head fell into his hands. A gin and tonic would be good right now. Or just straight gin. He needed a distraction.

She came back into the room and he lifted his head, calm washing over him. She was just what he needed. Her hair with its wild bun and seventies-colored scarf wrapped around it gave her a bohemian flair, a contrast to the conservative checkered shorts and plain white shirt she was wearing. He had yet to see her hair completely down. She always wore it up in some fashion, including in her videos. He wondered exactly how long it was, how wild it was, how it would feel in his hands—

"Maude made us a snack." She walked over to a little table with a teapot, cups, and a round cake holder on top. "It's not chamomile or Kava, but Earl Grey is good too. Would you like some?"

Her words brought him out of his thoughts, and he ran his hands over his thighs. He didn't need *that* kind of distraction. If she knew he was attracted to her . . . game over. "Sounds great." He popped up from the chair and went to stand beside her as she poured tea into the cups. "I can cut the cake if you'd like."

She glanced at him. "Sure."

They carried their tea and cake to the table and sat down. Hunter took a big bite, and orange sweetness exploded in his mouth. "This is incredible."

"They always are." Britt pressed her fork into her slice. "Sometimes I wonder if Maude puts a little extra *something* in her baked goods."

He stilled. "Does she?"

Britt shook her head. "It's an inside joke. Maude still has her D.A.R.E. T-shirt from the eighties."

"Dare?"

"To keep kids off drugs. It was a campaign thing back then." She paused. "I don't know how well it worked. I know it didn't for—" She quickly shoved a bite of cake in her mouth. "Mmm. Good!"

Her muffled exclamation seemed a little exaggerated. Then again, perhaps not. It was fantastic cake. He took another bite, his jitters completely disappearing. "I feel like I'm at a tea party."

"Is that a bad thing?"

"I've never been to one before. Only seen them in movies. But I'm up for an adventure."

She smirked. "I wouldn't call Earl Grey and orange dream cake an adventure."

"Adventures are what you make them."

Maude glided into the room, holding a feather duster the size of her head. "Don't mind me," she sang, waving the duster around in a weak attempt to clean. "Just tidying up in here."

Britt looked at Hunter and rolled her eyes.

He grinned. "This cake is delicious," he said to Maude, almost finished with his slice.

She turned, her eyes twinkling with delight. "Why, thank you," she said, punctuating her words with flourishes of the duster. "I'm glad you're enjoying it." Her gaze darted from Hunter to Britt, then back again, her smile growing even wider.

Britt leaned forward. "Sorry," she whispered as Maude turned around and started faux dusting again.

He scooted closer to her and lowered his voice. "About what?"

Maude started to hum a tune that sounded vaguely familiar. Then she softly sang, "Take a chance on me . . ."

Britt sat up. "Really, Maude? ABBA?"

"Oh . . . sorry." She looked over her shoulder with feigned surprise. "I didn't realize I was singing out loud."

Hunter burst out in laughter. "I thought I'd heard that song before. Been a long time, though."

But Britt wasn't laughing. She pulled out her phone and started typing on it.

"What are you doing?" Maude asked, fully facing them now.

"Telling X to come get you." Britt peered up at her.

She held up the feather duster. "No need, I'm leaving." She breezed toward the door. "You two have fun—"

"Bye, Maude!" But Britt was smiling now. After Maude left, she leaned back against the chair.

"She's something else," Hunter said, still chuckling.

"That she is." Britt giggled. "That feather duster was hilarious."

"Yep." He picked up his small teacup. It felt like a toy in his hand. He took a sip and promptly set it down.

"Still don't like tea?" she asked.

"Affirmative. But I do like coffee." He hesitated before saying his next words. He didn't want to push her before she was ready, but since she wasn't tense, she might be willing to agree. "It's time for your lesson now," he said. "What do you think about going to a café with me?"

⁓

Britt felt her shoulders scrunch up. Unbelievable. Here she was having a great time with Hunter, and she was only slightly annoyed with Maude's obvious attempt to spy on them. That had disappeared when she realized Hunter wasn't bothered at all. He had the best laugh too. *Did this man have any flaws?*

But one mention of going out in public, and she was back where she started—anxious, nervous, and on the verge of perspiring. *How attractive.*

He was sitting close to her now, and he surprised her by moving toward her a few inches more, his gaze holding hers. "You can say no. I won't mind, and I won't judge. But I think it would be a good thing for you. I know this small café that's off the beaten path. There isn't room for a lot of people." He glanced at her teacup, then back at her. "I'm sure they'll have Earl Grey."

Her shoulders lowered slightly, and she couldn't pull her eyes from his. The irises were so captivating up close, full of varying shades of brown and green. And those long lashes . . . perfect. She wanted to say yes. Badly. What was stopping her?

Me. I'm stopping me.

His smile was as gentle as his words. "Maybe another time."

She started to nod, then stopped. What was she doing? This stunning, kind man was trying to help her. She had to meet him halfway. "I'll go," she said, sitting on her hands again.

His grin sent a tingle straight to her toes. "Excellent. You'll have to drive, though. I don't have an extra helmet on me today."

"Good, because I'm never getting on a motorcycle."

"Never say never." He stood and picked up his empty plate and almost-full teacup.

"Oh, I can definitely say never. Because it's never going to happen." She joined him, and they set the dishes by the cake. "Maude will get these," she said, turning toward him.

Most of their in-person interactions had been when she or both of them were seated. This time she was paying attention to their height difference. The top of her bun was level with his sternum, and she had to look up at him. She'd already noticed his slightly scruffy whiskers, but now that they were standing close to each other again, she wondered what they would feel like against her skin. She'd never touched a man's face before. Not even her father's—at least not that she remembered.

Blinking, she got a grip. Staring at his stubble was weird, and she didn't want to come across as more peculiar than she already was. "I-I'll grab my purse and we can go."

"Lead the way."

When they reached the front of the store, X was standing behind the counter reading a homeopathic magazine. He was the only one in sight. "Where did Maude go?" Britt asked.

"I sent her on an errand." He put the magazine down. "A *long* errand."

Hunter chuckled. "Looks like you have your hands full, X."

X grinned. "Almost fifty years and counting. I wouldn't want it any other way. You two heading out?"

"Yes." Her hand went to her shirt hem.

In one smooth move, Hunter entwined his fingers with hers. "Heard of Yo Jo's?"

X thought for a second. "Don't believe I have. Coffee?"

"Yep. That's where we're going."

Hunter was still holding her hand like it was no big deal, and X either didn't see that they were holding hands or, unlike his wife, decided not to make a commotion over it. But to Britt, it was a massive deal. She'd never held a man's hand before either. And Hunter's was delightfully warm. A little rough, as expected from his job. Also, all engulfing.

The tingle that had traveled through her earlier felt like a lightning bolt, making it hard for her to remember that he was helping her with her anxiety, not anything else. Still, holding his hand was *thrilling*.

A customer walked into the store, making X's eyebrows rise with surprise. It was Monday, after all. With a nod to Britt and Hunter, he hurried over to her. "Welcome," he said with a big grin. "How can I help you?"

As X and the customer conversed, Hunter led Britt outside. Although it was close to five o'clock, there wasn't a cloud in the sky and it was still hot. He shielded his eyes with his free hand as they stepped off the sidewalk.

Britt glanced at their hands still together, unsure what to do. Surely he hadn't forgotten he was still holding it. But there was no reason to anymore.

He dropped her hand and headed for the car. "Still a hot one, isn't it?"

She nodded, a little disheartened that they weren't walking hand in hand anymore. She pressed her key fob to unlock the car. Feeling like she had to address the handholding, she said, "Thanks."

"For?" He walked to the passenger side.

"Keeping me from stretching out my shirt."

He smiled. "My pleasure."

For a split second, she thought he meant it.

Amy stood in her bathroom and applied a swipe of lipstick to her lips. Tantalizing Taupe. A misnomer if she ever saw one. It was her go-to, a utilitarian shade that was the exact opposite of tantalizing. Now that she was looking at her reflection, the color screamed High School Math Teacher.

She had a deep, rich red in her collection, but she'd only worn it twice and it was probably dried out. Tantalizing Taupe would have to do. She fluffed her silver-streaked brown chin-length bob and took a quick inventory of her outfit, trying to forget she'd spent way more time picking it out than she should have for meeting a friend at the movies. She'd landed on cropped tan chinos, a mint button-down blouse, and navy blue sandals, and she would bring a dark-blue sweater with her to wear in the theater.

"Here we go," she said, then gave her reflection a thumbs-up.

She got in her car and backed out of the driveway. Britt had told her she was going to K&Bs again today. It was almost six, and she wasn't back yet. Maybe she was working on an art project with Maude and X. That was usually the case when she spent a lot of time at the shop.

Over the past week they hadn't talked much. Britt had been busy with work and trying to figure out what to do for Savannah's shower, and Amy had, in a moment of insanity, decided to mulch her flower beds and fell into bed early each night, exhausted. She'd popped a couple of Tylenol Extra Strengths before she left the house.

As she drove to the Mango Movieplex, she once again wondered what she was doing. No matter how many times she told herself this was just an ordinary outing to a movie, she knew she was fooling herself. It wasn't a date either. But what did you call going out with a handsome single man who also didn't want to date? Friendship wasn't the correct term. Rendezvous with an acquaintance? Hanging out with a buddy?

Why label it?

She blew out a breath and turned into the parking lot. That was the correct conclusion. No labels or expectations. Just two adults—middle-aged adults—having a good time. Still, she took one more peek at her face and hair in the mirror, made sure she had nothing stuck in her teeth or hanging out her nose, and got out of the car. Immediately she was hit with a blast of heat, and it was only May. The next few months would be brutal. Otherwise known as summer in Texas.

Amy scanned the lot for his Mercedes, and found it parked in the row in front of her. She laid her sweater over her forearm, adjusted her purse strap, and headed to the building. When she walked into the cool theater foyer, she was glad for the relief and to see Max standing a few feet away, looking like he came straight from an AARP magazine shoot.

"Hi," he said, striding toward her. He adjusted his black-framed glasses, and whatever woodsy cologne he wore, it was nice. Like her, he was dressed casually—white T-shirt, casual gray jacket, wheat-colored pants, slip-on canvas shoes. He took a step toward her, as if he were going to hug her, or maybe kiss her cheek. Then he halted and glanced down at his shoes before saying, "Glad you could make it."

"Me too." Neither of them needed to be ill at ease, so she leaned over and gave him a peck. "Thanks for inviting me."

It was the right thing to do because he immediately gave her a carefree smile. "Ready to eat some overpriced junk food and enjoy some black-and-white suspense?"

"I'm always up for junk food. We'll see about the suspense."

They both ordered popcorn and a drink. Amy also got Junior Mints, and she noticed Max skipped the Milk Duds. When it was time to pay, she was relieved he didn't insist on buying her food. By the time they went into their theater, there were still ten minutes left before the show started.

"Back, front, or middle?" he asked.

The theater only contained a handful of people. "I like the middle," she said.

He allowed her to go in front of him, and she picked two seats that were as close to smack dab in the middle as possible. Two young women were already seated in the actual center seats.

They sat down and settled in, some older Top 40 hits playing in the background while the screen flashed local advertising. She took a sip of her drink. "I can't remember the last time I saw a movie in the theater," she said. "Maybe with my friend Laura? Must not have been that great of a movie, since I really can't recall."

"Crystal and I used to go a lot." He stared at the popcorn bag in his lap for a moment, then shook his head. "I told myself I wasn't going to talk about her tonight."

"Hey." She touched his arm. "You can talk about her all you want."

He turned to her, his smile warm. "Thanks, Amy. I know I need to move on, it's just that everything still reminds me of her. Even after all this time."

"I get it." She set her Junior Mints on her armrest. "Daniel and I have been divorced for twenty years, and I haven't seen or talked to him for almost as long. That night at karaoke brought up memories. Terrible ones, but that's par for the course. We didn't have a relationship like yours and Crystal's."

"I'm sorry."

"It's okay. There was a time I did love him. And for the first few years, we had some great times. We also had Britt. So not everything was horrible." As she was talking, she remembered the first time Daniel had taken her to a movie—one of those nineties teen comedies that were so popular at the time. She was sixteen, he was seventeen, and she could still remember how he kept inching his hand closer to hers, so slowly she almost grabbed it just to get their first handholding experience over with. But then he linked his fingers with hers, and he didn't let go until the credits.

Amy shook off the memory. "Now here *I* go, talking about my ex."

"In a way it's inevitable." He picked up a few pieces of popcorn. "They were an important part of our lives."

She nodded, but disagreed about Daniel being important to her—at least not from the fourth year of their marriage until their divorce. He'd left her to raise Britt on her own and had little impact on their daughter's upbringing. "How was work last week?"

"Busy." He finished chewing the popcorn and swallowed. "Then again, it's always busy. Are you enjoying your time off?"

"I'm getting a lot of projects done." She told him about the weeding and mulching, and that she'd also planted some annuals.

"You like gardening then."

"I hate gardening." She opened the box of mints and offered him one. He shook his head. "But I like having a neat, colorful landscape and I can't afford to hire help." That last part slipped out, and she instantly wanted to take it back. "I mean, I could, but I prefer to save the money."

"You're not . . ." He didn't finish, but looked at her, concerned.

"In financial trouble? No. I make a good salary, and Britt pays rent and all her bills. When Daniel and I bought the house, we got a good deal. I'm fine." She grinned. "I'm just cheap."

"Nothing wrong with that. I've been known to pinch a penny or two."

"Let me guess, you got your Mercedes on sale."

He chuckled. "No, I paid full price. Of course, the dealership makes it seem like you get a deal, but we all know how that works. I don't even really like it that much. I'd rather drive something more practical."

She side-eyed him, wondering if he was trying to downplay his wealth to make her feel better. "Then why don't you?"

"I've got an '83 Corolla in my garage. Still runs and has over three hundred thousand miles on it. I keep it to remind me of when I was working three jobs while going to college." He crossed his ankle over his knee. "It also needs a paint job and the inside smells like an '83 Corolla. If I ever drove it to work or the courthouse or pretty much anywhere else . . . let's just say people would be wondering why their lawyer and/or colleague couldn't afford a better car."

"Ah. Got it." His explanation made sense, but she still wasn't sure he was being honest about not liking the car. Not that he was lying to her, but it's just that she couldn't imagine not enjoying a luxury car if she could afford one.

"But if you ever want to take a spin in an old clunker, let me know." He grinned. "Or a highfalutin Mercedes."

She laughed. "Let me see, which one should I pick?"

His smile diminished a little. "I'm serious, Amy. Just say the word, and I'll pick you up."

The theater darkened and the previews started. But she was still looking at him . . . and still smiling. "I just might take you up on it."

Chapter 14

I hope that wasn't too torturous for you."

Britt glanced at Hunter, who was stretched out on the passenger seat of her car as they drove back to K&Bs. Her instant reaction was to think he was being sarcastic, but his expression showed he was serious. They were driving back from Yo Jo's, having spent almost two hours there. She had to admit the first thirty minutes were extremely uncomfortable. "I wouldn't call it torturous," she said. Then she sighed. "It wasn't easy, though."

"I know. But you handled it like a champ."

She rolled her eyes. They'd been drinking coffee, not running a marathon. Although from the sick feeling in her stomach and the sweat running down her back as they approached the café, a marathon might have been easier. She should have known the place was busy from all the cars in the parking lot, and when they walked inside, there were no places to sit. Turned out Yo Jo's Monday special was two for one espressos, and according to the barista, it was always packed.

Hunter had leaned in close and whispered, "We don't have to stay."

She'd almost fled at that moment. Then she looked up at him, saw the encouragement in his eyes, and stayed put. By the time they got their order, a two-seater table had opened up, and they sat down. Conversations hummed around them, and she was so aware of being surrounded by people she couldn't even talk. They sipped their drinks until the crowd filtered out, and only then did she regroup and relax enough to have a conversation with him.

She looked at him again, surprised to see his eyes were closed as he lay back against the seat. She jerked her gaze away and focused on the road. She could stare at him all day, and at the café, she did, because he kept telling her to keep her eyes on him instead of the crowd. The easiest request she'd ever received.

Even though she was consumed with her own anxiety, she still noticed that Hunter had attracted plenty of female attention. The barista even outwardly flirted with him, which made her feel invisible. It didn't matter that they weren't on a date. They could have been, and the woman's behavior was out of line.

Britt sighed again. Who was she kidding? That barista knew she and Hunter weren't a couple. Everyone in the café knew. A man as fine as him wouldn't be with a timid mouse like her. That only happened in movies and romance novels.

"Hey." His eyes were partially open, giving him a sexy, half-sleepy look. "That was a big sigh. Everything okay?"

Oops. She hadn't meant for him to hear it. "Yes. Just tired." Which was true. Coming down from prolonged anxiety could be exhausting.

"I think I dozed off a little."

"I haven't exactly been stimulating company."

Hunter didn't respond for a moment. Then he said, "Don't do that."

"Do what?"

"Belittle yourself. You were good company. Me falling asleep proves it."

She frowned and turned into the strip mall parking lot. "I'm not following."

Another long pause, and she had parked next to his motorcycle by the time he spoke again. "I probably shouldn't admit this."

Uh-oh. She put the car in park but kept it running for the AC.

He turned to her. "I've battled insomnia for a long time. Lately it's been worse. The last few days it's been terrible, although I have an idea why."

She wondered if he was referring to whatever had been bothering him earlier. He still hadn't mentioned the cause, and she didn't want to pry, even though she was curious.

"There's something about you that's calming," he said.

Britt almost scoffed. "Really? Because most of the time I feel anything but calm."

"That might be so, but outwardly you're cool as the clichéd cucumber." He gave her a crooked smile.

Oh no. Not the crooked, charming smile that made every nerve in her body blissfully misfire. Her palms grew damp again. Forget anxiety. This was . . . *yearning. Double oh no.*

"You also have a soothing voice. I . . ." He hesitated, as if he were unsure about what he was going to say. "Anyway," he suddenly continued. "The fact is that when I'm with you, I'm relaxed enough to fall asleep. That's a good thing. A *very* good thing."

Her entire body felt like it was glowing inside, and she was elated that she could help with his problem. Art lessons didn't seem enough for what he was doing for her. Despite the difficulty, today had been a milestone. She'd been able to go to a crowded place with someone besides her mother and Savannah, and in the end, she'd managed to somewhat enjoy herself. That was Hunter's doing, and she was grateful.

"So don't sell yourself short, Britt." His smile was in full force now.

And so was her galloping heartbeat. The space between them seemed to suddenly shorten, even though neither of them moved. Then she thought she saw his gaze drop to her mouth, only to meet her eyes again. It was so quick she was sure she imagined it.

But her body thought it was real.

He opened the door. "See you next Monday?" His voice sounded quick, like he was in a hurry.

"Sure—"

"Great. Bye." He shut the door, and in seconds he had his helmet on and had cranked up his bike. Then he sped off.

She fell back against the seat. Huh. Had she done something? Said something? She didn't think so. Then again, she wasn't sure. Maybe she'd given him a weird look and wasn't aware of it.

Her chest tightened and she headed home. Somehow, some way, she had to stem her growing, and futile, crush on Hunter Pickett.

⟳

Hunter opened the throttle on his bike until he was flying over the speed limit. He raced back to the apartment as if the cops were chasing him. They actually had at one time, when he was twenty and drunk driving the Porsche Taycan he'd gotten for his birthday two weeks earlier. He ended up crashing it into a tree, fortunately escaping with only scratches and a warning when he told the police officer he was Arthur Pickett's son. Now that he thought about it, he couldn't believe the man hadn't hauled him off to jail. Hunter certainly had deserved it then.

He took a curve sharper than he should have and quickly counterbalanced the bike, slowing down his speed. Talk about dumb. He was about to wipe out because he'd wanted to kiss Britt so badly, he was afraid if he hadn't dashed off, he might have given in, ruining everything. He still marveled that she had no clue how adorable she was . . . and desirable. *Sooo desirable.*

That was a huge problem.

He whipped into his apartment complex lot, parked the bike, yanked off his helmet, and jogged inside. He needed a cold shower, and not because of the muggy air.

When he entered the apartment, he saw Sawyer mashing the buttons on the video game controller and yelling into his headset at his competition. "Dude," Sawyer said, pointing the controller at the TV and swerving it around. "That was not cool!"

Hunter went to the fridge and grabbed a Coke, keeping the door open to let the cold air cool his body. But it had no effect on his mind, and he was back to thinking about Britt again.

She'd been expectedly nervous when they went inside the café, and he'd made a mental note to never take her to Yo Jo's on a Monday again. He was unaware of their special, and he didn't want her to think he'd pulled a fast one on her. When she decided to stay, he was proud of her. Once the place cleared out, she became more at ease, and they were able to talk. Surface conversation, of course. Favorite foods, colors, their work, stuff like that. He had no intention of talking about personal things, especially his family. She didn't seem eager to talk about her family either. Which made him curious, but he didn't ask.

"Hey!" Sawyer yelled at Hunter. "You're letting all the cold air out."

Hunter quickly shut the door. "Sorry," he mumbled, starting for his room.

"Hang on a sec." Sawyer yanked off his headset. "You all right?"

He had to smile. His friend was doing a great job of keeping tabs on him. "Yeah," he said. "I'm fine. Just a little distracted, but it's all good." Somewhat, anyway.

Sawyer narrowed his gaze, as if he were weighing Hunter's words. Then he gestured to the TV. "Want to join us?"

Shaking his head, he held up the can. "Gonna finish this and hit the hay."

"Okay, old man." Sawyer slipped on the headset and spoke into the mike. "All right, punk, game on!"

Hunter entered his room and shut the door. The apartment had two bathrooms, and as the "old man," he'd gotten the larger room with the attached bath. He stripped down and showered, trying to get Britt out of his system. But all he could think about was how he wanted to hold her. Kiss her. Comfort her. She brought out his protective side. Up until he met her, he didn't know he had one.

He shut off the water and toweled dry, then put on boxer shorts and climbed into bed. Popping the top off the Coke, he took a gulp, then set the can down on his side table and put his arm behind his head. Now that he had some distance between them, he could see he'd been a jerk rushing off the way he did. He picked up his phone and found her number.

Should he apologize? Or just let it go and see her next Monday like he said? They hadn't talked in between their lessons, but not because he didn't want to.

Hunter stared at her name. They weren't dating, and he doubted they ever would. She wouldn't want to get involved with an ex-con, he knew that for sure. But he couldn't help but compare her to the women he had dated—a term he used loosely. Going out was something he did regularly in between going to jail and before he became sober. He wasn't proud of his behavior with them either. Women had been playthings, and he'd gravitated toward the ones who were eager to participate. Still, he knew he'd hurt some of them, and he told himself he didn't care. It was their fault they got involved. He'd always been up front that he was only interested in one thing. And he made sure he was drunk or high every time it happened.

He squeezed his eyes shut, almost drowning in the intense mortification flooding over him. He deserved this feeling, this excruciating remorse. During his last stint in jail, he'd been visited by a chaplain, who had talked to him about Jesus and had explained how the Son of God had sacrificed himself for mankind's sins. Hunter had confessed to him and asked Jesus for forgiveness. He'd gone to church several times since on the few Sundays he'd had off, and he believed Jesus had forgiven him.

But he hadn't forgiven himself.

He kept staring at his phone. Being sober had cleared out the cobwebs, and he no longer wanted to be that playboy who was only out to satisfy himself. Until Britt, he hadn't met a woman who made him yearn to be a better man, not just clean up his act so he wouldn't land in jail again. It was all so strange. If she hadn't popped up randomly in his YouTube feed, he would have never known she existed.

His finger hovered over her name, and he finally tapped it.

Hey. Sorry about leaving so fast. I forgot I had a

He couldn't say date. It was a lie, and he didn't want her to think he was taken.

an appointment. With Sawyer. We play video games on Monday nights.

He winced and sent her the lame apology and even lamer excuse. Not exactly a fib since he and Sawyer often did play video games. They just didn't have a set date.

His eyes remained glued to the phone, waiting for a response. He sat up in bed, his back leaning against the cool wall. Then he face-palmed. He'd just told her he'd rather play video games with Sawyer than hang out with her. *Idiot.*

Hunter slid down and tossed his phone on the bed. Well, that was that. She probably wouldn't respond to him. He'd see her on Monday, though. Unless she cancelled the lesson. He shoveled his hands through his damp hair. She wouldn't do that . . . Would she?

He grabbed his phone. No response. Maybe he should go play a game with Sawyer and his friend. That would get his mind off his idiotic mistake—

The phone vibrated in his hand. A message notification popped up. He tapped on it, holding his breath.

No problem. I hope you have fun. See you Monday.

Hunter beamed, relief expelling from him. He almost typed *I can't wait*, but he caught himself.

See you then.

Another buzz.

Thanks again for tonight. I had a good time.

He stared at the phone, grinning like a fool. "Me too."

The theater lights went up, and Daniel gathered his empty pop-corn bucket and drink. He stood as the credits rolled for the latest superhero movie. He could barely comprehend the plot for this one, although he suspected it was the special effects, not the story, that enticed the theatergoers.

On a lark, he'd decided to take in a show at the Mango Movie-plex. He was usually on call during the evenings, but Arthur had given him the night off. He decided to catch the seven o'clock showing, and the theater was only half-full, as expected on a Monday night. When he reached the ginormous trash can near the back of the theater, he stuffed his trash in it and walked down the hall to the exit.

The movie had been playing at the far end of the hall, and he passed several other screening rooms, their doors still closed as muffled cinema sounds came through the walls. A few yards ahead and to the right he saw a door open and slowed his steps. He could see the illumined sign that said *Vertigo*. He'd almost chosen to see that movie, changing his mind at the last minute.

Then two people came out of the room. He didn't recognize the man . . . but he instantly knew the woman.

His heartbeat screeched to a halt, along with his footsteps. The man lightly put his hand on Amy's waist and guided her through a larger crowd. She turned to look at him, mouthing the words "thank you."

He jerked forward as someone collided with his shoulder.

"Excuse me," a tall, lanky kid said, giving him an apologetic wave and scurrying off with his friends.

Daniel realized he was standing in the middle of the hallway, the other theatergoers dodging him. He regained his composure and started walking, this time with hurried steps. Of all the theaters in the Dallas area, they had to be at the same one. And who was that guy she was with?

He caught sight of them again as they walked close together toward the exit. *Too close.* An ugly thread of jealousy wound through him, choking off the common sense that told him Amy had the right to go out with anyone she wanted to, and he didn't have the right to complain. Or interfere. *But I can still follow them.*

And he did, feeling a little bit like a spy and a lot like a chump, but that didn't stop him. The man was impeccably dressed. Daniel had been around Arthur and his ilk to know that the casual jacket he was wearing cost a mint, and that the shoes were even more expensive. Amy looked . . . Well, she looked incredible. He hadn't been this close to her in almost two decades, and even though they were a decent distance away, he still got a good view of her. Fit, trim, and those amazing legs . . . She was still every bit as pretty as she had been years ago.

They walked out the door, and he hustled after them, slowing his pace as they walked to the parking lot. Her brown hair was shorter than he remembered. It suited her. He wished he could get a look at her face, though, not her profile. He considered jogging past them so he could do just that, then he saw them walk toward a Mercedes . . . and he stopped cold. He spun on his heel, turned around, and walked in the opposite direction.

His pulse still careened in his body, but it was tempered with a hard splash of reality. Amy had always been and still was a beauty. He shouldn't be surprised that a rich, good-looking guy would want to be with her.

Wait—did Brittany know about Amy's date? Or boyfriend? It

was an unspoken rule that they didn't talk about Amy's personal life. But he'd never had much of an opening to either.

He rushed to his car, a 2003 Fusion that needed a tune-up, and got inside. He turned it on, cranked the air, and quickly dialed Brittany's number.

She picked up on the third ring. "Hi, Dad."

"Hey, Brittany, did you know—" he stilled, realizing he was about to put his daughter in a terrible position. If she knew about Amy's date, she'd feel obligated to tell him or lie about it. And if she didn't and Amy hadn't told her . . .

"Did I what?"

His brain grasped for a decent answer. "Did you know there's a new superhero movie out? I thought we could go see it."

Pause. "I'm sorry, Dad. I don't go to the movies. They make me anxious."

Oh. He knew that. He stared at the ceiling of the car and winced. "No, I'm the one who's sorry. I forgot."

"It's okay," she said in her soft, sweet voice. "I should be able to go to the movies. Normal people do that."

"Honey, you're more normal than most people I know. Besides, theaters are crowded, the sound is loud, and the refreshments are highway robbery."

"Maybe we could rent one and watch it together."

He nodded and positioned the air vent toward him. "I'd like that. How was your day?"

Another pause. "It was good, Dad. Really good. I think . . . I think I might have made a new friend."

Daniel smiled. "I'm glad to hear that." And it was something he needed to do too. Other than his boss and his family, he didn't engage with too many people. He was never one to have a passel of friends like Amy always had. She was a cheerleader and one of the most popular girls in school. He was shy and a gearhead, always working on cars instead of his studies. He'd been shocked when she asked him to sit with her at the school library when she was a junior and he was a senior. They started dating after that, falling in love with each other before he graduated.

And he'd idiotically thrown it all away.

"Dad?" Britt said, breaking into his thoughts. "If you don't mind, I'm pretty tired tonight. Can we talk later?"

"Sure thing. And let me know when you want to see that movie. I'll even let you choose which one."

She chuckled. "How magnanimous of you."

"I guess I'll have to google that," he said, only partly kidding.

Her laughter grew. "Thanks, Dad. I'll talk to you soon."

"Love you, Brittany."

As always, after he said those words, there was hesitation. "Talk to you later," she finally said.

He hung up, not blaming her for holding back from him. Hopefully one day he would hear those words from his daughter. Until then, he knew he'd have to earn them.

Daniel slipped his phone into his short's pocket and pulled out of the parking space. He couldn't resist driving around the lot to see if the Mercedes was still there. It was gone. Another wave of jealousy hit, but he brushed it away. He didn't know about his ex-wife's personal life, other than she hadn't remarried. That had surprised him, and he wondered if he'd soured her on marriage. He'd put her through the wringer, and he would never forgive himself for that.

Amy deserved to have a good life. If Mr. Mercedes made her happy, then he wouldn't stand in the way. Not that he had the chance to anyway. He'd blown that years ago.

Chapter 15

Amy walked inside her house, unable to stop smiling. Tonight had been fun, more than she'd anticipated. The movie was great, but the company was even better. It turned out Max liked to whisper comments during movies, which didn't bother Amy a bit, since she was inclined to do the same thing. She'd learned over the years to keep quiet, although sometimes she couldn't help herself when something ridiculous or wonderful happened on screen. Britt was tolerant of her habit, but it drove Laura to near madness, and one time she'd showed her the duct tape in her purse as a warning. Amy wasn't sure if her friend had been joking or not.

Daniel had never minded comments during movies, though.

She whisked her ex out of her mind and thought about Max again. When they were leaving the theater, she'd felt him touch her lower back as they threaded through the crowd. But he quickly dropped his hand and didn't touch her again as they walked back to their cars. They'd stopped by his Mercedes first—she wanted to get a better look at his fancy car—before they said their good nights and parted ways.

As she passed by the kitchen, she remembered what she felt when he pressed his fingers against her back. *Nothing. Nada. Zip.* Which confused her a little. While she was firm in her decision not to date, if she did change her mind, Max would be the perfect candidate. There was no doubt she found him handsome. He was polite. A true gentleman, actually. Smart, successful, and funny.

But she wasn't attracted to him. Not one iota.

She walked to her room, took off her makeup, changed into her lemon-yellow silk pajama set, and went to the kitchen to get a drink. It was barely past nine, and she wasn't tired yet. Maybe she'd read in the living room or watch another movie until she was ready for bed.

When she entered the kitchen, she saw Britt standing in front of the sink. "Hey, sweetie," Amy said, giving her a hug. "How was your day?"

Britt turned off the water and dried her hands. "Good. I was just about to make a snack. Crackers and cheese. Want any?"

She was still pretty full from the popcorn and Junior Mints, but she nodded. "Sure. I'll get the drinks."

A few minutes later they were seated at the table with a plate of sliced cheddar cheese and buttery crackers between them, glasses of iced tea at the ready. "So how's your project going with Maude and X?"

Britt froze, a cheese-laden cracker halfway to her mouth. Her eyes widened. "M-my project?"

"Yeah." Amy picked up a cracker. "Has Maude finally decided to do that mural on the back wall of the shop? She's been talking about it for years."

Her daughter paused, then quickly nodded. "It's in the planning stages." She shoved the cracker in her mouth.

"I should stop by soon. It's been too long since I've visited Plano's quirkiest couple."

"Uh . . . sure. Just not on Mondays."

"But that's when you're there," she said. "I figured I'd bring pizza and we can hang out in the art room."

"Education room," Britt corrected, snatching another cracker. Instead of eating it she was breaking it into crumbs. "It's closed on Monday for . . . a special project. But I'm not involved with that one." She let out an awkward noise. "Besides, X is gluten and dairy free, and Maude is allergic to, um, oregano."

"I could bring Chinese—"

"Perfect!" Her smile was too wide. "How about on Wednesday?"

"Okay." She tilted her head as she took a big gulp of tea. Her daughter was acting a little odd. "Everything all right?"

Britt set down her glass and smiled. "Yes."

Amy's concern evaporated. She hadn't seen such a bright smile on Britt in . . . months? A year?

"I'm planning Savannah's shower," she said. "Would you like to help?"

"Of course." Now it was Amy's turn to beam. "I talked to her mother at church last Sunday. Dawn said the whole family is excited, but a little sad that Savannah and Justin are moving away."

"I am too." She brushed the cracker crumbs into a neat pile on the table. "I'm going to miss her."

"I know you are, sweetie. I will too. But you can . . ."

"Visit?" Britt looked up.

Amy nodded, although she knew that wouldn't happen anytime soon. Not unless she went with Britt, and even then, she couldn't see the trip being easy. At times, she wrestled with not pushing Britt a little to be more social. Maybe they should have taken more trips during the summers when she was off from school. But up until five years ago, Amy had either taught summer school or took classes herself, and there was no time, money, or energy to go on a real vacation. By the time there was, Britt was still in therapy, and even more adverse to leaving the confines of Allen and Plano.

Britt stared at the crumb pile for a moment.

"There's plenty of time to decide," Amy said. "And you don't want to go too soon. They'll be newlyweds, after all, and who wants to be around all that *romance*."

"Yeah," she mumbled. "Who wants that?" Then she lifted her head. "Where did you go tonight?"

Amy paused. Should she tell Britt about Max and the movie? No, not until she figured out their relationship, if it existed at all. There was no point in bringing him up if she wasn't going to see him again, even as a friend. If they started hanging out more often, then she'd explain it to her daughter.

Britt was the major reason why Amy had never pursued a relationship, although she'd never tell her that. With her anxiety disorder and her father's abandonment, she didn't want to add to Britt's problems by bringing a man into the dynamic, only to have her attach to him and then be devastated if the relationship didn't work out. She wouldn't put Britt or herself through that again.

"I went to the Mango Movieplex," she said, deciding on a half lie. "They had a one-night showing of *Vertigo* that I wanted to see."

"Since when did you become a Hitchcock fan?"

"I like a suspenseful movie every once in a while." She swirled the ice in her tea. "And it was something different. I hadn't been to the movie theater in a long time."

Britt pressed her lips together but didn't say anything.

Amy wondered if Britt was blaming herself for that. She hoped not. Time for a topic switch. "Let me know what I can do for the shower."

"Savannah texted me a list of her bridesmaids, and she's still deciding on a theme." Britt shrugged. "She wants it to reflect her wedding theme, but in a particular way."

"That sounds like Savannah," Amy said. "In a way that makes your job easier."

"That's probably why she's doing it."

"Are you nervous about the shower?"

"Not as much as I thought I would be." She smiled again. "I want it to be perfect for her."

"Then we'll make sure it is."

They finished the snack and Britt headed to her room for the night, while Amy went to the living room. She glanced at the book lying on the table beside her recliner, a novel she was struggling to get into. It was one of those celebrity book club picks, and while the writing was good, the subject matter was a little dark, not exactly her preferred reading material. Instead, she picked up her phone and decided to watch a couple of Britt's videos.

She watched the latest one that Britt had uploaded last week about painting on wood. She was hand-lettering the words *Take Risks* on a thin, rectangular piece that looked like the kind of blank signs K&Bs carried. Her letters were perfect, and so was the painting that followed. Amy's grandmother had artistic aptitude, but nothing on Britt's level. Her daughter had incredible innate talent, but she was successful because she paired it with hard work, practice, and discipline.

She glanced through the comments, as she sometimes did after watching a video. Most of them were glowing, but occasionally, some blockhead would write something cruel or offensive. Amazingly, Britt did a great job of not letting those comments get to her, probably because she was so confident in her skills.

Amy just wished Britt could be more confident in herself.
The comments scrolled past her until her eyes landed on one.

Hi, honey. This is your best video yet. <3

She sat up straight and looked at the name. Sober4lyfe. Who
was this guy? Or girl? Quickly she shot off a text to Britt.

Who's Sober4lyfe?

⌒

Britt was shoving her arms into her vintage Jackson 5 T-shirt
when her phone buzzed. She pulled down the shirt and picked up
the phone.

Who's Sober4lyfe?

Oh no. Britt was still dealing with her guilt over lying to Mom
about Mondays and art projects. She'd even dragged Maude
and X into her deception. But she didn't want to share Hunter
with anyone. Not yet. Their friendship—and she had to keep
using that term or else she'd start writing his name all over her
sketchbook and drawing hearts around it—was too new. Too
special.

And now Mom had found Dad's YouTube handle. When he
told her he wanted to comment on her videos, she hadn't thought
much about it. No one would know who he really was anyway.
There were so many comments on her videos that most of them
got lost in the shuffle.

She paced, trying to figure out what to say. Maybe now was the time to tell her the truth. But she wasn't sure. She feared her mother would be furious with her, and then fight with Dad. She'd seen enough of that as a child, and she didn't want to witness it again.

More importantly, she didn't want her father to have a reason to leave again. Not when they were just establishing a relationship.

She had to type something, or her mother would be at her door any minute now.

Britt: I don't know.

Mom: He/she commented on your last video. Called you honey and then <3

Britt couldn't help but smile. That was sweet.

Mom: Don't respond. You don't know who's behind the screen name. He/she could be a criminal.

Britt: I won't. I rarely respond to comments, just mostly like them.

Mom: I see you haven't liked this one. You need to keep it that way.

Britt: Okay.

She tossed her phone on her bed and scowled. When would her mother stop badgering her about online safety? *I'm not a child.* She would never do something as careless as get involved with a delinquent. She'd even been super careful with Hunter, and he turned out to be one of the best things that ever happened to her.

Sitting down on her reading chair, she thought about their conversation at the café again. They were slowly learning about each other. Their different tastes in foods, colors, and activities. She would have to show him the light when it came to yacht rock, though. He had no idea what he was missing.

What they hadn't talked about was their families, and she was fine with that. Hers was so confusing right now, and she didn't want to get into the past. She was enjoying the present, and that was enough for her. They would get to know more about each other as time went on.

Her phone buzzed again. She got up and grabbed it off her bed.

Good night, sweetie. I love you.

How could she be upset with her now? She smiled and texted back.

Britt: Love you too. Thanks for looking out for me.

Mom: Always

She stared at the screen, keyed up over lying to her mother, getting treated like a two-year-old, and now feeling enveloped in love and security. Her mother was the only person in the world she fully trusted, and that included Savannah. No matter what, Mom had her back.

But she wished she had someone to talk to about this. She didn't want to bother Savannah with her family drama, although she knew her friend would drop everything and be there for her. That wouldn't be fair to her, though. This was Savannah's time to shine, and she needed to focus on the upcoming wedding, her move, and her fiancé.

Talking to her father about it was out of the question. If he knew her mother had discovered his screen name, he might stop commenting altogether. Britt didn't want that. She liked seeing his cute little messages.

She moved her thumb across the screen to her very short list of contacts and saw Hunter's name. They'd already put a period on the end of their day with their prior text conversation. She'd been relieved when he told her he had a standing time to play video games with his friend and hadn't left so fast because she'd said or done something weird. She didn't want to take up too much of his time. He had a life outside of her.

Her gaze stayed on his name. Then she tapped on it.

You awake?

He immediately answered.

Hunter: Yep.

Britt: How was the video game match?

Hunter: . . .

As she waited for him to reply, she got up from the chair, turned on the lights, then snuggled into bed.

I beat the pants off him.

Britt chuckled.

Britt: That must have been a sight.

Hunter: You can only imagine. On second thought, don't. ☺

She turned on her side and started typing.

Britt: Have you ever had something you needed to tell someone, but couldn't bring yourself to do it?

Hunter: Like a big secret?

Britt: Yes. Exactly.

Hunter gripped his phone and stared at Britt's text. Dread flowed through him. Had she somehow figured him out, and this was her way of leading up to telling him she knew about his past?

The thought was crazy and fleeting, but he still had a sick feeling in his stomach. If she ever decided to do an online search of him, she wouldn't find much. He didn't use social media and his father had made sure every trace of his past arrests and incarcerations had been scrubbed from the internet. As a top-notch criminal lawyer, he didn't need his son's bad publicity affecting his career.

The sick feeling switched to guilt for not being completely honest with her. Then it morphed into curiosity. Was she holding something back from him?

If this has to do with me, don't worry. You can tell me anything.

He realized it was an egocentric text, but he didn't want her to fret over talking to him. And eventually he would tell her everything, after he proved to her beyond a shadow of a doubt that he was a different person than the punk kid of his past.

No. It's not you. It's . . . someone else. Two people actually.

He was relieved, but he noticed she was being vague.

Hunter: I suppose everyone's got a secret or two they need to hold on to. Sometimes people keep secrets to protect someone else.

Britt: I think this is one of those cases. But how do you know when it's the right time to tell them?

The million-dollar question.

Hunter: I wish I had an answer for you. Only you can determine when it's time.

Britt: I've never kept a secret before. I've always been an open book. Although that's easy to do when you don't have many friends.

Up until recently, Hunter had also been an open book, but in a bad way. He snuck his first drink when he was twelve, when he was at a friend's house and they busted open a six pack from his parents' refrigerator while they were out for the day. Ever since then, he'd never tried to hide his drinking or intermittent drug use, at least not much. He always got caught, and upon reflection, he thought that was probably the point—to see how far he could push his parents, to find out how much they would cover for him.

What he never considered was how much pain he'd cause them. Or himself.

> Hunter: I'm sure whatever the secret is, you're keeping it for a good reason.

> Britt: Maybe. It's all so confusing.

He wanted to hop on his bike and meet her somewhere, to hold her hand and reassure her it would be okay. Texting was so impersonal and could be misconstrued, even though it was his primary mode of communication.

> Britt: I'll figure it out.

> Hunter: You okay?

> Britt: *thumbs-up*

> Hunter: Sorry I couldn't be more help.

> Britt: You were helpful. I just needed someone to listen.

> Hunter: I'm here any time you need me.

He paused, wondering if he'd gone overboard. This was all so new to him, having to measure his words and actions. He didn't mind, but the margin of error was razor thin sometimes.

Britt: Thanks, Hunter. Good night.

Hunter: Good night.

He set down his phone and turned over on his side, his covers bunched halfway up his bare torso. He'd been drifting off right before she texted, but now he was wide awake. He thought about watching another one of her videos but changed his mind. Earlier today he'd almost spilled the beans about falling asleep to her calming voice. If she found out he'd done that, it would set his progress with her way back.

Add another secret to the list. And he couldn't even say his reasons for keeping secrets from her were noble. He wasn't protecting her, although he tried to convince himself of that. He was chin deep in self-preservation. Maybe he hadn't changed that much after all.

He flopped over on his back and stared at the ceiling, barely visible in his darkened bedroom. He needed to set a deadline to tell her the truth, but he also needed enough time with her so that when he did reveal his past, she wouldn't be shocked and tell him to take a hike.

After Dad's party. That was in nearly a month, plenty of time for he and Britt to get closer. He could reveal some things about his family too, to enable trust.

He shut his eyes. This all sounded so calculated. But he didn't have a choice. Not if he wanted to keep Britt in his life. And he wanted to . . . desperately.

Chapter 16

For the next two weeks, Britt was floating close to cloud nine. She and Hunter continued their mutual lessons— she taught him art and he taught her confidence. He'd even started arriving earlier at K&Bs so they could have lunch together in the education room before instruction, and a few days ago they'd made a return appearance at Yo Jo's. She'd managed to make it through Double Shot Monday again and actually enjoyed herself.

Maude was all aflutter and did little to hide it. For once, Britt didn't care. If her friend wanted to think she and Hunter were an item, she could go right ahead.

Britt was wishing the same.

But she was also realistic. He hadn't said or done anything to make her think he considered her anything more than a friend. And she was okay with that. *Sort of.* It wasn't his fault that the more she learned about him, the more she liked him. She found out his father was a lawyer and his mother had been a stay-at-home mom all his life. He had two brothers and two sisters-in-law. He liked to run, swim, and play football and basketball, although he rarely did the latter two. He wasn't a great student, which was why he'd gotten his GED.

Then there were the personal things. He revealed that he didn't want to work at The Warehouse for the rest of his life, but he wasn't sure what to do. "I guess I could try community college," he'd said last week as they drank their decaf at Yo Jo's. "It's been years since I cracked a textbook, so I don't know."

"Is there anything you're interested in?"

His gaze met hers, his gorgeous eyes turning bright. "Art, believe it or not. I really enjoy it. I've even been reading online articles on classic painters during breaks at work. I'll never understand Pollack or Picasso, though."

"They're an acquired taste," she said.

"I don't have a toothpick's worth of skill or talent, but I think it will be a good hobby for me."

"It could be more than a hobby, Hunter. You're really good."

He ducked his head. "Nah."

His humility irked her a little. "Are you saying I don't know what I'm talking about? That I can't recognize good art when I see it?"

His head jerked up. "No. I'm not saying that at all. It's just hard to believe . . . Well, I can't believe I'm good at anything other than sports. And I'm so rusty now, I doubt I'd be competent at that either."

This was a side of Hunter he rarely showed. But she knew it wasn't an act. He quickly recovered by making a quip about being a former jock, but his words stuck with her. Somehow, she'd have to convince him that he had talent. Raw, unformed talent, but it was there.

The following Monday, they both sat down at the table while Maude prepared their usual snack. She'd been plying them with various baked goods during their lessons, enough that Britt had started taking walks around the neighborhood in earnest, sometimes with her mom. She still hadn't told her about Dad, and that gnawed at her. But like Hunter said, she would know when the time was right.

Britt set her huge canvas tote bag on the table as Hunter stood close by. He leaned in and tried to peek into the bag. She nudged him in the side and put her back to him, hiding the contents. "All will be revealed soon," she said, smiling.

But it quickly faded when she realized her back was against his torso, and he wasn't moving.

"Just a quick look?" he said, his mouth close to her ear.

A delicious shiver slid down her spine, making her forget her words.

"Fine," he said, his tone still light as he stepped away. "I guess I'll have to wait."

She took in a breath, fighting for her composure. "Smart move," she joked, but caught the shakiness in her voice. Nuts. She was slipping into old nervous habits. But this uncomfortableness felt different. For some bizarre reason . . . it felt good.

Britt forced herself to be calm as she pulled out a round, sunshine-yellow portable Bluetooth speaker and set it on the table.

Hunter eyed it. "What's this?"

"Today's the day we will immerse ourselves in . . . yacht rock."

"Aw man," he whined. "Not that."

She laughed as he pretended to pout. "You haven't given it a proper chance."

"I don't have to. Can't we compromise? Maybe some Van Halen ballads—"

"Those exist?"

"Not really, although they do have some lighter rock tunes." He folded his hands into a pleading gesture. "Please, Ms. Branch. Don't do this to me."

Britt picked up her phone and found her seventies playlist. "It's either that or disco."

He sat up straight. "Yacht rock it is. But next week we listen to my list."

She nodded. "Fair enough." She pressed Play, and a Christopher Cross tune filled the room.

"Oh, I love this song," Maude said. "It's from that movie . . . Drat, I can't remember the name. But X and I used to dance to it all the time."

Britt had legit forgotten Maude was still here.

Maude strode toward them. Today's caftan choice was beige with southwestern symbols scattered all over it. Her red glasses hung around her neck, and she had her long, gray hair tucked under a sage-green turban. "Is Savannah going to have a band at her wedding?"

Britt paused. "I don't know. She hasn't mentioned it."

"She must be having some kind of music." She glanced at Hunter, as if asking him for confirmation.

He shrugged his broad shoulders. "Don't ask me. I haven't met her yet."

Britt looked at him, wondering if that was a hint that he wanted to meet her friend. She'd talked about her to him enough, although she hadn't said a word about him to Savannah. Maybe it was time for them to be introduced to each other. And she would, soon. She started to reach into her bag to pull out the subject for her and Hunter's next drawing.

"If she doesn't have a band, then there will be a DJ," Maude said with an emphatic nod. "And lots of dancing. But first there will be the bridal party dance."

Britt's head snapped around. "What?"

"The dance where everyone in the party is announced. The maid of honor is paired with the best man . . . oh boy." She hurried to Britt's side. "Are you okay?"

She tried to nod her head, but her nervous system had crashed to the floor. No one had said anything about a dance, especially not with a man and in front of a crowd. She could feel the color drain from her face.

Maude put her arm around her shoulders. "Didn't Savannah tell you?"

"No." She reached for her shirt hem, another thing she hadn't done in a while.

"Maybe it's just a northern thing," Maude said quickly. "Or even just a Vermont thing."

"What if it isn't?" The pale-blue tank top she was wearing was cotton and didn't have any stretch. When she pulled on it, her straps dug into her shoulders. "I've never been to a dance . . . I don't even know how to dance—"

She felt Hunter's fingers clasp hers. "I do."

⌒

Hunter held on to Britt's hand, not caring if Maude was a witness or not. The second she mentioned dancing at the reception, Britt's face turned a grayish pale. If he hadn't pulled her hand away from her shirt, she might have busted her tank top's thin straps.

"And I know how to dance too, sweetie." Maude gave him a tiny nod, one Britt didn't notice. "X isn't too shabby on his feet either."

"Between the three of us," Hunter said, running his thumb over the back of her hand, "we can teach you."

"And you might not have to worry about it at all," Maude said, her encouragement sounding a little desperate.

Britt looked up at Hunter with wide, vulnerable eyes. "I don't want to be like this," she whispered.

He knew exactly what she meant. Over the past two weeks she'd admitted more than once that anxiety was her enemy, and that she'd do anything to vanquish it. But nothing ever totally worked.

Maude dropped her arm from Britt's shoulders. "Don't worry sweet pea. You got this." She walked over to the table where the speaker sat next to Britt's phone. "How do you work this thing?" Then a slow song filtered through the speaker, one he recognized. Something about dreams, he thought.

"This one's good." Maude spun around and clapped her hands together as she walked over to them. "Hunter, you stand here." She moved him a couple inches to the right, so he was standing straight in front of her. "Britt, you move one step forward."

Her eyes were still locked on his as she complied.

"Good. You're both in position."

Britt's scared eyes widened even more.

"Maude?"

They all turned to see X poking his head into the room. "We've got a customer."

"Can't you see I'm busy, *Xavier*?"

"She requested your help specifically. She has a long list of supplies for her project too."

"Drat," she said.

X's bushy, gray brows arched. "We've got a customer on a Monday, and you're upset about it?"

"No, but . . ." She glanced at Hunter and Britt and sighed. "Tell her I'll be right there." After he left, she leaned in close. "I trust you two will figure this out." She patted them on the shoulders, then wafted out of the room.

Hunter let go of Britt's hand. "Okay, let's—"

Click. The door latched shut.

Never change, Maude. He turned his full attention on Britt.

"I can't do this, Hunter," she said, moving away from him.

"Yes, you can." He took her elbow and drew her close. "I'm not good at dancing, and you don't have to be either. Almost nobody is paying attention anyway. They're all talking, laughing, hitting the bar . . . You get the point."

He felt her arm loosen up a bit. "Really?"

"Really. Trust me, I've been to a few over the years." Although, he'd never seen a bridal party dance together, so maybe Maude was right that it was a northern thing. And of course he hadn't been on his best behavior at any of the weddings he'd attended, especially family ones. "Who's the best man?" he asked. He almost didn't want to know who would be dancing with her. He shoved away the tiny arrow of jealousy piercing his heart. This was about Britt, not him.

"Justin's brother. He's older, in his mid-thirties. He's been married for years."

That was a relief. "Okay, so he's someone you know. That helps."

She nodded. "He's really nice. Their whole family is."

"See," he said, grinning. "Nothing to worry about."

The song ended and a jazz-infused tune started playing. He nodded with his head toward the speaker. "Got any other slow songs?"

"A few." She went to her phone and started searching. Soon another ballad filled the room.

For a second, he thought he'd have to guide her away from the table, but she finally walked toward him and stood in the exact place Maude had told her. "Now what?"

Now what, indeed. He took a step forward, telling himself that he was only going to show her how to dance—how to place her feet, where to put her hands . . .

His mouth turned to cotton. *Don't enjoy this . . . too much.*

Hunter took her hand and slowly placed it on his shoulder, not wanting to startle her. Her fingers lightly rested there, and he could feel the warmth of them through his black T-shirt.

She pulled away slightly and looked up at him, questioning in her eyes.

"It's okay to touch me," he said, his gaze not leaving hers. "I won't bite."

She let out a breath and returned her hand, applying a little more pressure.

"Good." He tried not to notice how nice she smelled. *Be real, she always smells nice.* Or how the lights in the room brightened up her dark hair, which wasn't pure black at all, but many shades of brown. Her art lessons had taught him about seeing colors in a different way than he had before. "I'll put my hand here." He rested his fingers lightly on the side of her hip, his palm spanning the curve.

Her gaze darted down to his hand and flew back up.

"Then I take your other hand in mine." He scooped it up and threaded his fingers between hers. "And then we move a little." He nudged her hip ever so slightly, and as they started to sway, he could feel the tension in her body begin to melt away. "See," he murmured. "Piece of cake."

She nodded, her gaze still locked on his. They moved tentatively to the music, then with a little more finesse.

After several seconds, he said, "You okay?"

"Yes." Her voice held a husky tone he'd never heard from her before.

Every nerve in his body sparked. *It's just a dance . . . just a dance* . . . But it wasn't, not for him. And he wanted to be closer to her. Unable to stop himself, he said, "I can show you another way."

Britt could barely breathe. She'd never danced with anyone before, so she didn't have anything to compare her dance with Hunter to. But she refused to believe she'd ever have a partner that could match him. Her fingers had been frozen in place on his shoulder, but she could feel the hard muscle underneath them. Her other hand was getting damp as he held it, but he didn't seem to mind, and, miracles of miracles, she didn't either. She didn't want to do anything or be anywhere else other than right here, dancing to decades-old music and gazing into Hunter Pickett's eyes.

Suddenly he said, "I can show you another way."

Her eyebrow raised, and he smiled, sending another shiver straight through her. "W-what do you mean?"

His eyes never leaving hers, they continued to gently sway as he moved his hand from her hip and took her hand from his shoulder, placing it closer to his neck. He did the same with her other hand. Then he put both of his hands on her hips.

"My sixth-grade dance move."

But his voice sounded deep. Raspy. Nothing like a kid and definitely all man.

"One more thing," he said, the words barely audible. He moved his hands to clasp behind her lower back, resting just above the waistband of her purple and white polka-dotted skirt. As he shifted position, he brought her closer until a slip of paper wouldn't fit between them.

"Is this okay?" he asked.

All she could do was nod. She didn't understand why, but her hands instinctively locked together behind his neck. She tried not to notice how his soft hair brushed against the back of her hand, or how she could see the tiny scar at the corner of his left eyebrow that she'd never noticed before. "I guess I shouldn't dance like this with Justin's brother," she said, surprised she was able to speak in a steady voice.

"You better not." A smile played on his lips.

She was about to ask him why he was showing her this kind of dancing if she wasn't going to do it at the wedding, but her words caught in her throat. She didn't need to ask, because the way he was looking at her told her everything she needed to know . . . and she wasn't imagining it this time.

The music stopped, but they didn't. His hand moved from her lower back to reach up and cup her cheek. "Britt," he whispered.

Her heart was hammering so hard she was sure the entire state of Texas heard it.

His other arm tightened its hold around her waist as his head tilted toward hers. He was going to kiss her, she was sure of it. His eyes were closed, his mouth now inches from hers . . .

And all she could do was say, "Why?"

~

Hunter's eyes flew open. What just happened? He was nose to nose with Britt, who was gaping at him with a mix of curiosity and confusion. The haze of desire started to lift, and now he was a little confused himself. He pulled away but didn't let her go. "What?"

"Why are you going to kiss me?"

He blinked. Then reality hit him, hard. He almost kissed Britt.

Not that he didn't want to. He so, so, *so* definitely did. More than once, if she would have let him. He was surprised because he'd gotten so out of control.

Hunter moved away from her and put a decent amount of space between them. He shoveled his hand through his hair. "Britt, I'm—"

"You were going to kiss me, right?"

His eyes darted to hers. There was nothing he could do but admit the truth. "Yes. I was. And I'm sorry."

"You are?"

"I respect you a lot—"

"I don't feel disrespected, Hunter. I'm confused."

He understood the feeling. "About what?"

She started to pull at the hem of her tank top, then shoved her hands behind her back. "I don't understand why you'd want to kiss me."

Was she serious? One look at her expression, and he knew she was. "I, uh . . ." This was new territory. He'd never had to explain his feelings. He just let his instincts take control, and the less talk the better. Never in his life had a female asked him such a question. "Did you want to kiss me?"

Her cheeks instantly turned fuchsia, and she averted her gaze.

"Because it's okay if you do." He took a step forward, and when she didn't jump back, he took another one. "I don't want you to think I'm using you."

"For what?"

He couldn't decide if she was really this naïve, or if it was some kind of act. "To kiss you, make out with you, go to bed with—"

"Whoa!" Her hands flew up, palms out.

"Because I'm not," he said in a rush. "I promise that never crossed my mind. Well, maybe once or—"

"Hunter!"

He was messing this up, badly. If only he hadn't given in to his impulses and tried to kiss her. She was starting to look distressed, and he had to get back on better footing. To prove himself, he told the truth. "When your channel first popped up in my feed, I thought you were cute, so I clicked on a video."

Her eyes widened, but she still listened.

"And then I started watching more. I was fascinated by your lessons, how easily art came to you, how well you described things, your creativity. That's why I reached out to you. I wanted to let you know how much I appreciated what you do. I was completely honest about that, and about wanting to make a change in my life. I . . ." He couldn't unload everything on her now. "I needed to do something different.

"And then we met and clicked. But you were wary, and you had a right to be. All I wanted was friendship, Britt. Or so I thought."

Her expression was softening. "What changed?"

"Being around you. You're not just cute, Ms. Branch." He smiled, but not the cocky, manipulative one he'd used on women before. This one was from the heart. "You're adorable. And talented, intelligent, and fun."

Shock registered on her face. "I'm fun?"

"Yes. When you're working on something creative, or teaching, or feeling at ease, you're a lot of fun. And even when you're anxious, I still want to be around you." He shifted on his feet, hoping she took his words the way he intended them.

Britt didn't say anything for a long moment. She wasn't pulling on her shirt hem either. Then she suddenly moved closer and peered up at him. "You're telling the truth, aren't you?"

"I'd say Scout's honor, but I was never a Boy Scout."

"I . . ." She lowered her head.

He took a chance and placed his fingertip under her chin and lifted it until he could meet her gaze. "You what?"

"I'm a mess."

"So is everybody else."

She frowned. "I'm weird."

"Trust me, you're not the weirdest person I ever met. Not by a long shot."

"But you're so gorgeous."

He scoffed. "Being good-looking ain't all that."

She crossed her arms and smirked. "Oh, really."

At least now she was relaxing a bit. "It's a cross to bear," he said, half exaggerating. "People make assumptions that you're shallow and self-centered."

Her expression grew serious. "You're neither of those, Hunter."

I used to be. But to hear her say he wasn't gave him hope. She was seeing him the way he wanted to be, and prayed he could continue to be. He closed the final distance between them. "I like you, Britt. I like you as an artist, as a friend, and as someone I really, really want to kiss. But only kiss," he added, before she got rattled again. "I'm not that type of guy." *Anymore.*

"I've never been kissed," she whispered, looking away again.

He'd figured that much. "Whenever you want a lesson, I'm here for you."

She laughed. "How noble."

"It's a sacrifice I'm willing to make."

Her eyes danced. Then she touched his arm, and he wondered if she was aware that her fingers were moving over his skin with slow, feather-light strokes. He held back a groan.

"What if I'm ready now?"

His neurons started firing again, a warm wave of happiness

washing over him. He drew her in his arms, this time for real. "Then I, Mr. Pickett, am at your service."

But he didn't need words to instruct her. He tilted up her face and bent his head toward hers. When she closed her eyes, he smiled, gently kissing her until she relaxed against him and started kissing him back . . . with *relish*.

And it was everything he dreamed it would be.

Chapter 17

Classic rock rolled through Daniel's earbud as he waxed Arthur's Bentley. He'd spent the afternoon washing and waxing all the Picketts' cars, including Lila's white Range Rover, the one automobile he hadn't had the opportunity to drive yet. "I love rock n' roll," he warbled as he worked the wax into the paint with a yellow microfiber towel. He didn't actually love it, but he was in the mood for it today. Country was his usual go-to.

He'd saved the Bentley for last, having decided that out of all of Arthur's vehicles, this one was his favorite. He loved the sleek, classic lines of the car and he appreciated that Arthur and Lila Pickett not only used all their cars, they also kept them around for a while. The Bentley was over a decade old, and the Range Rover was the newest at four years old. When he'd worked as a mechanic, he knew people who leased or bought a new car every year. He'd always believed cars were meant to be kept, taken care of, and enjoyed.

He sprayed the hood with a little more wax and belted out the next line of the song.

"Daniel?"

At the sound of Lila's voice, he spun around, and promptly yanked out the earbud. "Yes ma'am?" Hopefully she hadn't heard his incredibly out of tune singing. As usual she was impeccably dressed, her flair and taste for high fashion eclipsing Arthur's.

Today it was white slim pants, a tailored rose-pink blouse, and her ever-present Tiffany gold diamond bar necklace. How did he know it was Tiffany? It was interesting the kinds of tidbits he'd learned from driving the Picketts around.

She looked over the short line of vehicles, each one perfectly centered in their garage spaces. "I think this is the first time I've noticed how expertly you park our cars."

He smiled at the compliment. Lila was more reserved and formal than Arthur, so this was a surprise. Setting the wax and cloth on a small metal supply cart nearby, he said, "What can I help you with today, Mrs. Pickett?" When she didn't answer, he turned around and saw she was twisting her large, square diamond solitaire ring while she stared at the Bentley's headlights. "Mrs. Pickett?"

She blinked. "Oh, yes." Turning to him, she dropped her hands. "Arthur's sixtieth birthday is in two weeks," she said.

He began rolling down his pushed-up dress shirt sleeves. Although it was sweltering outside, the Picketts' garage was air-conditioned, so he hadn't worked up a sweat. "I didn't realize that."

"We're having a surprise birthday party for him that night. So far he hasn't figured it out, thankfully." Her pale-pink lips turned up in a smile and she tucked a lock of her short, silver hair behind her ear.

He'd have his work cut out for him that night. No doubt he'd be expected to provide the valet parking.

"I'd like for you to attend."

"Me?" he said, unable to hide his surprise.

"We've had several chauffeurs over the years. They've ranged from excellent to . . . Let's just say we fired one the same day we hired him. But Arthur likes you." She paused. "I do too, of course."

He was glad she added that part. He didn't want to do anything to upset his employers, whom he not only liked, but was starting to admire. Being around uber rich people had taken some getting used to, and he knew they all weren't as easy to get along with as the Picketts.

"I know Arthur would be pleased if you joined us," Lila said.

It would be poor form to turn down an invitation to such an important occasion. And although he knew he would stick out like a pineapple in a pear tree, he realized he wanted to go. "I would be honored, Mrs. Pickett. Thank you for inviting me."

"Black tie, of course. Do you own a tux?"

"No, ma'am."

"Dan Hutton's offers rentals."

Daniel almost choked. No way could he afford to even rent something from that place.

"There's something else I need to tell you." She was back to twisting her ring. "Our youngest son, Hunter, is also invited. I don't know if Arthur has told you anything about him."

Uh-oh. He blanked his expression and didn't answer, not wanting to betray Arthur's confidence, or lie to Lila. And now he knew why Hunter had been looking at tuxedos.

"Hunter has had his . . . challenges," she said. "But I feel strongly that it's important for him to be at the party. I can't go into details, but I know for a fact he's been sober and has stayed out of trouble for nearly two years now." She straightened, her hands at her sides again. "My husband and I believe in second chances."

Arthur had already proven that by hiring Daniel, and now he wondered how much Lila knew about his own past.

"But we've given Hunter more chances than we can count," she continued. "He squandered them all. If he really has changed, this will be the litmus test. That said, I can't promise he won't implode and cause a scene at the party. His relationship with our family is quite strained."

The pain in Lila's eyes mirrored the same anguish Daniel had heard in Arthur's tone after he'd talked to Hunter. *They love their son very much.* Enough to go through agony to help him, to the point of employing extremely tough love.

"I just wanted to warn you."

"Is there anything I can do to help? With the party," he quickly added.

"Your attendance will be enough. Oh, and please bring a plus-one."

"Thank you, Mrs. Pickett."

She glanced at the cars. "They look wonderful, Daniel."

He stood a little straighter, gratified she'd noticed his hard work.

Lila turned to walk away, only to face him again. "I want to apologize for my two daughters-in-law. Their tacky behavior toward you has not gone unnoticed. I have spoken with Payne and Kirk about it, and rest assured, they will be treating you with respect going forward."

He stilled, then wanted to protest that the women hadn't been that bad. For sure they were spoiled, whether it was because they were raised that way, their husbands indulged them too much, or both. But if Lila thought it was bad enough to say something, he wasn't going to contradict her. "Thank you."

She smiled, more relaxed than before. "Have a good evening."

He watched her walk away. Then he realized what he'd agreed to. Yikes. Pineapple in a pear tree didn't begin to describe how out of his element he would be. And she wanted him to bring a plus-one? He didn't have any plus-ones in his life . . .

But he did have Britt.

He shook his head. "No," he mumbled, and went back to finishing the Bentley, this time sans the music. He couldn't ask her to go with him. His inner introvert was already balking at the idea of spending an evening with a bunch of people he didn't know and had nothing in common with. No way would she be able to handle it.

Then he realized there would mostly likely be alcohol there of some kind. Apprehension kicked in. He'd been sober for years, but every day he craved a drink. By going to his boss's party, he would be putting himself in an uncomfortable situation, surrounded by his coping mechanism of choice.

Daniel stopped waxing and measured his options. He could wait a few days and back out of the invitation, saying he had a prior commitment. Which would mean he'd have to lie to Lila, something he didn't want to do. Like Arthur, she had extended kindness and trust beyond his job description. He didn't want to do or say anything to violate it.

He could suck it up and attend the party, ignore the alcohol, and try to enjoy himself. That was the mature, adult thing to do. And it's what he would do.

Then Britt came back to mind. Maybe he could convince her to go. Not because he needed a crutch, but it was always helpful to have someone to keep him accountable. Going to the party could be beneficial to her too. At the very least she'd get to see the Picketts' art collection. It was small, but from what he could tell by the way the cleaning staff carefully dealt with the paintings, they were valuable. He and Britt could put in an appearance, say hello, and then leave. Bonus—he'd get to spend more time with his daughter.

Daniel finished waxing the car, letting his mind mull over whether to invite Britt or not. After he was done, he put everything away and gave the garage a quick sweep. It was time to pick up Arthur, and while he hated dealing with Dallas traffic, it was a joy to drive the Bentley.

As he headed downtown, he still hadn't decided if he should ask Britt, but he had some time to figure it out. And find a cheaper place to rent a tuxedo. He blew out a breath. Whether Britt came or not, he was sure it would be an interesting night.

Lights? Check.

Sound? Check.

Script? Check.

Britt started to turn on her camera, then stopped when she caught her reflection on the computer monitor. Instead of cringing like she normally did, she smiled. Today she'd put her hair up in a ponytail with a pastel tie-dyed scrunchy and matching cap-sleeved T-shirt. Three weeks ago, she'd decided to do a tie-dye tutorial, and the shirt and scrunchy had been two of her test subjects. She'd ended up dying twelve items, including a twin bedsheet, and didn't like any of the results other than what she was wearing, so she scrapped the video. Maybe she'd attempt tie-dyeing another day.

But her dyeing disaster wasn't what she was thinking about as she looked at her reflection. She couldn't see her facial features, only outlines and shadows. Four words came to mind. *Hunter thinks I'm cute.* She could pinch herself. No guy had ever called her cute. The only person who had ever called her that was her mother, and she'd stopped once Britt reached adulthood.

She continued to smile, leaning her chin on the curve of her hand. He also said she was adorable, and that had blown her mind too. But not as much as when he told her she was fun. She'd never thought of herself as fun, and certainly had never heard anyone describe her that way. And Hunter Pickett, a funny, considerate, even-keeled guy insisted she was. Oh, and then there was the whole cover-model gorgeous thing he had going on. *Sigh.*

Her phone rang. She looked at the screen and smiled. *Hunter.* She quickly answered it. "Hi," she said, hoping she didn't sound too eager.

"Hey."

His deep voice made her toes curl and grip the bright-orange shag rug underneath her desk. Their kiss—more accurately, kisses—from yesterday flashed in her mind, as they had since the moment he'd sweetly pressed his lips against hers. Softly, tenderly . . . *double sigh.*

"I'm on my way to work but . . ."

A shot of alarm went through her. "But what?"

"This is going to sound corny." The sound of a door closing came through the receiver. "I just wanted to hear your voice."

She almost melted in her seat. "You could just listen to one of my videos."

"It's not the same, not by a long shot." Another pause. "Corny, right?"

"Wrong. It's not corny at all."

"Oh, good. I thought I'd have to turn in my cool card for that one."

Never. He was the coolest guy she knew, although that admittedly was a small pool of contestants.

"I also wondered if we could interrupt our regularly scheduled week and have lunch tomorrow?" he asked. "I know it's not Monday—"

"What time?"

He laughed. "Okay, that's a yes. No later than eleven since I gotta be at work at two. Are you okay with going out? I was thinking simple, like a deli or something."

She hesitated, the familiar nervous feeling starting up like clockwork.

"Or we could get something and eat it at K&Bs. I'm sure I could sweet-talk Maude into letting us use the education room."

"You could sweet-talk her into anything," Britt said. But even though she was sure Maude and X wouldn't mind, it was an imposition and a lot of trouble to go through when they could just eat at a restaurant. "Are you familiar with the 360 Deli? We could go there."

"Sure," he said, sounding a little surprised. "Want me to pick you up?"

Britt could hear birds chirping and the faint hum of traffic in the background. "You have a car?"

"Nope, but I got an extra helmet."

She spun side to side in her chair. "You're determined to get me on that thing, aren't you?"

"Don't knock it, Britt. I'm a safe driver. You can trust me."

No argument there. She trusted him, totally. Even now when she thought back to how she'd initially suspected he was a deceptive creep made her feel foolish. "I can pick you up."

A pause, long enough to make her wonder if he was going to tell her no. "Okay. I'll send you the address. I gotta run, but I'll text you on break. Bye, Britt."

"Bye." She hung up and slid halfway down the chair. Finally, she understood all the hype about romance, and she could hardly believe she was in one. After they kissed, Hunter had taken her hand and led her to the table. "We need to work on our lesson," he said, his tone serious.

How were they supposed to focus on their drawings after what had just happened? At her confused look, he said, "I need a distraction. A big one, if you get what I mean."

She didn't—not totally. Just that he was right, they couldn't keep kissing in the education room. Maude could walk in on them at any moment, and Britt would never hear the end of it. Besides, she didn't want anyone to know what they'd done. Not because she was ashamed or embarrassed. She wasn't. But being in Hunter's arms, the feelings his kisses brought out in her— they were private, only to be shared between the two of them.

So they drew a football.

Hunter had laughed when she pulled it out of her bag. "You like sports," she said, giving him her rationale for the unusual choice. "Footballs have lots of texture. This will be interesting to duplicate."

He agreed, and they started on their lesson. Britt fought to pay attention to their work and not to Hunter. Or more specifically his mouth. Eventually, she succeeded.

By the time they'd perfected the outline of the ball, Maude had popped back in the room, and Britt and Hunter hung out with her and X for an hour after their lesson was over. When he left, Britt thought she was the only one who noticed the way he'd looked at her before he left, and how long he'd looked at her. But Maude immediately plied her with questions that Britt promptly brushed off. X put the feather duster in her hand and sent her to the back of the store as Britt was leaving.

She stared at the screen again. She needed to film the intro and outro for two more videos, but she didn't feel like working today. However, there was something she'd been wanting to do, ever since she met Hunter.

Britt pulled out a drawing pad and plucked a charcoal pencil from the holder by her computer. She faced the blank sheet of paper, closed her eyes, and began to draw.

A few years ago, she'd read an article online about drawing with your eyes closed. The concept was to feel the object while you were drawing, which would lead to a more creative and less inhibited result. Right now, she couldn't touch her subject . . . but she remembered.

She held out her hand as she thought of him, imagining she was touching his face. She already knew his hair was soft, had felt the roughness of his chin and upper lip from his perpetual five o'clock shadow. Her right hand sketched as her left thumb traced the imaginary line of his mouth, then moved over the slope of his nose, her fingertips lightly dancing over his long eyelashes. She continued to outline his face with her fingers, the charcoal making light brushing sounds as she whisked it over the paper.

When she was finished, she opened her eyes and looked at her work. Her initial reaction was to laugh—she'd never drawn a portrait so out of balance before. But as she studied it, she realized the abstraction held its own fascination. His hair wasn't centered on his head but was just off to the side. His chin was bigger than his mouth, which wasn't accurate in real life.

Then her gaze landed on his eyes. She paused and leaned forward. Eyes were her specialty, and she'd always been confident in drawing them. But what she'd sketched surprised her. The eye shape was spot on, but that wasn't what caught her attention. It was the emotions she saw in them, ones she didn't associate with him. Uncertainty. Confusion. Vulnerability. Even a tiny bit of pain.

Britt frowned. Why had she drawn that? She'd only seen Hunter insecure about his art, and that made sense. He was just learning how to draw. But she couldn't remember ever noticing him confused or vulnerable. And the pain . . . She was clueless about that.

She turned from the picture, a little disturbed. She'd expected to create a drawing that was far from perfect, but one that would capture his charm, confidence, and beauty. Instead, she'd depicted the exact opposite.

Britt shut her sketchbook, put it back in her desk, and decided to do some work. By the time she finished the first intro, she felt better. It was just a drawing. An experiment, even. Next time she would draw him with her eyes open and depict him the way he truly was.

Because the picture she sketched wasn't the Hunter she knew.

Amy ran the back of her hand over her forehead, wiping away the sweat pooling above her brow. Another day, another weed battle. Actually, it had been almost three weeks since she'd last tackled the weeds, and fortunately there weren't that many left. Good thing because it was only ten thirty, and she was already dripping from the heat.

She yanked out a few invaders between the white impatiens that bordered the patio, then took a desperately needed water break. She plopped down on one of her patio chairs under the shade of the roof, grabbed her water bottle off the table, and took a big, refreshing drink. Then she slouched in the chair and looked at her handiwork. But Britt wasn't far from her mind

For the third morning in a row, Britt had left the house before eleven o'clock, and each time, she didn't say where she was going. Amy assumed it was K&Bs. Where else would she go? But she was spending more time there than she had in years, and that was curious. There was also something else different about her daughter—she was smiling. A lot. Even humming sometimes. Always one of those seventies songs she loved that Amy was indifferent about. *Give me U2 and Dave Matthews Band any day.*

But it wasn't just that. Britt was also looking different. Her skin wasn't as pale, and Amy chalked it up to the daily walks she'd suddenly decided she needed to take. No complaints from Amy because Britt needed the exercise and sunshine. But her skin tone couldn't make that much of a difference. Her clothes were still the same too. Britt always had her own style. Eclectically put together, if that was a thing.

Amy tapped her chin, trying to put her finger on what had changed with her daughter. A bee landed on her water bottle, and she waved it off. Then it hit her—it wasn't how Britt looked that was different. It was how she carried herself. Her steps were sure, her shoulders squared, her chin up. She hadn't noticed her pulling or tugging on anything lately either. In fact, if she didn't know any better, her anxiety-ridden daughter was *confident.*

Amy was glad but befuddled. What caused the change? Was it her decision to be Savannah's maid of honor? Amy and Britt had gone shopping last night for the shower, buying everything that matched Savannah's French-country-meets-Texas-cowboy theme. That sounded like a disaster to Amy, but Savannah was making it work and they were able to find everything. Britt had seemed confident then too, and unbothered by the crowds as she and Amy had a blast picking out favors, decorations, and partyware.

It was a miracle.

She stood, halting her thoughts. Britt was coming into her own, and however it was happening, Amy wasn't going to question it, only support and encourage the change.

She was about to go back to her flower bed when her phone rang. Picking it up off the table, she was stunned at what she saw on the screen.

"Well, well, well," she said, staring at Max's name. The phone continued to ring as she considered whether to answer it. She hadn't heard from him since their movie night almost three weeks ago. No call, no text. Not even a butt dial. It would serve him right if she didn't answer. He'd made it clear he wasn't interested in pursuing a friendship with her.

At the last minute, she slid her thumb across the screen. "Hello?" she said in a detached tone, as if she had no idea who was calling.

"Hi, Amy. It's Max Monroe. I'm sorry it's been a while since we spoke. I've been swamped with work."

Such an original excuse. But she wasn't mad at him per se. There had been no expectations for anything between them. She was mad at herself for being so annoyed that he didn't contact her. She'd even been questioning whether she said or did something wrong, and she hated when she did that to herself. Last week she'd finally let him go and hadn't thought about him. Now he popped back up in her life.

"Amy? You still there?"

"Yes."

"I am sorry," he repeated. "I'd hoped to get back in touch with you soon after seeing the movie, but I had an unexpected out-of-town trip, and then several cases that needed my attention. I really have been busy."

To his credit he sounded contrite, and she had no reason not to believe him, other than her apparently still-existent difficulty trusting anyone of the male persuasion. *Thanks, Daniel.* "Ugh," she said, shaking her fingers at her throat in a cut-off motion.

"Pardon?"

"Nothing. Is there something I can do for you, Max? I've got a flower bed emergency going on here."

To her surprise, he chuckled. "Weeds out of control again?"

"Always. But I shall prevail." She sat back down, feeling less tense. "Sorry work has been such a bear for you."

"Part and parcel of the job. I don't have much time to chat, unfortunately. But I wanted to ask if you'd like to attend a party with me. My boss, Arthur Pickett—did I mention him to you?"

"Yes. I think at the coffee shop." She couldn't say for sure, it was such an insignificant detail at the time they were getting to know each other.

"His family is throwing a surprise sixtieth birthday party in a week. It will be at their home in University Park."

She let out a low whistle. "Sounds fancy already."

"Oh, it is. Black tie, of course." He sighed. "I've been there once before, for a Christmas party. Don't get me wrong, Lila Pickett is the consummate hostess. But fancy events are not my thing."

They weren't Amy's either.

"It would be so much more bearable if you would accompany me. I enjoyed our last outing, and I think we'll both have a good time. Or at least try to."

"Since you're making it sound so attractive," she said, laughing. "Sure, why not?" She'd have to find a suitable dress, but she was always up for retail therapy. "I'm happy to go with you, Max. Thanks for inviting me."

She thought she heard him exhale a breath. "Great. Frankly, I thought you would hang up on me. If you even answered the phone. I promise I won't be so neglectful in the future."

"A text every once in a while would be nice," she admitted.

"Yeah, I'm not really a text person. But I could be."

"Please, join us in the twenty-first century."

Max laughed. "You're delightful, Amy. You always make me smile."

She basked in the compliment. "Thanks, Max."

He told her the details—date, time, exact address. "I'll pick you up an hour before. Considering traffic, that should get us there in plenty of time."

"Ooh, I get to ride in the Mercedes?" she said, sitting up in her chair.

"I could bring the Corolla if you prefer."

"As tempting as that is, I'll pass."

"Mercedes it is," he said with a light chuckle. "Thanks, Amy. We'll talk soon, and we will definitely see each other on the thirtieth."

"Bye," she said, ending the call. Well, that was a surprise. A pleasant one. Not only was she getting the chance to buy a ritzy dress, but she would also get a peek at how the 1 percent in the Dallas metro area live. She'd always wondered what those huge mansions looked like inside. And Amy would do her best to be *delightful*.

But for now, she had weeding to finish. She stared down the green interlopers in her flower bed. "Your doom awaits!"

Chapter 18

The alarm on Hunter's phone shrieked in his ears. He flopped his hand on his nightstand and felt around for it, and with one eye open, he peeked at the time. Seven thirty. He groaned, and after letting out a huge yawn, he threw off the covers and swung his legs over the side of the bed. Once the sleepy haze disappeared, he smiled at the first clear thought that came to his mind. *Britt.*

It was all so wonderfully strange. In the past he'd always looked at relationships sardonically. An odd take, considering his parents had a loving marriage and his brothers . . . Well, last he heard, they were both still married. He didn't know much about their lives anymore. But the fact remained that before he met Britt, he'd never pictured himself in a serious relationship. Now he didn't want to imagine his life without her.

Rubbing his eyes, he stood and made his way to the bathroom. They were meeting early this morning at Yo Jo's, which was starting to become *their place*. He almost laughed out loud. When had he become so sentimental?

Hunter stared at his reflection in the mirror. The word *grizzled* came to mind as he rubbed his hand over his stubbly chin. He often went two or three days without shaving, and even when he did shave, he didn't completely get rid of his whiskers. A lot of that was laziness. But Britt didn't seem to mind that he wasn't totally clean-shaven. More than once when she was in his arms, she'd trailed her finger over his cheek, his chin, his mouth—

He quickly splashed cold water on his face. Dating Britt was an exercise in restraint, a new concept for him. And a good one.

He took a quick shower and ran his razor over his face, making a mental note to shave in earnest and get a proper haircut before his father's party. He'd briefly thought about inviting Britt, but realized it was impossible. When his mother threw a party, it was an event, and there would be lots of people there. Not exactly Britt's comfort zone.

And there was another, bigger reason. She'd confirmed she was an only child, and her parents were divorced, but she didn't mention her dad. He suspected some bad blood there. He'd given her minimal, though honest, details about his life, and he already knew who her mother was, although Britt still didn't know he knew.

He grimaced and shut off the razor. He hated keeping secrets from her. And he knew the longer he held back, the harder it would be to explain why. He still intended to tell her everything after Dad's party, but as the time neared, his dread grew. Britt was so sweet. Pure. Naïve.

He was none of those things, and he couldn't just snap his fingers and make his past behavior disappear.

He cleaned up the hair around the sink, vowing to focus on the happiness of the present and stop borrowing trouble from the future. After slipping on a pair of black shorts and a green T-shirt, he put on socks and his short hiking boots and walked into the living room.

"Yes, ma'am. He's doing well." Sawyer was standing in the kitchen, his back to Hunter. "Thank you for the check you sent. It was very generous." Pause. "I'm happy to do it, ma'am."

Hunter scooted around him to get to the fridge.

Sawyer's eyes widened and he shut off his phone, shoving it into the pocket of his knee-length athletic shorts. "Uh, hey," he said, awkwardly leaning against the counter and crossing his arms over his chest.

"Who was that?" Hunter grabbed the glass bottle and pulled it out.

"Ah, no one."

He arched a brow at him. "No one sent you a generous check?"

Sawyer's gaze darted back and forth before he looked at Hunter again. "What's with the fifty questions?"

"I asked two." He poured the juice in a glass. "Sorry. I'm not trying to be nosy, just making conversation." He put the bottle back in the fridge. "You're up early."

Sawyer dropped his arms and relaxed his stance. "You haven't exactly been sleeping in lately. Mr. Keane's got you working a lot of extra hours, huh?"

Hunter nodded, letting his roommate think that work was the reason he'd suddenly become an early riser. He hadn't told him about Britt, although there was a chance Sawyer would have seen her pick him up the other day, even though he'd waited outside for her.

He drained the juice, gave Sawyer a goodbye salute, and headed outside to the lot. The summer heat had been relentless the past couple of days, and the forecast showed no sign of it letting up. He hopped on his bike, put on his helmet, and immediately started to sweat as the engine roared to life. Extremely hot or extremely cold days made him wonder if he should try to get a car, just a beater to use when it was uncomfortable to ride.

The silly giddiness he always felt when he was around Britt kicked in. Today he would suggest they go to a movie Monday night, after their art lesson. It was the logical next step in her quest to control her social anxiety. She'd been open about how much she hated being in a place where she couldn't easily escape, and theaters were number one on her list.

But if she said yes, that meant sharing popcorn. Hand holding for sure. Her head resting against his shoulder. Maybe a kiss or three during the show if he were lucky. How could she resist that?

He sure couldn't.

~~

Britt felt a tap on her wrist as she braided her hair into a side ponytail. She rarely ever arranged her curls like this, mostly because there were always the rogue ones that escaped her braid. But she was feeling carefree today, and a little adventurous. Also, happy. Very, *very* happy.

She glanced at her watch, her father's text bubble on the tiny screen.

Can I call you in a few minutes? Got something to ask you.

Britt responded with a yes and finished getting dressed to meet Hunter. It was Friday and they'd seen each other every day this week. It seemed like the time flew when they were together, and as soon as they went their separate ways, she wanted to see him again. Thankfully he liked to text and talk on the phone. She'd never used her phone so much until she met him.

Her father's text reminded her that she needed to tell him about Hunter. But not until she told her mom, and the right opportunity for that hadn't arrived yet. Britt's focus had mostly been on Hunter—or could she call him her boyfriend? Like nearly everything in their relationship, she wasn't sure what the protocol was.

She had just opened her car door when the phone rang. She sat down, fished the cell out of her purse, and turned on the car. "Hey, Dad," she said, a blast of warm air hitting her. She turned it down and shut the door. "What's up?"

"Not much."

When he didn't elaborate, she frowned. "Everything okay?"

"Ah, sure. It's fine."

He didn't sound convincing. "What did you need to ask me?"

Hesitating, he finally said, "My boss's birthday party is next Saturday. Would you like to go with me?"

That was the last thing she'd expected him to ask. "I don't really like parties."

"I know, honey, but this one is special. The family has a decent-sized art collection. I thought you might want to look at it. We can show up for a little while, see the paintings, and then bow out early."

She rocked her palm back and forth on the steering wheel. While the idea of seeing someone's private collection was intriguing— how rich was Dad's boss exactly?—the thought of meeting so many strangers in an unfamiliar place sounded like a nightmare.

"If you want to think about it, that's fine," Dad said. "Or you could just say no. I totally understand."

"N—" She couldn't even speak the word. *When am I going to stop running away?* "I'll go," she said, placing her hand on her nervous stomach.

"Really? That's wonderful," he said, excitement in his voice. "And I promise, whenever you want to leave, we'll take off."

"Thanks, Dad." Her stomach settled down and she smiled. Not only did he want to spend time with her, but he also thought about her interest in art. She'd longed for him to be a part of her life. Now he was, and it was better than she thought it would be.

"One other thing, though. It's black tie, so if you don't have a fancy dress, you'll have to get one. And it's on me, Brittany. Let me know how much it costs and I'll reimburse you for it."

His offer touched her heart. "You don't have to. I can afford it myself."

"I know," he said, his voice sounding thick. "But let me do this for you. I've missed out on so many things . . ." He cleared his throat.

"Okay."

"Thanks." Another pause. "I'm so glad you said yes, Brittany. We're going to have a great time. I'll text you the details later. Love you."

"I—"

He hung up.

She stared at the phone. She'd almost told him that she loved him, something she hadn't done since he had come back into her life. It was the truth. She'd always loved her father. When he was sober and attentive, and even when he was drunk and difficult, although she never liked him much during those times. She loved him even when he left. *That's why it hurt so much.*

There was something shifting inside her. She was opening her heart. Not just to Hunter, but to her dad too. And it felt so good, like a snuggly blanket wrapped around her, making her feel warm and secure. A weird analogy for such a hot day, but it was true. After years of keeping her distance from everyone other than the few trusted people in her life, she was finally understanding the freedom of letting down her guard and letting someone in.

With a smile, she drove to Yo Jo's, a tiny thrill racing through her as she saw Hunter's motorcycle in the parking lot. She parked the car and hurried into the coffee shop. He'd already gotten a table and their drinks—double espresso for him and an Americano for her.

"Hi," he said, when she reached the table. He stood and kissed her cheek, then scooted the chair next to his seat closer to him. As she sat down, he slid her drink to her.

"Thanks." She picked it up and took a sip, still smiling. She probably looked like an idiot, but for once in her life, she didn't care.

"Thanks for meeting me a little earlier than usual. Picking up the extra hours this week is going to put me in good stead with my boss." He grinned. "You look happy today. And cute." He touched her braid, running his fingers down the length of it. "I like it."

"It's kind of frizzy."

"Didn't notice." He moved his hand and reached for hers under the table. "So what has you in such a good mood, other than being in my presence?"

Those words from anyone else would have been a turnoff, but she knew he was joking. "Nothing special," she said, then hid her mouth behind the cup. "It's a nice day, that's all."

"If you find oppressive heat and humidity nice."

"Today, I do."

He squeezed her fingers, his expression turning serious. "I've been thinking about some things this morning."

"Such as?"

Hunter let go of her hand and put both of his on the table, folding them loosely. "There's a first-shift job opening up soon. I was thinking about applying for it."

"Oh?"

"That way I'd be on a daytime schedule and off on the weekends. We could go out Friday or Saturday nights. Or both, if you want."

It did sound appealing, although there was still the niggling anxiety knowing those were the two nights when most people went out. "When will you apply?"

"Today, if it's posted, which I heard it will be. If I get it, then I'll have next weekend off for sure." Then he paused, frowning a little. "Well, Friday night anyway. That Saturday I've got, um, plans."

She waited for him to tell her what they were, but he didn't, picking up his espresso and taking a gulp, somehow managing not to burn his mouth on the hot beverage. What plans would he have if he wasn't working?

"Anyway, it's not a done deal by a long shot, but it's worth pursuing. And that leads me to my second round of morning thoughts." He held the cup loosely in his fingers. "I want to go back to school."

Britt's brow shot up. "Really?"

"Yeah. I'm still not sure what I'll major in, though. Maybe business."

She nodded. "What about art?"

He shook his head. "Not practical enough, and I'm not talented enough."

"But—"

Hunter put his finger over her mouth. "Shhh, little cheerleader." When she smiled, he brushed his fingertip over her top lip. Quick. Light.

Shiver.

Putting his hands in his lap, he said, "Don't get me wrong, I still enjoy drawing and I'm going to keep it up. But I need to be realistic."

Britt touched his arm. "You're right. But I'm glad you're not giving up on art."

"Never." He put his hand over hers. "Once I make a commitment, I'm committed."

They talked and sipped their coffees, with Hunter taking a short break to get them two sausage rolls. By the time he had to go to work, he was firm in his decision to go back to school. "I'll get some info from the community college." He stood up.

"Let me know how I can help," she said as they walked out of the café.

"Just be by my side, Britt." They stopped in front of his bike. "That's all I need." He kissed her, then got on his bike, giving her a rakish wink before putting on his helmet and driving off.

Britt hugged her purse to her chest. *Sigh* and *swoon*.

She felt a tap on her shoulder and turned around. Two tall, tanned, gorgeous women about her age were behind her, carrying their coffees in their manicured hands.

"I'm sorry," one of them said, pushing aside a straight, caramel lock of hair from her forehead with a long white fingernail. "Is he your boyfriend?"

The question caught her so off guard she couldn't answer.

"He's so hot," the other woman said, fanning her face with her hands, gold bracelets jangling on her thin wrist.

They were staring at her as if she had six sets of eyes. "Yeah," Britt said, lifting her chin. "He is my boyfriend."

They exchanged looks, then looked back at her with plastered-on smiles. "Well, I guess there's hope for all of us then," the caramel-haired girl said.

The other one, a perfectly coiffed blonde with flawless skin leaned closer to her. "You go, girl."

Britt gaped as the two of them walked toward a silver SUV.

What. Just. Happened? Had they just made fun of her, like so many popular kids had done in school? Or were they just as in awe of Hunter's good looks as she was?

Then it hit her that it didn't matter what their intent was. She answered them and she survived. Even better, she hadn't felt an instant of anxiety. She still didn't—just some confusion. Wow.

So this is what normal feels like.

Chapter 19

W hat about this one?"

Amy peered over the dress rack and looked at the black off-the-shoulder formal gown Laura was holding up. "Not enough coverage," she said, sliding a few more unsuitable dresses to the side.

"Oh, please." Laura walked over to her and held the dress in front of Amy. "You'd look sexy in this."

"I don't want to look sexy. I want to look appropriate."

"Appropriately boring." Laura folded the dress over her arm. "Try it on anyway. For me, your dearest friend who is teeming with jealousy."

Amy's head popped up, but she relaxed when Laura winked at her. Amy almost hadn't told her about Max's invitation, considering their conversation on the patio a few weeks ago when Laura had admitted she was lonely. But the two of them had been shopping buddies for years. Besides, it was just another friendly outing with Max. She'd made that clear when she called and asked Laura to help her shop for a dress. However, Laura hadn't sounded convinced.

This was their fourth dress shop, including hitting the mall, and Amy was starting to lose hope that she would find anything. And while she wasn't going to compromise her standards, she'd humor her friend. "Okay." Amy slid over two more dresses, then stopped at a caramel-colored gown with a high, jeweled collar. It was sleeveless, but backless, like Laura's choice. "Ooh, I like this one."

Laura nodded. "It's beautiful. Even better—it's in your size."

Amy took it. A short while later after combing through all the gowns, she found one other dress, a red and silver number that looked more suitable for Christmas but was pretty and modest. She took them to the dressing room while Laura sat nearby.

When she put on Laura's suggestion, she immediately wanted to take it off. She'd never been a bosomy woman, but the neckline still felt way too low. The dress was also formfitting, and even though she was fit, the gown outlined the slight tummy bulge she could never get rid of. If she chose this, she'd have to fight with shapewear to get it to look good. Still, she showed it to Laura, who promptly gave it a thumbs-down.

"You're right," she said. "Too revealing."

Amy quickly took it off and rehung it, then slid the silver and red dress off the hanger. When she slipped it on, it was much more flattering. The top was completely covered in silver sequins sewn onto thin, silver fabric. The neckline was acceptable, and unlike the other two, it had three quarter sleeves. The red skirt flared out a little at her hips and the hem brushed against the floor. She nodded at her reflection and showed Laura.

"Definitely a contender," she said.

But when Amy put on dress number three, she knew she had a winner. The collar wasn't too confining, and it was decorated with the perfect amount of jewels so she wouldn't have to wear a necklace. The bodice was slightly formfitting where it needed to be, and the rest of the gown was flowy and comfortable.

When she came out of the dressing room, Laura grinned. "That's the one."

Amy nodded, turning around in the three-way mirror to see all angles. "I feel like a princess."

"You look like a queen." Laura got up from the chair and stood beside her. "Max is going to flip when he sees you."

Her cheeks pinked. "I don't want him to flip."

"Are you sure?"

She stared at the mirror, unable to answer. Now that she had the dress, she couldn't deny the anticipation threading through her. Or the happiness. She'd never worn a gown this fancy or expensive, and that included her wedding dress. She'd opted to go with a simple white sheath with no train or veil. That wasn't out of the ordinary these days, but back in the nineties, she was an anomaly. Considering how bad her marriage had been, she was always grateful her parents hadn't blown a lot of money on the ceremony.

"Let's get this puppy and go find you some shoes," Laura said.

Amy faced her. "I've got some black pumps at home." Then she almost laughed at her friend's appalled expression.

"Pumps? Absolutely not. You're getting some strappy sandals with no less than a three-inch heel."

"My feet will hurt all night."

"And it will be worth it. Now march in there and get dressed. We have more shopping to do!"

After finding the perfect pair of pain-inducing heels and getting Laura's hearty approval, Amy purchased the dress and shoes, trying not to throw up at the sight of the final bill. This was a once-in-a-lifetime opportunity. And as Laura kept telling her, she rarely treated herself and had never splurged like this.

"I can't wait to hear what Britt thinks of your outfit," Laura said as they left the shop and walked into a wall of Texas heat.

Amy pressed her lips together.

Laura cast her a side glance, and when they reached the car she said, "You're going to show her the dress, right?"

"Um . . . I haven't told her about the party." She unlocked the doors, opened the back passenger side, and hung the garment bag on the hook. "Or about Max."

"*What?*"

Amy quickly slid into the front seat and started the engine.

Laura's eyebrows had shot up almost to her hairline. "You haven't told her?"

"No." Amy put the car in drive and backed out.

"Why on earth not?"

"Because I don't know where this thing with Max is going." She avoided looking at Laura as she drove out of the lot.

"You've been out twice, and he invited you to a fancy-schmancy party. I think it's going well."

"Two dates don't define a relationship. I'm just being careful."

Laura leaned back against the seat. "I'd understand that if Britt were a kid. She's twenty-eight, though. I'm sure she'd be able to handle it if you and Max didn't work out. I think she'd be mad that you didn't tell her about him when you first met."

Amy didn't want to consider that Laura might be right. But she couldn't go against her mama bear instincts. Britt wasn't like other kids. She never had been. And Amy was aware of the judgment she occasionally got from others about her twenty-eight-year-old daughter still living at home. But Britt couldn't even go shopping without stressing out about being in public. How was she supposed to live on her own?

"I'll tell her after the party," Amy said. "If Max and I are still seeing each other at that point."

"I don't know why you're waiting—"

"Laura, I know what I'm doing."

Her friend paused. "I hope so."

They drove in silence for a few minutes. Then Laura said, "What kind of jewelry are you going to wear?"

Amy smiled, relieved that Laura had dropped the subject and wasn't mad at her. "Gold hoops?"

"Do you have any rhinestones?"

Amy smirked. "What do you think?"

"That would be a no then. We'll get you some. And you must get your hair and nails done too."

"I'll do that later this week." Oh boy. She could practically feel the cash sliding out of her account. Oh well. After decades of scrimping and saving, she finally had enough margin to spend frivolously like this. As they headed for an accessories store, she hoped it would be worth it.

⁓

"Oh, I just knew you two were meant to be together!"

Britt arched a brow at Maude as she set her sketchbook on the table in the education room. After she left Yo Jo's yesterday, she'd gone home and sketched out some preliminary dress ideas. Her dad was probably expecting her to go to a fancy dress shop to get her gown for the party, but after dress shopping with Savannah, Britt knew she wouldn't find anything she liked at those stores. With Maude's help, she'd create the perfect outfit, though. "What are you talking about?"

"You and Hunter. He's taking you to the party, right?" Maude sat down next to her.

Britt fiddled with edge of her sketchbook. "Um, no. It's not just a regular party. It's black tie." Hunter would never go to one of those parties, even if he did have the opportunity, and she couldn't imagine he ever would. Britt was still stunned that she was going.

"Then who are you going with? Savannah?"

"No. I'm going with Dad."

For once, Maude was speechless. Her eyes widened behind her red-framed glasses. "*Your* dad?"

Britt nodded.

"The one who hasn't been around for years?"

"Yes."

Maude frowned. "Does your mother know about this?"

"No, and please don't say anything to her." Britt explained about Dad coming back into her life. "I'm going to tell her when the time is right."

Maude shook her head. "Keeping secrets isn't good. It isn't right either."

"I know." She turned up the bottom corner of the sketchbook page. "I feel so guilty about it."

"Then tell her." Maude covered Britt's hand with her own. "Be honest with her."

"I will, after the party." She pushed the sketch in front of Maude. "Can you help me make this?"

Maude lifted a brow, then sighed and looked at the drawing.

Instead of taking her inspiration from the seventies, Britt went back a decade and designed a simple dress with a rich, crimson velvet tank top and a long, straight white skirt. Around the waistline she drew a bright pink belt with a bow on the side. Next to the dress she'd penciled in some long white gloves.

"Very Audrey Hepburn," Maude said, her expression relaxing. She took off her glasses. "I expected more ruffles and chiffon. That was the style in the late seventies and early eighties."

"I thought about that. Then I was looking at some online images and fell in love with this." She smudged the hem of the dress with her finger, giving it a softer look. "What do you think?"

Maude smiled. "I think you'll be stunning." She tapped on the gloves. "I have a pair just like these. Would you like to borrow them?"

Britt grinned, thankful Maude had dropped the subject of telling Mom about Dad and seemed excited about the dress. "Will it be hard to make?"

"Not at all. We'll need a pattern, but I'm sure we can find one online." Maude got up and went to the storage room, then returned with a tape measure around her neck. "I'll get your measurements. Then we'll look for a pattern, and tomorrow I can shop for the fabric."

"Can I go with you?"

Maude nodded, delight in her eyes. "Of course." She gestured for Britt to stand up. As she measured Britt's dimensions, she said, "X keeps telling me not to be nosy, but I can't stand it anymore. Are you and Hunter dating?"

Britt almost told her no. When she and Hunter hung out at K&Bs, they made sure to keep their distance. Maude had given up dropping hints and trying to force them into compromising positions. But after Maude's insistence on honesty, she had to tell the truth. "Yes," she said. "I'm pretty sure we are."

"That's wonderful!" Maude crouched and stretched the tape from Britt's waist to the tops of her shoes. "He's a catch for sure. Such a polite, friendly young man." She stood, her knees audibly creaking. "Quite delicious looking too."

Britt couldn't help but grin.

"I take it your mom doesn't know about him either." She wrapped the tape measure around Britt's waist.

"No. Neither does Dad. But I'll tell them," she added quickly.

"After the party, right?" Maude supplied.

"Right." She waited for Maude's censure, or even an eye roll.

But she simply wrote down the measurements on Britt's sketch. "Why aren't you sure you and Hunter are dating?"

"Because I don't know how all this works."

She went to Britt and smiled. "No one does, sugar. If we all knew the mystery about relationships, everyone would be blissfully happy. Every single couple is winging it as they go along, including me and X."

"Really?"

"Yes. Because people change over time. Sometimes quickly, sometimes at a snail's pace. It depends on how hard life hits them. X and I aren't the same optimistic young couple we were back in Vermont. Back then we thought we had all the answers, that nothing was going to stop us or make us unhappy. We were in love. That was all we needed."

Alarmed, Britt asked, "You don't love each other anymore?"

"We love each other more deeply now than we ever have. But love isn't all you need to make a relationship work. You must have communication, patience, and empathy, along with understanding and honesty. Above all, you have to be willing to make it work. If you give up, the relationship is over."

"I don't think Mom gave up on Dad," Britt said, suddenly feeling defensive of her mother. "He made it impossible for them to be together. Even I knew that back then."

"Then he wasn't being honest with himself. And he wasn't willing to work on whatever the problems were between them." Maude touched her shoulder and smiled. "I'm not judging Amy, not at all. She's told me a little bit about your father. Being with an alcoholic is difficult. Impossible, if they're not sober. Just ask X."

Britt was stunned. "You're an alcoholic?"

Maude nodded, her expression the most serious Britt had ever seen it. "A high-functioning one, which was why it was easy to hide it from him when we were dating. But soon we had the pressures of moving here, opening our store, and trying to conceive a child. When I found out we couldn't have children, I didn't care if he knew or not."

"I had no idea."

"I've been sober for most of our marriage. X could have left me, but he didn't. He stayed by my side. Not sure if I would have made it if he hadn't." She wiped her fingertips under her eyes. "Oh boy, I hadn't planned to spill those beans today."

"I'm glad you did." Britt hugged her. "My dad's been sober for a while now. I hope Mom can see him for the man he is today and not hold the past against him."

"That's why you're afraid to tell her."

Britt nodded.

"We'll just have to pray that they'll keep the past where it belongs." Maude stepped away. "Now, we have five days to get this dress done. Let's do it!"

She and Britt got online and searched for patterns similar to Britt's design. But it was hard for Britt to concentrate. She was still reeling from Maude's revelation. She was also thinking about her assertion that everyone in a relationship was winging it. That was how she felt—ungrounded. Maybe it had more to do with not being honest with her family about him than with Hunter himself. Because when she didn't think about the secrets she was keeping from her parents, and when she was with him and only thought about him, she definitely felt secure.

Maude was right—she had to come clean about everything, including telling her parents about Hunter, telling Hunter about her parents, and telling Mom about Dad. But the last thing she wanted was upheaval before such a big event. It was going to be hard enough settling her nerves, and the only way she could keep the anxiety from taking over the rest of the week was to not think about it, except when she and Maude were making the dress.

But once the party was over, no more procrastinating. She'd tell the truth. How bad could it be?

Daniel tugged on his bow tie as he pulled in front of K&Bs to pick up Brittany for the Picketts' party. After he'd called her yesterday and asked if he could take her to the party early, she instructed him to pick her up here. He hadn't questioned her, figuring she didn't want him to see Amy yet.

But he decided that next week he would ask her to tell Amy about him. Although he tried to, he still couldn't get the image of her and that guy at the movie theater out of his mind, and that had happened weeks ago. He kept telling himself he didn't have a right to know who he was or if they were together. But the curiosity was overwhelming and he'd almost asked Brittany about it a couple of times. He'd been patient enough waiting for her to reveal that he was in town. The longer it dragged out, the harder it was getting to maintain that equanimity.

But the truth was, he longed to see Amy. To talk to her, to ask her forgiveness, to have some sort of relationship with her, even if it was just so the three of them could all be in the same room. He also missed her and had missed her every day since he left. Now that he'd seen her twice, those feelings had come back and continued to grow, no matter how he tried to distract himself or talk himself out of them. He'd traded in the two most precious people in his life for whiskey, vodka, and gin. And he'd regretted it ever since.

But he wasn't going to think about any of that tonight. He was going to focus on Brittany and make sure they both had a wonderful time.

He pulled out his phone and texted her.

Daniel: I'm here.

Brittany: Be right there.

Daniel got out of the car and walked over to the sidewalk in front of the store. He would have walked inside but she had explicitly said she'd meet him out here. He tugged on his bow tie again. *This penguin suit is for the birds.*

The door opened and Brittany walked outside. Daniel's jaw dropped. She looked like she'd stepped out of *Breakfast at Tiffany's.* Even her hair was tamed into a sixties hairstyle, and it was stunning. He quickly went to her. "You look beautiful, honey."

Her cheeks turned red, and she glanced away. "You sure it's not too much?"

"No. It's perfect. You'll be the star of the party." When she cast him a panic-stricken look, he backtracked. "But only if you want to be. There'll be so many people there . . ." Great. He was saying all the wrong things. "I—"

She put her white-gloved hand on his arm. "I get it," she said, managing a tense smile. "And I'll be okay. Just don't leave me."

"I won't, Brittany. You can count on me." He crooked his arm, and she slipped her hand through it. He opened the door of his Fusion, and she got inside. After shutting the door, he jogged to the other side of the car, spotting an older couple standing at the window of the store, their noses practically pressed against it. Daniel nodded to them and smiled. They both waved.

Soon they were on their way to the Picketts'. "What are the names of your friends at the art store again?" he asked.

"Maude and X." She was fidgeting with the tips of the gloves on her right hand. "Maude helped me make the dress."

"You made that?"

"I designed it. Fifty dollars and some change."

He glanced at her, noting her wide smile. "Well done. Send me the bill, remember." He'd learned how to sew buttons out of sheer necessity, but he couldn't fathom what it would take to make something as complicated as a dress. Then again, he was always impressed with Brittany. "When we arrive, we'll go in the front and then straight to the gallery. It's upstairs."

"Your boss doesn't mind if we're early?"

"He doesn't know, remember? His wife, Lila, said it was okay. She was happy about it actually. She said art was to be enjoyed, and she was glad someone was going to enjoy it."

Brittany nodded. "I can't wait to see the collection."

And he couldn't wait to show her. He didn't know a Rembrandt from a Rodin, but he knew the Picketts' collection was expensive. He was sure Brittany could tell him all about the paintings and statues.

They were both quiet on the rest of the drive, but it was a peaceful silence. Daniel didn't feel the need to come up with small talk, and Brittany seemed okay sitting there tugging slightly on the fingertips of her gloves. When he pulled into the gated neighborhood, he glanced at her. Yep, her eyes were as big as saucers.

"Oh, wow," she said, looking out the front and side windows. "These houses are amazing."

"That they are." He remembered the first time he'd driven into the Picketts' neighborhood. He had to pick his jaw up off the floor.

A few minutes later, he pulled into the circular drive. It was weird being a guest instead of an employee. A valet dressed in a crisp black suit opened Brittany's door for her and held out his hand to help her out of the car. "Thank you," she said in a small voice.

Daniel quickly bounded out of the car and gave the guy his keys. He could see his daughter was already overwhelmed. Hopefully in a good way. "You ready to go?"

She looked up and nodded, her eyes sparkling with excitement.

He offered his arm again, took a deep breath, and together they went inside.

Chapter 20

A my held her breath as she stood in front of the full-length mirror hanging on the back of her bedroom door. She placed her hand on her abdomen, the silky feel of her formal gown smooth and soft underneath her palm. But inside, her stomach was on a roller coaster. Was this how Britt often felt? *My poor girl.*

Britt had left earlier today to work on her project at K&Bs. She'd been spending so much time there, Amy barely saw her anymore. Earlier this week when she told Britt she was going to stop by the shop and see her progress, her daughter had been adamant that she wait.

"Next week," she implored. "All will be revealed next week."

Amy acquiesced. Britt had no idea that her words held a double meaning because Amy had decided to tell her about Max. Even if tonight's outing ended up being a bust, she'd come clean about him. She'd never kept a secret from Britt, other than not telling her the worst details concerning Daniel's bad behavior. But she'd never been deceptive about herself, and the guilt was starting to get to her.

Switching her mental focus, she turned to the side and checked her profile. The caramel-colored dress complemented her moderately tanned skin—thanks to her constant battle with the flower beds. Her makeup wasn't too heavy, but not as light as she usually wore. And the fit was perfect. Comfortable even. The only downside was that the hem was a little too long, but that would change once she put on her heels. She'd practiced walking in the three-inch sandals a little bit around the house earlier today. Although she wasn't graceful, she wasn't an oaf either.

Glancing at the time on her watch, her eyes widened. Max would be here any minute, and here she was preening in the mirror. Okay, not exactly preening. More like trying to calm herself down. She couldn't remember the last time she was this nervous. *It's just a party . . . It's just a party . . .* Except it wasn't. Not by a long shot. And now she was wishing she'd told Britt about the party and Max so she could lean on her daughter for moral support.

She quickly slipped her feet into the gold straps, yanked up the back strap on both shoes, and turned to head for the door. Two steps in, she stumbled . . . and heard a ripping sound.

"Oh no!" She looked at the hem of her dress, breathing a sigh of relief when she didn't see a tear. Maybe she'd imagined it. But just as she almost stopped looking, she saw it—a small hole right above the seam on the right side. "Oh no, no, *no!*"

She lifted the dress up to her knees, her heels clacking on the wood floor as she hurried to the junk drawer in the kitchen where she kept a tiny sewing kit for emergencies. She flung it open and fished around. "Where are you!" she yelled, as if the drawer would just hand her the kit on demand.

The doorbell rang and she shot straight up. Max. She couldn't go to the party with a hole in her dress. Maybe she should just pretend she wasn't here. No, that was dumb. She sighed, still holding the bottom of the dress with her left hand, and went to the door. Taking in a deep breath, she opened it. "Hi, Max."

His brow shot up as he looked her over. "Interesting sartorial choice," he said, noting her dress.

She glanced down and realized the hem wasn't just past her knees, but on the edge of indecent territory. She instantly dropped it, the fabric hitting the ground. "Sorry for the show."

"I'm not." He grinned.

Amy couldn't help but chuckle. He wasn't leering at her, just making a joke. "C'mon in," she said, opening the door wider. "I've had a *sartorial* catastrophe." She shut the door behind him.

"I can't tell." He paused. "You look lovely, Amy."

Her face heated, and she actually dipped her chin in an *aw-shucks* kind of way. "Thanks, Max. I'm sorry, but do you mind waiting for a minute? I ripped the bottom of my dress, and I can't find the sewing kit. I think it's in my daughter's room. I know we're going to be late, but—"

He held up his hand. "Just tell me where to sit."

"The kitchen's that way. I'll hurry."

Max smiled again. "I don't mind being fashionably late. Isn't that what all the fancy people do?"

"I wouldn't know." She hurried to Britt's room, thankful that Max was so understanding, and yet still wondering why she wasn't attracted to him. Even in her embarrassment, she'd noticed how exceptionally handsome he was in his tuxedo. And as usual, he was being so nice. She should be head over heels for him by now. Or at least have a butterfly or two.

Amy entered the room and glanced around. She rarely came in here, respecting Britt's privacy, and she didn't want to be in here now, much less searching her room for a needle and thread. But she was desperate, and she'd add it to her list of explanations regarding Max when she talked to Britt about him.

The walls were covered with all sorts of Britt's colorful art. Most of her décor was seventies inspired, even down to the round orange shag rug in the middle of the floor. Everything was neat, except for her desk, and that only had a sketchbook and a charcoal pencil on it. She decided to start there first, carefully walking across the shag rug so she didn't get her heel caught on the fluffy fibers.

When she reached the desk, she was about to open the drawer when she saw Britt's sketchbook. She paused, taking note of the mostly complete sketch of a young man who made handsome Max look like chopped liver. Amy couldn't resist picking up the book and studying it for a minute. This was on another level, almost photographic in quality. *Yowza.*

She set the book down and opened the drawer. The sketch was obviously of a model from a magazine or the internet. Britt often used photographs to practice portraiture. *She'd hit the jackpot when she found that guy.*

Unfortunately, all she found in Britt's desk were more art supplies, and she was about to lose hope when she saw the small kit on her nightstand. Amy snatched it up, lifted her dress to a modest level this time, and clacked back into the kitchen where Max was dutifully sitting, staring at the refrigerator.

She bustled into the room and sat down in the chair. Then she remembered her southern manners. "Can I get you a drink? I've got some iced tea I made yesterday, but it's still good."

He shook his head. "I'm fine. There'll be plenty of refreshments at the Picketts'. Probably an overwhelming amount."

She grimaced, her nerves bundling up again as she pulled out a needle and the small spool of white thread. It was either that or black. "I can't believe I did something so stupid."

"You ripped your dress on purpose?"

"No." Amy poked the thread at the needle and missed. Twice. Ugh, she hated sewing. "It was an accident—"

"Then it wasn't stupid." He took the thread and needle from her, and in less than a second had it ready.

"Impressive," she said, taking it from him.

"I've had lots of practice." His expression turned solemn.

He didn't have to say "since Crystal died." She could see that plain as day on his face. "Usually, I ask Britt to sew on a button or fix a rip for me, but she's out working on a project."

"I look forward to meeting her someday."

She looked at Max. "I'm sure you will, soon." When he smiled, she returned it and quickly stitched up the hem. Her work wasn't perfect, but no one would be lying on the floor with a magnifying glass, judging her sewing capabilities. "Okay, I'm ready to go." She stood, only teetering slightly on her heels, using the table to steady herself. "Oops. New shoes, and they are totally going into the dumpster after tonight."

He chuckled, then stood and held out his arm. "Lean on me if you need to."

She rested her hand in the crook of his elbow. "Thank you. And may I say you're looking suave and debonair tonight."

"You may definitely say that."

As they left, she hoped the rest of the evening would be smoother than the beginning of it.

⁓

Hunter's Uber pulled up in front of his parents' huge mansion. Although it was only dusk, the entire estate was illuminated, from the hedgerow lined up along the front to the interior rooms. From the passenger seat in the back of the SUV, he could see the huge spiral staircase and massive crystal chandelier through the large windows on the front of the house.

He thanked the driver as a man dressed in a crimson sports

jacket, black pants, and matching black tie opened the door. Hunter had never seen this guy before. He figured the chauffeur he met that day at Hutton's would be doing valet duty tonight.

Stepping out of the SUV, he stared at the incredible house and gulped. He hadn't grown up here, since his father wasn't making the big bucks until he started his own law firm while Hunter was in high school. Still, he grew up more than comfortable. But this mansion was awe-inducing, and he'd only been here twice since they moved in five years ago.

He didn't belong here. He knew it, and everyone else would too. As soon as he told his father happy birthday, he was heading out.

Although he arrived early, another car pulled up behind him, prodding him to go inside. He wished he could call Britt or even text her. But she'd said she was busy at K&Bs tonight and wouldn't be able to answer her phone. He'd thought that was weird. What would she be doing that kept her from her phone? In the end, it didn't matter. He shouldn't be on his phone anyway. He needed to focus on his parents. He was only here because of them.

As soon as he walked through the door, he saw his mother . . . and his heart warmed. Until this moment, he hadn't realized how much he'd missed her. And with his mind clear instead of hazy with alcohol, he was suddenly hit with everything she had tried to do to help him over the years. It put a lump in his throat.

"Hunter." She sailed over to him in a whoosh of gray, sparkly satin and on a cloud of expensive, yet sparingly used, perfume. "Thank you for coming."

Normally she would envelope him in a hug and rest her cheek against his chest. Even though she was in high heels, he was still over a foot taller than her. But she didn't even shake his hand. She was keeping her distance, and he didn't blame her.

Seemingly out of nowhere, Kirk and Payne appeared, both their jaws set in stone. He didn't blame them for that either. They all had the same light-brown hair and hazel eyes, but his brothers were shorter, more dour versions of himself.

He looked at all three of them. "Thank you for inviting me. You won't be sorry."

"We better not be." A muscle twitched in Payne's cheek.

Kirk nodded. "Or you'll be the one who's sorry."

"Boys," Mother said in a firm, hushed tone. "Enough. Let's just have a good time tonight. Your father only turns sixty once."

His brothers nodded as they were joined by their wives.

"Nice to see you." Everly hooked her arm around Payne's waist.

Ashleigh, Kirk's wife, nodded. "You're looking good, Hunter." She went over and hastily pecked his cheek.

"Thanks," he mumbled, and from their bland expressions he could tell they were only being polite. He turned to Mother, and out of habit, he almost asked for a drink, stopping himself in the nick of time. "I think I'll get a Coke."

"I'll go with you." Mother gave a sharp look at Everly and Ashleigh, then turned to Kirk and Payne. "You don't mind greeting the guests, do you?"

Hunter could tell they absolutely minded, but they both nodded.

Mother walked alongside him as they made their way to the expansive bar in the corner of the great room. The house was over twenty thousand square feet and there were many common areas throughout. The bedrooms were upstairs, along with two rooms that served as the art gallery, a passion of his mother's. The whole house was designed in a traditional style, with marbled floors, crisp white walls, and lots of architectural details. Gold was everywhere in the house, softened by muted crimson reds, emerald greens, and slate blues.

He almost laughed as he realized how many details he was noticing at first glance. Britt really was influencing how he viewed the world.

"You just missed the most charming young lady," Mother said, her heels and his dress shoes making a sharp tapping sound on the marble floors. "She's dressed just like Audrey Hepburn."

Hunter nodded. He couldn't even conjure a clear image of Audrey Hepburn. He wouldn't be surprised if Mother was still trying to match him up with one of her high-society friend's daughters. She'd been doing that up until she and his father cut him off. Naturally, none of those women were interested in a high school dropout who couldn't stay sober.

"We think very highly of her father," Mother continued as they reached the bar. "I'll have a . . ." She glanced at Hunter.

"Your usual?" the bartender said. Hunter didn't recognize him, but the man obviously had worked his parents' events before.

"No. Diet Coke, please."

He looked surprised, then nodded. "And for you, sir?"

"The same." Hunter leaned close to her. "You don't have to teetotal on my account."

She smiled. "I'll have some champagne later."

He straightened and returned her smile.

The bartender handed them their drinks, and they turned around. More people were milling about, but Mother stayed by his side.

"Anyway, about the young woman—"

"I'm gonna stop you there." Hunter looked at her. "I'm not interested."

"You haven't even met her yet."

"I don't need to." He took a sip, wondering if he should say anything about Britt. *No more lies, right?* "I'm seeing someone."

His mother scoffed. "You're always *seeing* someone."

"It's different this time." His tone was low, softer than he intended.

She looked up at him, one perfectly manicured eyebrow lifted. "You're serious."

"Yes. I think . . . I think I might be in love with her." *Wow.* He hadn't expected those words to burst forth. But it was true. He knew he had to keep a lid on that in front of Britt, though. They'd only known each other for a month or so. Way too soon to fall in love. But he couldn't deny his feelings. Even now he was wishing he'd talked her into coming tonight, even though he knew he'd made the right decision not to. She would be uncomfortable the entire time. But he missed her. Wanted her by his side. *Forever.*

Mother stared at him as if she wasn't sure she'd heard him right.

"Lila! It's been so long!" An older woman draped in shiny black fabric with a diamond choker around her neck—real diamonds for sure—was floating toward them.

"Teresa!"

Hunter watched with slight amusement as the women kissed each other's cheeks, then tried to surreptitiously gauge their clothing, jewelry, and makeup. He'd seen this type of female interaction many times before with his mother and her friends. Once they'd taken mental inventory, they dove into conversation about people he'd never met and knew nothing about. He slipped away, planning to play wallflower until his father's arrival in . . . He checked his watch and grimaced. He still had thirty minutes left.

His nerves ramped up and he glanced at the bar again. One

shot of whiskey would calm them. But he couldn't stop at one, so he didn't need to start.

"Hunter?"

He turned to see a thin woman with long black hair wearing a plunging black strapless dress and platform heels move to stand beside him. *Uh-oh.* What was her name? "Hey, uh . . ."

"Cara." Her nose scrunched up. "That's all you can say after you ghosted me three years ago?"

Oh boy. Three years ago was one big blur, right before he hit rock bottom. "I'm sorry—"

"It's okay." She moved in close. "I forgive you. I'm just glad to see you again. You look . . . yummy." She inhaled. "Smell yummy too."

"Uh, thanks." He gulped down half his Coke.

"You know, I broke up with my boyfriend last week."

His gaze darted around the room, which was now filling up fast. He didn't recognize anyone to the point where he could escape Cara and go talk to them. He should have just stuck with his mother and Teresa.

"We could"—she ran her finger down the center of his shirt—"Pick up where we left off."

⌒

Britt tugged at the index finger of one of her gloves as she gazed at the painting in front of her. Like all the other pieces in the gallery, it was beautiful, and in the classical style. Although there weren't any museum-quality pieces in the collection, there were some expensive ones, most of them classical, except for two modern pieces—one in each room.

But as she tried to focus on the perfectly rendered eighteenth-century women having a pastoral picnic by a pond, she couldn't ignore the heightened sounds of people and music downstairs. A few minutes ago, someone had started playing the baby grand in the room near the bottom of the spiral staircase. Lila had offered to give her and Dad a tour of the house in the future when more time permitted. Britt considered that a polite offer—she was sure she'd never see the inside of this house again. She could tell that her father hadn't believed the woman either. It was a kind gesture, though.

"This one's nice," Dad said, sidling up to her.

Britt turned to him. "You've said that about all of them."

"Because it's true." He shrugged. "I don't know much about art."

"I'll be happy to teach you."

"And I'll be happy to learn." He glanced at his watch. "We should get downstairs. I don't want to miss Arthur's arrival."

She tugged on her glove again, then put her hands behind her back.

He peered down at her. "I'll be right by your side, Brittany. Promise."

"I know." She looked at the picture again, wishing she could stay up here. There were even a couple of chairs in each room, so people could sit and ponder the art. Or just visit with each other in a lovely setting. "Thanks for arranging this, Dad."

"You're welcome, honey. I'm glad I could do something nice for you." He was staring at the painting again.

She took his hand and squeezed it. When he looked at her, he didn't have to say anything. All the regrets and apologies for the past were right there in his eyes. He was making up for them now, and not just because he brought her to a fancy house to see art and attend a party. He'd consistently commented on her videos, texted her at least once a day, and they met in person once a week. He had more than proven himself.

She let go of his hand. "I'm going to tell Mom you're back," she said.

He turned to her. "Really?"

"Yes. Tomorrow." She faced him. "I'll convince her that you've changed. Because I believe you have."

Dad pulled her into a strong hug. "I can't tell you how much this means to me, Brittany. I won't let you or your mother down."

After a moment's hesitation, she leaned into him. When she put her arms around him, her eyes misted.

"Thank you, Brittany." He kissed her temple.

The hole in her heart that had been there when he left and had been growing smaller since his return, finally closed. *I love you.* But before she could say the words, he pulled away.

"Sorry," he said, looking over her dress. "I didn't mess you up, did I?"

"No," she said, blinking back tears. "I'm good." More than good. She had her father back.

A tall man wearing a white suit jacket, black pants, and matching bow tie entered the gallery. "Ms. Lila requests that you join the party downstairs."

At his words, her anxiety kicked in. But only a little. Her father was by her side. Everything would be all right.

He guided her toward the door, and they made their way down the grand staircase. Tinkling piano keys mixed with the hum of conversation, the sounds growing louder as she neared the first floor. She could see the whole front room, the dazzling dresses and smart tuxes blending as her heart hammered in her chest. These weren't her people. Not even close.

She was about to step on the marble floor when she turned to the right . . . and her heart skipped a beat. A gorgeous man who looked like Hunter was standing off to the side with a beautiful dark-haired woman hanging all over him.

He lifted his head, looked straight at Britt, and her heart stopped.

Chapter 21

Made it in the nick of time."

Amy's jaw dropped as Max pulled up in front of the Picketts' house. No, this wasn't a house. It was a bona fide mansion, and she'd never even been this close to one before. It was spectacular.

A young man opened her door at the same time Max got out of his car, leaving the engine running. He met her on the passenger's side just as the valet was helping her out of the car. Mindful of her hem, she lifted her dress a *tiny* bit. She'd shown enough skin for the night.

As the valet went to park Max's Mercedes, Max offered her his arm again. She took it, still marveling. "This is really something."

"I'd forgotten how impressive it is actually." He turned to her. "We better get inside. Arthur should be here any minute."

They walked in just as a sophisticated, impeccably dressed woman was trying and failing to shush the crowd. And it was quite a crowd, almost filling the large grand hall. Finally, someone from somewhere whistled, and everyone quieted down.

"Arthur is on his way," the woman said in a soft Texas drawl that managed to sound both sweet and elegant. "We'll be dimming the lights in five minutes."

"Where should we stand?" Amy asked.

Max shrugged. "Anywhere we can find a place."

They made their way toward the ginormous spiral staircase as a young woman wearing a vintage sixties dress and long white gloves descended the stairs, a man with close-cut, curly black hair in a tuxedo right behind her. The outfit looked like something Britt would wear, not that she would ever go to a huge, fancy party like this.

Then the man turned to look out on the crowd. Amy halted.

His gaze suddenly locked on hers. Her heart hammered in her chest. She'd recognize those green eyes anywhere, anytime, even though it had been almost twenty years since she'd last seen them. *Daniel.* Although, it couldn't be Daniel because he wouldn't be at this kind of party with these kind of people. Impossible.

The woman stopped at the bottom of the stairs, Daniel almost bumping into her.

Amy's hand flew to her mouth. Britt? No, it couldn't be.

"Something wrong?" Max asked.

She couldn't look at him. All she could do was stare at Britt, who was frozen on the bottom step, gawking at something on the other side of the room.

Amy's gaze followed hers just as the crowd cleared for a moment. She couldn't believe it. Standing near the wall with a modelesque woman basically glued to him was the man from Britt's drawing.

"Amy?" Max stepped in front of her. "You're white as a sheet."

"I—" She turned to Britt again and saw the familiar look of fear in her eyes. Daniel leaned over and whispered something to her. Britt gripped his arm.

Another whistle. This time a man's voice rang out. "Light's out in three . . . two . . . one . . ."

Darkness descended on the room, although it wasn't completely without light. Two of the outside lights were still on, but they didn't give off enough illumination for her to see Britt. She felt Max cover her elbow with his hand. The room was now so silent, Amy could hear herself breathing.

She wasn't thinking about Max, or his boss. *Daniel is here. With Britt.* Her daughter knew he was in town and hadn't said a word to her about it. How long had he been here? Why was Britt here? *How could she keep this from me?*

The door opened, and Arthur walked in.

~

"Surprise!"

The lights blazed bright again as the crowd's shouts echoed off the marble floor and high ceiling of the great room. But Hunter barely heard it and kept his gaze on the staircase, confusion swarming his mind. Britt was here? With the chauffeur? At least that's who he thought was standing behind her. She was still on the step, her expression petrified. Daniel—was that his name?— now had a protective arm around her and was whispering in her ear.

But her eyes are still on me.

"Now the fun begins." Cara, who had yet to get the hint that Hunter wasn't interested, stood on her toes and circled her arms around his neck. "Remember the last time we were together? Right in this house, in your parents' bedroom—"

"Stop." He moved her arms from him as politely as he could. And although his focus was on Britt, the shame of that night came barreling at him. He'd been so drunk he barely remembered what he did with Cara. But he recalled enough, and it made his stomach turn.

"Hunter—"

He pulled his gaze away from Britt long enough to look at Cara. "Sorry. I'm not interested."

Her perfectly shaped eyebrows flattened. "Were you ever?"

No more lies. "No."

Hurt spread across her face. "So you just used me?"

His chest compressed. "Yes."

A string of expletives that would embarrass a sailor flew out of her mouth. He didn't try to stop her. He deserved every insult. When she was done, he saw that a few people were watching. Thankfully, his family was still far enough away basking in congratulations that they didn't notice.

"You're the worst, Hunter Pickett." She spun on her heel and stalked off.

He adjusted his tie and glanced around at the small group of onlookers. Unable to defend the indefensible, he turned his gaze from them and back to Britt.

But she was gone.

⌒

"Brittany, wait."

Britt ignored her father's pleas as she tried to thread her way through the crowd, barely able to see through the tears in her eyes. She was also lost and had no idea where she was or how to escape. The house was so big, the guests so numerous, she could go around in circles all night and never find the front door.

"Brittany!"

She could hardly hear his voice above the din, and she wasn't being fair to him by refusing to respond. It wasn't his fault Hunter was a creep. No, worse than a creep. He was sadistic. There was no other word to describe him. He'd reeled her in like she was a brainless fish and toyed with her, when all the while he lived a totally different life. Did he even work at a warehouse? And that woman clinging to him—was she his girlfriend? His *wife?* She didn't know, and she didn't care. Not anymore. All she wanted was to get out of there.

"Britt!"

She halted, almost crushed by the throng of people moving around. But she could hear the one voice she'd never expected. "Mom?"

"Excuse me. Coming through." Her mother was shoving her way through the partygoers until she was in front of her, eyes blazing. "Brittany Danielle, what are you doing here?"

"Amy . . ." A sharp-looking middle-aged man came up beside her, bewildered eyes behind trendy dark-framed glasses. He circled his arm around her mother's waist in a protective gesture. "Are you okay?"

"No," she growled, not looking at him and keeping her ire on Britt. "Where is your father?"

"Right here." He moved to stand beside Britt.

Mom pressed her lips into a line so tight they turned white.

"I can explain," Dad said.

"I don't want your explanations," she shot back. "How could you do this to me? How could you . . ." She glared at Dad again, then took off.

"Amy, don't." Dad chased after her, both of them disappearing in the crowd.

Britt was pulling on her gloves so hard they were slipping off her arms. She wanted to run. She wanted to crawl in a hole. Most of all, she wanted to throw up. But all she could do was stand there and stare at the man who was with her mother.

"Ah . . . I'm Max," he said, thrusting out his hand. "You must be Amy's daughter."

She stared at his hand in a daze. He knew about her? A person didn't bring a stranger to a party like this. Max had to be Mom's boyfriend. *Why didn't she tell me?*

Max withdrew his hand and looked around, his expression uncertain. "Um . . . can I get you a drink?"

"Britt!"

Hunter. His voice spurred her to move. "Sorry," she mumbled to Max, pushing past him. But she didn't get very far before Hunter had grabbed her arm.

"Britt, what are you doing here?"

If someone asked her that question one more time . . . She turned and tried to jerk her arm away from him. "Let me go," she grumbled, unable to look at him.

"Not until we talk."

Her gaze went to his, and she was shocked at what she saw. Pain. Vulnerability. Confusion and apprehension. The same things she'd drawn into the portrait she'd made of him when she closed her eyes. Later she drew a more accurate one that exemplified his beauty, thinking that she'd finally captured the real man. But she had no idea what was real anymore.

"Please, Britt. If you don't want to have anything to do with me after we talk, I won't bother you again."

She didn't believe him. But for some inexplicable reason, she couldn't tell him no. She nodded and let him lead her out of the crowd and through the numerous living areas. The house seemed endless.

Finally, they stopped in front of a closed door. Hunter opened it, and they both went inside.

It didn't take long for Daniel to catch up to Amy. Halfway down the Picketts' driveway, she'd stopped to take off her shoes and throw them in the yard before marching off again. Daniel scooped them up and ran after her, saying her name over and over. When he reached her, he jumped in front of her, intending to make her stop.

But Amy had always been unpredictable, and she kicked him in the shin and blew past him again. The blow didn't hurt . . . too much. He spun around and grabbed her by the waist, the flowing fabric from her dress twisting around both of them.

"What are you doing?"

He glanced at the house. They were far enough away that no one could see them. He set her back down but held fast.

"Let me go." She squirmed in his arms.

"Not until you settle down."

"Settle down?" She glared at him, years of rage in her eyes. "You can't tell me what to do. Not anymore."

"Did I ever?"

Amy paused. "No."

If the circumstances were different, he would have smiled. Nobody told Amy Branch what to do. But at least she'd stopped moving. "If I let you go, will you stay?"

"No—"

He tightened his arms around her. He wasn't hurting her. He'd release her before he would do that. But she had to listen to some kind of reason. And now that she was calmer, her hands resting on his biceps instead of pushing against them, warm memories flooded him. He missed her so much. Even her red-hot temper. "I'll ask again. Are you going to stay?"

After a second's hesitation, she nodded.

Daniel slowly loosened his arms, ready to grab her again if she went back on her word. When she didn't, he dropped his hands to his sides and took a step back. "Sorry I had to do that."

She lifted her chin, still glaring at him. "You have no right touching me. Or ordering me around."

"I know, but—"

"What did you do to Britt?"

He frowned. "I didn't do anything to her."

"Have you brainwashed her? Bribed her?" Her hands were fisted at her sides.

"No, Amy. I wouldn't do that to our daughter."

"Oh, that's right." She sneered, crossing her arms. "You wouldn't do anything with Britt and couldn't be bothered with her. Until now." She heaved out a breath. "You must be here for a reason. What do you want?"

"I—" After tonight's fiasco, this would probably be the last time she'd speak to him. Hopefully she wouldn't be hard on Britt for keeping their secret. "I want us to be a family."

She scoffed, rolling her eyes.

"I'm serious. And don't be upset with Brittany. Please," he added, showing that he was trying not to tell her what to do. "I reached out to her three months ago."

Her nostrils flared. "Three months! You were sneaking behind my back for that long? I don't know why I'm surprised. You did that most of our marriage."

"I know, and for that I'm sorry. It's another reason I moved back. To apologize and try to make up for the past."

"Don't waste your breath."

Daniel opened his mouth to speak, but the bright lights from the house reached far enough that he could see the furious anguish in her eyes. He knew he'd hurt her. She'd refused to speak to him during their divorce, requiring that all communication be done through her lawyer. He'd easily obliged, still too much of an alcoholic to care at that point. But after all these years . . . she was still dealing with the pain he'd inflicted. "Amy," he said, going to her. "I—"

"Back off." She held out her palms. "I don't care what you're going to say. You should have been man enough to come directly to me instead of going through Britt. She's vulnerable. Fragile."

"She's stronger than you think."

Amy's eyes narrowed into slits. "You know nothing about *my* daughter."

"Three months ago, you'd be right. But I've gotten to know her, Amy. She's talented, kind, and strong." He paused, his chin trembling with emotion. "She's also a grown woman. She can make her own decisions."

"Amy!"

He turned around to see her date jogging toward them. It was the same guy from the movie theater. Clearly, they were in a relationship. Jealousy twisted inside him again.

"Are you okay?" he said, moving to her side.

Without a word, she turned to the guy, grabbed the back of his head, and kissed him. Hard. Full. And a knife stabbed into Daniel's heart when the man drew her against him, eagerly returning her kiss.

She pulled away, giving Daniel a triumphant look. "I am now."

The guy looked dazed and confused. "Do you want to go back inside? Or I can take you home. I got the keys from the valet, so we can leave now."

"Take me home." She grabbed her shoes from Daniel and stalked away, her date or boyfriend or whatever right on her heels.

Daniel thrust his hands through his hair, his senses reeling as he watched them walk away. His hope for reconciliation disappeared. Amy was right. He should have gone to her first, even though she'd just proved his assumption that she wouldn't be willing to talk to him or even be civil. Now Brittany was stuck in the middle again, having to choose sides—

Brittany! In his haste to talk to Amy, he'd left her at the party. He hurried back to the house, kicking himself for doing the exact thing he'd promised he wouldn't do. *I left her alone.*

⌒

Hunter turned on the light and shut the door behind him. They were in his father's office, which had more square footage than his entire apartment. He yanked at his bow tie, almost ripping it off. The thing was strangling him. Or maybe it was the mix of panic and fear making his throat feel like it was closing.

When he unbuttoned the top two buttons on his shirt, she backed away, running into the emerald green chaise longue opposite his father's mahogany desk. "W-what are you doing?"

He stopped his movements, realizing he was scaring her. "This stupid shirt and tie . . . It's like a noose around my neck."

But that didn't appease her. She looked like a beautiful ingenue that had just walked out of an old movie, albeit one with fear in her eyes and her gloves bunched around her wrist. "Britt—"

"Don't come near me."

This was eerily reminiscent of when she found out who he was—or rather who he'd presented himself to be. He held up his hands. "I'll stay right here. Promise."

"You said you wanted to talk." She bit her lip, hard. "So talk."

This wasn't the way he wanted things to go down, not by a long shot. But all he could do was tell her the truth. "I—"

"Are you married?"

"What?"

"That woman who was hanging all over you. Is she your wife?"

He shook his head. "No. Not even a girlfriend."

Hurt flashed in her pretty eyes. "You sure looked cozy."

"Britt, I used to know her . . ." He rubbed his left eyebrow. "I haven't told you the whole truth about myself."

"No kidding."

At her biting tone he said, "And what about you? Why were you here with my dad's chauffeur? You didn't say anything about going to a party tonight."

"You didn't either." She bit her lip again and then her eyes widened. "Arthur is your dad?"

"Yes. Lila is my mom. I didn't know they invited Daniel to their party."

"*What?* You know my dad?"

So Daniel was her father. "I met him once." Hunter tugged on his collar, even though it wasn't constricting him anymore. He dropped his arm to his side. "When I was reserving this tuxedo. See, my dad likes to shop—"

"I don't care." She put her hands over her ears like a child.

Unable to stop himself, he went to her. "Britt, please listen. I didn't tell you about my family because talking about them would lead to other things I wasn't ready to tell you."

"That's supposed to make me feel better?"

"I don't know anything about your family either."

She lifted her chin. "You never asked."

"And you never asked about mine."

Britt stared at him, and if they weren't fighting, he would have kissed her senseless by now, just to reassure himself he hadn't lost her. But the dark dread pooling in his gut told him otherwise.

"It was a game to you," she said, her voice barely above a whisper.

"You and me?" He shook his head. "No. Not by a long shot."

"I don't believe you." She started to shake. "I don't think I ever did. It never made sense to me that someone like you would waste his time with me. I always thought you could have any woman you wanted. Like that one tonight."

"I don't want her, Britt." He put his hands on her trembling shoulders. "I want you."

"I don't believe you." She shrugged him off. "And now that I know your obscenely rich—"

"That's my parents' money, not mine. I live in an apartment and work—"

"Sure you do." She moved away from him. "I'm such a fool." She shoved past him and opened the door.

"Wait, please."

She looked at him over her shoulder, tears streaming down her face.

"Britt," he rasped.

She shook her head and disappeared.

He sank onto the chaise, his head in his hands, trying to collect himself, struggling to figure out if he should go after her or not. He wanted to, but right now she wasn't going to listen to him.

Hunter lifted his head. Her father was Dad's chauffeur. He almost laughed it was so ironic. All this time he had a connection with her, although tenuous at best. Had she mentioned him to Daniel? He had to wonder, considering how secretive she was about her family. Even if she did, whatever she told him wouldn't be the complete truth. *Because I held it back from her.*

They would figure this out, though. He'd give her time to cool off, and he'd talk to her again. Explain everything and pray she understood. And if she did—no, *when* she did—he would spend as much time as it took to make things up to her.

"Have you seen my daughter?"

Hunter turned and stood. Daniel was in the doorway, looking as wrung out as Hunter felt.

"I thought I saw her coming from this direction, but she disappeared again." Daniel's eyes held a note of pleading. "She's wearing a white and red dress—"

"I know who she is." Hunter walked toward him, feeling slightly panicked that he didn't know where Britt was. "I was just . . . talking to her."

Daniel eyed his open-collared shirt. "About what?"

"Long story." He guided Daniel out of the room. "We need to find her first and then I'll explain everything."

"Seems to be the night for explanations," Daniel muttered, and they hurried toward the front of the house.

Britt ducked into the kitchen where a staff of four were preparing food for the guests. She whipped off one of her gloves and wiped her eyes with it, only to discover it was useless. Satin fabric didn't absorb anything. She ran the back of her hand over her face and willed herself not to cry again. She went to the bay window and hid behind a corner wall, pulled her phone out of her purse, and called Savannah. "Please answer, please answer . . ."

"Hey, Britt. Long time no talk."

She lowered her voice, not wanting to be detected. "Can you pick me up?"

"What's wrong? You don't sound good."

"I'm not. Here's the address, but I'll be standing in front of the house next door."

"You're in University Park? What are you doing there?"

She inhaled a shuddering breath. "I'll explain later. Please hurry, okay?"

"I'll be there ASAP."

Britt put her phone back in her purse and slipped through the back door, wishing she'd paid more attention to the layout of the neighborhood. Arthur and Lila's backyard—oh, and *Hunter's*—was as overwhelming as their house.

Unsure of the direction, she started walking. If she had to, she'd call Savannah back and give her better directions. But she had to get out of here *now*. Away from Hunter, the party, even her father. Away from them all.

Chapter 22

Amy gripped her shoes so tightly the straps dug into the palm of her hand. She still couldn't believe Daniel was back or that Britt had been seeing him on the sly for so long. He had to be manipulating her somehow. Being sneaky was his MO, not Britt's.

Anger coursed through her, and it wasn't until she was halfway to her house that she remembered she was in the car with Max. She hadn't experienced that type of blind rage since . . . since she'd been married to Daniel.

She glanced at Max, who hadn't said a word since they left the Picketts'. He stared straight ahead, the oncoming headlights on the other side of the road illuminating his face . . . and his stone-set jaw.

Looking at the strappy heels in her lap, she slightly relaxed her grip as reality replaced fury. *I kissed Max.* This was bad, really bad. Not the kiss, although she honestly couldn't remember it. She'd been so furious at Daniel for, well, everything, that she acted without thinking, wanting to drive the point home to him that she'd moved on. Which wasn't true at all.

Another truth hit her. She'd used Max, who had been nothing but kind to her since the second she met him. It was something one of her high school freshmen would have done. Immature and thoughtless.

Max remained silent as he turned into her driveway. Her outdoor light turned on, flooding the driveway with bright light. He put the car in park, then killed the engine. They sat in silence for a moment.

"Max . . ." She swallowed, mortified by her behavior. "I'm sorry."

"About the kiss?"

He was facing her now, and she could see his full expression. Gone was the mild-mannered Max she knew. He looked hurt, confused . . . and angry. "I—" She glanced at her shoes again. "I shouldn't have kissed you."

"I don't know what happened back there. To be honest, I don't want to. But it's probably a good thing."

"What do you mean?" she asked, surprised.

"I was starting to really like you. Not just as a friend." He ran his palm over his tuxedo pantleg. "I know we agreed that we wouldn't date, and I truly meant it at the time. But I was changing my mind. You're fun, Amy. You're witty and pretty, and I'd be crazy if I didn't fall for you."

Her heart squeezed. "Oh, Max—"

"Let me finish. I'd hoped you felt the same way, or at least could at some point. But when you kissed me, I knew you didn't. You weren't thinking about me, were you?"

"No." Her eyes burned. "I wasn't."

He faced the front just as the garage light turned off. "I don't think we should see each other again."

She started to protest, then simply nodded. "Good night, Max."

"Goodbye, Amy."

She hurried out of his car, the light turning back on. She'd barely opened the door when she heard him back out of the driveway and speed off. She leaned her forehead against the doorjamb. *Stupid, stupid, stupid.* She'd let her anger at Daniel ruin a friendship that may have eventually turned into a romantic relationship. *Now I'll never know.*

Amy went inside and shut the door. She didn't expect Britt to be home, and when she checked her room upstairs, it was empty.

She went to her bedroom, plopped onto the edge of her bed, and tossed her shoes on the floor. Her heart hurt to think that Britt was with Daniel. *How could she do this to me?* She slipped out of her beautiful, expensive dress, letting it fall in a puddle next to her bed, and shoved on an old T-shirt and shorts.

Then she lay down, hugging her pillow to her chest, her heart in pieces. "How could she betray me?" she whispered.

~

"I'm confused."

Britt didn't respond to Savannah as they left swanky University Park.

"If I have this straight," Savannah said, "you were at a party with your dad, and your mom showed up with her date? Boyfriend?"

"I have no idea what he is," she said flatly. "Mom never mentioned him."

"So she never told you about her guy and you never told her about your dad. Oh boy. That had to be a mess." When Britt didn't answer again, Savannah said, "Are you okay?"

"No." She wondered if she'd ever be okay again.

Her phone buzzed for the third time since Savannah had picked her up. She didn't bother to check who it was. It had to be her father, or her mother, and she didn't want to talk to either of them right now. She knew for sure it wasn't Hunter. He'd had his fun and laughs at her expense. He was probably out having a grand time with that woman he was with. Or maybe even multiple women. "Whatever."

"What's that?"

"Can you take me home?" she asked, on the verge of tears again.

"But you just said you wanted to stay at my house." Savannah maneuvered her car onto the freeway that was always crowded, no matter what time of day it was.

"I did, but . . ."

"Britt, talk to me. You're holding something back, and I think you've been keeping whatever it is inside for a while. Even when we were planning my shower, you were preoccupied, although I didn't think you were upset." She glanced at her. "Actually, you've been happier than I've ever seen you up until now."

Although she didn't want to talk about Hunter, she didn't want to dodge Savannah either. She was her best friend, and she'd dropped everything the minute Britt had called her. "Something else happened tonight," she said, twisting her gloves into a knot. "I . . . I found out my boyfriend isn't who I thought he was."

Savannah nearly veered into the next lane. She course-corrected as the other driver laid on the horn until he flew by her. "You have a *boyfriend?*"

"I thought I did," she mumbled.

"Why didn't you tell me? How could you not tell me?"

Britt winced at Savannah's furious words. "I'm sorry—"

"We're best friends!" She lifted one hand off the steering wheel, then dropped it back down. "Who is he? How long have you been dating?"

"He's a guy I met online."

Savannah looked at her. "Oh, Britt. Seriously? Why didn't you introduce him to me? I could have vetted him for you."

For some reason, her words irked Britt. "Because I thought I could handle it myself." Obviously, she couldn't. She'd been played, so badly played. Her heart ached so much she could hardly stand it.

"He was at the party tonight?" Savannah asked in a softer tone.

"Yes. His parents own one of those massive houses. He could live there too, for all I know."

"You don't know where he lives?"

She thought he lived at the apartment complex where she'd picked him up that one time. But he could have pretended to live there since he never invited her inside. "Just take me home, Savannah."

"But—"

"Please!" She couldn't stand to explain her folly, even to her best friend. It was so humiliating, so agonizingly painful.

Then she realized if she went home, she'd have to face her mother. She couldn't do that. "Never mind," she said, sitting up straight. "Can you take me to Maude and X's?"

"That wacky couple at the art store? And I mean that in the most complimentary way possible."

"Yes."

Savannah paused. "I will, but I really want you to stay with me tonight. We don't have to talk about the party, or the guy, or your parents. We'll just hang out and play games or something."

Britt considered it, but talk would eventually turn to Savannah and Justin's wedding and the upcoming shower next weekend. Her stomach started to burn. How was she going to face all that now? Her mother was angrier than Britt had ever seen, and she was supposed to help with the shower. And Britt knew she couldn't stand to listen to Savannah's happiness, even though she was glad for her friend. "I just want to go to Maude's."

Savannah didn't say anything, but the temperature in the car dropped at least five degrees. For the rest of the ride, Britt gave directions, and Savannah silently followed them. When she reached Maude and X's townhouse, she pulled to a stop.

Britt opened the car door. "Thank you."

Silence.

"Now *you're* mad at me?" Britt blurted out the words before she could stop them.

"Don't I have a right to be? You didn't tell me about your boyfriend, and you'd rather spend time with Maude and Z—"

"It's X—"

"I don't care!" Savannah closed her eyes, gathering herself. "Britt, I don't understand what's going on. This isn't like you."

With those words, everything inside Britt crumbled. She was right. Being a maid of honor, keeping secrets, going out and having fun, dating a gorgeous guy—especially that—were things she *did*. She'd been pretending to be someone she wasn't. That stopped now.

"I can't be in your wedding," she said flatly.

"Britt—"

But she was already halfway out of the car. "Find someone else." She slammed the door.

Tires squealed as Savannah zoomed away. Britt stared up at the night sky, barely seeing the twinkling stars sparsely scattered across it. Her insides turned to ice as she made her way to the front door.

When she reached it, she knocked several times before a light turned on in the picture window, and then the one above the porch came to life. The door opened and X was standing there, wearing striped pajama bottoms and a Simon and Garfunkel concert shirt. Maude appeared right behind him, surprisingly clad in an old-fashioned nightgown. "Britt?" they both said in unison.

She dissolved into uncontrollable sobs.

~

For the fourth time, Hunter texted Britt.

> Please text me back. I know you're mad and you have a right
> to be. I can explain it all if you'll just talk to me. At least let me
> know you're okay.

He set his phone back on his lap as Daniel drove them to Britt's house. He stared out the window as the scenery zipped by, panic and dread swirling within him.

"Still no answer?" Daniel asked.

"No. I just texted her again."

Her father blew out a long breath. "I'm worried about her."

"Me too." He and Daniel had searched the house and grounds looking for Britt but didn't find her. During that time, Hunter had texted her several times. When Daniel said he was going to see if she'd gone home, Hunter insisted on accompanying him. He knew she lived in Allen, but he didn't know her address. It was dawning on him how little they'd shared of their personal lives. Neither of them had asked too many questions, which made him wonder what else Britt was hiding.

It also dawned on him that he hadn't told his family he was leaving or even told his father happy birthday. He rubbed his temple. They wouldn't be happy about that. *At least I didn't make a scene this time.* Maybe that would be a point in his favor . . . but he doubted it.

Daniel pulled up to a stop light. As they waited for it to turn green, he said, "How do you know Brittany?"

Hunter had never heard Britt use her full name, and he'd never thought of her as a Brittany. But it fit. "Her channel," he said, cringing inside. No matter how he spun this, it was going to make him look bad, so he explained it as straightforwardly as he could. "She thought I was a creep at first."

"Are you?" The light changed and Daniel inched forward. Traffic on this main road was as packed as it usually was on a Saturday night.

"If I was, would I admit it?"

"Probably not." He put on the brakes as the car in front of him stopped. "Define your relationship then."

This was the first time he'd been put through his paces by a woman's father, and it was wracking his already wracked nerves. "We're dating." Hopefully they still would be after all this was over.

"She never mentioned you."

No surprise there. "To be honest, sir, she didn't mention you either."

Daniel's jaw jerked. "I wouldn't expect her to."

He hadn't anticipated that answer. "Neither of us talked about our families."

"She didn't know you're Arthur's son?"

"No." He looked out the window again. Numerous restaurants and stores with their vibrant neon signs lined both sides of the road. "I'm sure you've heard stories about me."

"Not stories," Daniel said. "Just facts. How long have you been dating my daughter?"

"A few weeks. But we've known each other a little longer." He told Daniel about the art lessons but didn't mention how he was helping Britt with her social anxiety. "I really care about her, Mr. Branch."

Daniel shook his head as the traffic began to move again. "It's

Daniel. Your father is my employer, Hunter. I should be deferring to you."

"Please don't. I can't stand all that formality. Never could."

Daniel nodded. "I've never been comfortable with it either, until I started working for Arthur. It's easy to be deferential when you're respected in return."

Hunter suddenly recalled what his mother had said shortly after his arrival at the party, when she mentioned the woman who looked like Audrey Hepburn. *We think highly of her father.* His mother wanted to fix him up with Britt without knowing they were already together. The irony of it all was unbelievable.

Daniel turned into a middle-class neighborhood, and a few minutes later pulled into a driveway.

Hunter didn't see Britt's car, only a sedan. "She's not here."

"I picked her up at K&Bs," Daniel said, turning off the engine. "I guess I better explain some things before we go inside. If Amy will let me inside, that is. My relationship with Britt's mom is . . . complicated. No, that's not true. We don't have a relationship because I ruined my marriage years ago. Amy hates me, and Britt never told her I was back in town. Amy found out about it tonight at the party, and she wasn't too happy about that, obviously. Things could get uncomfortable, so if you want to wait here—"

"If there's even a chance Britt is here, I want to talk to her," Hunter said, opening the car door. "I need to know that she's okay."

Daniel nodded, and they exited the car. He rang the doorbell five times before it finally opened, and the woman Hunter had seen earlier arguing with Britt and Daniel stood in the doorway, glaring at them.

"I should have known you wouldn't leave us alone," she sneered. Then she looked at Hunter, surprise crossing her features. "Who are— Wait . . . You're the guy from the drawing."

"What drawing?" Hunter asked.

"Forget it." She scowled at Daniel again. "Where's Britt?"

"I was hoping she was here," Daniel said.

Amy's anger turned to alarm. "I thought she was with you."

"I thought she got a ride home. We couldn't find her at the Picketts'—"

"Then where is she?" She clutched her chest. "Where is my daughter?"

Britt stared at the cup of peppermint tea Maude placed in front of her. At least she'd stopped sobbing, although her breath was still shuddering. She hadn't wanted to lose control, but she couldn't help it.

Maude sat down, her long, gray hair in a side braid draped against her granny nightgown. "Oh, honey. I take it the party didn't go well?"

Sniffing, Britt nodded, still staring at the tea.

Maude handed her a tissue from the dispenser on the kitchen counter. "Do you want to talk about it—" She sat up. "What is that horrid smell?"

"Valerian," X said as he walked into the kitchen carrying a small oil diffuser. "With a touch of Bergamot. It helps with anxiety and sadness."

"It smells like a cow pasture." She waved X away.

He looked a little insulted, but he left with his diffuser.

Britt agreed with Maude, but she didn't care about the smell or anything else. Another tear dripped on the table. She quickly wiped it away.

Maude took her hand. "Do you want to talk about it?"

"I'm such an idiot."

"No, you're not—"

"Don't," she said, holding up her hand. "Don't try to make me feel better. I was so stupid, Maude. He made a fool out of me."

"Who?"

"Hunter."

Her brow shot straight up. "Our Hunter?"

"He's not mine." She hung her head, several curls brushing against her cheeks. She'd only now noticed that her carefully created updo was wilting.

"I refuse to believe he would hurt you," Maude said.

Britt faced her. "He's not who he claimed to be." She told Maude about Hunter being at the party, who his parents were, and that he was with another woman.

Shock registered on her face. "I can't believe it," she said. "He told us he worked at a warehouse."

"I'm sure that's a lie too."

X reappeared with a different diffuser, this one much more palatable. "Lavender and lemon," he said in a pinched voice. "Conventional, but effective."

"Thank you, sweetie." Maude motioned for him to put it on the counter. "Give us a few more minutes." He nodded and left, then she turned to Britt again. "Have you talked to him?"

"A little, right before I left. But I don't ever want to see him again." Tears spilled down her cheeks. "I thought . . . I thought . . ."

"You liked him a lot."

"It's more than that. Not that it matters what I feel anymore," she said.

"Britt, it always matters how you feel."

"Not to him."

"Are you sure?" Maude asked. "I've seen how he looks at you. Cares about you—"

"It must have been an act." She moved to get up from the table. "If you're going to defend him—"

"Sit down, Brittany."

Maude had never used such a curt tone with her before. Britt obeyed.

"Look, I understand that you're hurting. But from what you're telling me, you haven't given him a chance to explain himself. And before you once again say that you don't want to listen to him, I'm going to point out that you're not being fair."

"How can you say that? He was with another woman!"

"Or you jumped to a conclusion."

Britt sat back, her arms crossed over her chest. "How would you know? You weren't there."

"Did you see him come in with her? Did he ignore you once he saw you? Or did he leave her and go straight to you?"

"How . . . how did you know that?"

Maude gave her a small smile. "I've been around the block a few times. The only way to find out the truth is to listen to him."

Her phone buzzed in her purse. Britt didn't make a move to answer it.

"Aren't you going to get that?"

"It's just Mom. Or Dad." She explained the other disastrous event—that her mother had found out about her father being in town. "Oh, and apparently Mom has a boyfriend I didn't know about. And Savannah's mad at me, so I told her to find someone else to be her maid of honor."

"Oh Britt, you didn't." Maude tapped her fingers on the wood table. "What a tangled web. Don't you people ever talk to each other?" When the phone buzzed again, she shoved Britt's purse toward her. "You need to let your parents know where you are and that you're all right. I'm sure they're worried about you."

"Fine." She yanked open her bag and pulled out the phone. Hunter's name popped up in the message list. Seven texts. Nothing from her father or mother, though.

"Call one of your parents," Maude insisted. "Right now."

She stared at Hunter's name again, stunned that he had texted her so many times when she assumed he was busy with his girlfriend. Then, to appease Maude, she made the call. "Hello? Yes, I'm all right. I'm at Maude's."

Chapter 23

Daniel put his phone in his pocket, nearly falling to his knees with relief after Brittany told him she was okay. She hung up right after telling him she was at Maude's, barring him from asking any other questions.

"Who was that?" Amy demanded.

He, Hunter, and Amy were standing in the foyer. That was as far as she would let either of them in the house, and it had taken some cajoling from Daniel to get her to agree to that. "Brittany," he said, and saw Hunter's head jerk up. The guy had been texting her since they walked inside.

"Is she okay?" Hunter said quickly.

And in Daniel's opinion, with great concern. He believed the young man when he said he cared about her. "Yes—"

"She called you and not me?" Amy threw up her hands. "I don't understand. What have you done to her?"

"Amy, just listen—"

She marched farther into the house.

Hunter frowned, clearly confused. As he should be. Amy wasn't making sense.

"I'll be back." Daniel fortified himself and went after her. He found her in the living room, her hands covering her face as she sobbed. His heart tore in two. Her pain was his fault—again. But instead of running away from the shame of constantly hurting her, the way he'd done during their entire marriage, he stood his ground. "Amy."

She lifted her face, her expression shooting daggers at him. She hadn't taken her makeup off from the party. Her hair was a mess, mascara streamed down her face, she was over twenty years older than the last time he'd seen her . . . and she was still the most beautiful woman he'd ever encountered.

"I'm sorry you had to find out this way." He wanted to go to her, but it would be a bad move. So he stayed put. "Brittany wanted to tell you herself at the right time."

"There would never be a right time." Amy ran her forearm under her nose, her eyes never leaving his. "How did you weasel your way back into her life?"

"I sent her an email."

"Oh, please. It couldn't have been that simple. You abandoned her, Daniel. Not just when we divorced, but soon after she was born. You chose booze over her. Over both of us."

"I know." His throat caught. "I think about my mistakes every single day."

"And I don't care." She straightened, staring at him in her uniquely defiant way. "If you think I'm going to let you hurt her again—"

"I won't. I'm sober, Amy. I have been for seven years."

"Sure. Like I'm going to believe that."

"That young man in there?" He gestured toward the foyer with his thumb. "That's Hunter Pickett. His father is Arthur Pickett, one of the premiere lawyers in the country."

"I know who he is."

Daniel waited for her to elaborate, but she didn't. "Arthur's my boss. I'm his chauffeur."

Amy let out a bitter chuckle. "He has horrible instincts then."

"No, he knows me very well. He was my lawyer when I went to prison."

She stilled. "Prison?"

"Seven years ago in Fort Worth. Drunk driving, third offense, BAC over .15." He rattled off the stats as if he were stating the weather forecast. But inside he was a swirl of shame, regret, and remorse, as he had been since the day he'd been arrested. "Arthur took my case pro bono. Not because he knew me. It was the luck of the draw . . . and I was very lucky. In more ways than one."

"You're a criminal on top of everything else." But Amy's tone didn't hold quite the same amount of venom.

"Arthur got the sentence down to two years, and it was enough for me to hit rock bottom and dry out. I went to AA meetings in prison. Met with the chaplain twice a week, more if he was available. Did my time with perfect behavior, and when I got out, I worked on rebuilding my life. That's when Arthur entered it again. He met with me and offered me a job." He stared at the floor. "I still don't know why. All he said was that people deserve second chances."

"I gave you so many more than that." She turned to him, fresh tears in her eyes. "Over and over, I forgave you, I believed your promises, I pretended that everything was fine. Until I couldn't do it anymore."

"I know. And you gave me more than I deserved." His throat burned. "I'm sorry for what I did to you and Brittany. I want to make up for it. That's why I came back."

"I don't want your apologies, Daniel." She composed herself. "I don't want you in my life or in Britt's. You ran out of chances a long time ago."

Hunter paced in the foyer, trying not to hear the conversation in the other room, but it was impossible. Thin walls, raised voices, whatever the reason, he heard every word, and he stopped in his tracks when he heard Daniel admit he'd gone to prison for a DUI, and that had been his rock bottom. His story was so similar to Hunter's it would have been eerie—except Hunter had heard the same stories from other people too. Alcoholics and addicts whose run-ins with the law had laid them low.

"Does Britt know?" Amy said, her voice distant but audible. "About prison? About the DUIs?"

"Yes," Daniel replied.

"And she forgave you?"

Pause. "Yes."

Hunter's eyes widened. If Britt was able to forgive her father, could she forgive him too?

He pulled out his phone and went outside. The air was muggy, and the cicadas were annoyingly loud, but he had to reach Britt. No texting this time. He pulled up her number and tapped it. He would call her until she answered—

"Hello."

He closed his eyes at the sound of her voice. "It's Hunter."

"I know."

Of course she did. Her tone was flat but at least she was talking to him. "Your dad said you're at Maude and X's."

"You're with him?"

"We were looking for you . . ." He didn't want to waste his time explaining the details. "Can we talk? In person?"

No answer.

After a few moments he said, "Please, Britt."

Several more seconds passed. "Yes."

"I can come to you." Then he realized he didn't have a car or his bike. He'd have to call an Uber. "What's the address?"

She hesitated before she gave it to him.

"All right, I'll be there as soon as I can—"

But he realized the line was already silent.

He stared at the phone, then quickly he brought up the Uber app.

The front door opened. Daniel stepped out, his expression haggard.

"Amy's calmed down a little," Daniel said, sounding weary. "At least she knows where Brittany is. Can I drop you off somewhere?"

Hunter held up his phone. "I was just calling an Uber."

Daniel gave him a faint smile. "I'm a chauffeur, remember? Driving your family around is what I do."

Hunter nodded and put away his phone. "Can you take me to Maude's? Britt's willing to talk."

His face brightened a little. "Sure."

They got into the car and were on their way, not speaking until Daniel pulled in front of a townhouse with a neatly kept lawn. He put the car in park but kept the engine running. "Full disclosure, since I'm tired of keeping secrets . . . I know you've been in trouble with the law."

Hunter swallowed. "Yes, sir. I have."

"And I have a feeling you heard part or all of my conversation with Amy, so you know I have too."

"Yes, sir."

His expression was stern under the streetlamp. "What are your intentions toward Brittany?"

Without hesitation, he said, "I love her. She's unlike any woman

I've ever met. She's talented, warm, generous, beautiful . . . She makes me want to be so much better than I ever hoped to be."

"Then be that for her, Hunter." His tone was forceful. "Don't throw away a good thing, like I did."

Hunter nodded, then opened the door and got out. Daniel waited until Maude, wearing a bland housecoat, opened the door. Then he left.

"Come in," she said, her expression guarded, something he'd never seen from her before. "She's in the kitchen."

"Thanks." He followed her to the back of the house, a little surprised by the calm décor and muted grays and whites. Very different from their colorful, eclectic shop. When they reached the kitchen, Maude disappeared.

He stopped in the doorway and looked at Britt. She was sitting with her head down, shoulders slumped, pushing her thumb back and forth on the edge of the table, several locks of gorgeous curls against her cheeks. Her gloves were wadded up next to a teacup, and the scent of lemon and lavender filled the room.

Taking in a deep breath, he approached her.

Britt didn't look up as she heard Hunter's footsteps against the linoleum in Maude and X's kitchen. When he sat down next to her, she could smell his cologne, even above the essential oils X insisted on diffusing. His scent wasn't overbearing, but it was different. Expensive smelling. Just another reminder that she never really knew him at all.

"Britt." His normally low voice had dropped even lower, his tone tentative.

She bit her bottom lip, almost to the point of drawing blood.

She kept her gaze glued to the table, unwilling to risk looking at him. She didn't want to get lost in his magnetic eyes or lose her senses at his charming smile. He knew how to get to her, and she had to keep her walls up.

"I guess I should start at the beginning." He paused, as if waiting for a response. When she didn't move or speak, he continued. "My parents are Arthur and Lila Pickett. I have two brothers, Payne and Kirk, both hugely successful. They're married, but no nieces and nephews yet. My parents always had high expectations for us. Straight As, college prep, Ivy League educations. Expectations I consistently failed to meet."

She couldn't stop herself from looking at him, and she saw the torment in his eyes. *He's faking . . . He's acting . . .* "Is that supposed to make me feel sorry for you?"

He blinked. "No. I'm just telling you about my family. We never talked about them, remember?"

She shifted her gaze back on the table.

"Payne and Kirk were stellar students. The only thing I was good at was sports, and in a family like mine, that's not a worthy accomplishment. But it's not my parents' fault for how I dealt with being different. I was always able to charm my way out of anything, so I used that to my advantage. And when I was old enough to use my looks as leverage, I added that to the mix. By junior high I was running with the wrong crowd. I had my first drink at twelve, my first hit of weed at fourteen. By high school I was an alcoholic and a drug user."

Her head popped up. "What?"

"I got kicked out of a lot of schools." He rubbed the back of his neck. "I was even in your mom's class for a while when I was a freshman."

"You knew my mom?"

"Barely. I made the connection about a month ago—"

"And never told me." She grabbed one of the gloves and started twisting it. When he started to take it from her, she snatched it away.

He withdrew. "Sorry," he mumbled, averting his eyes. "I didn't tell you because I wanted to wait for the right time."

She stilled. How many times had she said that to her dad about Mom?

"There's more. So much more. I got kicked out of so many high schools I had to get my GED. I broke the law numerous times—drunk driving, buying drugs, even petty theft once. Every time, my dad covered for me. Mostly out of self-preservation. Couldn't have his youngest son humiliating the family at every turn. And then there were the women—"

"Enough!" Hearing about his alcohol, drug use, and law breaking was one thing. But she couldn't bear to hear about how many women he'd been with.

"Britt, I'm being honest here. I'm ashamed of my past. All of it. By the time I was twenty-six, I was so lost. I hated what I'd become, but I couldn't stop it. Then I got arrested for petty theft at a liquor store. And for the first time in my life, my dad didn't show up to bail me out. I had to get a court-appointed attorney, and because my record was expunged, I ended up with a light sentence. But I still went to jail.

"When I got out, I was banned from my parents' house. I had to get a job, an apartment, and I couldn't get either of those until I got clean and sober. I had to grow up."

He continued to tell her how he'd pulled himself out of the mire—thanks to people at the church he started attending. "One guy gave me a job at a fast-food place he owned. I met with a group there, and we worked through a sobriety program. I was living at a weekly rate motel until I got the warehouse job. The nephew of a friend of my mother's was also working there. Sawyer. He's my roommate."

"You really live at that apartment complex?"

"Yes, Britt. Everything else I've told you about myself is true. Including my feelings for you."

She couldn't speak, could barely think. While he'd been telling her his story, he'd been absently running his fingers through his thick hair, and it now looked wild and untamed. He was wearing the tuxedo, except for the tie and jacket, his biceps tight against his crisp white shirt. In his honest anguish, he still somehow managed to be heart-stoppingly handsome.

"I love you, Britt," he said. "I know it's soon, but it's the truth. I don't want to hide anything from you anymore—"

"Stop." She pushed away from the table and went to the other side of the room. She had to, or else she'd fall under his spell again. "You don't mean it."

"I do." He jumped up and went to her. "I promise. I'm telling the truth."

And that's what scared her. Because she could understand his past—somewhat. Reconciling with her father, hearing his story, and seeing him turn his life around had made her realize that people could change for the better. She believed Hunter when he said he was clean and sober.

But she'd never been able to understand why he wanted her. She still couldn't, especially now that she knew what he came from. She would never measure up to the Picketts or live in the world that Hunter would return to. And he would, eventually. She knew deep inside he would be successful at whatever he decided to do now that he had reset his life. Eventually he would get tired of her fragility, her anxiousness, her lack of glamour.

He'd be surrounded by beautiful, sophisticated women. His type of woman. Something she could never be.

"Britt, please—"

She turned her back on him. Swallowed her tears.

"That's it?" His voice cracked. "I just bared my heart and soul to you."

Her whole body started to shake, but she didn't move. Didn't speak. Didn't back down.

"I guess I was a fool too."

Britt heard him storm out of the room and she gripped the wall in front of her. When Maude dashed in, she turned around, barely able to speak.

"What happened?" Maude asked, stricken. "That boy looked like death warmed over."

Somehow, she managed not to cry. Or maybe she just didn't have any tears left.

⁓

The next morning, Amy rolled out of bed, her eyes puffy and her head throbbing. After Daniel and Hunter left last night, she finally realized why the kid looked so familiar. Hunter Pickett, Arthur Pickett's son. She still wasn't sure how he was involved with Britt, but she was going to find out today. If Britt wasn't home by noon, she was going to march over to Maude's and make her leave.

In the back of her mind, she knew she couldn't, and shouldn't, force Britt to do anything. But she was still so angry. Seeing Daniel last night, hearing what had happened to him and how he had changed—that made everything worse. Because as he talked and told her his story, she realized even through her haze of anger that he looked good. Healthier than she'd ever seen him. His green eyes weren't bloodshot from alcohol and hangovers, his skin was lightly tanned, his body more filled out. Right before the divorce, Daniel had been skinnier than a rail. Living on a liquid diet would do that to a person.

She didn't want to have sympathy for him. She wanted to hate him for what he'd done to her and Britt.

Soon after she entered the kitchen to make coffee and find the Tylenol, the phone in her hand rang. Hoping it was Britt, she was disappointed to see Laura's name pop up. Then she realized her friend had to be wanting a detailed report about the night before. Amy ignored the call, set the phone on the table, and made coffee.

By the time the pot was full, Laura had called three more times. *Uh-oh.*

Hopefully something wasn't wrong with her or Farah. She quickly answered on the first ring. "Are you okay?"

"That was my question," Laura said, sounding concerned. "We were supposed to meet for breakfast an hour ago. Where are you?"

Amy stilled, the coffeepot in her hand. How had she forgotten her breakfast date with Laura? "I'm home," she said, the pot wobbly as she poured the brew into her cup. "I'm sorry, it completely slipped my mind."

"You had that much of a good time last night?" Laura teased.

She set the pot down and pinched the bridge of her nose, willing herself not to cry.

"Amy?"

"I . . ."

"I'm on my way over."

Amy shook her head. "You don't have to—"

"Yes, I do. I can tell something is really wrong."

She paused. "It is."

"Be there in twenty."

Somehow Laura managed to beat her estimate by five minutes. She didn't bother coming into the house but opened the backyard gate and walked over to Amy, who was sitting on one of the patio chairs staring at the thick green grass.

"How did you know I was here and not inside?" Amy asked.

"We've been friends for almost twenty years." She sat down. "I know you pretty well by now. What happened?"

Amy explained everything, including kissing Max, which Laura found more surprising than the fact that Daniel had returned.

"You kissed him?" Laura leaned forward, her eyes bright with anticipation. "How was it?"

"I don't know."

She frowned. "Huh?"

"I wasn't thinking about Max when I kissed him."

Laura winced. "Who were you thinking about—" She gasped. "Daniel?"

"Just about sticking it to him, that's all. Nothing romantic, if that's what you're implying." She shuddered. "That would never happen. And I know what you're thinking. It was a low thing to do."

"Very low," Laura said honestly. "Why did you do that to him? It's not like you to be petty."

She fisted her hands. "Daniel makes me crazy. He always has. I thought I was rid of him, Laura. But like a bad boomerang, he's back in my life. Britt seems to have reconciled with him."

"Have you talked to her about it yet?"

"She's at Maude's." The hurt returned. "I can't believe she didn't tell me about him."

"I can."

Amy jerked her head toward Laura. "What?"

"Look how nutty you're acting now. Do you think anything

would have changed if she'd told you before? Except for you kissing Max, you would still be just as angry."

"No, I wouldn't." But as she said the words, she knew Laura was right. And now she was realizing that Britt had made the right decision by keeping the secret until she felt she could reveal it. "She would have had to tell me eventually."

"True, but maybe she had a plan to make the news land a little more softly. She's spent her entire life hearing how awful her dad is."

"Excuse me?" Amy balked. "I never said anything that wasn't the truth."

"I know, but even when you didn't say anything, she knew. Everyone knows how bitter you are about Daniel."

Amy scowled. "If this is a pep talk, it's the worst one in history."

"It's real talk. Listen to me. You have to let Daniel go. All of him—the pain he caused, the dreams he destroyed. If you don't, it's going to eat you alive. I think it has in some ways. You won't even think about letting another man near you."

"That's because of Britt—"

"Oh no." Laura held up her hand. "Don't use her as an excuse. She's a grown woman."

"I know that." She kicked at a pebble near her chair. "What I don't get is why everyone feels the need to remind me."

"Maybe because you need the reminder." Laura sighed. "I'm sorry, Amy. I wish last night would have been better for you, and I know Daniel being back and Britt not telling you is a shock. I'm not trying to make light of your feelings, but this could be the chance you've been needing to put the past behind you for good."

Amy let her comments settle.

"Think about it, okay?" Laura smiled. "Did you at least get to see the inside of the house?"

"Yeah," she mumbled. "It's incredible. I thought only people in movies had houses like that." So that was the type of environment Hunter had grown up in. No wonder he'd been a spoiled brat. Well, maybe not a brat, but he sure had an air of entitlement to him. Now that she knew who he was, the memories of him being in her class became clearer—the charming smile, the lack of effort, the attempts at making her believe his lies about why he didn't have his schoolwork or couldn't study for a test. None of it had worked on her.

She heard a car door slam and shot up from her chair. "That might be Britt," Amy said.

Laura was already standing. "Good luck," she said. "I'll talk to you later."

As Laura left the backyard, Amy went inside. She and Britt both arrived in the kitchen at the same time. Her chest squeezed as she saw the state of her daughter. She was wearing the same dress she had on last night, but it was wrinkled as if she'd slept in it. Her hair was in a sloppy ponytail, and whatever makeup she'd had on last night was gone, save for a small smear of black under her left lower lashes.

Amy rushed to her. "Are you okay?"

Britt slowly lifted her head, her eyes empty.

Chapter 24

I'm so glad you're home."

Britt stiffened as her mother smothered her in a big hug. When Mom pulled away, she looked uncharacteristically uncertain. She also looked kind of terrible too, as if she hadn't slept all night. *Neither did I.*

"Did you have breakfast yet?" Mom said. "I can whip up some chocolate chip pancakes. I know how much you love those."

"I'm not hungry."

"You want some coffee then?" She went to the cabinet and took out a cup that said *I'm not bossy, I'm aggressively helpful* on the side. "I just made a fresh pot."

"No thanks." She set her purse on the table, then sat down. "I'm sorry I didn't tell you about Dad."

Mom quickly moved to sit next to her. "It's okay. I understand why you didn't."

"Really? I thought you'd be furious with me."

"Oh, I was. But Laura helped me see the light. I'm still not happy about it, though." She paused. "When were you going to tell me?"

"Today." She leaned her elbow on the table, her head falling against her hand. After Hunter left, Maude gave Britt the guest bedroom and offered her one of her smaller caftans to sleep in. "This one's from thirty pounds ago," she'd said, holding up a green and yellow one. "It will still be big, but it would be more comfortable than the dress." But Britt had refused, too tired to think about changing clothes. Turned out she was too tired and emotionally exhausted to sleep too.

Mom sighed. "Well, I was going to tell you my secret today too. Remember that guy from last night?"

Britt frowned. "How could I forget? Is he your boyfriend?"

"No. He is—was—a friend."

"Was?"

"Oh, Britt, I did something stupid last night. Really dumb." She pushed back her light-brown bangs from her forehead. "I kissed Max in front of your father."

"I'm not sure I want to hear this—"

"That's as PG-13 as it gets. The problem is, I don't like Max that way."

Confused, Britt asked, "Then why did you kiss him?"

"To get back at your dad. Which I didn't need to do. It's not like Daniel has spent the last twenty years pining for me."

Britt wasn't sure that was true. Anytime her dad brought up Mom, there was a twinkle in his eyes and a lightness to his voice.

"Anyway, I should have told you about Max. We went out a couple of times as friends."

"Why didn't you tell me?" Britt asked, surprised at the tiny prick of hurt she felt. She was so sure she couldn't feel anything anymore.

Mom looked contrite. "I didn't think you could handle me being in a relationship."

Annoyed, she said, "I'm not a child. I could have handled it."

"I know. I'm sorry for treating you like one." She sighed. "And for using you as an excuse. I'm the one who can't handle it, and that's something I'm going to have to work through. Are we okay, you and me? We've got Savannah's shower next Saturday—"

"We don't." Britt went to tug on her gloves, then remembered she'd put them in her purse. She couldn't reach the hem of her dress so all she could do was yank on her fingers under the table. "I'm not in the wedding anymore."

"Oh, Britt! What happened?"

"She's mad because I didn't tell her about me and Hunter." She couldn't bring herself to say the full truth. Savannah had a right to be mad at her, and during her sleepless night, Britt realized she had used her best friend's anger as an excuse to back out of the wedding. Her stomach twisted with remorse, but she didn't know how to fix things with her.

Mom's eyes narrowed. "What about you and Hunter?"

She pulled on her index finger so hard she almost knocked it out of joint. She had to tell her mother about him. Or at least some things about him. "Hunter Pickett. We were dating—"

"You were dating *him?*" Mom exclaimed. "Behind my back?"

"I-I didn't want to tell you—"

"I had him in one of my classes years ago. He was trouble back then. Big trouble." She sat back in her chair and huffed. "Well, now I know why he was with your father last night. How did you meet?"

Uh-oh. And their conversation was going so well. "Online," she squeaked.

"How many times have I talked to you about internet safety?"

"Mom—"

"Did he take advantage of you?"

"He's not like that. We broke up because he lied to me."

"That's not much better." Mom glanced up at the ceiling before leveling her gaze on Britt. "Why didn't you tell me you were dating someone?" She paused. "Were you ashamed of me?"

"Mom, please. Just listen. It's hard enough talking about it."

Her mother paused, then nodded. "Go ahead."

Britt told her mother everything about how they met and the art lessons at K&B. "That was my project. Teaching Hunter how to draw. And I didn't tell you about him for the same reason I didn't say anything to Dad or Savannah." Her eyes began to sting. Everything was so messed up.

"Call Savannah," Mom said in a gentler tone. "You two have been best friends since grade school. You can work this out."

"I don't know about that." Tears fell down her face. Ugh, now her chest was burning again. "I didn't want to tell her or anyone else about Hunter. I just wanted to have something special of my own for a little while. To see what it felt like to be normal for once."

Her mom didn't say anything, confirming what Britt had always known to be true. She wasn't normal. She never would be.

"You aren't together anymore?" Mom asked.

She shook her head, not missing the relief in her mother's eyes, even though she was trying to hide it.

"How about we rent a movie tonight?" Mom said. "We can drown our sorrows in a good old nineties rom-com. That was the best era."

Did her mother really think that Britt wanted to watch a romance right now? "I'm going to my room." She grabbed her bag and shot up from the table.

"Britt," Mom said. "You and Hunter . . . You weren't serious, were you?"

I love you, Britt. His words, said in his melty deep voice and with so much sincerity that she almost couldn't breathe, echoed in her mind. Her heart went ice cold. "No, Mom," she said, turning to leave. "We weren't serious at all."

⁓

After a long, sleepless night, Hunter found himself right back at his parents'. He sat on his bike, looking at the grand house again. All night he'd grappled with what to do. Call Britt and try to talk to her again? No. She'd made it clear she didn't want to see him. Even now as he stared at the abundant tulips that lined the circular drive—something he hadn't noticed last night—his chest felt like a brick had been dropped on it. What he'd feared would happen had come true. She could forgive her father and overlook his past. *But she can't forgive me.*

He did call someone else, though. Andrew, his sponsor. After he left Maude's, he called an Uber to pick him up at the end of the block, then had the driver drop him off at one of the bars he used to frequent before his last illegal escapade. He didn't know the bartender, or anyone else in the place. He wasn't focused on that either. There was only one thing he wanted, other than Britt.

"Gin and tonic," Hunter said as he sat on a stool. The place was off the beaten path, and even though it was Saturday night, there were only a few people there. "Hold the tonic."

The gruff bartender nodded and poured him two shots of gin, then walked away.

Hunter picked up the glass and stared at the transparent liquid. Sniffed it. All he had to do was down it in one gulp. *Just to dull the pain . . .*

He set down the drink. Threw some money on the bar and walked outside. His hands shook as he dialed Andrew's number.

He answered it on the first ring. "Hey, Hunter," Andrew said. "Haven't heard from you in a while. How are things going?"

Gravel crunched under his expensive rental shoes as he paced. "Not good. Can you come get me?"

For the next two hours, he and Andrew talked over coffee at a twenty-four-hour pancake house, and by the time Andrew had dropped him off at his apartment, Hunter was set to rights. He still craved a drink, but he'd made too much progress to slide backward now.

Andrew had also reminded him of one of his steps—making amends. Something he hadn't done yet with his parents.

He yanked off his helmet and hung it over one of the handlebars. No one around here would steal his helmet or his old bike. They probably wouldn't be caught dead with either one. He got off the bike and headed to the door. His parents were usually home on Sunday afternoons, and he had to apologize for last night.

He shoved his hand through his uncombed hair and rang the doorbell. He probably should have showered and shaved before he left his apartment, but once he'd made the decision to apologize, he didn't want to put it off. When he didn't get an answer, he rang it again.

Finally, the door opened. Sue, his parents' live-in cook, looked at him with surprise then blanked her features to neutral. As always, she was wearing her chef's uniform—a grayish-blue short-sleeved top with offset black buttons and black pants. Their regular housekeeper must be off today.

She peered at him over silver-rimmed glasses. "Can I help you?"

While her expression was detached, he could sense her disapproval. "Are Mother and Father home?"

"Are they expecting you?"

"No."

She glanced over her shoulder, then looked at him again. "I have strict orders not to let you in."

He grimaced. "I was here last night for Father's party."

"I didn't see you."

"I didn't go into the kitchen," he said. "And I was only here for a short while."

After she studied him for a moment, undoubtedly trying to gauge whether he was lying to her or not, her rigid demeanor eased a little and she opened the door all the way. "I'll tell them you're here."

"Thanks." Hunter followed her inside but stopped in the foyer as she continued farther into the house. He didn't see a single indication that there had been a huge party the night before. Everything was spotless and pristine, like his parents' houses always were. He could remember living in a very modest house when he was little, but it was just as immaculate. Kirk and Payne had always been neat and organized, while Hunter had been grounded numerous times for being messy. He continued to be, up until his arrest. Being in jail had knocked the sloppiness right out of him.

His phone was in his pocket, and he resisted pulling it out. Last night he kept checking his messages, praying that Britt had changed her mind and wanted to talk to him again. She hadn't, and he didn't want to be thinking about her right now. It hurt too much. But he couldn't stop either. He couldn't turn off his feelings like a light switch. Painful confirmation that he really loved her.

But once he was over her—*if* he got over her—he was never falling in love again. He was better off being alone than going through this misery.

The rhythmic click of his mother's dainty heels on the marble floor thankfully brought him out of his thoughts. As she neared, his stomach dropped at her ominous visage. She stopped a few feet from him. He didn't have to suspect her disapproval. It was all over her face.

"You have a lot of nerve coming here after disappearing last night," she said, her harsh gaze meeting his. "You never even told your father happy birthday."

"I know. And I'm here to apologize—"

"Don't bother. You never meant it in the past." Surprisingly, her chin started to tremble. "Kirk and Payne warned me not to invite you, that you would be undependable as always. But I didn't listen. I believed your father when he said tough love would work on you. I thought you'd changed. Sawyer—"

"What about Sawyer?"

She looked away.

"Mother," he said, a cold sensation washing over him. "What about Sawyer?"

Her gaze returned, filled with self-righteousness. "He's been keeping me updated on your *progress*. Which you've proven is no progress at all."

He stilled, remembering when Sawyer had been on the phone and was cagey about answering Hunter's innocuous questions. He'd thanked someone for their generous check. It never dawned on him that it was from Mother.

More pieces fell into place. Sawyer's constant interest in Hunter's sobriety, which Hunter had thought was done out of friendship. But it was only because his mother had bought him off. He'd always thought it was strange that Sawyer, whose parents were almost as rich as his own, was fine living in a nondescript apartment and working second shift at The Warehouse. The same shift Hunter worked. "You paid Sawyer to spy on me?"

"Yes." Her lower lip quivered, but she remained defiant. "I had to know if you were okay. And I won't apologize for it. The only thing I regret is inviting you last night. Obviously, you've been hiding your true self from Sawyer."

Hunter couldn't believe this. Not only had she spied on him, but she automatically assumed he'd vanished last night out of irresponsibility. His hands balled into fists at his sides. She was snapping to judgment without all the facts.

He was ready to bolt. He didn't need this, and he didn't need them. Five more steps and he'd be out of their super mansion and their lives . . . forever.

But his feet wouldn't move. Deep inside, he understood his mother's reaction, and up until this moment he'd never fully acknowledged the damage he'd done to their relationship. In the past he'd always been too sloshed or hungover to take responsibility. It was always everyone else's fault things went south, even though it was his decisions that mucked everything up. He'd disappointed her so many times, no wonder she was angry. She'd given him another chance, and he'd blown it.

Slowly he faced her, his fists loosening, his shoulders sagging. "I'm sorry," he said, facing her. "I messed up last night more than you realize."

Her mouth tightened.

"But it's not what you think. Sawyer's right. I'm clean, sober, and since I got out of prison, responsible. I don't ever want to go back to jail again, and the only way I can stay out is to stay away from my vices. All of them.

"That woman you mentioned last night, the one you said looked like Audrey Hepburn?" At her nod he said, "She's my girlfriend. Was . . ."

"Daniel's daughter?" Shock registered on her face. "How—"

"It's a long story." He swallowed. "She didn't know about my family or my past. I hadn't told her yet."

"And she found out last night."

"Yeah. It ended up being a mess, and she broke up with me." He scrubbed a hand over his face, exhaustion from the emotional merry-go-round he'd been riding for almost twenty-four hours finally settling in.

"Oh, Hunter." She went to him and pulled him into her arms.

He leaned down and rested his chin on her slim shoulder. Despite the awkward height difference, he closed his eyes, soaking in her soothing embrace. When was the last time his mother had hugged him? For sure before he was a teenager. He'd started holding her at arm's length back then.

"I'm so sorry." She rubbed his back the way she used to do when he was little.

His eyelids stung, and he knew if he didn't let go, he'd start to cry and that was the last thing he wanted to do, period. He carefully moved out of her embrace. "That's why I left last night. I had to explain everything to her . . . including my past." His chest felt hollow. "I should have been honest with her up front."

"Yes, you should have." She started twisting her diamond solitaire, something she always did when she was uneasy. "And I shouldn't have spied on you. Or at least I should have let you know that I asked Sawyer to look out for you. Don't be upset with him. He didn't want to. But I can be very persuasive."

"I'm sure the money helped," he said, unable to keep the bitterness out of his tone.

"From what I understand, he's using it to pay for college. He didn't want to ride on his parents' coattails. His mother said he's always been independent and different from the rest of their family."

"Sounds familiar." He managed a slight smile. "Is Father home? I want to wish him a belated birthday."

Mother smiled and put her arm around his waist. "He's in his study. I told him you were here, but that I needed to talk to you first."

They walked to the other side of the house where the study was. When Hunter stood in the doorway, his father got up from his desk. Immediately Hunter engulfed him in a huge hug.

"Happy birthday, Dad."

He hugged Hunter tightly. "Thank you, son."

When they parted, Hunter grinned. "We've got a lot of catching up to do."

⁓

Three weeks after the Picketts' party, Daniel was waxing their cars again. More than ever, he was grateful for their air-conditioned garage. The July heat was brutal, and today's temp was supposed to reach ninety-five degrees. Even though he'd lived in Texas all his life, he never liked the summers.

He was almost done waxing the Jag when his phone buzzed. He pulled it out, expecting it to be Arthur. Since he and Lila had reconciled with Hunter, the man had been in a nonstop good mood. Just last week Daniel had joined them for a round of golf at the country club. The lines between employer and friend were starting to blur, and Daniel was okay with that.

Still, he had to wonder if Arthur had noticed Hunter's underlying melancholy. Daniel didn't know him well, but maybe he was attuned to it because he and Hunter struggled with addiction, and he knew what it was like to lose someone you loved because of it. Then there was the awkwardness of Daniel being Brittany's dad, although Hunter didn't seem to hold it against him. None of that seemed to affect his game either—he'd easily blown out both his father and Daniel on the course.

But Arthur's name wasn't on his phone screen. Amy's was.

Daniel frowned. Brittany must have given her his number, since he and Amy hadn't talked since the night of the party. Before it went to voicemail, he quickly answered it.

"What took you so long?"

He sighed at her sharp tone. "Hello to you too, Amy."

She paused. "Sorry. You don't understand how difficult it is for me to call you."

Oh, he had a good enough idea.

"Have you talked to Britt lately?" she asked, still sounding edgy.

"A few times. Just texts, though." He set the waxing cloth on the cart.

"There's something wrong with her, Daniel. She won't talk to me. She spends all her time in her room or her studio and she's barely eating. She hasn't uploaded a video in weeks."

Daniel had noticed that too, but he wasn't completely familiar with his daughter's posting schedule.

"I wouldn't have called you, but it's your boss's son's fault she's like this."

"Ba— Amy . . ." Wow, he'd almost called her *babe*. When they were married, he'd used that endearment more often than he'd called her by name. "She's nursing a broken heart. Give her some time and space."

"You don't know her like I do," Amy snapped.

He prayed for patience, knowing that barking back at her would end the conversation. While he didn't like that Brittany was suffering, at least Amy was speaking to him. "You're right. I don't."

"We have to help her," she continued. "I . . . can't stand to see her like this."

"Me either." And he was concerned. "I'm new to this father thing, Amy. I'm not sure what to do."

She didn't answer, and Daniel thought she might have hung up on him. Then she said, "Meet me for supper tonight at Harvey's. And no, they don't have karaoke anymore."

He frowned. "I haven't sung karaoke since our divorce." Too many embarrassing memories. And they were all on him.

"Maybe together we can come up with a solution. Six thirty sharp. Don't be late."

"Okay," he said, and she ended the call. She didn't exactly hang up on him, but she didn't say goodbye either.

Daniel picked up the waxing cloth and returned to work on the Jaguar. He had approximately five hours before meeting Amy. Hopefully that would be enough time to come up with something to help his daughter.

Chapter 25

Hunter drove past K&Bs three times before finally deciding to park his bike in the lot. He was disappointed Britt's car wasn't there, but he was also a little relieved. He hadn't gotten the first-shift job, so Monday was still his only day off. For the past three weeks he'd been living in a weird limbo of watching her videos, wanting to reach out to her, and changing his mind. He even tried being mad at her for cutting him off at the knees and shutting him out. But whatever anger he had didn't last long. He'd made the mistake of not being forthright with her and he had to live with that.

But what he couldn't live with was not knowing if she was okay. She hadn't uploaded a new video or replied to comments on her most recent ones in almost a month. He'd given up texting her, figuring she'd probably blocked his number by now. He couldn't go to her house and try to talk to her, even though he knew where she lived now. She—or more likely, her mother—might call the cops on him for trespassing, and he couldn't afford to have that happen.

An hour ago, he checked her channel again. She'd taken it down. He'd lost his last connection with her. That's why he was at K&Bs. Hopefully Maude and X could at least let him know if Britt was all right.

Hunter walked into the store, trying to tamp down the nervous energy running through him. He wasn't surprised that it was empty. It was Monday, after all. He inhaled the sweet scent of vanilla and . . . ginger? Cinnamon? Whatever it was, it smelled like a snickerdoodle. Maude must have taken over X's diffuser today.

They were both behind the front counter, their eyes wide as they stared at him. *Uh-oh.* Maybe he shouldn't have come. Maude and X would be protective of Britt, just like Daniel was. That's why Hunter hadn't asked him about her, although the guy was cordial to him during their golf game. No matter what, Daniel would be on Britt's side. Hunter would feel the same way if he had a daughter.

Maude's shocked expression disappeared as she bustled out from behind the counter and went to him. "Hello, Hunter," she said, without her usual enthusiasm. X appeared behind her, looking hesitant.

"Uh, hi." Clearly, he shouldn't have come. "Have you, um, seen Britt lately?"

"Yes."

He blew out a relieved breath. "Is she okay?"

"No."

His stomach sank to his knees. "I guess you heard everything."

"She told us."

"Then you know I'm a recovering alcoholic and drug user with a prison record—" He stopped talking as X's and Maude's eyes grew to the size of saucers.

"Um, no," she said.

"Britt never mentioned that," X added.

Hunter squeezed his eyes shut. Now they probably wouldn't ever let him back in the store. He opened his eyes and looked at them. "I'll be going now—"

"Hunter." Maude put her hand on his arm. Then she glanced at X before shoving her hand inside her bra.

"Uh . . ." Hunter said.

"There it is." She withdrew a gold coin and showed it to him. The number thirty was engraved in the middle, along with the words "one day at a time."

A sobriety coin. The program he'd gone through at church didn't give out coins, but he'd seen them before. Some of the participants had been through other sobriety programs and had relapsed, but they still carried around their coins.

"You're among friends here." She shoved the coin back in her bra. "I like to keep this close to my heart."

The tension eased from his body as X nodded his approval. "Have you tried to reach Britt?"

"She's not answering my calls. Or texts." Hunter shoved his hands into his shorts pockets.

Maude fiddled with her glasses chain and glanced at X again. He gave her a single nod and slipped away. Then she motioned for Hunter to follow her to the front. When they reached the counter, she went behind it and faced him. "Do you love Britt?"

"Yes," he said emphatically.

"Then why aren't you fighting for her?"

Her blunt question caught him off guard. "If I could, I would," he answered honestly, then shook his head. "I'm the one who messed up here."

"I think there's some blame on both sides, Hunter."

"But—"

"Do you want her back or not?"

Hope suddenly grew in his heart. "Yes. I'd do anything to make that happen."

"Good." She grinned and put on her large red reading glasses. Today's beaded chain colors were red, white, and blue in honor of the Fourth of July, even though the holiday had already passed.

"So," he said as he rubbed his hands together. "What should I do?"

"Nothing."

He stilled. "Come again?"

"Well, almost nothing." She bent down and foraged through some stuff behind the counter. When she stood again, she was holding a pad of drawing paper, a pack of colored pencils, and a ballpoint pen. "You're going to write her a love letter." She slid the supplies toward him.

Hunter eyed the art supplies, doubt creeping in. "I've never been good at writing."

"You don't have to be. Just tell her everything you would say if she were standing right here." Maude pointed to his left. "Don't hold back. When you're finished, give it to me. I'll make sure she gets it and *reads* it."

He touched the colored pencils. "You really think this will work?"

"I have no idea." She clasped her hands together. "But it's worth a try. You're a good man, Hunter."

"I didn't used to be—"

"Stop. Whatever you were in your past, you're not that now. I've seen you with Britt. How you look at her, how she looks at you. Even before you got together there was something special between you. I'm an expert at these things, you know."

"Oh, really." He smirked.

"Britt's changed since you came into her life. She was growing into her own, learning to let go of her fear. You had a lot to do with that. But now she's retreating again, something she does when she's hurt or scared. Will the letter work? Maybe it will get you two talking. Or maybe it won't, and Britt will decide it's easier to hide from life than to live it, even though we all know that's not true. At least you would have given her the chance to decide."

Hunter frowned. He was the one who needed the chance, not her, and she was the one who was refusing to talk to him. But Maude was right, he needed to fight for her. He gathered up the materials. "Can I use the room?"

"Of course."

A few minutes later he was staring at the blank page, the past couple of months rolling through his mind—how much his life had changed since meeting Britt. Not just falling in love with her, although that was the most important thing. He hadn't given in to his instincts to run and drink away his problems when Britt broke up with him, or when he found out about his mother's subterfuge. Instead, he stayed sober and reconciled with his parents. He and Sawyer were cool now, after Hunter told him he knew about his arrangement with Mother and that he understood why he did it.

"Dude, I am so glad this is out in the open now," Sawyer had said, visibly relieved. "I didn't like keeping that secret from you, especially now that we're friends."

Friends. When he'd left prison, he didn't have a single friend left. Now he had Sawyer, Maude, and X. His parents too. He'd always felt like the odd man out, that it was him against the world, although he realized that was just his immature reaction to being different from his family. Even if things didn't work out with Britt, even if he had to carry the pain of losing her for the rest of his life, he wasn't alone anymore.

But he had to fight for her one last time.

He picked up the colored pencils and began his love letter.

⁓

"Sorry I'm late," Daniel said to Amy as he sat down at the table. "Traffic was a mess today."

"Uh-huh." She folded her arms on the table and glowered at him.

"Seriously, you can check the traffic report." He fought to restrain his temper and opened the menu. Was she going to treat him like poo on the bottom of her shoe for the rest of his life? Amy was a passionate woman, and she could hold a grudge. He just wished she wasn't so volatile toward him. "Did you order yet?"

"I'm not hungry."

He snapped the menu shut. "All right, let's get this over with so we don't suffer any longer than necessary."

She flinched, her scowl morphing into surprise.

"I've been thinking all afternoon about what we should do, and there's only one solution." He paused, bracing himself for her inevitable negative reaction. "We both talk to Britt. Together."

"Absolutely not." She uncrossed her arms, her hands closing into balls. "I won't be in the same room with you."

"You already are." He tried to smile, but the bitterness coming off her in waves prevented it. "Look, she needs our support—"

"I'm only talking to you now because Britt won't talk to me, and I need you to tell her to."

He blinked. "What?"

She grabbed a paper napkin and started shredding it. "At least she's communicating with you. Tell her she has to start talking to me."

"Amy—"

"You're going to refuse my one request?" Her voice broke, and she turned her head to the side when the waitress appeared.

"We need a few more minutes," Daniel said.

After the waitress left, Amy glared at him again. "I can't believe this," she said, her eyes filling. "All these years, you were never there for us. I ask you for one simple thing, and you can't even do that."

Guilt almost flattened him. But he stood his ground. "I want to, Amy. I want to do everything I can to make up for abandoning you and Brittany. But I can't tell our daughter what to do and who to talk to."

"Then what good are you!" She jumped up from her chair and rushed out of the restaurant.

Daniel yanked his wallet out of his pocket, threw a few bills on the table, and went after her. She was getting in her car as he reached the parking lot. He ran and blocked her.

"Get out of my way!" She tried to shove him aside.

He didn't move. "Not until you calm down."

"Don't tell me what to do!"

"But you want me to tell Britt what to do."

She halted, staring up at him. Tears dripped down her face. "I—"

He couldn't stop himself from wiping her cheek with his thumb, nearly melting with relief when she didn't stop him. "You're not alone in this anymore, Amy," he whispered. "I'm right here by your side." He pulled her close and wrapped his arms around her.

"I tried my best to be a good mom," she said, weeping against his shoulder.

"You're an amazing mom."

"I'm too overprotective. I worry too much about her. I—"

Daniel shifted her in his embrace so he could see her face. Her beautiful, anguished face. "It's going to be okay, as long as we handle this together. She's never seen us united. Right now, she needs us to be."

There were people filtering through the parking lot, the evening sun blazing down on them, and he was still wearing his chauffeur uniform except for the jacket and tie, and his clothes were sticking to him . . . but neither of them let go of each other, didn't stop gazing into the other's eyes.

Having her in his arms again felt so incredible, so right. How had he been such a fool for so long? He could have been with her all this time, and they would have raised their daughter together.

"Don't," she said, breaking into his thoughts. "Don't beat yourself up."

"You could always read my mind. It's kind of eerie."

"You're an open book . . . when you're sober." She moved out of his arms.

"I plan to stay sober, for the rest of my life."

Amy looked at him. "I think you mean that."

"I do, but it won't be easy." He held her gaze. "I'll have my problems, my temptations. But I will fight them, because I want to be a part of yours and Britt's lives."

"Daniel—"

"I don't expect to be welcomed with open arms, or even forgiven right now. Not until I've proven myself to you and Britt. I'm going to do that for the rest of my life, if that's what it takes."

Amy couldn't move. She was sweating, still crying a little, and emotionally spent. The last several weeks of Britt's silent treatment had taken their toll. She'd tried everything she could to get Britt to open up to her—offering to take her back to counseling, to go on a vacation, to help her with her channel, to mediate things with Savannah—everything except help her get back together with Hunter. That was the last thing Britt needed to do, to go back to the man who had demolished her heart.

Nothing had worked, and that's why she reached out to Daniel. But she hadn't expected him to want to talk to Britt together, or for her to fall apart in his arms, and she hated that she'd given in to her weakness. But even now, as they looked at each other and tried to figure out their next move, her body still tingled from his touch, the faded memories of how much they'd loved each other and the passion they'd shared washing over her in waves.

She couldn't give in to those confusing feelings, but she could agree to Daniel's suggestion. He was right that neither of them should tell Britt what to do. Amy hated when people did that to her. "When should we talk to her?"

Relief appeared in his green eyes. "As soon as we can."

"Right now?"

He nodded. "I'll meet you at the house."

She watched as he turned to leave, then leaned against her car, feeling the hot metal and glass through the thin pink cotton fabric of her T-shirt. Never in a million years did she think she'd be at the point where she needed Daniel's help, or that he would be available and level-headed enough to offer it. And the fact that he was right blew her mind. He was showing shades of the man she'd fallen in love with, before alcohol had taken over his mind and spirit.

She shoved down her thoughts, got in her car, and sped to the house, worrying her bottom lip as she tried to figure out what to say to Britt. What she hadn't revealed to Daniel was that Britt wasn't just giving her the silent treatment and refusing to upload videos. She looked awful. Pale, thin, her hair uncombed and her shirts so stretched out they didn't fit her properly anymore. Even at her worst levels of anxiety, she had taken care of herself. This wasn't just anxiousness. This was depression.

Her teeth clenched as she pulled into the driveway and waited on Daniel, who had always been a careful driver when he wasn't drinking. This was Hunter's fault, and she wanted to give that kid a piece of her mind he'd never forget. How dare he hurt her daughter like this? And once Britt was on her feet again, she would march right over to the Picketts' and tell him exactly how she felt about him.

The engine hummed as she reined in her ire. No matter how much she wanted to put Hunter on blast, she couldn't. For one, it would embarrass Britt. Two, it wouldn't do any good. Hunter Pickett couldn't care less what Amy thought about him.

Other than him being incredibly good-looking, Amy didn't understand how Britt could fall for him. He was cocky, manipulative, a troublemaker, and a huge flirt. The short time he'd been in her class she'd seen the female students fawning over him, and he had basked in their adoration, but only if they were pretty. The plain and unattractive girls he ignored. Now that he was a grown man, he was even more stunning. And while Amy thought Britt was lovely, she wasn't a typically beautiful woman. Coupled with her anxiety issues . . . What drew him to her? Was it a conquest? A joke?

Amy pressed the heel of her hand against her forehead, kicking herself for thinking Britt couldn't attract an exceptionally attractive man on her own merits. But Hunter wasn't an upstanding man. If he were, he wouldn't have hurt her so deeply.

Daniel pulled up beside her and got out of his car. Together they went inside.

"She's probably in her room," Amy said as they entered the foyer. "I'll get her."

"Amy."

She turned, disturbed by the uncertainty on his face. "What, you changed your mind?"

"No. We're going to talk to her. But I have to tell you something first."

Amy faced him, baffled.

"I've been trying to figure out the best way to say this." He frowned. "Or if I should tell you at all. But there's been too many secrets floating around lately. And if you found out that I knew—"

"Know what, Daniel? Just say it."

Hesitant, he nodded. "Hunter has a past. Similar to mine."

Her eyes widened. "He's an alcoholic?"

"Yeah. He's also got a record."

"I knew it." She threw up her hands. "I knew he was no good. Does Britt know?"

"She does, but—"

"Then thank God she's out of that relationship." She exhaled with relief.

"Amy, they might get back together. Hunter cares about Britt. In fact, he loves her. I doubt he'll give up on her so easily."

She couldn't believe what she was hearing. "You're taking his side? Of course you are. You're both the same."

Anger flashed in his eyes. "No, we're not."

"And he's going to hurt her over and over again," she continued, ignoring his words. "Just like you hurt me."

"Amy, just listen—"

"No! There's nothing you can say that will make any difference. And if Hunter Pickett dares step foot on my property, I'm calling the cops. He's not coming anywhere near my daughter."

Daniel exploded. "You haven't changed a bit, have you? Jumping to conclusions, swinging your anger like a baseball bat, closing off your mind to anything you don't want to hear. I bet you don't even remember how many times I tried to sober up, tried to do better. But it was never enough. I never made enough money, I didn't do enough around the house—"

"You didn't! You were always drinking, Daniel. Except for the first couple years of our marriage, you were never sober."

"That's not true," he insisted.

"You were too drunk to remember!"

"I—"

"STOP IT!"

They both turned to see Britt standing in the hall, her body shaking.

"Stop . . . fighting . . ." She burst into tears and sank to the floor.

Chapter 26

Britt sat on the couch in the living room, staring at her lap, unmoving. She couldn't bring herself to look at her parents or even tug on her shirt hem. It was bad enough she put her channel on private. Ever since the Picketts' party, she wasn't motivated to do anything, especially art. But she was getting so many DMs and questions in the comments of her videos, she had to do something. She was losing ad revenue, but she felt she had no choice.

And now her parents were fighting again. Shame filled her as she sniffed back more tears. Hearing her parents fight like they had when she was a child had kicked her into the past, when she would cry herself to sleep at night while they had World War III in the other room. After all this time, nothing had changed. They were still at each other's throats, and she was still that little girl who couldn't hold in her tears.

"Britt," Mom said, her voice sounding thick. "Please. Talk to us."

Us. Hearing her mother say that word was strange. The fact her parents were in the same room together not battling right now was a miracle. And she knew why. They were worried about her.

She was worried about herself.

Britt didn't like ignoring her mother, but Mom had been overwhelming ever since the night of the party. Hovering and smothering, and the only way to stop her was not to engage. At least her father sent her minimal texts, like *hi* and *thinking of you.* Britt managed to respond to those with one-word answers. Maude too.

Hunter had completely stopped texting her. No surprise since Britt refused to answer him. She couldn't seem to do anything, including work. Every time she thought about art it brought Hunter to mind, squeezing her heart until she was sure it would burst. Then there was Savannah, whom she hadn't heard from at all.

She'd lost her boyfriend, her best friend, and if she didn't get it together, she would lose her job. But she didn't care. She was falling down an abyss and she didn't know how to stop.

"Brittany," Dad said. "Your mother and I want to help you."

The calm concern in his voice compelled her to look at him. "I don't think I can be helped," she said, her voice so tiny she could barely hear it.

"Oh, honey," Mom said. "Sure you can. This is just a small setback—"

"Small?" Britt's eyes narrowed. "My life is a wreck, Mom. How can you call that small?"

"I didn't mean . . ." She turned to Dad, silently pleading.

Then he did something that shocked Britt to the core. He took Mom's hand. Even more unbelievable, she didn't shake him off. "Regardless of our relationship, we both love you. I know I have a long way to go before you fully trust me, but your mother has always been here for you, and no matter what happens, she always will be. We both will."

Britt wiped her weepy eyes with the back of her forearm. "It hurts so much."

"I know." Mom grabbed a tissue and blew her nose. "A broken heart is the worst."

Dad winced.

"I wish I'd never met him." She'd said the words over and over in her mind, but this was the first time she'd spoken them out loud. "It wasn't worth this."

"Are you sure?" Dad said.

She nodded. But even as her head moved up and down, she had doubts. If things were different, if they weren't from two opposite worlds, maybe they would still be together.

Releasing Mom's hand, he leaned forward. "Have you talked to him?"

Britt shook her head. "I can't."

"Why not?"

Because he's not who I thought he was. "We would never have worked out anyway."

He frowned. "You really think so?"

"C'mon, Dad. You work for his father. You see how they live. They literally have an art gallery in their house. And you've met Hunter. He's gorgeous, smart, charming—"

"Manipulative," Mom muttered.

"He's not like that. He's always been kind and considerate of me. He's also extremely patient, easy to talk to . . ." *And a fantastic kisser.* Her parents didn't need to know about that, though.

Dad and Mom exchanged a look.

"Do you love Hunter?" Mom asked.

Surprised by her question, she wanted to say no. But she couldn't. *No more lies.* "Yes," she whispered. "But it doesn't matter anymore." She got up from the couch and left, heading for her room. While she appreciated their help and that they'd stopped fighting when she asked them to, there was nothing they could do.

Britt went inside her room and perched on the edge of the bed, motionless, staring at her desk. She'd thrown Hunter's portraits away, but they were seared in her memory. She glanced at her closet and saw her maid of honor dress hanging in its garment bag. It had been delivered yesterday. No returns.

Her life had been normal for a few weeks, and she'd been happier than she ever imagined. But taking risks and moving out of her comfort zone had only resulted in pain she couldn't have fathomed.

"Brittany Danielle Branch!"

She jumped at the sound of her name. *Huh?*

"To the window. Now!"

Was that . . . Maude? She got up from the bed and opened her window, the steamy summer air hitting her square on. Sure enough, Maude was in her driveway, holding a megaphone and wearing a brick-red and lemon-yellow flowered caftan. The hot breeze caused the hem to flutter around her ankles.

Britt leaned partway out the window. "What are you doing?"

She brought the megaphone up to her mouth. "Getting your attention."

Mom and Dad came outside, looking confused and alarmed. "What's going on?" Mom demanded.

Maude turned to her, still talking through the megaphone. "I have a special announcement—"

Mom held her ears while Dad took the megaphone from Maude.

"Sorry." Maude held up a letter. "I have a special delivery for Brittany Danielle Branch."

"You could have put it in the mailbox," Dad said, looking up at Britt.

"Oh no." Maude's voice was plenty loud as she shook her head, her glasses bouncing on her chest. "I have to hand deliver this to her, and she has to read it in my presence."

"I have a doorbell, you know." Mom was also gazing up at the open window.

Maude ignored them and stepped forward, staring straight at Britt. "Would you have answered the door and talked to me?"

Britt paused. Shook her head.

"Exactly." She took the megaphone from Dad and resumed using it. "I'm going to stand out here in the blazing heat until I hand you this letter and you read it."

"Good grief." Britt shut the window and hurried to the door. Maude would keep her word and probably end up having a heat stroke in the process. When she went outside, Mom was trying to talk sense into her.

"You're going to melt, Maude," she said, glancing around. "And then there are the neighbors."

"Are they still nosy?" Dad asked.

"Only Mrs. Dalton across the street, but she stays inside on hot days like this."

Britt walked over to Maude and took the letter. "Fine. I'll read it later."

Maude pointed the megaphone at her, but Dad whisked it away again.

"I'll keep this safe for you," he said, putting it behind his back.

"How about you two go into the kitchen." Mom smiled, although it was a little off. "I'll fix some iced tea, and you and Maude can visit."

"Marvelous idea." Maude headed toward the door, then looked at Britt over her shoulder and motioned for her to follow. "C'mon, sweetie," she said to Britt. "Your letter awaits."

⌒

"That will be twenty-two dollars."

Daniel pulled out a twenty and a five and handed it to the young woman behind the ticket counter. After she gave him the white tickets with purple print and his change, he turned to give one to Amy.

She snatched it out of his hand. "I don't know why I let you talk me into this. We should be at home."

He hid a smile, wondering if she realized what she was saying and how it sounded. "We need to give them some time alone." Once Britt and Maude had gone inside the house—that woman was quite a character—he'd ushered Amy to his car and told her they were going to the movies. After some expected back and forth, she got into the passenger's seat in a huff and didn't speak to him the entire way to the Mango Movieplex, nearly a thirty-minute ride. She also didn't argue with him when they arrived, just got out of the car and followed him to the ticket counter.

"Don't you want to know who the letter is from?" she asked. "What it says?"

He guided her to the snack counter. "It's none of our business. Popcorn?"

She rolled her eyes. "Oh, all right."

"Two small popcorns, two Cokes, and one Junior Mints."

"I didn't ask for Junior Mints," Amy said.

"You can eat them later." He turned to her as the concession attendant filled their order. "You need a distraction, or you'll fret about the situation all night."

They got their refreshments and headed for the show. Amy stopped him when they reached the theater door. "You know this is a rom-com, right?"

He glanced at his ticket. *Wrong Way, Cupid.* "Wait, I thought I asked for *Jack Robin: Pirate Mercenary.*"

Amy scoffed. "What a stupid title."

"You think *Wrong Way, Cupid* is better?"

"No, but I think I see the confusion." She pointed at the sign. "This is theater six, Jack what's-his-face is theater seven."

"Maybe we can trade tickets—"

"It's almost starting." She grabbed his hand, and they marched inside. Previews were playing on the screen, although there were only four people in the theater. That wasn't a good sign. Exactly how bad was this movie?

Armed with her Junior Mints, she led him to the middle of the theater, and they sat down just as the movie started. Ten minutes in, he knew it was going to be terrible—one of those movies where every joke was lame and nothing surprising happened.

"We should have traded in our tickets," Amy whispered, after one of the characters literally slipped on a banana peel. At least the Cupid character was wearing shorts instead of a diaper, but he was still hauling around a mini golden bow. "Sorry."

"It's okay." He dug into his popcorn and tried to focus on the movie. But even if it had been a masterpiece, he wouldn't have been able to pay attention. He was wondering about Britt, although he felt a little better after talking to her. His baby girl was hurting, but the way she had defended Hunter to Amy gave him some hope that the two of them would figure things out. She loved him, and he knew Hunter cared about her. They just had to get talking again. Maybe Maude could facilitate that.

But Britt was only in the back of his mind. Right now, his senses were filled with salty popcorn and Amy's vanilla-scented perfume. He kept looking at her, smiling when she chuckled at a dumb joke. Ironically, for an intelligent woman, she'd always enjoyed lousy comedy, which made him think her apology was for his benefit more than hers.

Suddenly the film shut off, and the lights came on. An usher jogged to the front. "Excuse me," he yelled to the six people in the theater. "We're having projector problems, but we'll have them fixed real soon. Just hang tight, y'all." He ran back up the outer aisle.

"Now what?" Amy slumped in the chair. "I was actually enjoying the show."

"I know." He grinned.

She turned to him. "I bet you're hating every minute of it."

"Pretty much." But he liked watching her having fun.

"How do you think Britt is doing?" She reached for her purse. "I should text her—"

He took her hand and threaded his fingers through it. Yeah, he was taking advantage of the moment, but he was also trying to keep her from bothering Britt.

Amy glanced at their clasped hands. "Point taken. You can let go now."

Daniel angled his body toward her. "Do I have to?"

She didn't move, her luminous eyes on his. Then she disengaged her hand. "I can't, Daniel."

"Can't what?"

"Let down my guard with you." She stared at the blank screen.

He faced the front. Neither one of them spoke or touched their food. Minutes ticked by and the four other people left the theater, leaving the two of them alone.

"Amy?"

After a moment she said, "Yes?"

He had to tread carefully with his next question, but he couldn't hold back from asking it. "Why didn't you get married again?"

Amy kept her gaze on the screen, unable to look at Daniel. She supposed this question would have come up eventually, especially if he ended up being true to his word and stayed sober, engaged, and dependable. But she didn't believe he would. He'd made so many promises, had let her down so many times. What made this time any different?

He's different. She couldn't deny that. He wasn't the unsettled, insecure, and at times fearful man she'd married. To be fair, he hadn't been any of those things before they tied the knot. They were young, but he had confidence back then. Swagger even, but in a good way. *A sexy way.* Then he changed, and everything went careening downhill.

"It was never enough. I never made enough money, I didn't do enough around the house . . ."

His words slammed into her as they resurfaced. They got married when she was in college, and he was working part-time as a mechanic, learning on the job. Then she was pregnant with Britt and trying to make straight As, like she had all her life. She was exhausted and working so hard, while he seemed to barely do the minimum.

The fighting started. The hurtful words said in anger on both sides. The visits to the bar, the cases of beer and bottles of liquor that kept appearing . . . and disappearing.

But when Britt was born, he was a new man. So attentive, so sweet. She still had a picture of their tiny girl lying on his bare chest while they both slept on the couch. Why she kept it, she didn't know. Those were the good times. But they didn't last.

More memories surfaced. Her working on her master's while she was teaching full time. Britt going to daycare. Daniel still in a dead-end job and drinking again. The fights were epic back then. Eventually the only thing keeping their marriage together were the sizzling ways they would make up, and even that had ground to a halt by the time Britt was in kindergarten.

"Never mind," he mumbled, breaking into her thoughts. "I shouldn't have asked."

She looked at him. He was fiddling with the popcorn kernels in the box on his lap but not eating any of them. All these years she had blamed him for failing her and Britt. But she'd never taken responsibility for her part in the destruction of their marriage. She never gave him enough credit or encouragement. But she sure was generous with the criticism.

"No," she said softly. "I'm the one who's sorry, Daniel." His eyes widened so fast she almost smiled. "I made a lot of mistakes too."

"Amy—"

"I contributed to our problems, but made you out to be the sole villain. I shouldn't have done that."

He took her hand in his. "Let's make a promise to each other, okay? We don't look back, only forward."

She nodded, and the lights dimmed again, Cupid and his white shorts appearing on the screen. She glanced at their entwined hands again. This time, she didn't let go.

~

"You've been staring at that envelope for ten minutes, Britt."

She lifted her gaze from what she was sure was Hunter's handwriting and looked at Maude, who was on her second glass of iced tea. At least her face wasn't beet red anymore. What a crazy thing to do, hollering through a megaphone to get her to read a letter. "Where's Mom and Dad?" she said, moving to rise from the chair. "They haven't come inside yet."

"I'm sure those completely *grown* adults have figured out

something else to do." Maude tapped the letter. "Quit procrasti-nating. I made a promise."

"To Hunter?"

Maude paused, then nodded.

"So you've seen him? Did he stop by the store?" Her curiosity was getting the best of her. "Did he look—" She bit her lip.

"Yes, I've seen him, yes he stopped by the store—to check on you, young lady—and yes, he looked as scrumptious as ever, although quite sleep deprived."

A butterfly faintly fluttered in her stomach, then disappeared. She didn't want to worry about him, or think about his scrump-tiousness, if that was even a word.

"Britt," Maude said, a touch of fatigue in her voice. "Just read the letter so I can go back to X. He's making pot roast tonight, and I'm partial to those little potatoes he cooks with the meat."

She nodded, not wanting to come between Maude and her spuds. She picked up the envelope. "I have to read this in front of you?"

"That's the deal. Silently—although I wouldn't mind if you read it out loud—"

"I'll read it to myself." Her fingers shook as she flipped open the flap and pulled out the letter, which wasn't a traditional letter at all, but several lists.

What I Like About You
- The way your eyes sparkle when you smile.
- How you stick out your tongue just a tiny bit when you're concentrating.
- Your art, from A-Z. Everything you create is amazing.
- You smell really, really nice.
- Your hair. Just . . . wow.

She caught herself smiling, then glanced up to see Maude giving her a sly grin. She shot her a pinched look and continued reading.

How You Make Me Feel
- Excited (yes, in all ways!).

Britt blushed.

- Comfortable. I can be myself around you.
- Warm. Inside and out.
- Capable. I feel like I can do anything with you by my side.
- Love. I feel love.

Her heart hitched. The last list had only one item.

What I Want
- You, Britt. In case you haven't figured it out yet, I'm so into you, and always will be.
  I love you, H.
  P.S. Excuse the drawings. I'm missing my art lessons.
  P.P.S. Please give me another chance.

She looked at the next three pages. One was a beach scene, and he'd executed it perfectly, the combinations of colors and shading bringing the sea to life. Floating on the waves were two stick figures on surfboards, their stick arms touching each other where their hands would be. She hadn't taught him how to draw people yet. She couldn't help but chuckle. He'd sketched a heart around the couple and wrote *Hunter <3 Britt.*

She folded the letter, put it back in the envelope, and gave it back to Maude.

"What are you doing?" Maude pushed it back at her.

"I don't want it," she lied.

The woman looked like her head was going to explode. "That boy wrote you a whole bunch of sweet nothings—"

"How do you know?" Britt asked. "Did you read it?"

"Of course not. I could tell he did by your expressions while you were reading. The twinkle in your eye, the smile on your face . . . You're trying to hide how much you care about him. And, I might add, you're not succeeding. At all."

Britt got up from her chair. "You don't understand."

"What's there to understand? You two love each other. Why are you letting a misunderstanding tear your relationship apart? Unless you're using that as an excuse to push him away. You are, aren't you?" She got up from her chair and went to her.

Britt faced Maude, trying to keep her chin up. "He's turning his life around."

"That's a good thing, Britt."

"He's going back to college, and he'll do well. He'll find his path, and he'll have the resources, intelligence, and ambition to succeed."

"Don't you want that for him?"

"Yes," she said, her throat tight. "More than anything. But he'll end up getting bored with me, tired of my issues—"

"Or he'll love and cherish you for who you are." She peered at Britt. "What are you truly afraid of?"

Everything. But that wasn't totally true. Over the past couple months she'd discovered there were plenty of things in her life and the world that she wasn't afraid of.

Maude patted her cheek. "When you figure it out, you'll know what to do." She collected her megaphone and held it up. "From my cheerleading days. Those taters are calling my name, Britt. See you soon."

She watched her leave, then sat back down at the table, looking at Hunter's letter. Maude obviously left it on purpose.

Britt pulled it out again. Reread it several times. Looked at the adorable picture he drew. *He's so perfect.*

Her head shot up. No, he wasn't perfect. He had problems and issues. Big ones, actually. *Just like me.* She'd put him on a pedestal, one he never asked or wanted to be on. And even though he hadn't told her about his past or his family, she'd held things back from him too. They were more alike than different.

They were also better together.

She got out her phone, texted Dad, then waited a few minutes for a response. When he didn't text her back, she didn't panic. There was time for them to talk. She hurried to her bedroom, grabbed some clean clothes, and went to the bathroom, catching a glimpse of her neglected self in the mirror. No more wallowing. No more excuses.

She was going to start living again.

~

By Thursday, Hunter had given up on hearing from Britt. He had to figure out how to regroup, but he wasn't sure how. He'd deleted YouTube from his phone, even though she hadn't put her channel back up. That was a start. But it didn't keep him from thinking about her, wanting her, wishing for her to come back.

Before his shift started, he'd enrolled in a Business 101 fall class at the local community college. He almost didn't do it, but then realized he had to keep moving forward with his life. He had come too far to turn back or fall off the wagon. He was returning to school because he wanted to, not because it was expected of him by his parents or anyone else.

He finished moving a tall stack of pallets with the forklift. Time to go on break. He turned off the machine and jumped down, and he was heading for the break room when Sawyer came up behind him, putting his arm around his neck.

"What's up, my dude?" he said, a huge grin on his face.

"On my way to get a Coke. You want one?" For some reason Sawyer was turning him in the opposite direction of the break room. "Hey, what's going on——" He froze as he saw an adorable woman with curly black hair approaching them, wearing a yellow and orange safety vest over a powder-blue T-shirt and white shorts, her hands behind her back. "Britt?"

Sawyer's arm slipped from Hunter's shoulders. "She's all yours."

He looked at his friend. "How did she get in here?"

"I pulled some strings. I kind of owe ya." He clapped Hunter on the back. "Don't blow it this time." He took off.

Hunter started to run to Britt, then slowed down, trying to keep his cool. She could be here to read him the riot act for all he knew.

She suddenly stopped a few feet in front of him and whipped out a megaphone. "Attention, everyone!"

He startled. What in the world?

"I have an announcement to make."

"Britt," Hunter said. He glanced around. The entire floor had stopped working and was gathering around, staring at them. Her worst nightmare.

The megaphone wobbled a little in her hand, but she stood firm. "Hunter Pickett . . ." Her eyes widened slightly as she took in the number of people looking in her direction. But she closed them briefly before meeting his gaze again. "I love you."

She loves me. His heart soared as he scooped her up in his arms and held her tight. Applause broke out around them. Then he set her on the ground, soaking in her bright, beautiful, *relaxed* smile. "How did you do this?" he said, still holding her close.

"I asked Dad to talk to Lila, and she talked to Sawyer, and he made it happen." She tightened her hold on his waist. "I'm so sorry, Hunter. I shouldn't have pushed you away. But I was afraid I'd lose you."

"And I was afraid of losing you." He looked around again. "FYI, everyone's watching us."

She nodded, keeping her eyes on him. But she wasn't completely at ease, and he could feel her trembling in his arms.

He held her tighter. "We could have met at K&Bs, or your house, or my apartment. You didn't have to do this in front of anyone."

"Yes, I did." She lifted her chin. "I wanted you to know I'm not hiding anything from you, especially my feelings."

His heart warmed, and his fingers brushed against the curl resting against her cheek.

"I needed to do this for myself too," she continued. "I can't promise I won't be nervous or anxious or even scared at times, but I'm not going to hide anymore."

Impressed with her determination, he said, "And I can't promise I won't struggle either. It's one day at time for me, and it always will be."

"I know." She smiled. "But we'll be there for each other. We don't have to go through any of it alone."

He touched his forehead to hers. "You know what this means,

though." At her questioning look, he whispered, "I'm never letting you go."

"You better not."

"Kiss her already," Sawyer hollered.

"Gotta do what the man says." He smiled, bending down to kiss her. And when she kissed him back, he knew she was his forever.

Chapter 27

"Y ou may now kiss the bride."

Britt beamed as Justin moved Savannah's veil from her face and sweetly kissed her. She felt Hunter's hand close over hers as they sat behind the bride's family. After the pastor pronounced them husband and wife, she waved as the happy couple passed by them. When Savannah blew her a kiss, Britt's eyes filled.

Hunter pulled out a handkerchief. "Here," he said, handing it to her.

"Thanks." She dabbed at her eyes, not wanting to mess up her minimal makeup. Right after she'd left Hunter to finish his shift—and after his mind-blowing kiss—she went straight to Savannah's and apologized. Her friend was surprised and forgiving.

"I promise I'll never keep another secret from you again," Britt had said. And she meant it.

Savannah hugged her. "I've already asked Trudy to be my maid of honor."

"It's okay. I understand. Can I still come to the wedding?"

"Of course. I couldn't get married without you being there." They sat down on her parents' plush white leather sofa. "Now, I want all the deets about this Hunter guy."

Britt had given her the "deets," and two days later, she and Hunter met Savannah and Justin for breakfast at Yo Jo's. Hunter and Justin hit it off right away, and Savannah gave her an enthusiastic two thumbs up.

She had also put her channel back up, and started making videos again, with even more enthusiasm than before. Although it did take her a while to clean up her DMs.

"Britt." Hunter tapped her on the shoulder, pulling her out of her reverie. "Time to go."

She got up from the pew and stepped into the aisle. Mom and Dad were sitting right behind them. Dad winked at her, and Mom gave her a little wave as she blew her nose. Her parents had been spending more and more time together lately, with Dad dropping by the house after work at least three times a week for supper. They still fought occasionally, but more about differences of opinion than anything serious, and they weren't vicious to each other anymore. Britt didn't know what all of it meant, other than it felt like she had a complete family again, and it was wonderful.

Half an hour later she and Hunter walked into the Elegance Ballroom for the reception. Britt had helped with the last-minute decorations, including hand-lettering all the table cards, adding two tiny, entwined gold-leaf wedding rings at the right-hand corner of each one. "Everything looks beautiful," she gushed as more guests filtered into the room.

Hunter agreed, taking her hand. "Do you want to sit down? Or circulate?"

"You know the answer to that." While she had come a long way in overcoming her social anxiety, she would never be a mix-and-mingler.

They found their seats while the hall filled. Finally, Savannah and Justin showed up, and the reception was in full swing.

The bridal party didn't dance, but the DJ hollered for everyone to hit the dance floor. Hunter leaned close to Britt. "Remember our first dance?"

She grinned. "How could I forget?"

He stood and held out his hand to her. "Dance with me. It's been a while since I showed you my sixth-grade moves."

Britt laughed and slipped her hand in his. He led her to the floor, and she easily melted into his arms. Suddenly there was a tap on Hunter's shoulder. He turned around.

Dad was standing there. "May I cut in?"

Hunter nodded and smiled at Britt. "She's all yours."

"I hope I didn't interrupt anything," Dad said, taking her hand as ABBA's "Take A Chance On Me" started to play.

"I can dance with him later."

"True. I don't think he's going anywhere."

"He better not." She smiled. The song was too up-tempo for a slow dance, so they just made up the steps as they went along.

Dad cocked his head. "I haven't heard this song in years," he said above the music.

"I heard it yesterday."

"Where?"

"On my yacht rock playlist." She grinned. "I can share it with you sometime."

They finished up the song, and another slow dance started to play. "I guess I better turn you over to Hunter," Dad said.

"Wait." Britt grabbed his hand, then pulled him into a hug. "I love you, Dad."

He hugged her back, and she thought she heard him sniff. "I love you too, sweetheart."

As if on cue, Hunter appeared, and Dad stepped away.

He drew Britt into his arms. "Everything okay?" he asked.

She watched her father walk to her mother, motioning for her to come with him. Mom smiled and nodded. Britt looked up at Hunter and kissed him. Then she pulled away. "Definitely."

⟍⟍⟋

"Daniel Branch, where are you taking me?" Amy half resisted him grabbing her hand and leading her from the table. Not to the dance floor but, of all places, to the janitor's closet.

He shut the door and turned on the light. "May I have this dance?"

Muted music wafted through the closed door as she looked at the shelves of cleaning supplies and the bucket and mop on the other side of the small space. "How did you find this room?"

"I scoped it out."

"You planned this?" She shook her head, chuckling. "We could just dance on, like, the dance floor."

"But it wouldn't be private." He moved closer to her. "We haven't danced together since our wedding."

Over the past several weeks, they had decided to rekindle the friendship they'd had in high school before they'd fallen in love. It was also a chance for him to earn her trust and for her to give it, although that remained unspoken between them. So far, it was all working out, and her favorite moments were their family dinners, something that had been few and far between when they were married.

She'd also made amends with Max, using Laura as a buffer. She invited both of them and Daniel over for dinner one night, and after apologizing to Max, she made sure he and Laura sat next to each other. When Max walked with her out the door, Laura turned around and mouthed an excited, "Thank you!" The two of them had been dating ever since. Even Daniel congratulated her on a successful match.

But now she and Daniel were alone in the confining closet,

and she couldn't deny she was deeply attracted to him. More so now than when she was younger, and raging hormones had taken control. Now her middle-aged hormones were creating all sorts of other havoc, but that had nothing to do with how her heart was galloping in her chest or her fluttery stomach. Even her toes were curling in her sensible silver low-heeled pumps.

"You didn't answer me." He took one step closer. He'd let his curly hair grow out a bit, and now it was a thick mass of black-and-silver locks that looked oh so good on him. Not to mention his gunmetal gray suit, which happened to go so well with her pale-yellow cotton sundress.

"I didn't?" She moved forward a little, smiling as she looked into his eyes.

"Nope."

Her breath caught as he lightly put his hand on her waist. Then his fingers brushed over her hips until he was touching her lower back.

"Daniel," she whispered.

"Yes?" he answered, his voice husky, low, and sweetly shiver inducing.

She put her arms around his neck. "We could just skip the dance and go on to the fun part."

He grinned, drawing her against him. "Which is?"

The door flew open, jerking them apart. "Oh, *excuse me,*" Maude said, fluttering her eyelashes in faux innocence. "I thought this was the little girl's room."

"It clearly says Maintenance on the door," Daniel groused.

Her eyes widened. "It does? I guess I misread it. I forgot my reading glasses at home."

Amy smirked. "They're hanging around your neck, Maude."

She glanced down. "Silly me."

"You saw us come in here, didn't you?" Amy tried to hide her laughter.

"Perhaps."

"Wait," Amy said. "I didn't know you knew Savannah."

"Any friend of Britt's is a friend of mine and X's. She's a charming young woman who is now learning how to make FIMO beads in my jewelry class." She turned to Daniel. "By the way, no one touches my megaphone and gets away with it."

"So sorry," he said as he started to close the door on her.

"Don't do anything I wouldn't do!"

Click. Daniel faced Amy again. "I'm thinking that's a really short list."

"Like maybe three things."

He took Amy in his arms again, angling his head toward hers. "Now, where were we?"

Her hand shot up between their faces, and his lips landed on her palm.

"Huh?" he said against her skin.

She removed her hand. "I need to tell you something first. Remember when we were at the movies?"

"How could I forget *Wrong Way, Cupid?*"

"Hey, I made up for it," she said. "We saw that Jack Bluebird movie."

"Robin. But go ahead."

Growing serious, she said, "You asked me why I never remarried, and I never answered because I couldn't admit it to myself at the time. I always used Britt or work as an excuse not to start dating again." She touched the collar of his shirt, then moved her fingertips to the side of his neck, playing with the curls resting against it. "But the truth is . . . you were always the one for me, Daniel. Despite everything, you still had my heart."

He took her hand and pressed it against his chest. "And you always had mine. It's why I never remarried either, even after I quit drinking." He kissed her hand. "I love you, Amy. I always have . . . and I always will."

Her heart sang. She'd never thought she'd feel this way again, and she wouldn't have with anyone else. "I love you too."

He kissed her until she was weak. And they didn't leave the closet for a long, *long* time.

~

SEVEN MONTHS LATER

Camera? Check.

Lights? Check.

Sound? Check.

Britt took a deep breath and started her video.

"Hi, friends. Welcome back to my channel, and thanks for watching. Today is a different kind of video because it won't be about art. In fact, it's my last video for the foreseeable future." She shifted in her chair, keeping her eyes on the camera.

"Last year I made a video about taking risks and making changes. I took my own advice, and I'm happy to announce that I'm teaching art classes in person at K&B Art Supplies in Plano, Texas."

"My turn yet?"

She glanced at Hunter, who was sitting next to her in a wheeled chair, his foot tapping on the floor.

Looking back at the camera, she said, "I also want to introduce you to my boyfriend, Hun—"

"Hunter Pickett," he said, sliding into the frame, a gorgeous smile on his face. "I'm the assistant manager at K&Bs, and if you stop in and say 'Britt Branch is the cutest artist ever—'"

"*Hunter!*"

"—you'll get 30 percent off your total purchase."

Her face blooming with heat, she shoved him out of the camera's eye. "Uh, so that's Hunter—"

He leaned over and pecked her cheek, then waved at the camera again. "Bye, y'all." Then he wheeled away from the desk.

She glanced at him, unable to stop laughing. "He's a mess."

"I'm your mess," he hollered off camera.

Britt continued the video, explaining a little bit more about her new job and how all the videos would be archived and available. Before she signed off for the last time, she said, "The last thing I want to say to all of you is thank you. This channel wasn't just a job, it was a passion. Thank you for being by my side through it all."

She turned off the camera and looked at him. "The end of an era," she said, a little lump in her throat.

"Yeah." He touched her hand. "You ended it perfectly."

Not wanting to get too emotional—she'd already gone through the gamut of feelings when she had decided to take Maude's offer and realized she had to end her channel—she smirked at him. "Do X and Maude know about your 'discount,'" she said, using air quotes.

"They will soon." He wheeled over and faced her, bringing himself close. "They adore me and love you, so they'll be fine with it."

He studied for a quiz in his business class while she prepared the video for upload. Before hitting the button, she looked at him. "Get ready," she said.

His eyebrow lifted. "For what?"

"You'll see."

In less than ten minutes, her notifications blew up. They watched as the comments rolled in.

That's your boyfriend, Britt? He's so dreamy!
Where can I find me one of those?
He can give me a discount any time.

Hunter fidgeted in his chair. "This is embarrassing."

"I can take down the video," she said, not wanting him to be uncomfortable. "It won't be a big deal to reshoot it."

"No, it's okay." He read a few more. "So far nothing about my job," he muttered.

Before meeting him, she would never have guessed that he found his looks more of an irritant than a benefit. That hadn't been the case when he was younger, but now he wanted people to take his mind and talents seriously, not just his appearance. Being an assistant manager and getting his business degree was helping, and he genuinely enjoyed learning about the art business and retail. But there were times when he was more mortified by the compliments than appreciative.

Another one came in.

I don't believe that's her boyfriend. She's never said anything about him until now. Maybe he's a friend or a cousin, and she's pretending she's got a hot guy for clout. I'm so disappointed. I would never have thought Britt would stoop to lying to hor fanc. Uncubccribod.

Hunter slid the keyboard toward him on the desk and started typing.

"What are you doing?" she asked.

"Responding." He scowled, banging on the keys. "She can't call you a liar and get away with it."

Britt put her hand over his, stopping him, then took the keyboard away. "Lesson number one—don't respond to comments you disagree with."

"It's not a disagreement. It's the truth."

She logged off the site and turned off the computer just as her mother called for them to come downstairs and eat.

"You're not upset?" he said as they left her studio.

"Nope." She stopped at the top of the stairs and turned to him, standing on her tiptoes. "You and I know it's real. That's all that matters." She kissed him, intending it to be a sweet peck like he'd given her on the cheek, but it immediately turned into something more.

"Ahem."

They parted and looked at her mother, who was staring up at them with slight disapproval.

Britt's cheeks heated, and they hurried to the kitchen. Dad was there, off from work, and plates of meatloaf, mashed potatoes, and green beans were in the center of the table. They said grace, and her mother picked up the meatloaf platter.

"Daniel," Hunter said.

"Britt," Daniel said at the same time. The men looked at each other, and he said, "You go first, Hunter."

Hunter's Adam's apple bobbed up and down, his expression suddenly anxious. "Mr. Branch—"

"Daniel," he said, frowning. "You've always called me by my first name."

"I want to do this right." He glanced at Britt, who was confused. Then he gulped. "Mr. Branch, I love your daughter. I'd like to ask for her hand in marriage."

Britt froze. They'd jokingly talked about getting married, but she thought it was just banter. But now he was looking at her, and she could see he was serious. "You're doing this over meatloaf?"

"Uh, yeah," he said, more doubt entering his eyes. "Is there a rule against that?"

"No." Britt bit her bottom lip. "I'm just shocked."

"Honestly, I was going to do this later, but I can't think of a better time than now." He fiddled with his jean's pocket and pulled out a small ring case.

"Oh!" Mom gasped.

"Is that what I think it is?" Dad said.

Hunter opened the box. A gold ring with a tiny, round diamond solitaire winked under the kitchen lights.

"You're proposing over *meatloaf?*" Mom exclaimed.

"Marry me, Britt," Hunter said.

Daniel cleared his throat.

"If it's okay with you, Mr. Branch," Hunter quickly added.

"*Daniel,*" he repeated.

"Daniel."

Dad turned to Britt and nodded. So did her mother.

Britt's eyes filled. "Yes. I'll marry you."

His grin almost took her breath away and he slid the ring on her finger. It was a little loose, but she'd get it sized later. He leaned toward her as though he was going to give her a full kiss, then glanced at her parents. He kissed her cheek instead.

It would do . . . for now.

"Well," Mom said, getting up from the table, still looking surprised. "I wasn't expecting that tonight. But welcome to the family, Hunter."

He stood, and Britt's heart filled as they embraced. Then he shook Dad's hand.

"Congratulations . . . son." He smiled.

They all sat down, and Britt didn't think she could be happier. Seeing her parents getting along so well, getting engaged, it all seemed like a dream.

Mom said, "Now that the surprises are over, who wants mashed potatoes—"

"Amy."

Everyone looked at Daniel, who was tugging on his collar and looking a little nervous. Then he started to dig into his pants pocket.

Britt drew in a sharp breath. Was her father going to propose? She looked at her mother, who was holding a serving spoon full of potatoes over her dish.

"Daniel," she said, her eyes wide. "Surely not—"

He took out a tissue and blew his nose. When he saw everyone staring at him, he said, "What? Did you think I was going to do this?" He moved the handkerchief and revealed a familiar diamond ring.

The potatoes hit the dish. "Oh, Daniel," she said, taking the ring from him. "How did you get my old engagement ring?"

"I had a little help."

Britt beamed. Her father had asked her two weeks ago if she knew if her mother had kept her wedding rings. After a little snooping in her jewelry box while Mom was out running errands, she'd found it. "I didn't think you were proposing tonight, though," she said.

"Hunter inspired me." He looked at Mom. "I don't want to wait either. Will you marry me, Amy? Again?"

She threw her arms around Dad. "Yes! Of course I will!"

After lots of wedding talk as they finished supper, Britt put on her coat and walked Hunter to his bike. He had a car now, a used one he bought two months ago with her father's guidance, but he rode the bike as often as he could. "You know, my mom will probably want us to have the reception at their house," he said.

"That would be wonderful." She'd gotten to know Hunter's family. His parents weren't the snobs she'd expected them to be, and she chastised herself for jumping to that conclusion. Then a thought occurred. "Would it be too weird to have a double wedding with my parents?"

He straightened the purple-and-red scarf tied around her neck and took her in his arms as a chilly March breeze ruffled his hair. "Probably. But I'm fine with it if they are. We can get married anytime, anywhere, with anyone you want. On one condition."

"What's that?"

He glanced at his bike. "Ride with me."

"Hunter—"

He walked over to the bike and pulled two helmets out of the saddlebag. He held the smaller one out to her.

"Anywhere?" she said, walking toward him. She trusted him enough to marry him, to be with him for the rest of her life. It was time to get over her fear of his bike. He would keep them safe.

"Yep." When she took the helmet from him, he grinned. "I would have proposed a long time ago if that would have gotten you to ride with me."

"Don't push it."

He lifted her onto the back of the seat and moved to sit in front of her. He put on his helmet, reached behind her and grabbed her arms, then wrapped them around him. "Hang on tight," he said, revving the engine.

She locked her fingers together, leaned her cheek against his back, and they took off. *I'm never letting go.*

Acknowledgments

So Into You was a book that came to my mind almost fully formed. Trust me, that never happens! Some characters and stories take a while for me to warm up to and fully understand but I was "so into" Britt/Hunter and Amy/Daniel right from the first sentence. A huge thanks to my editors Becky Monds and Karli Jackson for their valuable input and encouragement. To my dear friend and critique partner, Amy Clipston—thank you for your wonderful insights and for being the best cheerleader ever! And my biggest thanks to you, dear Reader, for choosing and reading *So Into You*. My hope is that you enjoyed reading this story as much as I did writing it. P.S. If you haven't listened to Yacht Rock, what are you waiting for? Visit my website: www.kathleenfuller.com to find Britt and Hunter's favorite playlist.

Discussion Questions

1. When Britt learns about Savannah's engagement, she feels left behind. Have you ever experienced a time when you thought life was passing you by? What was it, and how did you handle it?

2. Britt's social anxiety is extreme. What advice do you have for someone struggling with social anxiety? If you've experienced it, what helps you?

3. Laura thinks Amy might be using Britt as an excuse to avoid dating and romantic relationships. Do you think this is true, or is there another reason or reasons she's avoiding romance?

4. Hunter is clean and sober but he's aimless when it comes to his future. When he meets Britt, he gains some focus. Have you ever struggled with being confused or uncertain about the future? How do you handle it?

5. Hunter feels like he's an outsider in his family. What are the reasons he feels this way, and do you think he's now able to grow closer to his parents and brothers?

6. Although she's an introvert, Britt has several great people in her corner—her parents, Savannah, Maude and X, and now Hunter. Who are some of the people in your life who care about you? In what ways do they support you?

7. Both Daniel and Hunter have similar addiction problems and have turned their lives around, but they still have to rebuild their relationships and regain trust. What are some ways they can continue to be trustworthy to their friends and family?

8. Britt is passionate about art, Amy loves teaching, Daniel enjoys working on cars, and Hunter is gravitating toward business. Discuss something you're passionate about and explain why.

About the Author

With over two million copies sold, Kathleen Fuller is the *USA TODAY* bestselling author of several bestselling novels, including the Hearts of Middlefield novels, the Middlefield Family novels, the Amish of Birch Creek series, and the Amish Letters series as well as a middle-grade Amish series, the Mysteries of Middlefield.

Visit her online at KathleenFuller.com
Facebook: @WriterKathleenFuller
Instagram: @kf_booksandhooks

Don't miss more sweet romances from Kathleen Fuller!

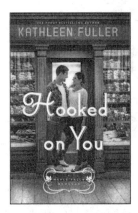

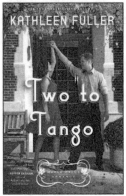

Available in print, e-book, and downloadable audio

THOMAS NELSON
Since 1798

LOOKING FOR MORE GREAT READS? LOOK NO FURTHER!

THOMAS NELSON

Since 1798

Visit us online to learn more:
tnzfiction.com

Or scan the below code and sign up to receive email updates
on new releases, giveaways, book deals, and more:

@tnzfiction